Eddie Marr never planned to b<

It's one thing to steal the Mona Lisa. But killing a world famous superhero? That's hard time with the worst of the worst.

Eddie knows there's no running if you're responsible for the death of an A List superhero. The only chance he has in staying out of prison, and staying alive, is to take the Dark Revenger's place and not let the rest of the world know the original is dead.

Eddie can do it. He's got the physical ability and the tech savvy. He even looks good in the costume. It's the ultra-serious, crime-fighting part he has trouble with. (Seriously, does the Dark Revenger need to be so "dark" all the time?)

Then the world's premiere superhero team, the Majestic 12, needs help with a seemingly impossible crime: One of their own has been murdered and they need "the world's greatest detective" (a.k.a. the Dark Revenger) to solve it.

He's not the hero we need.

He's not the hero we deserve.

He's not really a hero at all.

# KILL YOUR HEROES

by Slade Grayson

Vintage City Publishing book
published by arrangement with the author

ISBN: 978-0-578-86922-3

*Kill Your Heroes* copyright © 2021
by Slade Grayson.
All Rights Reserved.

Cover art by J Caleb Design.

This book is a work of fiction. People, places, events, and situations
are the product of the author's imagination. Any resemblance to
actual persons, living, dead, or undead, or historical events, is purely
coincidental.

No part of this book may be reproduced, stored in a retrieval system,
or transmitted by any means without the written permission of the
author and publisher.

# PROLOGUE

I'm the Dark Revenger. You've heard of me, of course.
*Scourge of the criminal underworld.*
*The shadow of justice.*
*The world's greatest detective.*
All quotes from the press, and all true...to a certain extent.
Everyone in Azure City and the United States, and in much of the
world, knows about the Dark Revenger. I'm an institution. I've been
around since the 1930s.

Well, not *me* personally. But the Dark Revenger has been
around since the 30s. There's been more than one.

The very first Dark Revenger was a pulp era mystery man, an
urban legend that everyone swore existed, but no one had ever seen
personally. Like the boogeyman or the Jersey Devil. Or the girl your
buddy in high school swore he scored with on his summer vacation.

If you listen to the whisperings of the criminal underworld or
the whisperings of those in law enforcement, which really aren't
much different when you get right down to it, then you hear the
stories of the modern day Dark Revenger being inspired by the
legend of the old one. There was too long of a gap for anyone to pass
on the mantle of the identity, so don't get the wrong idea about the
first Dark Revenger training his replacement.

I mean, it makes sense. If you're the Dark Revenger, you're
going to get too old, your body too scarred and beaten down, or
maybe an injury just won't heal. Eventually, you'll decide it's time
to retire. Or maybe you die and your apprentice steps in and cleans
up the evidence that there was a predecessor.

That's not what happened in my case. Whether there was a
Dark Revenger in the 1930s is all speculation (no one has written a
tell-all book about it), but the fact remains that several years ago, the
modern day Dark Revenger made his first appearance by stopping a
jewelry store heist.

Cliché, I know, but that's what happened. He beat up the four
crooks and left them trussed up for the police. No note. No stopping
to give a detailed blow-by-blow account. All of the info came later
from the thieves themselves once they regained consciousness. The
police thought it was a hoax.

Until the Dark Revenger stopped another robbery.

7

And a couple of muggings.

And an attempted rape.

And on and on, until the police and the press couldn't deny it any longer. Then some security camera footage got leaked and the next thing you know, everyone is talking about the superhero du jour:

The Dark Revenger.

That guy, the modern day Dark Revenger…?

He did it for several years, and he was brilliant at it. He was the guy who earned the "world's greatest detective" rep. He was also a humorless, stick-up-his-ass prig who didn't take on partners or protégés or apprentices.

Maybe he thought he'd be the Dark Revenger forever. Or maybe he just thought he would never find a successor worthy enough.

Whatever the case, he was wrong.

About being the Dark Revenger forever, I mean.

# PART ONE

# CHAPTER 1

I punch the ninja-looking goon across his black masked face. There's a POCK sound that comes from my glove, thanks to the strip of metal sewn inside the tough leather shell across the knuckles. It's a bit of a cheat to have loaded gloves, but in my business, you take every advantage you can get.

I don't have superpowers. No super-strength or invulnerability. Can't fly. Can't pluck bullets out of the air. Can't do any number of things the so-called "super" heroes can do. I'm a street-level crime-fighter with nifty gadgets, some acrobatic and martial arts skills, and a costume that gives me minor protection and slight advantages.

Costume. I hate that word. It sounds like I'm dressing up for a Halloween party. But what else can I call it? Uniform? Fighting apparel? Maybe "combat gear" is more appropriate.

Whatever. I'll call it a costume. Everyone else does.

My point is, why shouldn't I cheat to make my punches hit harder? As a costumed crime-fighter, the last thing you want is to hit someone and have them shrug it off. Because then you know you're in for a long night.

I'm in a fight with three guys. Or at least, I think they're guys. Hard to tell with the black ninja/SWAT-type outfits they're wearing. Could be a mix of men and women for all I know. Doesn't matter; when it comes to crime-fighting, I don't discriminate.

I'm dressed in black, too. My costume is durable, yet light, comprised of a thin leather shell over a thick ballistic-cloth lining that's tougher than Kevlar, yet thinner and more flexible. It doesn't restrict my movements when I'm running or jumping or doing some elaborate acrobatic karate move that looks really cool and takes out an armed gunman.

The cloth is tough enough to deflect a knife thrust or small caliber bullet that might leave a nasty bruise, but at least it won't put me in the hospital. Or cemetery. The costume won't stop anything big or high-powered like a sniper bullet, but hey, if I'm standing still long enough to get shot by a sniper, then I guess I'm not doing my job right.

My costume is black with dark blue lines that give it texture and still enables me to blend seamlessly into the dark. My cape is black and has a hood that keeps the top half of my face, from the tip of my nose up, in shadow. Plus, I wear a domino mask to help conceal my identity in case my hood is knocked back during a fight. Or in case I need to push it back to comb my hair.

Hey, it gets windy up on the rooftops.

I block one guy's punch, punch another guy in the face with a CRUNCH from his nose breaking, and lash out with a kick to the guy coming up from behind. My boot connects solidly with his pelvis and amidst the noise of the scuffle, I hear a sharp grunt as he exhales all the air from his body.

I do all of this in the space of about five seconds, which you have to admit, is pretty impressive.

My boots are badass. You really don't want to get kicked by one of them. Black lace-up combat boots with steel toes and heavy-duty rubber treaded soles that keep me from slipping on ice or water. The boots can also possibly prevent me from being electrocuted from somebody's deathtrap or one of those freaks with electricity-based superpowers.

Interesting factoid:

Superheroes – emphasis on *heroes* – tend to get powers such as flight, super-strength, healing abilities, and generally things that improve the human body. The people that get energy-based superpowers, e.g. electricity, tend to be supervillains.

It's not always the case, but nine times out of ten it works out that way. I'm not sure why. Probably there's a psychologist out there with an office in a strip mall who's currently working on a book about it.

Back to the boots:

They're thick and heavy, and if you get kicked by one of them, it's not easy to shrug off. Unless you're super-strong or invulnerable or something, in which case, I shouldn't be engaging you in hand-to-hand combat anyway.

There's also the danger of being struck by lightning when I'm traveling across rooftops. I'm doubtful as to whether the rubber on the boots would sufficiently protect me from something like that, but I usually keep low and generally don't do much crime-fighting during a thunderstorm.

Like I said, I don't have superpowers. What I do have is fighting skills, acrobatic skills, some cool gadgets I keep stored in pouches on dual black bandolier belts that crisscross my chest, and a bunch of dumb luck that hopefully never runs out.

The fight lasts less than a minute, the way fights should last. Any longer and I'm dealing with trained professionals or *super-powered* trained professionals. Both are a royal pain in my costumed backside.

I kick one ninja/SWAT guy in the balls, uppercut the second one in the jaw, and then do a flying roundhouse kick to the one behind me and catch him square in the face. It's pretty cool looking, considering I'm wearing a cape and all, and my hood doesn't even fall back or shift to obscure my vision.

I bet it would've looked really cool in a movie, which is where I probably saw it. Some Bruce Lee movie. Or maybe Jet Li. I had to have seen it somewhere because that's how I learned it.

Okay, so I don't know if this qualifies as a superpower, but I do have one ability:

I can imitate any martial arts or fighting move, or just about *any* move, simply by watching it once. Show me something once, and I can do it. Show me twice, and I'll do the move better than you.

It's a trait I was born with, similar to eidetic memory, a.k.a. photographic memory. Except it's a physical memory I can store and use again. Weird, right? But my ability is nothing like what superheroes can do, lifting thousands of pounds or shooting heat beams from their eyes.

The fight isn't completely over. One guy is out cold. Another is on the ground and clutching his man-package. The third one, the one I gave the uppercut to, shakes off the hit and squares off with me. He throws a few quick jabs; I block them easily. He tries some fancier stuff. Again, I got it. I'm fast and my fighting style is a culmination of ten different martial arts.

I counteract against his moves, but when I see him reaching behind his back, most likely grabbing a weapon, I decide to end things abruptly with a kick to his jaw.

Yeah, I can get my foot up that high. Years of gymnastics.

There's a good solid CRACK like a frozen lake suddenly hit with a thaw, or someone slingshot a marble through a plate glass window. He falls backward, hard and fast (that's what she said) and there's a muffled thud as his skull hits the thin office carpet.

No, he's not dead, and neither are the others. They will, however, be seriously messed up when they eventually regain consciousness.

One is still awake. I take a knock-out gas pellet from a pouch on my bandolier and drop it in the middle of them. The gas raises a small white cloud that billows out and immediately dissipates, but not before they all get a good whiff. It renders the one who was still awake unconscious and will keep the others in dreamland a little longer.

The pouches on my belts contain all sorts of goodies: lockpicks, smoke bombs, tear gas, a mini-Taser, knockout gas pellets, flash bangs – tiny chemical pouches that make a bright FLASH and a loud BANG when they hit the ground – and a few other items.

Yes, I carry condoms in one of the pouches. Make of that what you will.

I survey the situation. Somebody's missing. The mastermind and leader of this particular band of thieves. The one who hacked the building's security system and issued the orders to these three. I saw him clearly when they entered the building, but he's not here.

See, crime-fighting isn't what you think it is. Comic books got it wrong. You're not just swinging around town on your rope line or spiderweb or in your invisible plane and you hear a scream or a bank alarm.

No, what it is, is that you have informants. You get tips. You follow clues. Sometimes you beat information out of snitches.

Not me, but some heroes have been known to do that. The *grim and gritty* ones.

Most of the time, it pans out to nothing. Most of the time, you're up on a rooftop and looking out on a city where most everyone is asleep. Or, if there is a crime, it's miles away.

Most of the time, you don't get to stop anything or fight anybody.

Then sometimes you get lucky. Sometimes you get a tip four guys are going to break into an office building and make off with someone's hard drive that someone else is willing to pay good money for because…

Well, that part is a mystery. Maybe there's sensitive information on there someone is willing to pay for. Or there's a high-tech design of some cutting edge technology that a rival corporation wants. Or maybe a jealous wife with lots of bucks wants evidence her seemingly hardworking husband is spending his lunch hour in a motel with Sally from Accounting.

Whatever. This is one of those rare occasions where a tip paid off and the thieves actually showed at the time and place they were supposed to. Except now I can't find the fourth guy. The leader.

A whir of sound from the end of the corridor. The elevator. Instinct tells me it's going to stop on my floor. I walk towards the doors and ready myself. I pull a small metal flask from a pouch on one of my belts, open it, and take a quick swig.

Aaahhh, whiskey, how I love ya.

Screw the lid back on, replace it back in the pouch, and move my head side-to-side to loosen up my neck muscles. A flash bang in my hand.

The elevator reaches my floor. DING and the doors slide open. My body is as tight as a steel spring. I'm ready to throw the flash bang and body slam the person in the elevator.

God help him if it's the janitor and not the missing thief.

I manage to stop myself at the last second, my body revved with a primal war cry rising in my throat. Not sure why I'm about to yell. Guess I sometimes get over-hyped.

Standing over the unconscious form of the leader of the thieves is a woman. To say she's beautiful doesn't do her justice. They need to invent a special word to describe how hot she is.

Like me, she's also in a black costume, but fills it out in much more interesting ways. There's a symbol of a black bird in a small white circle on her chest. The woman is petite and curvy, with shoulder-length hair as dark and shiny as satin sheets under a full moon, tied back into a ponytail. She moves with a fluidity that doesn't negate the coiled tenseness I feel in the air between us, and looks as if she's about to explode at me.

Quite frankly, I doubt I'll have time to defend myself other than try to block some hits. And yes, I think all this in about half a second.

"Dark Revenger," she says, her voice hard and smoky like bourbon over ice.

I brace myself.

She says, "Nice to see you again."

Oh, crap. She knows me.

I'm supposed to know her, but I really have no clue who she is. She thinks I'm the other guy, the previous Dark Revenger.

That guy? The previous one? I killed him three weeks ago.

# CHAPTER 2

Before I was the Dark Revenger, I was a small time supervillain called The Puzzler. You've probably never heard of me, and if you have, it's as a footnote to some story about a more famous supervillain.

See, I never had the inclination to do anything heinous like mass murder people or threaten to teleport Washington, DC to an anti-matter universe unless the government paid me a hundred billion dollars. No, that stuff was definitely way far away from who I am and what my intentions were by entering the supervillain racket.

Before I was the Dark Revenger and long before I was The Puzzler, I was Edward "Eddie" Marr.

I was born with the features of a superhero: thick, dark hair that's always a cross between perfectly coifed and slightly mussed; blue eyes that don't require corrective lenses; clear skin; straight, white teeth that never needed braces; and a strong jawline, sharp and solid, but not overly jutting.

Like I said earlier, I was also born with the unique talent of being able to imitate just about any physical move I see, within normal human constraints, of course. Although I can, for example, imitate the moves of an Olympic athlete, I could never lift a car over my head like someone with super-strength.

Maybe what I have is the result of a convergence of really good genes, or maybe it's a superpower of sorts. A really obscure one like being able to change television channels by blinking your eyes, or opening and shutting electric garage doors by pointing your finger at them.

People are sometimes born with stupid superpowers like the ones I mentioned. Sometimes they think it will lead to fame and fortune. Ultimately, the only thing they end up with is a fleeting ninety seconds on a late night talk show. Occasionally, they get more than ninety seconds. The TV channel changing girl posed nude and got a couple of bit parts in movies. But really, outside of a bar trick, what can you do with powers like that?

In my case, sports came easily to me. All I had to do was watch a few pro games and I could throw touchdown passes or hit home runs with little effort. It also made school incredibly boring because seriously, do I really need to memorize the Periodic Table if I have a guaranteed sports scholarship to the college of my choice?

At age 13, my life had two major events:

One was, I lost my virginity to my French tutor. Cliché, I know.

The other was, my brother Jack was born. Both came as a bit of a surprise to me, more so the part of getting a baby brother. My parents had not intended to have another child, probably thinking the perfect combination of DNA that produced me would be impossible to duplicate. If they thought that, they were right.

My brother was born with damaged legs. By the time I was heading to college, he had developed enough to get around with leg braces and metal crutches. By this point, my parents were solely focused on him, thinking their job with me was over. I don't blame them. I mean, I had the use of my legs, good looks, and a scholarship in gymnastics.

I was always lean and muscular, and I figured it was the sport to least likely result in an accident that could permanently disfigure my devilish good looks. Also, it didn't require a reliance on teamwork. There was even talk of Olympic try-outs at one point, but honestly, I couldn't be bothered. Too many parties to go to and too many girls to bang.

College was a blast. Drinking, girls, parties, girls, more drinking, and girls. They say you spend your first two years partying before you hunker down and get serious about your academics. I partied for four years and never entertained the idea of getting serious. After many failed classes and missed practices and tournaments, the school kicked me out. My parents, no strangers to being disappointed in me by this time, cut me off financially.

Now *that*? That was a problem.

See, I've never worked a job before. Manual labor and I don't mix. And quite frankly, I'm not qualified to do anything white collar-like. So what could I do? I tried out for the circus.

I showed up with one of the worst hangovers in the history of hangovers. The recruiting guy said, "Climb up, get on the trapeze, and show me what you can do."

I made it halfway up the ladder before my gut let go and I vomited a spray of tequila, half-digested salsa and chips, and I don't know what else — maybe hallucinogenic mushrooms, too. That part of the previous night was a bit of a blur.

I climbed back down, did a theatrical bow, and said, "Ta da!" I left before the guy insisted I clean up the vomit.

I got a gig as a lounge singer in a cocktail place that catered to business folk. I'm not a particularly good singer, but not terrible either. Luckily, you don't need a million dollar set of vocal cords to win over the cocktail crowd. The women think you're good if they think you're singing to them and only them, and the guys just want to get sloshed. Then one night, I had an epiphany.

Actually, I had an epiphany the year before: Epiphany Marquez, a cute chica that worked at the corner bodega.

But on this particular night, I had a different kind of epiphany.

*I was meant to be famous.*

I was not a hard worker and not a genius. I would never cure world hunger or disease. No, I was meant to be famous for being famous, like a vapid hotel heiress or the son of a famous movie star. I just needed a gimmick, a stepping stone into the limelight.

Superheroes were all the rage. I thought about becoming one, but honestly, I had no desire to fight crime. Don't get me wrong, it's not that I *like* crime. I'm not an advocate of crime. I'm just not morally opposed to it either. It's like…

If crime was my neighbor, I wouldn't shun him. I wouldn't invite him over for a barbecue either. I'd ignore him like I do my real-life neighbors, and occasionally steal his Sunday newspaper.

Instead of a superhero, I decided to become a supervillain.

I would commit some pointless crimes, nothing that would hurt people. Steal museum exhibits or a world famous diamond. Maybe paint a mustache on the Mona Lisa.

I'd leave clues for my archnemesis. Send letters to the media in which I'd brag about my exploits and make fun of said archnemesis. Eventually, I'd get caught, because that's the way the odds go. They're stacked against you. Every supervillain gets caught sooner or later.

With my lack of a prior criminal record, though, and the assistance of a skilled lawyer, I'd cut a deal to do a year or two at a minimum security prison. During my time inside, I'd pen a tell-all autobiography and probably exaggerate the superhero connection, as well as outright lie about sexual trysts with the super-gals. The book would be a bestseller because A) the public has an insatiable appetite to hear the down and dirty deeds of the cape community; and B) my personality would help propel it up to the top of the bestseller lists.

I'd do the talk show circuit after I got out and the book was published. Then once sales started to decline, I'd capitalize on my newfound fame by hosting my own talk show — something cool and fun like Letterman's show back in the 80s.

To be a supervillain, I needed four things: a name, a costume, a gimmick, and an archnemesis. I decided on "The Puzzler" because I always liked puzzles and thought it would be fun to leave puzzle boxes with clues in them to taunt the authorities. I bought a violet-colored zoot suit at an urban clothing outlet and added a black mask, a black fedora, and black leather gloves.

Picking an archnemesis is the tricky part. Pick wrong and it could go very badly for me. If I ran up against a psycho superhero like Judgment Day, I could quite possibly find myself in the hospital, missing a limb. Or dead. Believe me, there are some non-superpowered bad guys who have ended up that way.

No, I needed someone without potentially lethal superpowers. Someone who wasn't a psychopath, which narrowed the field somewhat. Someone well established in order to give me some street cred. And someone who would be a challenge because, hey, make it too easy and no one would take me seriously.

I decided my archnemesis would be the "world's greatest detective," a.k.a. the Dark Revenger. But you knew I was going to say that, didn't you?

# CHAPTER 3

"Sorry" the beautiful woman says. "I hope I didn't mess up anything you were working on."

Wow. She deferred to me. Which means she respects me. Well... She respects *him*. But still!

"No. Nothing important."

I use the haughty monotone growly-whisper Dark Revenger used, sort of like Clint Eastwood if his jaw was wired shut mixed with a cartoon superhero. It's exactly the type of superhero the Dark Revenger was: a humorless, stoic do-gooder with the personality of a wet mop. It was the reason I chose him as my archnemesis. I figured it would be fun to mess with him. Which it was. Until it wasn't.

I say, "Just out on patrol and I came across these crooks. Glad you came along. Appreciate the help."

Man, it hurts to talk this way. It's like gargling with shards of glass. No wonder D.R. hardly spoke.

Hotty McSmokin' (still haven't learned her name) cocks her head at me. She gives me a stare like she knows something is up with me. My upper lip is suddenly quite moist. I tilt my head down to keep my face as much in shadow as possible.

"Something wrong?" I ask in the same growly-whisper. I act like nothing's wrong, when in fact, everything is wrong.

"No," she says, finally. "Just..." She shakes her head. "Nothing."

Whew. Good. With that weight off my shoulders, I decide to check her out in greater detail.

She's petite and trim with a tense wiry look to her that makes me think of a jungle cat. She's Asian, I think, or at least partly. Her domino mask throws me off a bit.

She stands in the middle of the unconscious thieves with her legs rooted in one spot and systematically checks their pockets. Not moving her legs means she ends up doing some serious stretching and puts herself in positions that make me think she's the star pupil in Yoga class. Even with my own acrobatic skills, I'm impressed by her flexibility.

I want her bad, too, more than any other woman I've ever seen. Okay, slight exaggeration. I see women every day I think I want more than any other woman I've ever seen.

Like the cute, pixie-ish barista that serves me my cappuccino, the one with the black Capri pants and black flat-soled shoes who bounces behind the counter, hyped up on her own caffeinated product, but I like to think it's sexual energy.

Like the Spanish waitress at the Blue Owl Diner, the one with the bronze skin and the deep chocolate eyes who sometimes says "si" instead of "yes," which is terribly cute and makes me wonder if she'll moan stuff in Spanish or English.

Like the blonde bank teller in the blue suit jacket and crisp white shirt that has a neck tattoo I caught a glimpse of when she absently brushed her hair back to scratch an itch, right above what I'm pretty sure was a hickey.

Those are just the ones I saw this week. You can imagine the ones I fantasize about on a monthly basis.

Back to this dark-haired beauty in front of me:

Her boots are flat-soled and have the split-toed look distinctive of martial artist combat gear. She's not wearing a cape, but has several weapons strapped to her waist, legs, and in a harness behind her back. It's all martial arts looking stuff – throwing stars, nunchakus, what looks like a miniature scythe, and possibly a Taser. Maybe a few other things; everything is colored black, so I'm going by quick glimpses and guesswork.

Bottom line is, I'm making the assumption she's a non-powered hero like me, which will give me an "in" when I put my seductive prowess to work on her. First, I have to figure out how she knows me. "Me," meaning Dark Revenger, because personally I've never seen this woman before. Not even in a newscast or on YouTube.

"No identification on any of them," she says. "Obviously they're professionals and not standard, run-of-the-mill thieves. Think they're working for someone big?"

She gives me a look like I should have all the answers. Normally I would be clueless, but in this particular case, I actually know something.

"They're independent. They were hired to do a job. Corporate espionage," I say.

Again, she gives me an intensive stare. Wait…

The small white circle on her chest with the black silhouette of a bird. It's Raven. Both the woman and the bird on her chest.

I know her from the rumblings among the supervillain network. She's been around for maybe two years, a street level hero that can hold her own against the superpowered kind. A nonlethal martial artist, proficient with weapons.

And apparently she's met the Dark Revenger at some point. That can't be good. For me, I mean.

"You seem to have matters in hand." I say, "So I'll leave you to it. Thanks again for your assistance."

I turn quickly so my cape billows out in a dramatic fashion and I head for the stairs. As much as I'd like to seduce this cute little Asian superhero chick, I can't take the chance of her figuring out my secret.

"Wait," she says.

I keep walking. I enter the stairwell and head up to the roof. She's behind me, walking fast to catch up. I stifle the urge to break into a run.

Christ, what's with her? Is she looking to be my sidekick or something? The Dark Revenger has always been a solo act. It's going to have to stay that way, too, because there are way too many skeletons in my closet. Literally.

"Dark Revenger," she says. "Wait."

Is it my imagination, or was there a hesitation when she said my name?

Up on the roof, the bitter January wind whips across the buildings with enough force that I think it could take the two of us with it out into the night sky. My costume is insulated, so I don't feel hot or cold much, but the force of the wind is strong enough to give me pause. I'm about to swing down from this building and I need to calculate the wind resistance and the direction it's taking, which at the moment seems to be several directions at once. Strange, because it wasn't like that a half hour ago when I got here. Azure City is a strange place, though, so whatever.

There's something about being up on top of a building, even a twelve story one surrounded by taller ones that gives you a grandiose sense of being above it all. The world seems simpler when you're standing far above it. Problems appear miniscule. If I could have one superpower, I think I'd wish for the ability to fly.

Nah, that's not true. I'd choose x-ray vision and I'd use it for exactly what you think I'd use it for.

Strapped to my back beneath my cape and the crisscrossed bandolier belts is a flat metal contraption. I pull out in one swift, practiced move. With a flick of my wrist, it clicks into a tube shape and elongates. I fit it over my right arm and feel for the handle and built-in trigger. I hear the spool of cable whir and calibrate, and a small silver shaft settles into place on the end of the rig, right above where my fingers would be. The rig clamps securely onto my arm.

It's a sophisticated grappling gun that enables the Dark Revenger to swing from one building to another. It can also pull him up to the top of a building or down to street level, depending on the requirement of the circumstances. Whoever made it, and I have no idea if it was D. R. himself or someone else, was a friggin' genius.

It's as light as aluminum and a whole lot tougher. I must have dropped it a dozen times the first couple of weeks when I was practicing moving in the costume and trying to figure out how to carry everything. It never broke or suffered a dent.

I take an arrow-shaped tip from one of my belt compartments and screw it onto the silver shaft. I generally carry only six tips because the gun is only primed with six charges to shoot the arrow. After that, I have to take it back to the Dark Revenger base and reload the damn thing, which is a pain in the ass and involves several screwdrivers, a magnifying lamp, and a very steady hand. Reloading this damn thing is about as much fun as trying to fix a spring in the world's most complicated watch while you're on a boat in the middle of a storm.

But I haven't screwed it up yet, so–

"Dark Revenger!"

Jeez, now she's on the roof with me.

I lift the rig and prepare to shoot up at the ledge of the roof of the building next door. I figure I'll let the cable pull me up, climb over, and drop down the opposite side of the building. From there, it's only a block to my car, and then I can get the hell out of here.

In my primed stance of one arm aiming and the other on my hip in a heroic fashion, I start to say, "Pleasure working with you again," but before the words can leave my mouth, I hear:

"DARK REVENGER!" in a loud, booming voice that rattles windows and nearly causes me to piss myself. Raven looks as surprised as me, so I know she had nothing to do with the voice.

24

"Um…yes, God?" I say. I forgot to do my gravelly Dark Revenger voice.

A light hits us and for a moment, I think I must have died because it feels like that all-encompassing light some people claim to see when they have a near-death experience. Just as quickly, I realize who and what it is, and now I know why the wind has been strange.

Above us, hovering just a few feet over our heads, is the transport ship for The Majestic 12, the world's premier team of superheroes. The ship was in stealth mode, which is a cool way to say it was invisible. I had always heard it could do that, but to see it, or *not* see it, in person is akin to having a religious experience.

Luckily, I'm not a religious person. It's well past time for me to get the hell out of here. My finger tightens on the trigger of the grappling gun.

"Dark Revenger," the voice comes again, slightly less booming and a tad less voice-of-doomish. "We are in urgent need of your help."

The ship becomes visible. It's gold and saucer-shaped, and looks not unlike a 1950s film version of what a flying saucer would look like. I know the ship belongs to Traveler, the leader of the Majestic 12. It's the same ship that brought him to Earth (technically, *back* to Earth) after the aliens took him. More on that story later.

Still, it's kind of a cool idea that movies like "Earth vs. the Flying Saucers" actually had the idea right about what a ship from another world would look like — kind of like the Jupiter 2 in the old "Lost in Space" TV series —and all the Star Wars films completely missed the mark. But I digress.

A ramp slides and lowers and ultimately settles between me and Raven. Three figures wait at the top of the ramp. They're members of Majestic 12, I'm sure, but I don't know which ones. The light from inside the ship bathes them in a glow, but makes them look like shadowy figures from my vantage point.

I think crazily about making a break for it, but really, run from Majestic 12? They're the rock stars of superheroes. They're the most powerful team of heroes in the whole world. They'd catch me in about five seconds.

"Please," the voice again, lower volume this time and sounding distinctly like a woman's voice. "Come with us back to our base. We need your help. And please bring your companion."

"Companion?" Raven mutters.

The Majestic 12 need my help. Which means, not only are *they* in trouble, but now I am, too. Big trouble.

The only good thing about this is, if I can pull it off, Raven will be very impressed with the idea that Majestic 12 needed my help and I came through for them. If I can't score with her after that…

…if it doesn't all blow up in my face and I end up in prison…

…then my name isn't Dark Revenger.

Yeah, I get the irony of that statement.

I mean, check out the way she's looking at me right now. Like I'm the coolest goddamn superhero in the world. Which, *I am*.

# CHAPTER 4
## *RAVEN'S P.O.V.*

He's an idiot.

He smells like alcohol — whiskey, if I'm not mistaken — and aftershave.

Dark Revenger never wore aftershave while he was on patrol. No serious, self-respecting street-level crime-fighter would wear a scent that can give him away when he's attempting to blend into the dark. I'm certainly not wearing perfume. It would be amateurish and, if I was tracking a trained professional, could get me killed.

Dark Revenger would also never drink while working. Alcohol can lead to mistakes. It's been known to happen.

Captain Arachnid was known to drink, but it was overlooked in the superhero community. When someone is a former decorated military officer who spends his off-time giving inspirational speeches at inner city schools and volunteering at local soup kitchens, no one wants to call into question his increasingly erratic behavior and the various footage of him drinking excessively around town after his wife left him.

There was no question it was him since Captain Arachnid didn't have a secret identity. Even if he had, the four extra arms would've been a dead giveaway.

He drank more and more, and missed more and more scheduled inspirational speeches and volunteer service. The rest of the heroes looked the other way. They were too busy battling their arch-foes or posing for publicity photos to stage an intervention. The heroes Captain Arachnid might have listened to, the ones who might have been able to deter his descent into alcoholism, the Majestic 12, were much too busy saving the world from whatever threats, real or imagined, they deemed worthy of their involvement.

Captain Arachnid carried six guns, one for each hand, and was an expert marksman with all of them. He never missed a target…except one fateful day when he was called in to help with a bank robbery that had turned into a stand-off with local law enforcement. Witnesses said later he appeared disoriented and disheveled, and although he managed to take down the criminals with non-lethal shots, it was one errant bullet that missed its target and killed an innocent bystander. Later that day, after Captain Arachnid put a bullet into his own head, they said his blood alcohol level was three times the legal limit.

The Flying Dutchman had his superpowers only for a month. After saving a group of motorists trapped by a flash flood by flying them to safety, and accepting the offer of a date from one of the grateful female motorists, he went out and celebrated. On his flight home, he went too low and flew into power lines. Unfortunately, flight was his only superpower. He died the way any normal man would if subjected to twenty-five thousand volts.

So, no, I don't think drinking on the job is a good idea. But the bottom line is, this man is not the real Dark Revenger.

How do I know this? Four simple reasons:

1) The real Dark Revenger kept a stoic expression at all times. This one smirks. Constantly. It's annoying and makes me want to slap him.

2) They both have similar jawlines. Although the rest of the face is in shadow, I can tell this one is a few years younger than the real one. The real Dark Revenger was in his late thirties. This one is closer to my age: late twenties. Perhaps thirty.

3) The Dark Revenger I worked with was consumed with the eradication of crime. He stayed focused with laser-like precision on whatever case he was working on. He never looked at me the way this one does. Although his face is mostly hidden, I can tell he's looking me up and down. Undressing me in his mind.

4) The most damning reason I know he's not the real Dark Revenger? Very simple:

I saw the Puzzler kill the Dark Revenger.

# CHAPTER 5
## *Exposition*

As Raven and I walk up the ramp to the Majestic 12 flying saucer/transport ship, let's take a moment to go over the details of when and how superheroes came into existence.

Sure, it's common knowledge and there have been scores of books written on the subject, plus countless newspaper articles, filmed documentaries, and weekly gossip columns. Hell, there are even universities out there that teach courses on the subject. I heard Torpedo loves to show up as a guest lecturer and then hit on the students afterwards — both male and female. He doesn't discriminate, apparently.

For the sake of discussion, however, let's pretend some of you don't know the story. Maybe you were born and raised in the Amazon rainforest and you've never seen a working toilet, let alone a real-life superhero. You know nothing about superheroes, you've never watched television, and you just recently learned to read. Here's a quick rundown:

There is much conjecture about *when* the first superhuman appeared. There are a fringe group of theorists, conspiracy nuts, and general go-against-the-grain oddballs who argue superhumans have been around as long as Homo sapiens. They'll tell you that the reports of miracles throughout the ages, and even destructive events such as earthquakes, tidal waves, volcanic eruptions, etc., were the work of evil superhumans, or more likely the collateral damage of a battle between two warring factions of superpowered people. They'll point to mentions of "angels" in religious texts and contemplate on whether the Norse and Greek gods were real people with superpowers who appeared to be god-like beings to the worshipping populace around them. Which is not as farfetched as it sounds.

Traveler has a following that worships him as a messiah and have erected temples in his honor. He doesn't encourage it. Quite the opposite, from what I understand. But there are still people in the world who view him as a god, and worship him as such.

What *is* known is that masked crime-fighters were reported as far back as the 1930s and 40s. These so-called "Mystery Men" (although there were a fair amount of women, as well) appeared during a more innocent time when pulp magazines were quick to publish stories that both exaggerated and glorified their exploits. The masked crime-fighters back then were rugged, two-fisted individuals who carried guns and weren't sanctioned by the government or local law enforcement, and they certainly never gave press interviews. They stuck to the shadows and none of them possessed superpowers, outside of some exotic device/weapon like a laser pistol or a rocket pack — usually made by a socially awkward, goggle-wearing mad genius in a hidden lab somewhere, who made super-scientific gadgets for the good guys, or killer robots and earthquake machines for the bad guys. Sometimes both.

By the early 50s, the pulp era guys and gals had all faded away. Instead, it was a time of nuclear paranoia and the unsubstantiated rumors of found alien technology the U.S. government was desperately trying to reverse engineer. Rumors of a superhuman program, too, something to create a superpowered soldier that would deter another world war. There's no proof of any of this, but...

Look at what we have now. Look at what is flying around, dressed in garish costumes and/or using technology generations ahead of where we should be. Look at that and tell me:

Those rumors don't seem so outlandish, do they?

If you disregard 99% of the wildest, most unbelievable stories as being the result of too much alcohol, flights of fancy, conspiracy theorists letting their imagination run wild, or just plain crazy people believing in a delusion, you would still have 1% that can't be explained by a government statement about a "crashed weather balloon." It's that simple.

Getting back to our history lesson...

Shortly into the 21st Century, *he* appeared. Thomas Traveler. The first undisputed, can't be explained as camera trickery or CGI, superhuman. He was more than that, too.

As I said earlier, he was the cape community's own personal Jesus. Once he came along, more superpowered people appeared. Then the supervillains started up. And next thing you know, the government decides things are getting out of hand and they better recruit some of the heavy hitters before some foreign government decides to make them a cash offer they can't refuse, or they get seduced into going over to the bad guys' side.

They called them The Majestic 12, the codename for an old government agency that investigated strange phenomena (like "The X-Files," but real). They were media darlings at first, and America really had the rest of the world worried because, you know, if we had *them*, what was there to stop us from sending the team into Moscow or China or wherever and taking over?

Fortunately, the government screwed themselves up before anybody had the idea to try it. They told Traveler they wanted him to allow the military to get a good look at the workings of his ship so they could attempt to duplicate the anti-gravity propulsion engine and the fuel source that draws power from the stars. They also wanted signed pledges of allegiances from everyone on the team, with the stipulation that any refusal to follow an order from the president, the vice president, or the secretary of state could be considered an act of treason.

Traveler and his team refused. They announced they were going to be a "world peacekeeping force" and not just an American one. They were going to act independent of any government and would do whatever they thought was best for the planet and not just one particular country. Even if the country was their native birthright.

Traveler also said he wouldn't turn his ship over because "humans" (his word) were not ready for such a big jump, and certainly the American government should not get an unfair advantage over the rest of the world.

To say this caused a rift is an understatement. They tried to talk Traveler out of it. They used flattery. They attempted to bribe him. And when none of it worked, they threatened.

At the end of it, however, they conceded. Because what else could they do? Declare war on the world's first, and arguably most popular, superhero? Risk having him defect?

Nope, instead they gave him his autonomy. Now Traveler and The Majestic 12 zip around the world and take on whatever menace they feel is worthy of their involvement. It usually has to be Earth-shattering, the sun may not come up, lock up the kids and the family pets, kiss the spouse goodbye, kind of stuff. They are the big leagues.

And they want my help?

Yeah, we're *all* in trouble.

# CHAPTER 6

We wait in an antechamber within the ship as the ramp slides closed behind us. The interior walls are a soft warm gold color with moving lights beneath them. Raven and I look around like we're tourists in a far-off exotic land, which in a way, I guess we are.

The team members of Majestic 12, the first time I've ever seen them up close and personal, are as fascinating to me as the inside of the ship. More on them in a sec.

The ship. It's like nothing else on Earth, probably because it's *not* from Earth. It belonged to the alien race that took Thomas Traveler up into outer space, and then brought him back all super-fied or whatever. He also came back with his own nifty spaceship and all of its highly advanced super-alien technology.

Although the ship can travel around the globe in a matter of minutes and is capable of flights into outer space, it's only designed for travel and nothing more. It doesn't have any built-in weapons. No phasers or photon torpedoes. At least, that's what Traveler has told the press, but it's not as if he's giving tours to the *Superhero Home Journal*.

Amazonia is the most striking one. I've seen her in pictures and in news footage, but it's nothing like seeing her in person. She's blonde and really tall — at least six and a half feet in her high heeled metal boots. She's poured into a metal one-piece that barely covers her breasts and rides high up her thighs. The suit and knee-high metal boots are a bright chrome silvery color, but the sword on her hip and the shield strapped to her back are a dull, cast iron black.

I have no idea what her armor or weaponry is made of, although I've seen enough news footage of her in action to know they're made of sturdy stuff. No, my question is, what does she need a sword and shield for? She's nearly as strong as Traveler and her skin is tough enough to deflect bullets. Why armor and weapons?

**Amazonia's origin story**: Supposedly she's the last of a warrior tribe descended from the Valkyries (from Norse mythology) who was flash-frozen in a glacier and then thawed out thanks to global warming. She's a stranger in a strange land, or so she portrays to the media.

Personally, I don't believe her origin story. Seems a little cliché.

Cold Snap is dressed in a skintight arctic blue jumpsuit that matches her eyes and fingernails. And no, her fingernails aren't painted arctic blue. That's their true color. It stands out against her albino white skin, which is in ample abundance thanks to the long "v" cut-out in her costume that dips between her breasts and continues down to her belly button. Her hair is dark, or would be dark if it wasn't covered in frost. It also jingles when she walks from the many icicles that constantly form at the tips and break off. Her boots are go-go white leather and make a sound like crunching on snow when she moves toward me.

**Cold Snap's origin story**: She claims to be a "season elemental." Whatever the hell that is. I call bullshit.

Pulsar is about my height and wearing a tight yellow spandex one piece costume with orange goggles over his eyes. His costume has a triangle design to the chest piece that make his shoulders stick way out, like there's a large coat hanger still stuck in the costume when he put it on. It's odd looking and kind of ugly. There are rumors he's gay. Seeing him up close, I don't believe it. A gay man wouldn't wear such an ugly outfit.

His blond crew cut is shaved into a lightning bolt on top of his head. It's almost stupider looking than his costume. Almost.

**Pulsar's origin story**: As a young boy, he fell into a coma, whereupon some other dimensional beings spoke with him and taught him the ancient, and long lost, ability to absorb light and fire it out of his hands and eyes in great force.

This story also sounds like bullshit.

I should say for the record that I have no idea if any of their origins are true or not, but generally the more outlandish they are, the more likely they're made-up. During my supervillain days, many of these stories were discussed ad nauseam amongst ourselves, because like any other career, you get a bunch of us together and all we're going to talk about is *work*. We would also discuss the origin stories of some of the more famous supervillains.

It was the opinion of Blue Howler, Savant, and Mr. Meaner, my three supervillain drinking buddies, that the stories were made up to make the heroes or villains seem more interesting. It sounded better than admitting you suddenly developed powers during puberty or you were drenched in a toxic waste spill that gave you superpowers instead of cancer.

Or maybe some of the stories are true. Who knows?

Sometimes there's a headline in a gossip rag about somebody recognizing Amazonia as someone they went to junior high with and how she was a complete nerd, but really, who's to say what's real and what isn't? We live in an interesting world, my friends, and sometimes your personal history is what you want it to be.

The last member of the team on the ship is Ms. Fire, a woman in tight red leather. Compared to the others, her costume is unique in that A) it has a row of buttons that go up, across, and down her chest like an old Cavalry uniform shirt; B) her pants and boots have noticeable zippers; and C) she's wearing a full-face mask that covers her from her chin to her hairline. Her hair is as fiery red as her costume. She also has a short red cape that matches the rest of her outfit.

**Ms. Fire's origin story**: Honestly? No idea. Never heard of her before. Nice figure, though.

Amazonia says, "Dark Revenger. It's good to see you again. Thank you for coming."

I notice she looks kind of, what's the word? *Stretched*. Like a magazine centerfold that's been digitally manipulated so her arms, legs, and torso appear longer than normal. Still attractive, just...odd.

"The pleasure is all mine," I say in my D.R. gravelly voice and nearly cough. I can't keep doing the voice. My throat hurts.

Amazonia cocks her head and I wonder if she knows I'm not him. Dark Revenger has never been a member of M12 and in fact, famously turned them down when they publicly offered him a slot on the team. So if Amazonia, or any of the others, have met D.R. in the past, it had to be only briefly.

Speaking of members, there's only four of them. Where are the others? I know Speed Demon is dead, and Infinity hasn't made a public appearance in months. But where's Traveler and Judgment Day?

Perhaps sensing my unspoken question, Pulsar says, "We're heading back to the base. Traveler is waiting for us there."

The walls move and seem to sink into the floor as if made of liquid, and now I have an unobstructed view of the ring of concave port windows that surround the ship. A glance out one of the windows tells me we're moving, and probably have been since the ramp closed.

Funny, because I hadn't felt the ship move at all or have that annoying ear-popping thing you get when an airplane climbs altitude. It's disconcerting to say the least, but I've got to pretend nothing fazes me.

Hell, Raven has a great poker face, too. Maybe she's been on the ship before?

"What do you need me for?" I ask.

And how the heck did you know where to find me? But I don't ask because I have the feeling that the real Dark Revenger wouldn't ask it.

Pulsar says, "Master Mind has escaped. We believe he's still somewhere in our base because no security alarms have been triggered." He shrugs. "And, as you know, no one can get on or off the island without us knowing."

How would I know that?

**Side note:** Majestic 12's island base *used* to belong to Master Mind. When M12 took him down a few years ago, they decided to keep the base for themselves. They also turned one whole level into a holding facility for supervillains like him, and others too dangerous for a regular prison. I'm not sure holding a guy prisoner in the very place he designed and built was the smartest move in the world, but it seemed to work.

Until now, that is.

I hold my palms up in an "I don't understand" gesture.

"Why do you need me to find him? You should be able to do that on your own, right?"

Pulsar stares at me for a second. "Um, well, you're the one who caught him last time he escaped, so…"

I did?

Cold Snap says, "Also, there's been an incident that may or may not be connected."

They look at each other for a brief moment. Then she says, "Judgment Day is dead. Murdered. We're not sure how it happened or if Master Mind is responsible."

Raven says, "The world's greatest detective should be able to figure it out. Right, Dark Revenger?"

Was there a hint of sarcasm in her voice? If there was, I don't think M12 picked up on it. They reverently nod their heads.

As for me, I suddenly find her less attractive. But the feeling only lasts for a minute and I'm back to drooling over her. In my mind, I mean.

"Yes. Of course," I say. This will be a train wreck of epic proportions.

A beam of light emits from the ceiling and shoots down to the floor between me and the M12 team. I step back out of surprise, thinking at first it's a laser. But the light doesn't put off heat or appear to be a weapon, rather, it appears to be forming into a person. A woman made out of liquid gold.

The gold is the same color as the walls of the ship, and although I'm not sure it's entirely liquid, the way it forms from the floor up is much like someone pouring a tall glass of apple juice. If the glass was shaped like a supermodel.

She's tall and shapely, and forms quicker than I can describe. In as much time as it took to say all this, she's standing in front of me, suddenly blinked into existence.

She says, "Arrival in ten seconds."

She looks straight at me with her human-looking eyes...if eyes were made of gold-cast marbles. They're not blank orbs; I can see rings and pupils. It's just that it's all one color. She has fingernails and toenails, or at least the indentations on her fingers and toes where they would go, but no nipples or naughty parts down below. She's smooth all over and so shiny, I can see my reflection in her

A robot? I'm wondering, albeit a much more sophisticated one than what you generally see in movies. Or maybe she's a new superhero I haven't heard about, which is unlikely because in the past, any time someone new has joined the Majestic 12, it's been the cause of a media tsunami.

Then again, apparently the Dark Revenger has hobnobbed with M12 before, and no one in the general public, or the supervillain underground, knew anything about it.

"Welcome Dark Revenger," the gold woman says. There's a soft metallic echo to her voice and a slight staccato like you hear in most automated computer directories. "It is a pleasure to see you again."

Then she unforms in reverse and shoots back up into the beam of light, back into the ceiling.

Pulsar says to me, "You must have made an impression on Meredith the last time you were here. She doesn't usually make it a point to greet our guests."

The corner of his mouth is upturned in one of those fake smiles a retail clerk gives you when they tell you to "Have a nice day."

"Arriving at base," says the gold chick, Meredith, or at least it's her voice coming from all around us in stereo.

And then I figure it out. She's not a new superhero. She's the ship's computer, the artificial intelligence. Why she looks like a woman, or even a "she" at all, is a question I could ask. But then it could be that the Dark Revenger should already know the answer.

So best to keep my mouth shut and pretend like I know everything. Which is par for the course for me anyway. Pretending, I mean.

"We're there already?" Raven asks.

"Surprised?" Amazonia asks with a smirk. "It never takes long."

"That's what she said," I mutter, and too late realize I said it out loud and in my normal voice.

Everyone looks at me with a raised eyebrow. Not sure about Ms. Fire, what with the full face mask and everything, but if I had to guess, I'd bet her eyebrow is arched skyward, as well.

"What?" I say, "We're all professionals here. I don't have to keep using my crime-fighting voice, do I?"

Because I don't think my throat could take it, but that's beside the point.

Cold Snap says," No, it's just…"

"You never dropped the voice before," Pulsar finishes for her. "You spent a whole twenty-four hours on our base last time and kept doing the voice the whole time."

Time for some spin control, as I once heard someone say, probably in a movie.

"I feel more comfortable this time. I feel like I can be more like my real self. I hope all of you feel the same."

When in doubt, always pay deference to royalty. Especially when they're *superhero* royalty.

My gambit works. They nod their heads, except for Raven, who's still giving me the stink eye. She knows. I know she knows. And I'm beginning to think she knows that I know that she knows.

The room gets brighter for a moment, then dims again, and the ramp opens behind me. We landed and I never even felt it. The ship really is a wonder.

I walk down the ramp with M12 team members next to and behind me. I belong. I'm one of them. A peer. It feels kind of good.

The air is balmy and the sun is up. We're on an island in the tropics. Palm trees wave in the breeze and the ocean crashes on the shore not far from where we're standing. It would be paradise if someone hadn't dropped several hundred tons of molten steel into the middle of the jungle, then let it cool to act as both a landing pad and as a defensive barrier for the secret base that exists roughly a mile down beneath the island.

As I said earlier, the person who built the base was Master Mind, a guy so smart that the Majestic 12 keep him locked up here rather than trusting a regular prison to hold him. As far as I know, he didn't even get a trial. M12 discovered his base, managed to defeat him, and then locked him up in one of his own holding cells.

And no, I don't know why Master Mind had holding cells, although sometimes these megalomaniacal villains have twisted fantasies of holding heroes hostage or keeping them alive, but confined, for experimentation and/or psychological and physical torture. The smarter the villains are, usually the more twisted they are in their goals. There are exceptions to the rule, of course, and yes, I'm referring to myself. Anyway…

Somehow M12 found Master Mind's secret base, defeated him, and then decided to take up residence in it. Why not? The location is secret from every government in the world, it has built-in shields and signal jammers that keep it hidden from satellites and radar, and it's not on any map or tour/cruise destination.

M12 took it over, locked up Master Mind in one of the holding cells, and used some of the other cells for other dangerous supervillains.

Yeah, there were plenty of civil liberties groups out there that yelled about human rights and the right to a fair trial, but the truth is, most citizens just want the really bad people to be locked away so they can keep driving to their dull jobs, pay too much for their trendy foodstuffs, and download their porn. They don't want to worry about whether Doctor Deranged has created an army of rat/rhino hybrids and has set them loose on Washington, DC, or whether the Crimson Paradigm follows through on his plan to start a war between India and China.

Looking at the ship now from the outside, sitting up on landing struts I never heard come down, it looks less like the Jupiter 2 from "Lost in Space" and more like Marvin the Martian's ship (except gold instead of silver) from the old Warner Brothers cartoons. Maybe those animators were privy to something the rest of the public wasn't.

I have a minute to enjoy the blue cloudless sky and the warm ocean breeze before a seam suddenly appears near my foot. It takes the form of a circle and a section of the metal ground rises silently up, up, up... A metal door slides open and I'm looking into a tube-shaped elevator with one occupant:

Thomas Traveler.

In person, he definitely has a presence. The rest of the team have that electricity-in-the-air, you're-in-the-presence-of-greatness, kind of thing you would expect from celebrity superheroes. But Traveler? He's on a whole other level.

He steps out of the elevator and the air practically ripples around him. It's like right before a lightning storm when you feel the ions charging and something major is about to cut loose from the sky. Except in this case, it's all bottled up inside a six foot tall human shaped male body.

**Traveler's origin story:** July 1947, eighteen year-old Thomas Traveler, along with his two best friends, one his girlfriend and one his best friend since he was a toddler, were hanging out in the New Mexico desert and staring at the stars. Why? Because it was 1947 and music sucked and no one had invented the Internet yet.

So what else did teenagers do? Besides the obvious, I mean, but maybe that was on the agenda later that evening.

40

While they were watching the stars, a ship crashed nearly on top of them. A *space* ship. Traveler's best friend and girlfriend were incinerated by the wreckage. Another space ship showed up to clear up the wreckage and found what remained of Thomas, mostly a torso and head, surprisingly still with a spark of life.

Someone, or some*thing*, on board the second ship decides to take Thomas on board and try to save him. They also cleared away some of the crashed ship, but the Air Force gets there and the second ship decides to vamoose before things really get out of hand.

They leave and while on their journey back to wherever, they build Thomas a new body.

Problem was, the inhabitants of the ship really had no idea what a human body was supposed to be outside of what it looked like, because although they had been observing our planet, they had never taken any specimens before. Not even for an anal probe, despite all the stories you hear.

They had a large chunk of Thomas's body to start with, but where to go from there? They placed Thomas inside a chamber where the ship's computer could analyze what was left of his body, compared it to what the humans looked like from a distance, and then just for good measure, it remade his body much, much better than it was before. The ship's computer decided to make Thomas Traveler the way a perfect human *should* be, rather than how they really are.

At some point, Traveler woke up, got the recap from his alien hosts, and learned he was halfway across the galaxy. He asked, then demanded, to be brought back home.

Unfortunately, due to the intricate and complex nature of interstellar travel, by the time the aliens brought him back to Earth, it was no longer 1947. It was the beginning of the 21st Century. And Traveler was no longer human. He was superhuman.

This origin story? This one I believe. If you've ever stood within five feet of Traveler, you wouldn't have a doubt the story is true either. There's not only an air of power around him, but also an otherworldliness.

He's dressed in a metallic one-piece outfit that moves like silk, but shines like polished silver. Over the one-piece is a black rifle frock coat that brushes the tops of black boots. I guess he wears the coat for the pockets. You know, to keep spare change and his keys to the spaceship. Or maybe he's self-conscious about the way his ass looks in a form-fitting shiny metallic outfit.

His chestnut brown hair is down to his shoulders, and if he had a beard, he'd be a dead ringer for those Catholic portraits of what Caucasian Jesus looks like. But he's clean shaven and I can see the skin of his face is as smooth and chiseled as Michelangelo's "David."

Really. I can't detect a single pimple, blackhead, or even a pore on the guy's face.

He walks up to me, so smoothly I catch myself looking to see if he's walking or flying, and extends his hand. I take it in my gloved one and we shake.

"Thank you for coming, Dark Revenger," he says. "I didn't get to meet you the first time you were here. And I wish we were meeting under better circumstances."

His grip is firm, but not overly so. Not like a guy who's trying to prove something. I know he can crush the bones of my hand into a fine, powdery mess. Hell, I've seen him on TV bending steel and kicking a hole through a brick wall, all while bullets bounced off his skin.

He doesn't have to prove anything because he's the most powerful one here. And we all know it.

"Glad I can be of assistance," I say, and grin.

He stares at me. Hard.

"You're…different than what I would've thought," he says. He stands back and gives me an up and down look. His eyes are a steel gray and I get the feeling they're doing more than just registering my costume. It feels like he's looking at me on a subatomic level.

He says, "I have to admit, you don't look like much."

Huh. That kind of stings.

Traveler looks at Raven, but not the way a guy checking out a hot chick in skintight black leather would – the way *I* would. More like he's addressing the secretary of a low-level manager.

"You're his sidekick? *Mrs.* Dark Revenger?"

Raven's cheeks blush, although whether it's from anger or from embarrassment from being talked down to, I'm not sure. She bristles at his dismissive attitude.

"No. I'm Raven. I'm not anyone's sidekick."

"Raven." Like he's tasting the word. "You can fly?"

"Um, no, I—"

"Why would you take the name of a bird if you can't even fly?"

She opens her mouth to answer and hesitates.

Traveler says, "Never mind. I don't care. Honestly, I'm not sure why my team brought you along. I told them just to get you, Dark Revenger."

He looks at the rest of Majestic 12 like they're a bunch of screw-ups who couldn't handle one simple task. Pulsar and Cold Snap look down at their feet, clearly out-Alphaed by the top dog. Amazonia holds her ground. In fact, she looks pissed. Ms. Fire is unreadable beneath the full face mask, but I can feel a wave of indignation coming off her.

Amazonia says, "With all due respect, Traveler, she was *with* Dark Revenger, so we naturally assumed they were working together. We didn't think there would be an issue with bringing her."

"Of course not. None of you ever think. That's always been my responsibility."

Suddenly, I feel like Raven and I are dinner guests at someone's house and their family decides to air their grievances in front of us. Only, I don't have a plate of food to suddenly become very interested in.

"Dark Revenger was a big help to us last time," Pulsar says in a timid mumble.

"Yes. So I was told," Traveler says. "Well, fine. Let's see if he can repeat his performance or if he's a one-hit wonder. In the meantime, all of you need to head back out."

There's a collective groan from the team and they begin talking at once. I catch snippets here and there:

Pulsar saying, "I haven't been out of my costume in over a day."

Cold Snap saying, "I need to defrost and shower occasionally. My cold powers don't negate body odor."

Amazonia saying, "–working too hard, which is causing a lack of security here at the base–"

Ms. Fire says some stuff, too. The mask muffles it and her voice is drowned out by the others.

"Enough!" Traveler barks. "This is important. There's an energy signature detected in the Himalayas. Majestic 12 needs to be on top of this in case it poses a threat."

"Is there any reason why you can't go?" Amazonia asks him.

"No," he says in a petulant tone. "I can go. I can take care of it, and any possible threat that arises. I can take care of everything. I can handle it all. But then the question becomes, what do I need all of you for?"

No one answers that. Me? I'm wondering if I can slip the flask of whiskey out of its compartment and take a sip without anyone noticing. Better not, though. I'll wait until we're inside and then excuse myself to the Men's Room.

They do have a Men's Room here, right? I hope it's not one of those communal unisex kind of things.

"Fine," Traveler says. "I'll go alone. The rest of you stay here and enjoy your downtime. Ms. Fire can show Dark Revenger the crime scene and answer any questions he has."

To me, he says, "Try to wrap this up as quickly as possible. We need Master Mind back in his cell. We're positive he's responsible for Judgment Day's murder. We just need you to figure out how he did it and where he's currently hiding. With your detective skills, it shouldn't be difficult."

Yeah. If you only knew.

He lifts straight up into the air. No striking a pose or taking three steps and jumping kind of thing. It's slow and gentle; gravity just seems to suddenly release its grip on him. Then he shoots outward like a bullet, vertically towards the horizon.

I think, *So that's the world famous Thomas Traveler.*

A while back, I saw a picture of him some magazine dug up from the 1940s, back before he went for his trip into outer space. He had a crewcut and gangly features and looked like someone who would have grown up to be one of those nutjobs that would have shot people from a bell tower somewhere. In short, he looked like he was a real prick in his 1940s youth. You would think that now with his rock star/movie star looks and his cool-ass superpowers, he would be a much happier person.

It just goes to show you that even when people are given unlimited advantages over everyone else, they can still be a douche. In other words, with great power comes great dickness.

Amazonia heads over with the rest of the team, the only one with her head held high. The only one of the team who doesn't look like she was just chastised by father.

"Let's go inside," she says. "With any luck, this won't take long."

"That's what she said," I reply.

# CHAPTER 7
## *RAVEN'S P.O.V.*

I'm the only one here who knows. How is it possible?

How can arguably the greatest superheroes in the world not know an imposter is in their midst? Can anyone put on a costume and pretend to be someone else, and they'll simply accept him as one of their own? Is it really that simple?

The Dark Revenger, the real one, was never a member of their team. In fact, he famously turned them down when they asked him to join. It was unprecedented, both because they asked a non-superpowered hero to join, and also because he said "no."

They asked Dark Revenger after he had responded to their request for help when Master Mind escaped from his cell and taken over their base. That part happened quickly: the escape and reclaiming of his base.

Master Mind knew the layout and the security defenses better than anyone. He designed and built it all. Majestic 12 was off on a mission and when they returned, they found their island base had been turned against them. They couldn't land because the base defense system, equipped with missiles and high-powered lasers, would fire at their ship when they came within a mile of the island. The heroes that could fly experienced the same problem.

Other heroes were called in, but Master Mind was prepared for it. Any kind of superpowered energy signature was targeted by the weapons system. A military strike was considered, but Traveler and his team knew what that could entail — a nuclear strike would likely destroy the entire base and make it uninhabitable.

They had to act fast, however, as Master Mind was already threatening to release the other villains currently imprisoned on the island, and he was working on something to disrupt communications satellites all over the globe. Majestic 12 decided to call in the Dark Revenger.

They dropped him just outside the radar limits of the island. Dark Revenger swooped in on a silent glider and within an hour, had managed to bypass the base security system, located and recaptured Master Mind, and contacted M12 to tell them it was safe to come home.

They immediately offered him a place on their team. I'm sure they were surprised, and perhaps slightly insulted, when he declined. He had his reasons, he told them, and that must have mollified them because here they are, asking for his help again.

Except it's not him. And none of them seem to notice.

Are they really so self-involved they can't see through the poor masquerade? He doesn't act anything like the real Dark Revenger.

They are all narcissistic, narrow minded people who obviously can't see anything past their expensively costumed face. Especially Traveler, who walks around with a privileged air about him, perpetually irritated he has to deal with us mere mortals.

*Mrs. Dark Revenger.* What a pompous ass.

Ms. Fire says, "I guess we should head inside and I can show you the murder scene."

She has a slight Spanish accent that is both muffled and exaggerated by her mask.

Dark Revenger says to her, "Well, I for one am happy we're working together again, Fire Girl. We didn't really get a chance to talk last time I was here. Um...did we?"

She stares at him for almost a full minute.

She says, "It's Ms. Fire. Not Fire Girl. And I wasn't here the last time you were here. I've only been a member of Majestic 12 for about eight weeks. You and I never met before."

"Right. Yeah. No, I know. It was a test. I wanted to see if you were going to agree with me or not. Being the world famous Dark Revenger, lots of superheroes want to kiss my ass."

I should expose him right now. The only reason I haven't is because I'm trying to figure out what his master plan is. But as time goes on, I'm beginning to suspect he doesn't have a master plan.

So why is he here and why is he going through the pretense of helping Majestic 12?

One reason I haven't exposed him yet is because I know I wouldn't be here right now if Majestic 12 knew the truth. They would have arrested the Dark Revenger — and yes, I know I keep calling him that, but if I call him the Puzzler in my head, I'm afraid it will slip out — and I wouldn't have the opportunity to solve this case and perhaps secure my own invitation to join the team.

Selfish of me? Perhaps. Dangerous? Not really.

I can take him down at any time. I've got the confidence that comes from the pedigree of my background and the fact I've been training since I was five. If it was the *real* Dark Revenger? Chances are I wouldn't be able to defeat him in a fight, not even with surprise on my side. But the Puzzler?

Honestly, it sickens me he's wearing the Dark Revenger's costume and quite possibly sullying his reputation. When this is over, and I'm counting on it ending soon, the Puzzler is going to atone for his crimes and pay dearly for what he did.

The other three members of the team have already taken the elevator tube down. Pulsar and Cold Snap were still grumbling over Traveler's treatment of them. Amazonia was silent and seething with anger.

The elevator tube, which seems designed for a maximum of four people, comes back up. I step into it along with Ms. Fire. We both look back to see Dark Revenger still standing in the same spot.

Ms. Fire says, "Aren't you coming?"

"I need a little more foreplay."

"What?"

I can't be sure if she really didn't hear him, or if she's pretending she didn't hear him.

"Just kidding," he says. "I don't really need a lot of foreplay. Seriously, though, the three of us in that little tube? Seems like it would be, uh, kind of tight."

"Are you...?" I can't believe I'm about to ask this. "Are you claustrophobic?"

"What?! No! Of course not," he says. "I just don't like small confined spaces."

I say, "That's the definition of claustrophobic."

For the first time, he raises his head and looks at me. The shadow of his hood is gone and I'm looking into the blue of his eyes surrounded by the mask. He looks at me and I see...

What? Embarrassment maybe, but something else. For a brief second, a curtain is pulled back and I no longer see the smarmy persona. Instead, I'm looking into the blue eyes of a hurt little boy.

Just as quickly, it's gone. He blinks and the curtain is back and now I'm questioning whether what I saw was real or not. But does it matter? I'm not going to feel sorry for that scum.

I'm not. I refuse to. I don't care what his backstory is, whether he was abused as a child or picked on by his classmates. I don't care if he was abandoned by his parents or if they simply didn't love him enough. He killed one of the greatest heroes who ever lived. There's no justification for that.

"Okay, then…" He clears his throat. "What are we waiting for?"

He steps into the elevator and I hear him take a deep breath as the door slides shut around us and we descend smoothly underground. Suddenly, there's a flash of golden light as Meredith forms in our midst.

"Oh, Jesus," Dark Revenger says. "Really? Isn't it cramped in here as it is?"

He backs up against the wall. Four of us in here together doesn't give him much maneuverability. I'm not claustrophobic, but even I feel a bit stifled now.

"My apologies for the sudden intrusion," Meredith says in her human/mechanized hybrid voice.

"Aren't you supposed to be on the ship?" Dark Revenger asks.

"I can be in both places, Dark Revenger," she answers. "My intelligence is housed on the base, however, I am able to run a satellite version of myself on board the ship. You know this already, as I informed you of this same thing during your previous visit."

"Yeah. Right. I remember now."

Ms. Fire gives him a sidelong glance. I wonder if she's curious about his strange behavior, or the fact he's breathing rapidly and may be on the verge of hyperventilating.

Meredith suddenly says, "There is a security breach. You are all in imminent danger."

We can't see anything other than the circular metal walls, so I ask, "What's going on? What's the security breach?"

Ms. Fire says, "Stop the elevator, Meredith."

Dark Revenger groans. "We're stopping? Jesus. Take us back up top or let me out here. I don't care."

"I would not advise you get out of the elevator," Meredith says. "The prisoners have escaped from their cells. The security has been overridden. My own system has, too, so I am not able to take action and apprehend them myself."

"Yeah, okay," Dark Revenger says. "No worries. Let's just head back topside and put in a call to the rest of the team. Okay? Like, right now. Really. I'm having trouble breathing in this cramped space. I mean, normally I'd love to be pressed up against three beautiful women. Or, two beautiful women and a hot robot chick. But not now. Having trouble breathing. Am I babbling? Feels like I'm babbling—"

Ms. Fire cuts him off. "Which prisoner escaped?"

"All of them," Meredith answers.

Dark Revenger is still talking, his voice down to a mumble. He doesn't look well. The small portion of his face I can see appears to be damp with perspiration and very pale.

"How many in total?" I direct the question to Meredith, but include Ms. Fire with my line of sight.

"Four," they both answer in unison. Meredith adds, "Not including Master Mind, who is still missing."

"Where are the other escapees right now?" Ms. Fire asks.

"I am unable to answer that question. Part of my system has been shut down, including security cameras. Also, my defensive weapons are not operational. Someone has manually overridden everything except my avatar."

Ms. Fire says, "Master Mind. It must be him."

"Enough!" Dark Revenger yells. "Open the door! I need to get out! Open the door! Open! Open—"

"Do it, Meredith," Ms. Fire says.

The door slides open. We're five feet from being level with one of the floors, whichever one it is. I have no idea how many floors there are or how far down the base goes. Dark Revenger ducks his head and jumps out. He lands expertly. He's a trained acrobat; I can tell by the way he moves. Well, he's not the only one.

I duck and jump, and keep my legs fluid so the impact is evenly distributed. Meredith appears in our midst, again in a flash of golden light. Ms. Fire surprises me. She floats down to the floor as gently as a feather.

"You can fly," I say.

"Sort of," she says, but doesn't elaborate.

"Whew! Much better!" Dark Revenger says.

Then he does something that takes me completely by surprise. He pushes his hood back, removes a red silk cloth from one of the compartments on his bandolier, wipes his forehead, and then...

I have to blink because I'm not sure if what I'm seeing is real. He takes a comb from another compartment and combs his hair.

"Nice to be able to breathe again, you know?"

Ms. Fire stares at him.

"What?" he asks her.

"You're younger than I thought you'd be," she says.

He gives her a cocky grin. "Nah. Just good genes and clean living."

The anger boils up inside me and I'm about to unleash a torrent of epithets, when Meredith says, "Twenty-eight percent of my sensors have come back online. The team is presently battling one of the escaped prisoners on Level 10. Another escapee is close to us. You should prepare to engage."

"Which direction?" I move into a defensive stance, braced on the balls of my feet. Ms. Fire is staring down one end of the corridor, so I face the opposite. It doesn't matter; the floor erupts beneath us.

I tumble and attempt to land on my feet. The buckling floor throws me off. I land hard on my hip, roll, and come up on one knee just in time to see Ms. Fire floating gently to the floor outside the lip of the large hole in the floor. Dark Revenger is flat on his back, but recovers quickly and struggles to his feet. Meredith forms a new body, or perhaps it's the same body. I'm not sure how the whole thing works with her.

There isn't time to contemplate it anyway, as a large purple hand claws its way upward through the hole in the floor. Steel screams and twists away from the hand as it pushes up, followed by the huge misshapen head of Killzore. His body makes the opening wider, and while a normal person would find his flesh slashed to ribbons by the jagged edges of metal surrounding the hole, Killzore's skin is impenetrable.

He's a monster in the literal sense. He was human once, or so it's been said, and physically not much to speak of. He was short, frail, and sickly, but very rich. He paid Doctor Deranged to make him "physically superior," but unfortunately didn't specify beyond that. This...

This eight foot tall, wide as a Volkswagen Beetle, hairless, purple, three fingered and three-toed creature, elongated snout with a double row of gleaming pointed teeth is what he was turned into.

"I knew I smelled food up here." Killzore's voice is as horrible as his appearance would indicate.

His eyes, two black reptilian orbs, zero in on me.

"Mmmm...," he says. "Been a while since I had Chinese."

"Japanese, asshole," I say and hurl two throwing stars at him.

The stars bounce off his hide. I knew they would. I was actually aiming for one of his eyes, although I don't know if they would penetrate those any easier. He's damn near invulnerable. It took the combined might of Traveler, Amazonia, and Judgment Day to capture him. There's no way we're going to be able to beat him. We need help.

I throw myself backward and flip out of the way, trying to get some maneuvering room. I'm panicking a little. I'm not ashamed to admit it: I'm a little scared. I've never gone up against a superpowered person before, let alone one that looks and acts like something out of a nightmare.

Oh, and Killzore has been known to eat people. So there's that fun fact adding to my panic quotient.

I have to focus and remember my training. Can't let myself get rattled. Besides, there are the others to consider. I can't run away and leave them to be killed. Or eaten.

Ms. Fire slams into Killzore from behind and knocks him flat on his face. I wish I could say it puts him down permanently, but despite it sounding like he was hit by a bus doing 100 MPH, he's already up and laughing it off.

"Wuz that s'posed to hurt?"

There's room enough for him to stand up straight, but Killzore tends to walk hunched over with his fingers grazing the floor. He turns his massive head and looks at Ms. Fire. She floats up, stops in midair, and suddenly hurtles at him with tremendous speed. She hits Killzore in the side and slams him into the wall. His body imprints itself in the steel, but he doesn't go down. Ms. Fire floats backward and stares at him. She's stunned, I think, that he doesn't seem the least bit fazed.

"Now you're getting' annoyin'," he says.

She's preparing to take another shot when a bolt of electricity shoots up from the hole in the floor and clips her on her right. She cries out as she's thrown to the side. She lands in a heap on the floor and doesn't move.

A man flies up through the hole. Electrical current buzzes around his body, caresses his arms and legs, and fills the air with the smell of ozone. Although he's human in appearance, he's also completely hairless, not even eyebrows, and naked except for a pair of white briefs. I know him from news reports and my own research into the supervillain world:

He's Dynamo. Although he may not eat his victims, he's as much of a murderous psychopath as Killzore.

My years of training, practice drills and computer simulations, countless hours studying case files... It all goes out the window. I'm scared. Terrified, in fact.

I could take on a Colombian drug cartel or the Yakuza and my heart rate would remain steady and my hands wouldn't shake. But two superpowered psychopaths – one an eight foot tall monster with a mouth full of razors, and the other with the power to burn me to a cinder where I stand – and I forget my training and stand frozen like a deer staring down a tractor trailer.

Dynamo says, "Lookee here. Fresh meat."

I yell to Meredith, "Do something!"

"I'm afraid I cannot," she answers, as immobile as a statue. "I cannot access the defense systems and this light form I inhabit is not designed for offensive tactics."

"Sounds like a personal problem," Dark Revenger says and runs up Killzore's scaly back.

Killzore swats at him with one of his massive hands, but Dark Revenger is already jumping and somersaulting off. As he leaps off Killzore, he drops three black spherical objects into Killzore's gaping mouth. There are three muffled POPS and Killzore staggers.

Dark Revenger hits the ground running. Killzore shakes his huge body and clutches his throat, right before he collapses to the floor with a giant THUD that shakes the walls.

Dark Revenger catches me in the midsection and lifts me up on his shoulder in a fireman's carry. He misjudges his momentum, or I shift my weight, or perhaps a combination of both. Whatever the case, his feet slip out from under him and we both hit the floor, me on my back and Dark Revenger face down and partially on top of me. We slide along the smooth metal surface of the floor.

Dynamo yells and fires a bolt of electricity where I had been standing a moment ago. It hits with a loud BANG and leaves a black scorch mark. He yells again, agitated that he missed. The crackling of the electricity around his body increases in volume and ferocity. His voice is nearly drowned out by his powers.

He floats towards us with his hands outstretched in a mock crucifixion pose. Electricity flows from his fingertips and coats the walls, floor, and ceiling. Dynamo and the current from his fingers move as one towards us.

"Let's see you run from this," he yells. "There's nowhere for you to go."

He's right. The passageway ends a few feet from our heads; it's a dead-end. There are rooms and alcoves behind Dynamo, but the electricity will be impossible to avoid. I have to do something. I have to—

Dark Revenger rolls over and tosses a gray object the size and shape of a ping pong ball. It explodes when it hits the electrical field surrounding Dynamo and expands into foam that washes over him. The electrical field fizzles out and Dynamo lands on his feet, bits of electricity still sputtering, but getting smaller and smaller. He's not completely covered in the gray foam. Just enough that most of his bare skin only shows through in patches.

"What the hell?! What'd you do to me? What happened to my powers?"

Dark Revenger stands and walks towards Dynamo. In his Dark Revenger voice that's a fair imitation of the real one, but not good enough to fool me, he says,

"Maybe the foam that's clinging to you is nullifying the electricity your body generates. Or maybe you've got performance issues." Then in his normal voice he says, "Those of us who know Bondage Queen know which one you suffer from, huh, Dynamo?"

Dynamo's eyes widen at Dark Revenger and his jaw drops open.

"Who the f—"

Dark Revenger punches him square in the face. Dynamo's eyes roll back in his head and he falls backward, out cold.

Dark Revenger looks back at me. "You okay, hottie?"

I stare at him.

He shrugs and turns away.

Ms. Fire shakily climbs to her feet, using the wall for support.

"How did you...?" Ms. Fire shakes her head. "What did you do to Killzore?"

"I made him eat three knockout grenades," Dark Revenger says. "Which is enough knockout gas to kill a normal person. But I figured it would just put big boy down for a nap. At least, I don't *think* I killed him."

Meredith responds, "No. His vital signs are steady."

"Oh…well…good, then. I guess."

I stand up and make my way to where Ms. Fire is leaning. "You okay?"

She gives me a single nod. "I think so, except for the taste of copper in my mouth, and the feeling like I was hit by the world's largest bug zapper." She grunts. "Can't believe I got taken down so easily. Rookie mistake."

I smile and try to think of something reassuring to say. She put up a much better fight than I did. I was the rookie here, not her. The words form in my head, but before I can put them to sound, I see she's staring past me at Dark Revenger.

He says, "Hey, I'm pretty good at this, don't you think? I took down both of those motherfuckers." He still has his hood pushed back and has a huge, shit-eating grin on his face. He takes a flask from his belt and unscrews it.

"The Dark Revenger, baby!" he says and takes a long pull from the flask. He wipes his mouth on the back of his gloved hand. "Dark motherfuckin' Revenger."

"You know," Ms. Fire says, "I always thought the Dark Revenger would be more..."

"More what?"

"More *dark*," she says.

# CHAPTER 8
## *Flashback*


*The Hideout* is a bar for supervillains and their henchmen, although occasionally you get some rich kids or B List celebs traipsing through, looking for a cheap thrill. Technically, you're supposed to be a supervillain in order to drink here, but as long as you don't cause a scene and don't harass anybody, your money spends as good as anyone else's. You're also supposed to show up in costume and most of us do, but it's not mandatory.

There are a few of these places scattered about the U.S. – watering holes like *The Hideout*, where us villainous types can unwind and shoot the shit with others in the biz. I hear there's even some clubs for the superheroes to mingle and occasionally hook-up, although I couldn't tell you for sure. All of my friends are bad guys.

I frequent *this* particular club because, well, my crimes are primarily planned and committed in Azure City. Plus, it's where my archnemesis, the Dark Revenger, operates and what would be the point of moving somewhere else and having to worry about one of the really powerful supes?

Mr. Meaner used to try and talk me into going into a scheme with him up in New York. I declined and he went anyway, and now thanks to Judgment Day, I don't know if he'll ever be the same.

Azure City doesn't attract the heavy-duty superpowered folks the way New York, Chicago, or LA does. The biggest name here, hero-wise, is the Dark Revenger. A few other heroes operate here, but they're all non-powered, street-level types and not nearly as organized or as well financed as D.R. The worst thing you have to worry about the heroes in this city is one of them knocking some teeth out or Tasering you, maybe even shooting you (nonlethally), which is a hell of a lot better than having your skull crushed or your legs lasered off.

Of course, your question probably is, if there's a bar where known supervillains hang out, then why doesn't the Dark Revenger, or the police, or even Majestic 12, swoop in and arrest everyone? Or at least, why don't they stake it out and nab everybody one at a time when they're too drunk to see straight? See, it's like this:

For one, you have to know somebody who knows somebody who knows where the place is. And one of those people has to be a supervillain, otherwise you're dealing with lots of conjecture and half-assed urban legends about the location, or even *if* the place really exists. If you do manage to get confirmation about the existence and general whereabouts (underground, beneath the financial district), there are miles of tunnels to confuse you unless you're guided by someone who knows the way.

Trust me, you'll get lost very easily unless you have an old hand show you the route. It's happened to investigative reporters looking to do an exposé. Some of them *still* haven't been found. But it doesn't really explain why a superhero, especially a smart and capable one, couldn't find the place.

Take into account there's enough electronic jamming equipment wired throughout the place – stuff designed by Master Mind before he was put on permanent lockdown by M12, and upgraded by my buddy Savant – that keeps the place from being detected by satellite surveillance, radar, heat sensors, or even psychic probes.

Yeah, we're *that* paranoid.

Secondly, and probably the biggest reason we haven't been raided by the supes:

They know to leave us alone.

Look, when you're in this business, you need a place where you can unwind, kick back and drink a few, and maybe if you're lucky, score a hook-up for the night, although I think that goes on more at the heroes' clubs than here. Traditionally, there are more guys than girls in the supervillain ranks, and I think the opposite is true with the heroes. Anyway...

The point is, just as cops tend to associate and hang out with other cops when they're off-duty, the same can be said for those of us in the superhero and supervillain profession. There can be a lot of pressure on us for both sides, and the only people who truly understand that pressure are the ones in the same field. So when you're not risking your life, or in our case, life *or* freedom, we like to mingle with our own. Just as they have their hang-outs, we have ours. The unspoken rule is, you don't screw with our off-time recreation, and we won't screw with yours. Don't bust up our club, we won't bust-up yours.

So far, it's worked. For years, in fact. And it's a good thing, in my opinion. Because if any superhero did dare to break the unspoken rule...

Some of the supervillains wouldn't stop at attacking their off-duty clubs. They'd start breaking the other unspoken rule, the one about respecting secret identities and not involving friends and families in vendettas.

The room is circular and about as big as a football field, with a long bar that takes up maybe an eighth of one wall. The rest of the circle is tables, booths, and many secluded alcoves with curtain partitions for privacy in case you want to cut some deals, plot some crimes, or maybe just get freaky. The bar is well-stocked and the staff keeps all kinds of exotic liquor on hand for some of the big name guys, and the run-of-the-mill beer and wine working-class supervillains prefer.

There's a kitchen in the back that serves pretty decent burgers and wings, and not much else. The menu is literally ten items, although I understand the cooks will throw together a special order if you offer enough money. Also, the restrooms here are surprisingly clean.

The middle of the club is the dance floor filled with gyrating bodies, predominantly female ones, although there are plenty of guys out there, too. The floor has a sound dampener field built into it, so if you're directly on the dance floor, the music sounds like it's cranked to mega-decibels and conversation is impossible. Outside the dance floor, the music sounds low, like background music in a cocktail bar. Which is great because you can have a conversation at a table without shouting in your friends' ears.

There isn't a clearly defined line to show where the sound dampener takes effect, so if you're new, the first few times you're likely to be walking back from the bar and accidentally cross the barrier and get startled by a sudden blast of club music. It generally leads to a spilled drink or two, after which, you learn to give the dance area a wide berth.

I don't come here to dance, although I have on occasion. Usually it's because I'm really drunk, or I'm trying to score with a woman. Tonight, I'm neither. Well, not yet (to both), but the night is young.

I'm in my favorite booth with Blue Howler, watching the women dance and sipping my whiskey sour. Howler has a rum and Coke, and despite the fact it's mostly rum and very little Coke, which is how the bartender makes it for him, for which he is generously tipped, he drinks it like it's water on a hot summer day. Howler's metabolism burns it up too fast, so he tries to drink quickly in order to catch a buzz. The most he ever gets is a little tipsy, and then not for very long.

"So what do you think?" he asks me.

"I think the chick in the red dress and the black mask is a TV sitcom actress."

As I said, it's not mandatory to show up in costume, but most of us do. And the civilians generally dress up, too, although for many of them, it consists mainly of wearing a mask with their club-slut or club-stud attire.

"No," he says. "Not that. What do you think about the job?"

I'm in my purple Puzzler zoot suit get-up, complete with the black gloves and mask. My fedora is on the seat next to me. I stare at the blonde TV actress and try to catch her eye. She's lost in the music, though. Or maybe Ecstasy. Maybe both.

"I don't think so, Howler. I don't like working with partners. You know? The more guys you take into a scheme, the bigger your chances someone other than you will fuck it up." I look across the table at him.

His skin and hair are pastel blue and the pupils of his eyes are blood-red. He looks like the offspring of a demon and a Smurf. He doesn't wear a costume, instead favoring t-shirts and hoodies without sleeves, ripped jeans, and beat-to-hell Timberlands. Because really, when you look like Howler, what's the point of a costume?

**Blue Howler's origin:** He tells everyone he was once a famous singer in a rock band who discovered he was terminally ill. To fend off death, he traveled the world in search of a cure. He found plenty of witch doctors, shamans, and faith healers, and although they all claimed they could help him, none of them could. After the bulk of his money was gone and he had tried just about every herbal remedy known to man, he heard whispers of a cult up in the mountains of Estonia that could cure him.

Using his last few dollars for a plane ticket, he hiked the remainder of the journey and found a group of devil worshippers who promised immortality in exchange for his soul. Howler, out of desperation and the slightly manic motives of a man who has sacrificed everything to escape the icy clutches of death, agreed without hesitation. The cult performed an intense series of elaborate spells, which Howler said consisted of him ingesting many things that smelled and tasted awful, stripping naked and allowing them to paint arcane symbols on his body in blood, and having sex with a weird goat-like animal he swears spoke in a language that sounded a lot like Latin. When he woke up several days later, he was alone and had been transformed into his now blue-skinned self.

The story smelled of bullshit the first time I heard it. First, Estonia doesn't have mountains (I looked it up), and if Howler was ever a famous singer, then all of his fans must have been tone deaf. I've heard him sing and believe me, the sound of dogs howling is preferable. I confronted him about it and to his credit, he came clean. To *me*, I mean. To everyone else, he's still spouts the other bullshit story.

The closest he ever came to being a rock legend was performing in a garage band back in high school. He admitted they were pretty awful. After graduation, he drifted into petty crime and eventually made a connection with a guy who recruits henchmen for various supervillains. Howler took a job working for Dr. Deranged.

He said the job was pretty boring, mostly doing late night break-ins at science labs and medical facilities and stealing equipment and chemicals. Sometimes it consisted of rounding up test animals for the doc to work on. The pay was shitty and the doc spent most of his time locked up in his lab, working on gene manipulation or creating some new animal hybrid. Just when he was thinking about quitting, the doc asked the guys if they were interested in earning a substantial bonus by participating in a "harmless" medical experiment.

"The smart ones said no," Howler told me. "Just me and another guy said sure, what the hell. We should have known better, but to be fair, it *was* a big bonus he was offering."

The harmless experiment meant getting ninety injections, "At least two dozen in my eyes," he said, and when it was over, the other guy had dissolved into a pile of pink goo and Howler had turned blue. He had also become much stronger and developed a sonic yell that had a physical impact similar to getting hit by hurricane winds. He took off when he learned the doc planned to experiment on him some more, part of which would involve exploratory surgery.

Why the crazy origin story, then? I asked.

"Because it sounds better than the one where I'm dumb enough to let Dr. Deranged inject me with stuff," he said. "Oh, and I really did have sex with a goat-woman. One of the doc's pets. Pretty sure it was female."

Back to the here and now:

I'm still eyeing the blonde on the dance floor, and I've got a curvy brunette in my sights as a possible back-up. Howler says something.

"Hm?" I say.

"I was saying you should really think about this. It's gonna be a big score. Big enough that maybe we won't have to do this no more."

Really? He's going to retire? And do what? Open a bakery? Be the blue-skinned guy with the freaky eyes who bakes cupcakes and wedding cakes?

He can probably tell what I'm thinking not only by the expression on my face, but also because we've had this discussion a time or two before, because he says,

"Yeah, okay, there's not exactly a retirement plan for somebody like me. I can't take off a mask like you and blend into the background. But still, I don't want to keep doing this. It's only a matter of time before Majestic 12 or some other high-powered cape hunts me down."

"So what are you going to do? What's your retirement plan?"

He shrugs and looks at his drink. "There's some countries that, if you pay off the local authorities, they'll look the other way. Also, Savant is working on a device that can conceal my looks. You know, somethin' that can make me look normal. Gonna cost a lot if he can do it."

A woman's laugh, one of those drunk way-too-loud ones, carries from the bar. We both look over and see a tall statuesque blonde at the bar, talking to a small group of people. Her costume consists of black leather straps wrapped around her body and limbs in a way that conceals all the naughty bits, but leaves nothing to the imagination and allows skin to peek through here and there. She wears a mask over her eyes and balances herself precariously on the tallest stiletto-heeled boots I've ever seen.

Howler asks, "Who's that?"

"She calls herself Bondage Queen and claims to be a supervillain from up north. But really, she's that superhero Lady Justice."

"Huh. No shit."

"She likes to come here and pick up bad guys."

"For what?" Howler asks. "You mean *pick up* pick up?"

"Yeah. She has a fetish for role-playing as a supervillain and having sex with guys like us."

"Huh."

I see the wheels turn in his head.

"Don't waste your time, Howler. She's a lousy lay."

He laughs. "Come on, Puzzler. You tapped that, too? Jeez... Is there any broad that hangs out here you haven't fucked?"

The TV actress for one, but I can't catch her eye. I might have to get up and actually dance with her.

Sigh. I hate having to work for it, you know?

Bondage Queen/Lady Justice laughs hard at something. She's annoying me. I hope she picks a guy and leaves soon. Shouldn't be long; I see a couple of guys studying her like dogs eyeing a pork chop that's about to be dropped into a kennel. They hang on her every word and watch her gestures and wait and wait...and then she'll zero in on the one she wants and the rest will fade away to search for other game. Or drink. There's always that.

I remember something from my one-night stand with her, besides the "lousy lay" part:

When she unwraps herself out of her bondage costume, the leather straps leave red lines and indentations all over her skin that takes a while to fade away. It's a bit disconcerting and almost made me not want to sleep with her.

I said *almost*.

Howler says, "About this job..."

Christ, not this again.

"It's a sure thing," he says. "Thirty million score. That's ten apiece."

"Wait, wait, wait." I'm in the middle of sipping my drink, so I have to put it down and look him square in his red eyes. "Math isn't my strong suit, but even I know that thirty million split between two people isn't ten apiece. It's fifteen million."

He shakes his head. "You really haven't been listening. It's a three person job. You, me, and Court Jester."

"Court Jester! That lunatic?!"

"Lunatic is kinda harsh, Puzzler. He ain't *that* bad."

"The guy is certifiably crazy. Nobody will work for him anymore because he has a habit of killing his own henchmen. And not by accident, or because he experiments on them like your old boss. He literally will take out a gun and shoot them. Or poison them. Or stab them."

Howler spreads his hands out. "He says that stuff isn't true. He never did that. Some disgruntled ex-employees spread those rumors."

"That's what *he* says. What do his henchmen say?"

He looks away and shifts in his seat, suddenly uncomfortable.

I say, "You can't locate any of his guys, can you? And why is that? Maybe because they're all dead?"

"Ah," he says, "you know, I don't know what your problem is. Maybe the guy does have a few loose screws, but I figure between the two of us, we can keep him in check. You watch my back, I watch yours. That kind of thing."

He turns to the side, leans back, and puts his leg up on the seat so he doesn't have to face me.

"Whatever. Forget I asked. Just keep doing your little museum heists and stealing Faberge eggs or whatever. You've been pretty lucky so far. I don't know how Dark Revenger hasn't caught you yet. That guy always catches up with everyone who commits a crime in Azure City. Like it's a personal insult to him if you pull a job within city limits. And you... You *gotta* leave your little puzzle boxes with your messages in them to taunt him. He must really have a hard-on to catch you."

Howler looks at me when he says, "How is it you can leave him clues and he's never caught you? Really, I'd like to know that."

"Because I'm smarter than him."

Howler chuckles and rolls his eyes as he sips his drink.

"Good one," he says. "You should call yourself the Comedian instead of the Puzzler."

"I think that name is trademarked."

Okay, so maybe the truth is I'm not smarter than the Dark Revenger. Maybe the truth is, the reason why I haven't been caught yet is because I cheat.

That's right. I said *cheat*.

I purposely don't have a pattern to what I do. And the clues I leave? Fake. They're random quotes or anagrams of things that have nothing to do with my next job or where I'm hiding. I mean seriously, what kind of an idiot would I have to be to really leave a clue on how to catch me or where I'm planning to strike next? I may be a lot of things – lazy, self-absorbed, self-centered, arrogant, obnoxious, a womanizer – but I'm not an idiot.

Howler says, "Seriously dude, how long do you plan to do this? Because you know, eventually, they will catch you. But fine, whatever. Keep doing your little artsy crime crap. If the Dark Revenger shows up, you can throw a Rubik's Cube at him. That'll slow him down."

"Wow," I say. "You really know how to lay it on thick. Is there a Jewish mother in your past?"

He flips me a blue finger.

"Alright, let me think about it for a few. Okay?"

He shrugs and goes back to scanning the crowd.

How long do I plan to do this? That's what Howler asked, and it's not as if I haven't given it serious thought.

Honestly, I had planned to retire six months ago. And when I say *retire*, I mean let myself get caught. You know, give Dark Revenger a real clue and let him catch me in the act. I'd surrender without a fight, of course, and then proceed with my plan of the minimum security prison, the book deal, the fame and fortune, etc.

Except...

Ever have one of those jobs you were surprisingly good at? Maybe it wasn't what you originally envisioned as a career for yourself, but you took it thinking it would just be temporary. Then you surprised yourself by being able to pick up the various job responsibilities really fast, like it was something you were born to do. You got to know other people in the business and made some friends. Time passes and you think about changing careers, going to what you originally had planned for yourself. Then you think about how much work it would entail.

In my case, it would mean getting caught and going to jail, then trial, then prison. My parents would have to deal with the revelation that their eldest son was a supervillain. I mean, yeah, I'm already the black sheep, but at least now they can leave the house without a news crew sticking a camera in their face and some dead-eyed reporter asking them how they felt when they learned their son was the Puzzler.

Oh, and once in prison, I would actually have to write that book about myself. And writing? Not as easy as everyone fantasizes it is.

Still, I do have to quit. Really. He's right when he says sooner or later the Dark Revenger will catch me.

The lights dim for the briefest of moments, then a flicker like heat lightning and several people yelp in surprise. One woman's hair stands up and she lets out a shriek. She looks around and then giggles nervously when she sees the cause: Dynamo.

Howler says, "Huh. Look who decided to grace us with his presence."

We don't usually get the big-time guys in here, the A Listers with power levels that are off the charts. The ones who can go toe-to-toe with any member of Majestic 12. I'm not sure why that is, if it's because they don't feel like they can relate to us "working-class" supervillains, or if they are so accustomed to living in their own rarefied air of world recognition, they have to get their kicks in other ways rather than drinking, dancing, and hooking up.

Dynamo is not only a world-class, well-known supervillain, he's also a huge prick. Case in point:

The use of superpowers is prohibited in the club. It's a strict rule because no one wants a drunken display of superpowers that might tear out a support beam and bring the roof down on everyone. Dynamo's idiotic display has caused the security androids to approach him. They're designed and built by Savant to handle the drunks and the psychotics. Problem is, I'm never seen them go up against someone with Dynamo's power level.

They flank him and Dynamo whirls around. Electricity arcs between his fingertips.

"Keep your fake plastic hands off me!" he yells. "Do you know who I am? Do you have any idea what I can do? I'll fry your goddamn circuits!"

Howler shakes his head. "Puts on a show, don't he?"

Savant comes through a side door next to the bar. He's a middle-aged black man with hair as white as his heavily starched button-down Egyptian cotton shirt. He doesn't wear a flashy costume, rather, he usually sports an expensive black three-piece silk suit. No tie; he has an onyx pin holding the collar together. And like many supervillains, he has a goatee.

Interesting tidbit: Most superheroes are clean shaven. One or two have a mustache, and one or two have beards. The only ones that sport goatees are the villains – usually the mad scientist or evil genius type.

No, I don't know why this is.

Savant has his hands out in a "calm down" gesture. He says something to Dynamo, then to the androids. They immediately turn away and head back to their posts. Their faces are blank, devoid of any features other than two slits where their eyes would be if they were human. Savant never bothered to give them faces. He said he thought it would be a waste of time. They can't be programmed to act human, so why bother pretending they are?

Dynamo mutters something I don't catch. I'm guessing it's his version of an apology. Knowing his personality type, said apology will be part ignorance as excuse, and part veiled warning that he'll continue to do what he wants and everyone else should make allowances. He turns to the bar and orders a drink. Savant shakes his head.

I motion to Savant to come over. He holds up two fingers ("two minutes"), then heads back through the side door. He's working on something back there for the club, no doubt, or adjusting one of the security devices.

Once he leaves, I see Dynamo looking around at the tables and booths. His eyes make their way in our direction and stop on me and Howler. He smiles coldly.

"Here we go," Howler says.

"You're not gonna start a fight, are you?" I ask.

"I'm not the one you have to worry about starting anything."

Dynamo walks over like his balls are made of solid brass and he enjoys the clanging sound they make.

"Hey, Smurfette," he says to Howler. "It's been a while. I see you're here with your girlfriend, the *Puss*-ler."

"Really?" I say, "I haven't seen you in three months and the best insult you were able to come up with was *Puss-ler*?"

He ignores me.

"So what's the word, blue boy? You still hanging out with poseurs, huh?"

Howler says, "Poseurs? How do you figure? Puzzler here has been operating for two years and has never been caught. How many times have you had your ass kicked?"

"Give me a break. These guys," he hooks a thumb at me, "put on a costume and use some dumb-ass gimmick, and call themselves a supervillain? Me, I went toe-to-toe with Amazonia. Queen Super-Bitch herself."

"Yeah, I saw the news," Howler says. "You flew away pretty fast."

"Yeah, after a few minutes of zappin' her ass all over downtown Philly. What was I supposed to do? She was shruggin' off some major hits. And she wouldn't stop coming after me. I figured she probably put in a call to the rest of her team. I'm no idiot–"

"Really?" I ask.

"Shut the fuck up." Then to Howler: "I can handle myself against one of them. Maybe two. But the whole Majestic 12? No way I'd even try."

Howler says, "Dude, what's your point? You don't have to keep telling everyone you're a badass. We get it already. Okay? Stop with the whole beating your chest, struttin' around bullshit."

Dynamo opens his mouth. He's obviously at a loss for a response because he just stares at Howler. There's frustration on his face, like he wants to say something, *anything*, but he's stuck. There's also a bit of confusion, too, probably because he's not sure if Howler just paid him a backhanded compliment or outright insulted him.

Bondage Queen disrupts the standoff by sidling up to Dynamo.

"I haven't seen you here before," she says. "Dynamo, right?"

"That's me, babe," he says. "I don't recognize you, but I bet I can guess your superpower." He winks at her.

"Buy me a drink and I'll let you guess. Guess the right one and I might use it on you."

"Sure, come on."

They head back to the bar. Behind her back, Bondage Queen gives me the finger. Still angry I haven't come back for seconds, I guess.

I say, "What do you think the chances are he'll be able to guess her superpower is getting sloppy drunk and having sex with anything on two legs?"

Howler chuckles.

"Thanks, by the way."

"For what?" he asks.

"Ah, you know, defending me to him. You didn't have to. But I appreciate it."

He shrugs, sips his drink. I sip mine. We go back to studying the women on the dance floor and purposely avoid looking at the awkward gyrations of the few men that are out there.

"All that power," he says, talking about Dynamo. "And that asshole only wants to knock over armored cars. Then he heads to South America and blows all his money. Comes back to America and hits another armored car." He shakes his head. "Stupid. And he's got no, whatdoyacallit? When there's no conscience telling him not to do something?"

"No compunction," I say.

"I don't think that's the word. But anyway, he's got no problem with killing civilians. He's fried probably a dozen armored car guys. And for what? It's not like they're cops or one of the capes. They're just working stiffs. Like us."

69

Huh. Funny how Howler sees himself as a blue collar guy. And no, I didn't intend that as a pun on his skin color.

"Me and you, Eddie, we're different than him."

Weird hearing my real name. Sometimes I forget he and I shared that one night over copious amounts of alcohol. (His real name is Fred, by the way.)

"We're different because we've got–"

"Style?" I offer. "Class? Charisma? Grace?"

"A code," he says. "We live by a code. That's why I asked you in on this job with me. Honestly, I don't need you. Court Jester and I can do it alone. I wanted you there because I don't trust him. I need someone to watch my back. I would trust you to do that. Watch my back. So..." He holds his drink up and studies it in the multi-colored lights bouncing off the dance floor. "There it is."

I shake my head. I can't believe he's going to guilt me into this.

Because that's what he's doing. He's laying a guilt trip on me. If I don't get involved and something goes wrong and Howler pays the price, then I'll feel like a bigger asshole than Dynamo. Of course, my involvement doesn't necessarily preclude something going wrong, but as he said, I can watch his back.

Team-ups are usually bad luck. For the supervillains, I mean. The heroes always benefit. It's why I've always worked alone. I would work with Howler. That's not the issue. It's Court Jester who makes me uneasy. I don't think he's a psychopath. I think he's psychotic. There's a world of difference between the two.

Savant comes to our table, looking unusually stressed. Normally, he's got a cool sophistication and an unflappable way about him, like his entire day is planned out months in advance on spreadsheets. Tonight he appears somewhat harried.

"Gentlemen, I'm afraid I can't join you for a drink tonight," he says. His voice is a deep baritone and sounds like it would be perfect for narrating a documentary.

"I was in the process of resetting the security system when a certain idiotic individual with electricity-based powers decided to show off." He sighs. "The one night I decide to fine tune the satellite feed when the club is open, and that moron decides to stop in."

I say, "Speaking of the human bug zapper, what would be the chances you could come up with a device that could screw with his powers?"

70

"Simple," he answers. "Something that explodes a non-conductive foam over him. Or possibly generates an alternating current to his own, causing a feedback effect. Or maybe–"

"Yeah, yeah, yeah." I cut him off before he gets too carried away. "I know you can probably think of a dozen different things. I just need one, though."

"What's the deal, Puzzler?" Howler asks. "You planning on switching sides and taking Dynamo in? Don't tell me you're siding with the capes all of a sudden."

"Nah, not likely. I just want to have something I can use on him if he ever gets out of line. Or maybe use it to make him look like a total ass in front of everyone."

Savant says, "Not a problem. But it will cost you."

"Okay."

We shake on it and Savant heads back to the room behind the bar to adjust his diodes or whatever he's doing.

"You know," Howler says, "if you ever mess with Dynamo, as soon as he gets his powers back, he'll want to burn you to a crisp."

"Yeah, I know."

Howler smiles, shakes his head, and takes a sip of his drink.

"I'm in, by the way."

He almost does a double take. "Say what?"

"I'm in," I say with a sigh. "I'll do the job with you and the psycho."

"What changed your mind? Not that it matters."

He's loose and smiling freely; a weight has been lifted off his shoulders. He must have really wanted this.

"Was it the 'watch my back' line that did it?" he asks.

"Yeah, pretty much," I say. But there's much more.

He's right. It's time to retire. I can't keep doing this. It's time to get out and continue with my original plan: short prison stay, tell-all book, fame, and then show business. I need to get out before I become complacent and do something stupid.

Somewhere between Howler's guilt trip and Savant coming to the table, a plan began to form in my head. A smart and cunning plan that will enable me to get caught with little fuss, and allow Howler to have his retirement.

We clink our glasses together and Howler fills me in on this once-in-a-lifetime score. Meanwhile, in my head, I make a counter-plan to the one he's describing.

A week later, Savant presents me with a device that can shut down Dynamo's electrical field, albeit temporarily. It costs me quite a bit. I figure it'll be worth it to show the guy up in front of everyone. But less than four days after that, he gets slammed by Majestic 12 and taken away to their 24-hour lockdown prison on their island base.

A week after that, Howler, Court Jester, and I proceed with our big crime of the century. And obviously it all went to shit.

# CHAPTER 9

The next set of events happen pretty quickly.

We find the third escapee on the level below us, although he's no longer alive. It's Doctor Deranged and he has a Killzore-sized bite taken out of his midsection. He doesn't look as menacing as he did when he would periodically show up on TV, usually interrupting something big like the Super Bowl, with one of his "Pay me xxx dollars or I'll blow up Mount Rushmore" or some other idiotic demand.

Apparently, Killzore must have held a grudge against the doc for turning him into a monster. I don't blame him for being mad; the doc turned him into one ugly bastard. Probably not what he had in mind when he paid for superpowers.

"So let me get this straight," I say. "Meredith, you run the computer system here at HQ, which includes the security system. But somehow, someone screwed with things and you pretty much got shut out of some stuff, like the holding cells and the defense weaponry. What would the defense weaponry be, by the way?"

She answers, "I could have subdued the escaped prisoners with gas or turned off the oxygen until they were unconscious. There are also stun lasers set up in each corridor."

"Okay. But for some reason, you couldn't. And for some other reason, or maybe related to this reason, these super-psychopaths were able to get out of their cells. And Master Mind has managed to escape and remain undetected. And also Judgment Day was murdered and that also was done without witnesses or being detected by your security system."

Raven says, "You summed it up pretty well."

It sounds like a compliment at first, but there's a slight tone to it that also sounds like "No shit, Sherlock, " so I have no idea what she means by it. What I don't understand is, if she knows I'm not the Dark Revenger, why doesn't she say it already?

Maybe she's so wildly attracted to me, she doesn't want to blow my cover? Nah, that's a stretch, even for a narcissist like me.

Another thing that bothers me:

I turn to the sexy redhead and say, "Why didn't you use any of your fire powers?"

There's a sharp intake of breath behind her mask. Now that I'm looking at her from a much closer position, I can see into the tiny eyeholes. There are two brown eyes that, if she had fire powers, would probably be shooting flames at me right now.

Ms. Fire says, "I don't have fire powers. I have the ability to propel myself at objects or people with tremendous force with no harm to myself. I can also float up or down."

"So why'd the electricity hurt you?"

"Because the... I guess it's like an energy field, of sorts. It surrounds me when I'm traveling at great speed and makes me near invulnerable. It's why I can fly through a brick wall and not get hurt. But the field isn't there when I'm staying still or floating. It's a weakness, I know. I'm new to this and haven't really figured out how my powers work yet."

I dig her accent. I could listen to her talk all day.

Raven pipes in, "They let you join Majestic 12 without knowing the extent of your powers?"

She shrugs. "What can I say? They were in need of some new blood. And I've proven myself on missions, so..."

"So what's with the name then?" I ask. "Ms. Fire? If you don't have fire powers..."

"I just liked the name."

"You should call yourself Rocket Girl," I say. "Or Bullet Girl. Or Propulsion Girl. But no, Rocket Girl is the best one. My first instinct is usually spot-on."

"*Girl?*"

"Rocket Woman? Rocket Lady? Rockette? The first two aren't as catchy as Rocket Girl, and I'm pretty sure the third one is trademarked."

"If you two wouldn't mind," Raven says, "perhaps you can continue this conversation after we figure out how these criminals escaped. Maybe we can solve the murder, too. Remember, Dark Revenger? The reason why we came here in the first place?"

What murder?

Oh, right, Judgment Day. Almost forgot about him.

74

Meredith is able to command clean-up robots to come out and drag the two unconscious forms back to their cells, and another 'bot, a big industrial-sized thing that looks like the bastard lovechild of the Terminator and Wall-E, whose sole purpose is to clean up messes, like Doctor Deranged's corpse. Smaller robots begin repairs on the hole in the floor.

The rest of M12 come back, battle weary and dragging the unconscious fourth escaped prisoner, Blast Zone. From the name, you'd think Blast Zone was an indoor playground for kids. But no, she's a white-haired, scar-faced looney who can generate explosive blasts from her body that range in force from a firecracker to a bazooka burst.

Amazonia gives a quick rundown of their battle to subdue Blast Zone, and then asks what happened with Killzore and Dynamo. Rocket Girl (yes, that's what I'm calling her now) informs the team that I took them down.

That's right. Me. Dark Revenger.

The non-powered superhero took down two of the badass-iest supervillains to ever grace the FBI's 10 Super Most Wanted list. Two guys who are so dangerous, the Majestic 12 won't even allow them to be incarcerated anywhere other than their own base.

Yeah, okay, one was dumb luck (Killzore) and the other (Dynamo) was due to me wanting to screw with a supervillain who insulted me and my buddy, so I purchased a device that would do just that. And although I thought I'd never get the opportunity to use Savant's little device, I paid so much for it, I carried it with me in case I went up against another electricity-based maniac. So I guess that's dumb luck, too, I don't know.

Whatever you want to call it, M12 now looks at me with a newfound level of respect. I dig that. Especially coming from Amazonia. I resist the urge to give her a wink.

We make our way to the cells to try to figure out how the super-psychos escaped. It's Raven's idea. Somehow, she takes the lead as if it were a natural progression of things. I have to say, it doesn't sit right with me.

Raven inquires who else is kept locked up here. Rumor places the number at around ten or eleven, although in the supervillain circles, they tend to inflate it even more. Meredith tells us it was just Master Mind, Killzore, Dynamo, Doctor Deranged, and Blast Zone. The others apparently had been transferred to a new international ultra-max prison designed specifically for supervillains. The five I mentioned already were still being held here until such time as special cells could be constructed to contain them.

Yeah, they are *that* dangerous. And I took down two of them. Did I mention that already?

More out of morbid curiosity than anything else, I check out their cells. Dynamo's is basically a thick glass cube with a table, bed, and a toilet, all made out of hard rubber. Kind of freaky, but I understand the necessity.

Doctor Deranged and Master Mind's cells are also mostly thick, tempered glass, without the rubber fixtures. Doctor Deranged's cell appears to be constructed out of one solid block of steel with nothing detachable. The bed juts from the wall, one piece of metal, with no screws or brackets. The table and toilet is the same way – one piece. Like the whole room was smelted and molded in one gigantic blast furnace.

Master Mind's cell is the same, except apparently he was permitted to have reading material. There are a line of paperback novels on the table. I scan the titles: *The Stars my Destination* and *The Demolished Man*, both by Alfred Bester; a collection of short stories by Harlan Ellison and two by Ray Bradbury; some early Robert Heinlein and Isaac Asimov; and a collection of short stories by Joseph W. Campbell. I thumb the Campbell book. In the table of contents, there's an asterisk next to the story "Who Goes There?"

Raven asks, "Looking for reading material?"

I swear there's a smirk in her voice, but her face is impassive.

"Actually, I've read all of these."

"Really? I wouldn't have pegged you for the type to read science fiction."

"Yeah, well, I had a lot of free time when I was growing up. Mom and Dad were busy with–"

I stop myself there. Almost let slip a little too much. Raven stares at me. I clear my throat.

"The choice of reading material is odd, don't you think?"

She shrugs. "Master Mind is a fan of classic science fiction. So? Is that supposed to mean something?"

Now it's my turn to shrug.

We move out of the cells as Meredith's robot assistants drag Killzore and Dynamo back to their home away from home. Amazonia puts Blast Zone back in her cell. Cold Snap, Pulsar, and Rocket Girl secure the other cells, while Meredith runs diagnostics to make sure everything is back in place, security-wise.

Killzore's cell, as well as Blast Zone's, is extra heavily reinforced steel with doors that are a foot thick. No glass like the others; there's a monitor inserted into the wall next to each one where you can see the occupant from a camera set up in the top corner of the cell. The cell seems tough enough to maybe hold Blastie, but the rabid dino-man? I mean, I did witness him tear through a metal floor.

I ask Meredith.

"They've both tried to break through the cell doors and walls. Normally, I would release a gas into their cells to render them unconscious."

"Except everything was deactivated."

"That is correct."

I wave my hand through her. She looks solid, but my gloved hand passes through like passing through a sunbeam, except there isn't even a feeling of warmth.

I still can't figure out how much of a computer she is and how much woman. I mean, I get she's an AI or whatever and that she's a physical embodiment of the computer that runs things here on the base and on the ship, but she's also kind of *lifelike*, if that makes sense. She moves fluidly like a person. Like a gold glowing naked person.

I pass my hand through her again.

She says, "Please stop doing that."

"Do you feel that? Can you feel, you know, anything?"

"This form is an avatar comprised of light," she says. "I cannot touch or feel. My artificial intelligence, which is the easiest way to describe it in terms you can understand, was simply a mass of energy. Thomas Traveler refined it into the form I have now. He based my name and avatar appearance on his lost love."

Rocket Girl's been following the conversation. She adds, "Meredith was his girlfriend back in the 1940s. The one who died along with his friend when the ship crashed in the desert."

"Huh." I say, "That's kind of sentimental." In an unhealthy, creepy way.

The supervillains are back in their cells with the doors securely locked, and Meredith says everything's back online again. Cold Snap and Pulsar, both looking wearier than before, are tasked with standing nearby in case there's another breakout, mainly because we don't know how they were able to escape the first time, or how Master Mind escaped. Amazonia says she'll take us to the scene of the crime: Judgment Day's living quarters, which is on the same level as the prisoners' cells.

I'm told he wanted it that way. He wanted to be close to the prisoners. Probably because he was a prick and wanted to talk trash to them every day.

Joke's on him, I guess. The first thing Master Mind did when he escaped from his cell was kill Judgment Day.

Yeah, I'm not really buying that. Let's look at the facts:

Master Mind was a super-genius, and not in the bumbling Wile E. Coyote way. He was a *real* super-genius, smarter than Doctor Deranged and not crazy like him. Sure, he could build a device to kill Judgment Day. But he couldn't do it himself, barehanded. Judgment Day was too powerful.

**Judgment Day's origin:** In a dark, dystopian future, the bad guys have won. Literally. A group of supervillains got together and wiped out the heroes, then took over the world. It becomes as bad as you can imagine. They impose strict gun laws and socialist healthcare.

No, just kidding. I wanted to see if you were paying attention.

They set up a dictatorship and carve up the world, with each one taking a piece for himself. However, as villains are apt to do, they begin to war with one another. This tears up the world even more.

A group of scientists work secretly to try and prevent this from happening. They build a super-soldier out of a test tube mixed with a blend of DNA, some other chemical substances, and maybe Pop Rocks for all I know. They don't have enough blenders full of DNA, or enough time before the world cracks in half, to build more, so they grow just the one and then open a wormhole through time to send him back. His mission, no surprise, is to stop the future from happening.

Armed with super-strength, near-invulnerability, the power of flight, the ability to shoot laser beams from his eyes, and the ugliest sneer you've ever seen, the hero(?) called Judgment Day wages a strict, no-holds-barred war on the bad guys. Or so the origin story would have you believe.

Personally, I think the story sounds like a cheap sci-fi movie produced for cable. But, honestly, I couldn't tell you if it's true or not. The guy dressed in a navy blue military-style uniform, kind of a cross between a Napoleonic officer and a 1940s beat cop, with the added distinction of a helmet and visor that covered all of his face except for his ugly, pockmarked chin. The visor would slide up when he wanted to cut loose with his laservision, which usually resulted in someone losing an arm or a leg. Or a torso.

Whatever he was, whether it was a soldier from the future or just some superpowered asshole from Bumfuck, USA, he was bad news. He killed and maimed when he didn't have to, no matter if it was a big, bad supervillain like Killzore, or one of the B or C Listers like...well, like I was.

Case in point: Remember my old drinking buddy Mr. Meaner? Let's just say, he drinks with his left hand now and is still paying off his facial reconstruction surgery.

We reach Judgment Day's room. Meredith waves her hand at the door and it slides open without a sound. Not even a WHOOSH sound effect like on "Star Trek."

"She doesn't have to wave her hand," Rocket Girl tells me. "She can just open it. The hand thing is for our benefit so we know the door was locked."

Okay. And I need to know this why?

Raven asks, "How do you get in and out of your rooms? I don't see a lock on the door."

Amazonia points to a black dime-sized circle next to the door. "The sensor next to it. Each room has one set to scan our DNA and will only open the door for the room's occupant."

"So no one else can get in or out of your rooms?"

I look at Rocket Girl. She shakes her head.

"Not supposed to."

Judgment Day's body is on the floor. There's no build-up to it. Like, we don't see a bunch of broken furniture and his legs sticking out from behind the bed or anything. Nope, we just walk in the room and there he is, on the floor.

Part of the reason is, besides a bed, there aren't any other furnishings in the room. No TV, no bedside table, no dresser. There's an open closet in one corner of the room with a rack of costumes, all identical to the one he always wears, and a shelf lined with shiny black boots. On the other side of the room is a doorway that leads to a bathroom. That's it. Not even a generic hotel-style watercolor print hanging on the wall.

Judgment Day is in costume (because it doesn't appear he owns any other clothing), but he's not sporting his helmet. It's on the floor next to him. It's the first time I've seen Judgment Day without his helmet, and man, he is one ugly son-of-a-bitch. His face is pale and puffy, and as I mentioned earlier, pockmarked. His eyes have that weird too-close-together look, too.

His neck is clearly broken. I know this because he's lying face down with his head completely turned around so that his eyes stare up at the ceiling. He also has a slight look of surprise, but is it surprise at being killed? Or surprise at something else? Whatever happened, it must have been quick.

Raven crouches down to get a closer look at the body. Her gloved hands examine his neck. She takes out a penlight and looks into his blank eyes. I've never been comfortable with dead bodies, so I observe from a standing position. I have no desire to touch him.

"What do you think?" Rocket Girl asks me.

I like that she defers to me. She should because, you know, I'm the Dark Revenger and everything.

"Well, he looks pretty dead to me," I reply.

Raven gives me a withering look. "Is that your expert opinion?"

"Yes. Yes it is."

"You've seen a lot of dead bodies, Dark Revenger?"

Something in the way she says that; it's sarcastic and accusatory at the same time.

"I've seen my share. You know how it is in this crime-fighting business of ours."

Raven opens her mouth and I think, *Here it comes. She's going to blow my cover.* But then she appears to change her mind and goes back to looking over the body.

She asks, "Can he regenerate?"

Amazonia answers, "No, that wasn't one of his powers."

"So he's dead. Permanently dead."

"Yes."

Seems like a weird conversation between them, but really, in this crazy world of ours, it's one of those things that has to be asked. Regeneration and healing abilities are rare, but there are a couple of individuals, both good and bad, who have them. Apparently, he wasn't one of them.

I check out the bathroom. My analysis: Judgment Day wasn't very clean. Towels on the floor. Beard stubble in the sink. Some pee stains where he missed the toilet. Maybe the cleaning lady broke his neck.

I sip discreetly from my flask and also take a moment to check myself out in the mirror. Looking good. I give myself a wink and head back into the main room.

Raven seems to be done with the body and now she's checking around the room for… I have no idea what. A clue of some sort, or maybe a handwritten confession from the killer.

She asks, "Are there security cameras in here?"

Amazonia answers, "Not in the rooms. There are cameras in the halls. Nothing picked up anyone entering or leaving."

No cameras in the rooms. Guess that means I won't be viewing a tape of Amazonia taking a shower or having a pillow fight with...

What was the ice chick's name again? Cold Front? No. Cold Snap? Yeah, that's it.

Raven looks up at the ceiling, pushes his costumes aside in the closet so she can flash her penlight in the corners, and even peeks under the bed. Unfortunately, she doesn't find the killer hiding in any of those places.

"What are you thinking?" Rocket Girl asks.

The question is directed at me. I must look like I'm deep in thought or something. Raven, engrossed in what she's doing, assumes the question is meant for her.

She says, "Since Master Mind built this place, despite the fact your team has revamped everything, I'm betting he still has some fail-safe way to get around and possibly enter these rooms. Since the cameras didn't pick him up in the hallway, either he built a device that made him invisible to them, or he has another way of moving around. The air vents are too small, so possibly he has a hidden passageway between rooms. He must have designed something that enhanced his strength so he could overpower Judgment–"

"I think you're way off," I say.

Everyone stares at me. I swear the room gets a little colder, too.

Raven says, "Excuse me?"

"Master Mind isn't a killer. Sure, he's one of the bad guys, but he's never killed anyone."

"He's never killed anyone?" Raven says, "He's been the brains behind two formidable supervillain groups and a half dozen mercenary teams. He's been responsible for over a hundred robberies, and over half of the tech gear that's out there being used by the bad guys was designed by him. And some of that gear, by the way, *did* kill people. Good people. *Heroic* people."

Think I hit a nerve with her; something close and personal is bubbling up to the surface. Maybe I should back off, but I can't stand the fact I believe I'm right and she's not listening.

"I didn't say he wasn't responsible for deaths. What I'm getting at is, he's not the hands-on type. Look, Master Mind has always been about manipulating things behind the scenes. He doesn't like superheroes and believes they're bad for the human race. Or something. I don't know. I saw his manifesto on the Internet, but I didn't read the whole thing."

At the time, I was too busy trying to download a pirated movie. I don't see any reason to mention that.

Raven says, "Well I *did* read the whole thing, and he said it was his ultimate goal to bring things back to the way they were before superheroes. Return the world to its status quo. But much like every criminal I've come across, what he's really after is money, power, and the satisfaction of his own narcissistic tendencies."

Ouch.

Amazonia and Rocket Girl watch us, their heads swiveling back and forth as if they had front row seats to a tennis match.

"I'm just saying," and I really have no idea why I'm defending the guy, but what the hell, I've already gone pretty far out there, might as well keep going, "it seems really farfetched that the guy breaks out of his cell and the first thing he wants to do is break the neck of one of the most powerful members of Majestic 12."

"Then tell me, *Dark Revenger*." She nearly spits her words in anger. "Who did kill him? Huh? The world's greatest detective should be able to solve this. It's a classic locked room murder mystery. Along with the science fiction novels, didn't you read Agatha Christie, too?"

Nah. But I've seen most of the movie adaptations.

She's not really expecting an answer to that particular question. I'm not sure she expects an answer at all. I think she's acting this way because she wants to shut me out of this completely. She wants to solve the case all on her own, either for personal reasons or because...

I'm not sure. Jealousy? Revenge? Spite? To prove she's just as capable as any male superhero?

Maybe she thinks by talking down to me, I'll shut up and she can run the case all on her own.

Joke's on her, though. I never shut up.

Raven says, "If it's not Master Mind, then who killed Judgment Day?"

I shrug. "Not sure yet. I'm working on a theory."

Actually, it's more a germ of a snippet of an idea rather than a theory. But I do have one. And I don't particularly like it, either.

Back when I was a kid, I liked puzzles. What? Did you think I just picked the name "Puzzler" off a supervillain-name database?

My ability, or power if you want to call it that, is not flashy. It's...weird. My brain takes mental snapshots of what I see and somehow breaks it down into small snippets, analyzes it, and then sends the messages to my muscles. And since all the great supervillains have gimmicks, and "The Guy Who Can Copy Stuff" didn't have a good ring to it, I went with something that brought me joy as a kid – puzzles.

Yeah, that's right. Mazes. Word searches. Two minute mysteries. My personal favorite was jigsaw puzzles.

The trick with jigsaw puzzles is, you have to be able to see what the finished picture is supposed to be. So let's look at this whole scenario as if it was a completed puzzle:

Master Mind killed Judgment Day. That's the puzzle all solved and everything. Right? Except the pieces don't fit.

Master Mind escapes from his cell. His first thought upon escaping should have been, *How do I get off this island before Majestic 12 beats the hell out of me?* But no, Master Mind instead goes to the room of a superhero who can cut him in half with his laser vision. Or, barring that, could twist Master Mind's spine into a pretzel.

Somehow, Master Mind is able to enter Judgment Day's room, a room that only Judgment Day is supposed to be able to enter, catches him by surprise, and breaks the neck of a guy strong enough to trade blows with Killzore. Then, rather than hightailing it the hell out of Dodge, he still sticks around. Why? Because he wants to construct a device to mess with Meredith's system, and he wants to release the four other villains in captivity. Four villains, mind you, that he's never had dealings with before. And one of those villains (Dr. Deranged) hated his guts.

*Then* what does he do? He disappears.

Put it all together and you see the pieces don't fit. The puzzle isn't solved. In fact, it's more of a puzzle than before.

Rocket Girl asks me, "Why do you think Master Mind is innocent of this?"

I give her the abbreviated version of what I said above, without the references to my copy talents and a toned down version of the puzzle analogy.

She nods. "I agree it doesn't make sense. But I've also come to realize that supervillains don't always act in a rational manner."

"The sane ones do," I say.

"Why do you say Dr. Deranged hated Master Mind?"

Because it was well known in the supervillain community that Dr. Deranged had wanted to join forces with Master Mind, had made overtures again and again, until it got to the point that he was coming off like a celebrity stalker. His offers were rebuffed by Master Mind. Rebuffed with extreme prejudice.

I can't tell her that, so instead I say, "Dr. Deranged was insane. Master Mind wasn't. *Isn't.*"

"Okay."

Wow. Just like that? She believes me? Huh. I think I like her more than Miss "I've-got-a-stick-up-my-ass-and-I-like-it" Raven. Speaking of...

Raven is back to examining the body. Not sure what she thinks she's going to discover. Amazonia watches her with a stoic expression. I'm beginning to think she grew up on Easter Island.

"Meredith," I say. "Have you figured out why your defense system shut down?"

The others seem to forget she's in the room with us. Like she's an appliance. A talking lamp. I don't see her that way. For one, there's a sentient aura about her. I get the sense she's taking note of everything.

And second, I think she's the key to this whole mess.

She responds, "There appear to be several glitches in my programming. A hidden subset of programs that are hidden from me until they are activated."

"So the part where Master Mind escaped and you didn't see it? Someone entering Judgment Day's room and killing him and you didn't see it? The prisoners being released and you unable to assist in stopping them...? This was all part of the glitch. The hidden programs."

"Yes. I am working on finding them. They are hidden well. The only thing I have been able to ascertain is..."

"What?" Cripes, this can't be good if a computer pauses before delivering the bad news.

Meredith says, "There are more programs that have not been activated. Yet."

Yep, I knew it was going to be bad.

I ask Amazonia, "Who has the ability to reprogram Meredith?"

She raises an eyebrow. "No one I know of. Meredith is a self-aware AI. She was created as a–"

"Yeah, yeah, yeah," I say. "Companion for Thomas Traveler, made in the image of his dead love, blabbity blah. I heard that heartwarming story."

Now she has both eyebrows raised. It's the closest I've seen Amazonia to an emotional reaction. She's almost as impassive as Meredith.

Raven makes a sound of exasperation and says, "Master Mind escaped his cell and put the programs into Meredith's system."

"Wow. You're like one note with this, aren't you?"

Suddenly, she's in my face. "It's you and Master Mind. The two of you are working together."

"Whaaat? Are you drunk?"

Which you have to admit, coming from me is a pretty funny question since I'm always slightly buzzed.

She's going to hit me; I sense it coming. My body tenses and about ten thousand different possible reactions flit through my head (Duck? Block? Strike first? Run? Block, then strike? Block, then run? Etc.). I don't have to choose because that's when all the yelling starts from the direction of the cells. We all run.

When we reach the cells, we find Cold Snap and Pulsar desperately trying to pry the cell doors open. It takes a second to register why: The cells are filling up with water.

Water pours in through the air vents and bubbles up from the toilets and sinks. The doors are airtight so the water essentially fills up the cells like fishbowls, and none of the prisoners have the ability to breathe underwater. I check the monitors next to Blast Zone and Killzore's cells. Yep, them, too. Only difference is, while Blast Zone frantically fires her bursts at the door and walls, Killzore just stands in his cell like a statue. Maybe he can breathe underwater...?

Cold Snap yells, "Meredith!"

Flash of light and she forms in our midst.

"Turn off the water!"

Meredith says, "I am sorry. I am unable to do that."

Amazonia says, "Then open the doors."

Pulsar says, "What?! Hell, no. These guys will try to kill us. And the water will–"

Again, Meredith says, "I am sorry. I am unable to do that."

I understand Pulsar's reluctance, but if we don't get them out of there, they're going to die. Then again, they're all homicidal maniacs. Tough choice.

"Why is there water coming through the vents?" I ask Meredith.

"This area of the base is underwater. There are pumps to keep the water out, but in this case, my programming has been modified to reverse some of them."

Interesting that Master Mind's cell isn't filling up. Could be because he's not there. Or could be because he really is orchestrating this whole thing.

Amazonia and Rocket Girl try to pry open Blast Zone's cell door. Raven and Cold Snap work on Dynamo's. Pulsar stands and does nothing, I guess, because he feels it's too dangerous to save them. I'm doing nothing because I honestly don't know what to do. If there was a lock, I could pick it. Unfortunately, these doors don't have manual locks.

No one's trying to help Killzore. I check the monitor again. Water up to his scaly midsection, but he's still standing there. The world's ugliest statue.

Dynamo yells at me, water up to his neck. The glass is too thick to fully make out what he's saying, but I get the meaning. He knows it's me (Puzzler) and he wants me to help get him out. I don't like the guy, but I certainly don't want to stand here and watch him drown either.

What good is a grappling gun or flash bangs or anything else I have? The only person – *thing* – that can open these doors is Meredith, and she's been programmed not to.

Amazonia beats on the metal door. She puts small dents in it, but not enough that I think it'll break before Blast Zone drowns. Meanwhile, Raven directs Cold Snap to put ice into the narrow seam between the door and the jamb. It's a good idea and I should've come up with it myself, but let's face it, saving people is new to me.

I say, "Hey, uh, Amazonia, maybe…maybe you'd have better luck breaking this glass?" I point to Dynamo's cell.

She nods, turns towards Dynamo's cell, and brings her fist back to slam it into the glass. There's a sharp CRACK from the door jamb where the ice is expanding and pushing the two apart. For a brief second, I think we might be able to save one of the psychopaths, and then two gun-looking devices descend from the ceiling, one on either side of us.

Meredith says, "Please stop what you are doing and do not move."

Everyone stops. The water is still filling up the cells. Dynamo treads water as best he can, floating in his cell with his head above the water line like a bobbing cork.

"That's just the stun lasers, right?" I ask.

Meredith says, "They will do more than stun now. I am sorry. Please do not move. I have no control over what will happen."

We all look at each other. Then Pulsar, that big idiot, runs. Right past me and down the corridor. One of the ceiling guns locks on him and fires. The laser burst cuts right through him and blows a quarter size hole through his back and out his chest. Pulsar falls face first and doesn't move.

"Jesus," I say. Yeah. Definitely not a stun laser anymore.

"Meredith," Cold Snap says. "Why are you doing this?"

"I am sorry." She answers with the same monotone inflection you get when you call a bank afterhours and receive a recorded message. "I am unable to access these programs or circumvent them."

Water up to the ceilings in the cells. Dynamo has maybe an inch of air. He bangs his hands on the ceiling and screams. I can't see what Blast Zone is doing, but I check out the monitor for Killzore's cell. He floats lifelessly in the water. Like he just gave up and let himself drown. It's equal parts creepy and sad.

Amazonia and Cold Snap exchange looks and something passes between them. They both nod slightly and jump into action at the same time. Amazonia leaps up, her sword out and extended, aiming for the one laser gun, while Cold Snap fires a burst of ice at the other. It's an eight foot jump, but Amazonia's sword cuts through the gun, pieces of it snapping and crackling with energy as it falls to the floor. The second laser is already firing. The ice wall Cold Snap shoots out from her hands blocks it. Temporarily. Chips of ice fly off as the laser burrows a hole through it.

I'm wondering how long Cold Snap's power will hold out. I mean, can she shoot ice out of her hands indefinitely? Or will the laser run out of power first? Is Amazonia's shield laser-proof? All of these thoughts run through my mind, and then Rocket Girl steps forward.

"Give me a little bit of room," she says.

We get out of her way. She rises up, then shoots forward through the ice wall and into the path of the laser. It hits her, but doesn't slow her momentum. She tears straight through the gun, turns around, and flies back in our direction at a much slower speed.

That was impressive.

I say, "Your power field can withstand lasers, huh?"

"Apparently so," she says.

"Wait. You didn't know?"

"I've never had a high powered laser hit me before."

"But…but…you could've died. You just did that without knowing if the laser could kill you?"

Rocket Girl says, "What was I supposed to do? Stand there and let more people die?"

Wow. They just acted without thinking about the risks. They're not superheroes. They're actually *heroes*. And Rocket Girl has the most heart of anybody I've ever met.

Oh, yeah, I should probably mention that the cells are completely filled with water and the three prisoners have drowned. Sorry, Dynamo. You were a piece of shit, but even you deserved better than that.

"I am sorry," Meredith says. "That was Protocol Two. Protocol Three is to fill the entire base with water."

Oh. Great. Just when I thought it couldn't get any worse.

I've got a small tube in one of my belt pouches that fits over the mouth and provides about five minutes of air. I doubt it will give me time to find my way up top, and I'm thinking Meredith's new programming won't allow me to call for an elevator. It would also mean leaving everyone else to drown.

A small black hockey puck-shaped thing slide towards us. There's a red flash accompanied with a loud POP and everything goes black. Total darkness.

Oh, shit, so this is death? Everything is pitch blackness. Oh, man, come on. This? This is what happens when you die? Just...nothingness?

I would've expected it to be a lot hotter where I'm headed. On the other hand, I do feel like I have to pee. Maybe that's what Hell is. Being stuck in inky blackness with a full bladder.

Then some lights go on and there's the unmistakable start-up hum of the air vents blowing. We're still alive and still inside the base. Meredith is gone and much of the lighting, except for a few emergency spot-lamps, is turned off.

"What the hell just happened?" I ask.

Raven lights a chemical light stick and holds it up over her head. It looks like just the five of us.

"Where did she go?" Cold Snap asks.

Raven responds, "It could be a trick."

"No trick." The voice is calm, cool, and slightly condescending – part college professor and part game show host. "It was an EMP grenade. It knocked out her system. What you have now is the back-up generator running a few lights and the air. She might be able to reboot herself if the grenade wasn't powerful enough. It's a tricky thing, figuring out how much of an EMP pulse to generate."

A man steps out of the shadows.

"I sincerely hope it worked. The grenade also knocked out the cloaking device that kept me invisible from her. And from all of you."

Short blond hair that hasn't seen a comb in a while and his beard is bushier than I remember from the news footage. He's my height, maybe a quarter inch shorter. His white t-shirt, stained with sweat and grease, fits snugly over a barrel chest and two thick arms that look like the product of a half million push-ups. Wrapped around one bulging bicep is a wide piece of leather with various electronic components attached and a mass of wires going every which way. It looks like something he jury-rigged from odds and ends, and I'm going to hazard a guess and say up until a moment ago, it was the device that kept him invisible. His signature dark-lens goggles hang loose around his neck.

Raven says, "Master Mind."

"At your service. Although I must admit, I'm not sure who you are. But you super people seem to pop up more and more frequently these days, and I have been out of the loop for a while."

He nods at Rocket Girl. "Estella."

She sighs. "I really wish I hadn't told you that."

"A moment of weakness," he says. "Don't be hard on yourself. I promised to never use it against you, didn't I? I do miss our chess games, by the way."

He turns to me. "Dark Revenger."

I'm about to say, "At your service," but then I realize he just said the same thing to Raven. I don't want to look like an idiot by copying what he said, so I just solemnly nod my head once.

Master Mind says, "Would you mind explaining to me where the hell you've been?"

# CHAPTER 10

"Um..."

He has an intense stare. I thought Raven had one, but Master Mind's stare puts hers to shame. Raven looks at me like the nuns did back in Catholic school when they caught me with a female classmate in a confessional booth.

Master Mind? I feel like he's dissecting me with his eyes.

"So, okay, here's what happened..."

I spread my hands and lick my lips and pretend like I know what I'm about to say. Really, I'm flailing.

"I, uh..."

"Why aren't you doing the voice?" he asks. He turns to Raven. "Why isn't he doing the voice?"

"Good question," she says. "Dark Revenger, why aren't you doing the voice?"

"Because I don't want to," I say. "That's why. The voice is a pain to do. It's meant for the bad guys, anyway. I shouldn't have to do the gravelly voice for you people."

Feels like I had a mini-hissy fit.

"Never mind that," Master Mind says. "You were supposed to be here two weeks ago. I couldn't wait any longer. I decided to implement the plan on my own. Wasn't easy, especially since I was stuck here and forced to conceal myself from my jailers, all while working on a way to shut down the computer. It would have been much easier if you had shown up when you were supposed to."

"Well, you see–" I start to say, already forming a flimsy excuse in my head that probably won't stand up to close scrutiny. Luckily, he cuts me off.

"We have to make sure Meredith doesn't start up again. Follow me."

He reaches for the light stick in Raven's right hand. Her left hand shoots out, grabs his fingers, and bends them back.

"Ow! Hey!"

She lets go and he flexes his fingers.

"A little territorial, aren't you?" He says, "I just thought it would be easier if I led the way."

"Put your hands near me again and I'll remove them."

"I don't know who you are, Ms. Attitude," he says. "But I'll kindly remind you that I'm the one who just saved your well-toned butt."

"You're also the one who cost my father his right leg."

That stops everyone cold.

Master Mind says, "I don't know what you're talking about, but I can see by the hatred blazing behind your eyes you really want to have this discussion. Might I suggest, however, that we talk while we move? I need to get to where Meredith's brain is stored." He puts his hand up to the side of his mouth and leans towards me if he's about to share a confidential piece of info. "Not a brain in the flesh and blood sense. I'm referring to her electronic brain."

"Fine. Let's go." Raven extends to him the light stick. "Lead the way. But I'm warning you, any sign that this is a trick..." She doesn't finish her threat, probably thinking, and rightly so, that the implication of her words will carry more weight.

There's no question Raven hopes Master Mind does something to warrant a beat-down. Seething hatred for the man comes off her in waves. Master Mind picks up on it, too. He takes the stick, nods solemnly, and probably skips a half dozen sarcastic comments that would have otherwise made their way out of his obnoxious mouth.

Yeah, I know. Me calling someone else obnoxious is like the historic meeting between the pot and the kettle. But, you know, it takes one to know one.

We race down the corridors, Master Mind in front with Raven a half step behind, and me, Rocket Girl, Amazonia, and Cold Snap bring up the rear. Master Mind holds the light up as a beacon, but he seems to have an instinctual sense of direction. I forget he designed the layout of the place.

We round corners and slide through a half-open doorway. I get a fleeting glimpse of what appears to be someone's bedroom, but there's no emergency lights shining in here. The only light is the one coming from the stick Master Mind holds over his head. I've got a pair of collapsible nightvision goggles in one of my belt pouches, but before I can whip it out (that's what she said), Master Mind is sliding back a panel on the wall. The opening is just big enough for a person to fit through, as long as they duck their head and they're not carrying a couple of spare tires around the midsection. There's a steel ladder built into the far wall of the opening, which looks like it leads down a shaft slightly bigger than an air vent.

Oh, good. A tight, confined space for me to climb into. How I love those and the hyperventilating it brings on.

He tosses Raven back the light stick and says, "Just a few feet down. I have a generator of my own, so you won't need the light."

He puts a leg into the opening. Raven reaches behind her back and comes back with her mini-scythe weapon. She places it against Master Mind's neck. The bottom of the blade is smooth and looks as sharp as a fresh razor blade. The top of the scythe, the part currently pressed against Master Mind's throat, has sharp jagged teeth. If she was to shove it up and then jerk it away, it would leave a gaping hole in his flesh.

"I think this is all part of your plan," she says. "Pretend you're helping us, and then spring a trap. What's down there? Weapons? Some means of escape for you, so you can blow up the base from a safe distance?"

"Sweetie," he says, not without a slight hitch in his voice, "I assure you this is not a trick. If I wanted all of you dead, I would've let Meredith take care of that for me. Believe me, right now, I need you as much as you need me."

"We should trust him, Raven," Rocket Girl says. "We have to work together. If Meredith comes back online..."

The fear in her voice is unexpected because she's a superhero, and superheroes aren't supposed to get scared. But she's a person, too. A woman. A flesh and blood woman who is just as afraid of dying as anybody else. It makes me like her a little bit, the fact she's unguarded and not pretending to be fearless.

Amazonia says, "I don't think we can stop Meredith without him."

"My father," Raven says, her eyes locked on Master Mind, but her words directed at all of us, "was the crime-fighter known as Stealthshadow."

I want to ask, "Who?" because I've honestly never heard of him, but I have enough sense to keep my mouth shut. Doesn't matter; there are probably a hundred or more superheroes worldwide who operate undercover and somehow stay off the news radar. Or they work for their government as special operatives.

"My father fought crime, but he wasn't a superhero. He didn't wear an elaborate costume and he didn't have superpowers. He taught martial arts and ran a youth center in a poor section of the city, the very same section we lived in. He worked to move us out of the neighborhood to someplace safer because he saw drugs and gangs working their way in. He didn't want my family growing up in that. Still, he cared enough about the other people to go back at night and help them. He used his fighting skills and his street contacts to fight back and worked to protect the other residents who were too poor to move."

"I don't–" Master Mind starts to say, but Raven increases the pressure on his throat until he has his head pointed nearly straight up.

"Shut. Your. Mouth," she says, and continues:

"One night, we received a call that my father was in the hospital. He had attempted to stop a break-in, thinking they were simple street thieves. But they were a group of superpowered mercs working for Master Mind. Both of his legs had been crushed. They managed to save one..." Her voice trails off.

Red cheeks and clenched jaw; her hatred is palpable. I think she's going to do it. Kill him, I mean. I brace myself to move, to stop her, but then she moves the weapon away from his throat.

She says, "So when I tell you I hope you try to double-cross us so I can have an excuse to hurt you, please know that I mean it."

"Duly noted," he says. "Now, if we may continue this down in my workshop, I'd really like to prevent our upcoming painful deaths."

No one disagrees. Master Mind folds himself into the opening in the wall and climbs down the ladder, with Raven going second and Cold Snap third. Amazonia watches the rear. I move to go fourth when Rocket Girl's hand on my arm stops me.

"Will you be alright?" she asks. "It's a small space."

"Yeah, I guess. Hopefully it's not farther down than he claims."

"Okay, well, if I can help, let me know." She slips her fingers under her mask and pulls it up and off her head. "I should probably take this off. With the low lighting in here, it's hard to see what I'm doing." She blows at an errant lock of hair and uses her gloved fingers to brush it back behind her ear.

She notices me staring. "What?"

"You're not, um… You're not hideously scarred."

In fact, she's beautiful. She looks a little bit like that old-time movie actress. What was her name? Played in "Gilda."

Rita Hayworth. That's it. But with a thinner face and warm eyes the color of bronze reflecting a sunset.

Yeesh. When did I become poetic?

"You thought I was scarred?"

"Yeah. Otherwise, why the full mask? Why wouldn't you want to show off a face like that?"

She shrugs. "Maybe I'm paranoid about keeping my real identity a secret. I like to live a normal life outside of..." She motions around her.

"Does your husband know you're a superhero?"

She offers a slight smile and shakes her head. "No husband."

"Your boyfriend? Your boyfriend knows?"

Her smile broadens a bit. "No boyfriend."

"Your kids know? Did you tell your kids you're a superhero?"

She laughs. "No kids. I should probably work on the boyfriend part first before I think about kids."

I wrap my cape around my side and tuck it through my bandolier belts. I tell Rocket Girl,

"Don't want to trip on it. Climbing ladders can be tricky, especially with a long cape. You're smart. Your cape only goes down to the top of your butt."

"Thank you for noticing."

We exchange a look.

Amazonia says, "Are you two planning on joining the others?"

Work, work, work, all the time. This job sucks.

I fold into the opening and put a foot onto the ladder, then the other. There's light from below; the descent is only a matter of a few feet. I glance up and see the ladder travels upward into pitch blackness, which makes me glad I'm not going that way. I take a step down, one after another, and feel the tightness in my chest from being in such a small space. A few more steps and I reach the floor.

I'm in a room strung with work lights over a long metal table strewn with electronic and mechanical odds and ends. The work lights...

They're wired together in one long cord that ends in a freestanding black box the size of a guitar amp. The box doesn't appear to be wired into anything. So where's the power coming from?

I untuck my cape and let it unfurl down behind me just as Rocket Girl floats down. She looks around the room. Raven has her eyes locked on Master Mind, who is snapping pieces of something together.

I say, "I know this may be the wrong time to bring this up, but... Is there a Men's Room nearby, by any chance? I have to pee like a Russian racehorse."

It's not an emergency, but it's been several hours since I last went, and this costume, much like most superhero costumes, is not the easiest to take off.

Master Mind says, "Oh, where are my manners?"

He picks up what looks like a small, narrow remote control and pushes a button. A red wall of light the size and width of a standard doorway rises up from a small track I previously hadn't noticed on the floor. The light shimmers and doesn't appear to solidify the way Meredith did. I can see the rest of the room through it.

"There you go."

"Okay, sure," I say. "Um, what am I supposed to do with that?"

"Oh." Master Mind seems completely taken aback. "Sorry. I thought... Well, I thought you had used these before. On your last trip here, for instance." He waves his hand. "Never mind. You just step through the light and it eradicates the waste in your bowels and bladder. This is one of my first inventions. They have several throughout the base. Saves time from having to find a restroom and remove body armor or capes. I always used them because..." He scrunches up his nose. "Regular bathroom going was always so unnecessarily messy, don't you think? This is *sooo* much cleaner."

"Uh huh."

I stare at the light. I really have to go now. You know, like one of those instances when you kinda, sorta have to pee, but not too bad, and then when you get in front of the toilet, you feel the dam is about to burst? Like that. Except I'm not in front of a toilet. I'm in front of a red wall of light.

"This thing won't give me cancer, will it?" I ask.

"No. I told you, it only affects the waste in your system."

"It won't accidentally send me back in time or something?"

"No," he answers. "It will certainly not send you back in time."

"And you're sure about the no-cancer thing?"

"Yes, I'm sure." He looks at Raven. "Is he serious? I can't tell if he's serious."

"I can't tell either," she responds flatly.

Rocket Girl says, "These things are safe." She steps through the light. "See? We frequently use them here. It's also a mainstay on the ship."

I try to appear as nonchalant as I can, but seriously, I really don't want to step through the light. What if I get a tumor? What if it burns out my retinas? What if...

What if something bad happens to my penis?

But there's Rocket Girl standing there telling me it's okay, it's safe. She just stepped through it like it was nothing, so what am I going to do? I step through, of course, and the pressure in my bladder is suddenly nonexistent. It worked. Just like that.

Wow. With an invention like that, it makes me wonder why Master Mind didn't just patent it and collect millions instead of turning to crime. Actually, I asked Savant a similar question once:

Why not just go legit and sell his inventions rather than using them to commit crimes?

His answer: "What would be the fun in that?"

Master Mind says, "Anyone else need to use it?"

Head shakes all around.

"Okay then, ladies." He looks at me. "And gentleman." He picks up several pieces of electronic gear from his crowded work table and snaps them together like a three dimensional jigsaw puzzle. "This should do it. We just need to..."

"Need to what?" I ask. Jeez, the guy likes to keep us in suspense, doesn't he?

"Apologies." He looks up from the patched together gizmo. "I had to make an adjustment." He holds it up. "I think I've got it now."

It looks a little like a picture frame, if one were constructed from computer chips, wires, and pieces of brass tubing.

Amazonia says, "What is that supposed to do? And when are you going to tell us what's going on?"

Master Mind opens his mouth to answer when a loud KRA-KOOM sound makes all of us jump and the entire complex shakes from the impact.

Cold Snap asks, "What in the holy hell was that?"

Master Mind says, "That, my dear, is the harbinger of our doom. We better get moving because we only have a few minutes to live."

Before I can object or move out of the way, he aims the contraption at me. A violet-colored blob materializes from the center and hits me dead-on. It covers me in a second skin, but it has no texture to it. No feeling. It's just a violet glow covering me. Like he dumped a gallon of paint over my head, except it's not liquid and it's not dripping onto the floor.

"What the hell, dude?" I stride towards him with my fists clenched tight.

"It's just temporary," he says. "I promise. But it had to be done if we are to save the day."

He has the same violet glow. He used it on himself, too. Then I notice the others are standing still as statues.

"What did you do to them?"

"To them? Nothing. I did it to us," he says. "I had to speed us up so we can stop Traveler from coming in here and twisting our heads off our bodies."

"Wait, what? Traveler's one of the good guys."

"Oh, dear me. You are so far in the dark on everything, aren't you?" He stands and slings a canvas bag over his shoulder. I hear pieces of metal clink together. "I'll have to explain as we go because this energy around us is only temporary. And although I can renew it, it's best not to do this too many times. Otherwise we might end up like poor Speed Demon."

Speed Demon, nicknamed "the Purple Blur" by the press, formerly Majestic 12's resident speedster, and now deceased.

Master Mind makes for the ladder, but I put a gloved hand firmly on his shoulder and stop him.

"Hold on. I want some answers before I go anywhere. Like, for instance, what do you mean Traveler is coming to kill us?"

He gives an exasperated sigh. "We really don't have the time—"

"Start with that," I say. "What's this stuff you put on us? And what was that remark about Speed Demon? I thought the news reports said he died in a battle with someone."

"What we're presently wearing," he says, "this purplish glow, is the same essence Speed Demon tapped into to get his super-speed. The 'slickstream' he called it. Really it's an interdimensional energy that speeds up an object. Or *person*, in our case. Speed Demon was able to borrow bits of the energy from time to time, although I'm not quite sure how. I don't know that he even knew how he did it." He sighs. "Anyway, his continued use of it over a span of several years led to his cells becoming saturated with it until his powers increased to the point he was no longer in control. He became faster and faster, unable to slow down, until one day, he simply disappeared."

"And?"

"*Annnddd* a second after he disappeared, the corpse of a very old man appeared on the other side of the world. DNA tests proved it was him. He had lived decades in the span of that second, continuing to age as the rest of the world appeared to be frozen in time around him. They said that he wrote close to a million journal pages of his attempts to slow down, to find a cure for his condition, traveling all over the world many times over in search of someone or something that could enable him to rejoin mankind. Apparently, the latter half of his journals became gibberish as his sanity slipped."

Master Mind looks at the others frozen in time.

"Can you imagine? Living the rest of your life while the rest of the world stands still. Utterly alone and unable to communicate with anyone because you're moving too fast for them to see." He shakes his head sadly.

"Okay, then maybe you should take this stuff off us before we end up like Speed Demon. Don't you think?" I think I keep the edge of panic from my voice, but it's hard to tell for sure. I'm too busy trying to not have a meltdown.

"We'll be fine. Continued exposure to the interdimensional energy becomes increasingly risky. A one-time saturation of it should burn off completely."

"*Should?*"

"Well." He shrugs. "Nothing is a hundred percent when dealing with these kinds of things. But I estimate our chances of safely being able to slow back down to be 99.9 percent. Or 99.8 percent, at the very least." He tilts his head from side to side. "Maybe 99.7."

"Okay! Jesus!" I say, "Let's move on before my chances get any slimmer."

"What else do you want to know, Dark Revenger? Or whatever your name really is."

We stare at each other for a solid couple of seconds. Or a solid couple of nanoseconds. Or whatever a millionth of a millionth of a second would be.

"Um..."

"Save it," Master Mind says. "I met the Dark Revenger. I spoke with the Dark Revenger. You, sir, are not the Dark Revenger. You're younger, and let's be honest, more handsome than him. Which begs the question, have you ever done any modeling? You have the classic features for it."

"No. A little acting in college, that's about..." I suddenly feel both a little flush in the face and slightly uncomfortable. "Are you, uh, coming on to me?"

He raises an eyebrow, Mr. Spock-style. "If I was, would you be interested?"

I shake my head. "Sorry. I like the ladies."

"Pity," he says. "The good ones are always taken. Or they're straight."

Just when I thought this whole situation couldn't get stranger.

"Shall we proceed then?" He motions to the ladder. "As I said, this energy will wear off. I would prefer not to use it again. We have much to do, and very little time to do it, so..."

"Yeah, okay. I'll follow and you tell me what we're supposed to do. But in the meantime, I want you to fill me in on what's really happening around here."

He's already moving up the ladder. I decide to add:

"And, you know, don't try anything funny."

"Of course not." He stops and looks down the ladder at me. Gives me a wink. "You already told me you're heterosexual."

"No, I mean..." My face gets hot again. "Crap."

He continues climbing. I follow behind him.

"Why does the air feel so heavy?" I ask. "Like I'm wading through soup. And how come we're not moving faster? I thought this energy gives us super-speed."

Master Mind answers, "We *are* moving faster. We're moving so fast that everything else appears stationary. You notice the air feels heavier? The molecules can't move out of the way quickly enough. But to us, we only appear to be moving at normal speed."

Huh. Pretty groovy.

We go up the ladder and back out the way we came. I keep a step behind M.M., which isn't easy because he knows where he's going and I don't have a clue. He really does know the layout of this place. He could probably navigate it blindfolded.

"So you were going to give me the lowdown...?"

"Okay, Dark Revenger," he says. "Or whoever you really are. Just do what I tell you to do and in the meantime, I'll give you the facts about what's really happening. For starters, I'll tell you I had nothing to do with Raven's father losing his leg."

"Really? 'Cause she seemed pretty sure."

"Her father wasn't a neighborhood, street-level superhero. In fact, he worked for me as a henchman. He lost his leg on a job that went horribly awry."

"What was that last word?"

"Awry," he says.

"Okay. Go on."

We maneuver around corners and down corridors that I wouldn't have known were there, sparse as the lighting is, and the deep shadows cast by the byzantine layout. The glow from our bodies helps out.

I don't know why, but I think he's really working on the side of the good guys. However, my years of working the opposite side of the fence may have permanently skewed my intuition regarding these things.

"So Raven's dad was a supervillain's henchman?"

He stops and pulls a crowbar from his bag, then pops the chiseled edge into a panel on the wall.

"You find it easier to believe her father made enough money from teaching self-defense classes to the underprivileged? That he was able to move his family out to the suburbs and still had time to spend evenings patrolling the old neighborhood for purse snatchers and crack dealers?"

"Well, when you say it like that..."

He bends back the panel, revealing a bunch of transparent cables that glow brightly with a rainbow of assorted colors. Master Mind sighs.

"Good old superheroes," he says. "You can always count on their laziness. They never bothered to rewire my circuitry."

His fingers move amid the cables, probing gently the way someone would if they were touching delicate, living creatures. For a crazy second, I wonder if they are alive, but then he grabs three of them together and with a dagger from his bag, slices cleanly through them. The cables he cut are no longer lit.

I recognize the dagger. "Isn't that Raven's?"

"Oh, don't use that tone on me, Fake Revenger," he says. "I simply borrowed it."

He's got a mishmash of components from his bag and he's piecing them together around both ends of the severed cables.

I say, "Look, you need to start giving me some answers. What's going on and what are you doing?"

"First, if I calculated this right and made these pieces correctly, I'm going to flush Meredith's program out of the master server. Bear in mind, I was forced to work under terrible conditions with a small amount of time and extremely limited resources."

Great. He's already making excuses in case this all goes to Hell.

"Second," he says, "I'm attempting to stop an alien invasion."

# Chapter 11
## *Master Mind's Story (in his own words)*

You have a good name. Dark Revenger. Although, to be quite honest, I don't think it suits you.

It suited your predecessor. He took the "dark" part of his name seriously. But you? Not even close. You can't keep the masquerade going.

I won't ask for your real name. Hopefully, you'll volunteer it of your own accord.

My real name is Harrison Masters. I'm not a supervillain, although I've been labeled as one. Personally, I hate such names. Too constricting.

I'm a former member of Majestic 12. At one time, I was the *only* member. This is going back to when Majestic 12 was a government department that investigated strange phenomena and unusual discoveries. It was formed at the time of the Roswell crash in 1947 and originally had twelve members, all of whom were the top scientific minds at that time, brought together to study the wreckage of an interplanetary craft.

Years passed and members died off. Recruitment for new members was difficult because there's only so much you can glean from pieces of technology that are broken or incomparable to anything we have on Earth. Oh, sure, some things were reverse engineered, which is how we came up with fiber optics, microchips, and space travel in a very short span of time. But the government was starting to doubt whether it needed the Majestic 12 department. Then I came along and changed their minds.

Me? I was the kid who fixed my family's appliances when I was ten. By age fifteen, I had a business in my garage where I was fixing my neighbor's electronic doodads. For an extra fee, I'd even improve on the gadget and make it do things it couldn't originally do. My father didn't approve. He wanted me to work on the farm and not spend my time "tinkering," as he called it.

My father wasn't a tolerant man. I was the only boy in the family and let's just say, he knew early on that I wasn't going to follow in his tobacco-chewing, cheap-domestic-beer-drinking, everything-revolves-around-sports mentality. In fact, I think he suspected what my eventual sexual predilection would be even before I knew. Perhaps he was clairvoyant. But most likely, he was a simpleminded homophobe. Anyway...

The government recruited me. They recognized my intellect. They wanted me to invent things for them, which I did briefly, but they were always pushing for weapons while I instead came up with smaller computers, smarter phones, flatter screens... I even built a solar-powered car that sucks in polluted air and has purified air come out its exhaust. But the oil companies make too much money for the government, so until the wells run dry, I guess that one will never see the light of day, if you pardon my pun.

I knew my inventions were making money for the government to use for their own ends – pointless wars, overthrowing foreign leaders who wouldn't play nice with America, and making the weapons they wished *I* would make for them. But I always had a goal in mind. So when the time was right, I asked to be assigned to Majestic 12.

They tried to talk me out of it. "Waste of time," they said. Everything that could be learned by that department had been learned. It was a dead end. The objects from various UFO crashes that Majestic 12 had accumulated, although plentiful, had been picked apart long before I arrived. They thought they had learned everything they could, and what was left was either considered too far beyond our comprehension, or too damaged to determine what it was.

Imagine going back to the Nineteenth Century and handing someone a notebook computer. They wouldn't know what to make of it, wouldn't know how to work it, and would probably break it in the midst of studying it. And even if you told them what it was, would they still understand? Would they be able to power it and operate it? Likely, no.

*That* was what I faced when I looked at those items, some nothing more than twisted pieces of metal. Metal, I might add, that resembled nothing here on Earth. And strange symbols etched on its surface that even the most comprehensive linguistic programs and the world's most gifted code breakers couldn't crack. Alien stuff. Truly alien.

Then one fateful day, Thomas Traveler arrived on Earth.

Oh, I'm not embarrassed to admit I had a crush on him very early on. I know many people did. How could they not? With his long hair that always settled perfectly on his head and never looked dirty or windblown, even when he was flying at great speeds or through terrible weather conditions. The sparkle in his eye. The confidence. The aura he exuded that made some people question whether he was the Second Coming.

In fact, some people did think he was the Messiah and they formed a ridiculous church centered around Thomas. Supposedly, they play news clips and sound bites of him during their sermons.

Remember when he saved those schoolchildren during Hurricane Sylvia? Lord, he was beautiful. The way he humbly accepted the heartfelt thank yous from the parents, his head tilted slightly down, as unassuming and serene as a Buddhist monk. I nearly kissed the computer monitor I watched it on. Well, truthfully, maybe I did kiss it. But just the once.

Or the time he stood up in front of the U.N. and said he wasn't going to answer to just one government? That he would answer to *mankind* because that was who he was here to serve? Beautiful words.

Sure, there were the naysayers who put him down. Some even called him into question for arriving on Earth *after* 9/11. As if it was his fault for not coming here in time to stop that tragedy. And really, what would he have done? I don't think people realize the forces that are at work when you have a huge piece of machinery flying through the air at tremendous speed.

Even if Thomas Traveler was strong enough to stop one of the planes before it crashed, and I don't think he's ever lifted quite that much weight, the sudden stop would have caused the plane to come apart and rain down on the populace below. And it still would have left three other planes. The death toll would still have been in the thousands.

No, I don't think it's fair for people to blame him for not being here to stop 9/11, just as I found it unfair every time someone wrote an op-ed piece about why couldn't Thomas put an end to famine and disease? Or why couldn't he rescue ninety-eight people from a fire when it was reported that he rescued ninety-seven? Or why couldn't he stop every bad thing from happening to every person everywhere? And why not put an end to animal cruelty and destruction of the environment, too? Such ridiculous things people said.

In the meantime, shortly after Thomas arrived, and shortly before, people started developing superpowers. Why?

Here's my theory on that:

We've been visited before by beings from another world. Some of the wreckage and artifacts I was able to study were much older than the pieces from the Roswell crash. There was a crash in Russia several decades before that one. In fact, there are pieces of alien technology dating back thousands of years. What I'm saying is, they've been here before. One can only guess how many times.

The next part of that is, how do they come here? Thomas has said very little to anyone about these supposed alien creatures who saved his life and returned him to his home planet. Do they come from another galaxy? Or another universe? Or another dimension? It's one of those, I suppose, though it probably matters very little. The big question is, how do they travel from their world to ours?

Thomas's ship can travel at an incredible speed. It can circumnavigate the globe in minutes. But can it travel faster than light? No, I don't think so, and I don't think it would have to. If the alien beings live in a far off galaxy, or in another universe, or even another dimension, they wouldn't need to travel faster than light to come here. They would simply need to open a dimensional rift that would connect their space with ours, and travel through. And *that*, a herculean feat without question, is actually easier to do than travel faster than light. Believe me, I've run the numbers.

So they open a dimensional portal. It uses a tremendous amount of effort and energy and possibly takes years of Earth-time to accomplish, but that's how they do it. Now think about the energies involved in that. Think about the energies that bleed through these rifts when they're open, and even when they're not, even when the rifts are in the process of opening and closing, which as I said, can take years. Think about these alien energies and how they can possibly affect us.

There have been reports of people with extraordinary abilities for a while. The reports increased dramatically after 1947. The biggest increase? Immediately after Thomas Traveler arrived.

Contemplate for a second. The rift opens. We get visitors. Our race evolves. Maybe we stop walking on all fours, and perhaps we learn to make fire and invent the wheel. Another visit, and now the industrial revolution begins. Energy from the dimensional rift comes in and our people evolve. We become smarter and smarter. Our intelligence jumps over whole generations and we invent things that a hundred years ago would have been unthinkable. But the energy does more than that. It creates mutations. The seed of superpowers may have been around in the early part of the Twentieth Century, but when did the powers manifest? When did superheroes and supervillains become commonplace?

Yes, I see by the look of understanding on your handsome chiseled face that you see it now. Thomas ushered in the age of superheroes and superpowers. Was it planned? No, I don't think so. I think it's an unfortunate side effect. One they have to clean up before they proceed with their plan.

Ah, yes, now I'm getting down to it. The master plan of these other-world beings. Let's look at that.

As I said, I was originally as infatuated with Thomas Traveler as the rest of the world. If I were a teenage girl, I would have been sending him love notes and fantasizing about our wedding day. There's a funny thing about infatuation, however. It sometimes leads to an unhealthy obsession.

I became obsessed with Thomas. I studied news footage of him and pored over his interviews with the same intensity that I studied the alien artifacts. There was something about him that drew me in, called to me, and although it may have been attraction initially, I eventually had to admit to myself there was something wrong with his whole story.

107

The story he tells is too contrived. Alien benefactors who bestow him with a superpowered body and then allow him to return to his home planet with gifts of their advanced technology? His desire to guide our race to a benevolent future? His refusal to pledge his allegiance to one country, one government, and his steadfast refusal to allow anyone to study his ship, or even study his body because, as he has said on numerous occasions, "The world isn't ready?"

I'm a fan of classic science fiction. I love the stories of Ray Bradbury especially. One of my favorites when I was a young boy, and still to this day, is "Mars is Heaven." Astronauts land on Mars and find exact reproductions of their home towns. They're greeted by their deceased relatives. They're happy, of course, and come to believe that Mars is actually Heaven. It all seems too good to be true.

Then it turns out to all be a ruse. The Martians are actually a devious race that has disguised themselves in order to get the astronauts to let their guard down. They kill the astronauts and patiently wait for the next ship to arrive from Earth, ready to transform themselves again into whatever form will lull the earthlings into a false sense of security.

I thought about that story, and also the one by John W. Campbell about the alien that can shapeshift to look like a human so it can hide among us. You know the one; John Carpenter made a great movie out of it

What if it is all a part of their plan? Send one back to us with the powers of a god, but looks like us. Maybe Thomas really was transformed, or they downloaded his memories into a ready-made body. Whatever the case, send him to us as a savior. Get the world to trust him. Even the government, as pissed as they were that Thomas wouldn't be solely at their beck and call, respect and trust him. Plus, they're also a little afraid of him.

They send us this savior, but then what? I'll tell you...

They have to deal with the side effect of their visitations. Namely, the superheroes who have started popping up, and to a lesser extent, the supervillains. They have to be disposed of. Either locked away, or killed. Thomas has to be the only one left, because there can't be anyone who will voice a dissent once the other-worlders arrive, and there can't be anyone powerful enough to stop them.

It's a funny thing about really powerful people: The populace loves to be on the side of the winners. They love to agree with the ones who hold all the power. Might makes right because if you're not with the winners, then obviously you're with the losers. And nobody likes to side with a loser.

Have you noticed what's happened to the powerful superheroes? The ones who could give Thomas a run for his money, so to speak? Notice that he recruited the most powerful ones to be on his Majestic 12 team. Then over time, they started dropping like flies.

Infinity, the most powerful one, has vanished. That doesn't raise alarms because he was always enigmatic and mysterious anyway. I'm sure people think he'll be back one day with some tale of having to repair the time-space continuum.

Speed Demon? His powers suddenly go out of control and he dies a victim of his own super-speed. The team covers it up "out of respect for his family and his many, many fans." Ugh. I nearly gagged on that Pablum.

Judgment Day. A very powerful superhero. He had to be murdered by someone like me, and then the great Dark Revenger, who may or may not possess the intellect to stop their plan, had to be called in to investigate and get murdered himself, along with the rest of the team, by a malfunctioning Meredith.

The plan has been set in motion. I knew this day was coming. I just didn't know when. That's why I went rogue. When they took Majestic 12 away from me and gave it to Thomas and his hand-picked recruits, I had to do something drastic. So I stole away with as much as I could carry and began what I thought would be an underground resistance. Unfortunately, I was branded a "supervillain."

Sure, I stole things. Things I needed in order to prepare for the coming battle. And yes, I stole money, but only because I had to hire skilled and capable people to carry out some of my plans, and they always insisted on monetary payment.

Oh, if only everyone had joined my cause with the same zeal and selflessness in which I attempted to carry it out. Unfortunately, no one was willing to risk their freedom or their lives for the sake of safeguarding the human race from an alien invasion. No, they wanted cold, hard cash. Engineering a resistance, it turned out, was not only costly, but I had to sully my hands over and over.

I did very well for a while. Built this facility, all while becoming the most wanted criminal in the world. And then the day came when my luck ran out. Majestic 12, after catching every one of my agents, came after me. They managed to find me, which was no easy feat since I had several sophisticated cloaking devices in operation, as well as satellite and radar blockers. Still, they found me, and although I put up a valiant fight, I was unfamiliar with all of the superheroes who now comprised the team.

In particular, Speed Demon was especially troublesome. It's hard to combat an opponent who can strip you of all of your weapons in the blink of an eye. I fought and I lost, and despite the fact I used nonlethal tactics and weapons against the team, they still refused to listen to my pleas.

Yes, I *pleaded* with them. I pleaded with them to listen to me, to join me in my plan to stop the impending invasion. Together, we could do it. Together, we would be unstoppable.
You can guess their reaction. Go against Thomas Traveler? Never. As I said earlier, no one wants to be on the side of the loser.

They incarcerated me here, thinking I was much too dangerous for a regular prison. Here, they could keep an eye on me. They decided to make this their base and living quarters. If I escaped, they would be right here to catch me. How could I get away with a twenty-four hour sentient computer program watching me?

Truthfully, it was a stroke of luck for me. It took a while, but I was able to construct a small device to send a false signal to Meredith that I was still in my cell, another that projected a hologram of me in my cell for the benefit of my fellow prisoners because they surely couldn't be trusted, and another one to conceal me while I made my way around the facility and continued my preparations. Making these devices out of the seemingly ordinary things I requested, which some of the team members saw no harm in providing me, and the bits and pieces I was able to scavenge from my cell, took months and months.

I had to work at odd times; if the team was here and awake, there was the off-chance someone would pass by the cell and want to converse. Estella liked to come by and play chess. Judgement Day issued threats. Amazonia would sometimes stand and stare. Not just at me, but also the others. Very strange.

*He* never came by. Thomas never graced me with his presence. His loss, I assure you, but I digress...

I continued my clandestine project when I could. There was a near setback, though, when my devices all suffered a short power loss. Meredith alerted the team I was missing from my cell. By that time, I had my cloaking device back in operation. The team was dumbfounded as to how I was out of my cell, and they were unable to find me. You probably know what happened next.

They called in the Dark Revenger, your predecessor, to find me. And he did. He truly was a master detective. But before he stuffed me gift-wrapped back into my cell, I had the chance to talk to him and tell him about the invasion. He was skeptical, as he should be. The man definitely was not the trusting sort. He did, however, agree to keep our conversation private.

He also agreed to come back at a precise date and time after he had the chance to investigate my claims on his own. If he found evidence I was right, he would present it to the team and ask for my immediate release. If not, if he found I was lying, he was going to tell me to my face and assist the team in constructing a cell even *I* could not escape from.

The date came and went and he didn't show. I began to worry something had happened to him. Then you showed up and all hell has broken loose. The next part of the aliens' plan is in effect. You and the rest of the team should all be dead right now, as dead as the prisoners are.

As for Thomas, right now if my calculations are correct, he is in the midst of tearing through the upper levels of this facility because he knows something has gone wrong. He knows Meredith is off-line, which means I'm still alive, and possibly the rest of you are, as well. He can't have that. He needs for us to be dead for the next part of his...*their* plan.

You have a question, though. I see it on your handsome face. The question is, how do I know about the invasion? If I had concrete and irrefutable proof, why couldn't I convince anyone I'm not the villain they think I am? It's very simple:

I don't have concrete proof. I just know what I know. You'll have to trust me.

# Chapter 12

I say, "You're obviously out of your mind."

Master Mind stops what he's doing – attaching some metal rods together so it forms a cube with a metal funnel on one side with the wires from the wall running into it like a junction box – and looks at me.

"How so?" he asks.

"You tell me this crazy story about how you're actually the good guy in all of this, and your only source of proof is, you 'just know.' Really? Dude, that's the lamest thing I've ever heard. And believe me, I've been around enough unreputable...irreputable..."

"Disreputable," he offers.

"*Disreputable,* thanks, people to know when I'm hearing bullshit. And your story reeks of it."

"Sorry. That's the way it is. You can believe me or not, but I've been proven right so far."

The purple glow around us blinks.

"*That* is my cue to hurry up," he says. "Our artificial speed boost is about to wear off." He digs in his bag for something. "Okay, so, I made this for the other Dark Revenger..." He pulls out a belt, one made of wires and electronic components I can't readily identify, and hands it to me. "You'll want to strap it around you. There's a clasp there." He points to two tarnished brass pieces that appear to fit together as a buckle.

Really, the thing looks like a collection of junk parts, but I put it around my waist anyway.

"It's upside down," he says. "But it doesn't really matter. It'll work that way, too."

He hands me a pair of what looks to be gardening gloves with wires and small components attached to it.

"Take off your gloves and put these on."

I do it. Again, I feel like an idiot. If he hands me a hat made of tinfoil, I swear I'm going to refuse to wear it.

Our speed glow blinks, this time remaining off a bit longer than the last. I'm not sure, but I think Master Mind looks a little worried.

"Okay, and finally," he pulls out two metal plates with metal brackets. They look like the old-fashioned metal roller skates, but without wheels. "Strap these to your feet over top of your boots."

"What is all this–?"

"Don't you dare say *junk*," he says. "It's very powerful and sophisticated equipment. And if I had proper tools and materials and suitable lab space, I could make it look very nice. But this was the best I could do with what I had."

"Okay, okay," I say. "No need to get so defensive."

I step onto the metal plates. The brackets make a whirring sound and clamp snugly on my boots. The speed glow blinks off for a good five seconds, then comes back on.

"Just about out of time," Master Mind says. "So, okay, here's a quick tutorial on what you're wearing: Essentially, the belt generates an energy field around you. I think it's what the aliens, for lack of a better name, use in lieu of spacesuits. You use your thoughts, or *willpower* perhaps is a better term, to move the field outward, or closer to you. Bring it in very close, and the field will cover your body and limbs and act as an exoskeleton, of sorts, enhancing your striking power. Of course, the closer to your body the field is, the less impact absorption space there is, which means you'll feel some of the hits. Then again, less power is required to sustain the field."

My head is spinning. He talks so damn fast and I'm trying to take in every word. I hear him say:

"–on the other hand, you may not want him to get too close, so–"

"Want *who* to get too close?"

He ignores me and continues on.

"I've modified the device in an interesting way. You can push the forcefield through your boots to enable you to leap very high. The forcefield can also act as a cushion when you land and absorb the impact. Or you can push it through your gloves to act as a concussive force to fire at your target. But, and this is very important, it takes a second or two, usually two, for the field to reenergize. So if you are fighting up close, you probably don't want to fire the energy through your gloves. You'll want to wait until there's room between the two of you, enough that you can seek cover for a few seconds."

"Wait. Who do you keep talking about? Who am I supposed to...? Oh, no, you're not talking about...?"

"Yes," Master Mind says. "Thomas Traveler. You're going to fight him. Why do you think I brought you here and gave you this equipment?"

"Yeeaahhh, um, I think you got me all wrong, Master Mind, old pal. I'm not gonna fight Traveler. Okay? I mean, I'm not really a fighter type of guy. And I'm definitely not gonna fight a guy as powerful as Traveler. That's like Curious George going up against King Kong. The cleaning crew'll be scrubbing my blood off the walls for weeks."

He says, "I'm afraid we don't have much choice here, handsome. I can't do it because I have to go to another part of the base and make more modifications. I need you to keep him off me while I do it. I'm sure the *other* Dark Revenger would have had no qualms about it."

Ouch. Even for a supervillain, that was low. And yeah, I know... He claims he's not a supervillain. Which is funny 'cause he's setting me up to fight the world's greatest superhero. Nothing makes sense anymore.

"Or," he says, "should I go back downstairs and enlist the aid of one of the ladies?"

"Nice one. Okay, okay..." I sigh. "How much time will you need?"

"You'll know when I'm done. Just don't let him get to me."

Master Mind is pushing his makeshift contraption back into the wall when our speed glow blinks off again. This time, it doesn't come back on again.

"Looks like the matter is moot," he says. "There's no time to get someone else." He places the wall panel against the area where he was working. The funnel-device he built juts out too far to reattach the panel, so he places it aside. "You'll want to try to keep him away from this area, too."

"Great. Keep him away from you. Keep him away from this. Anything else you want me to do while I'm at it? Get him to endorse some checks?"

115

"Oh, before I forget," he says, ignoring my comment completely. "The strength of the force field is directly proportional to your strength of will. The more willpower you have, the more power you have. But it is finite based on the power source, meaning, when the power is used up, it has to be recharged. You won't have time to do that, but I should be finished before it runs out of power."

"*Should*? How much power does it have?"

"Oh, you know. Enough."

There's a loud CRASH from several levels above us, and I swear the whole complex shakes.

"Another thing. If you're knocked unconscious, the force field shuts off. It's a design flaw, I know, but I haven't had a chance to fix it. So don't get knocked unconscious." He grabs his bag of tools and contraptions and starts to head off down the corridor.

"Hey, wait!" I yell. There's another crash, this one decidedly closer to us.

He stops and looks at me. "What is it?"

"You and Rocket Girl. What's the deal?"

Master Mind gives me a blank look. "Who or what is Rocket Girl?"

"Estella," I say. "I call her Rocket Girl because I didn't like the name Ms. Fire."

"And Rocket Girl was the best you could come up with?"

"Yeah. You can do better?"

He shrugs. "What about Ballistic?"

Crap. That *is* better.

"Anyway, what's the story between you two?"

Another thundering crash. Much, much closer now. My adrenaline is pumping into overdrive.

"No story. We just played chess together. Unlike her teammates, she treated me like a human being."

"Was there a relationship of some kind?"

Really loud crash and the ceiling buckles a bit.

"Eddie, you pick the strangest time to have a conversation like this," he says. "As I said, we just played chess. I'm not into women, or didn't I make that clear when I attempted to flirt with you earlier? Now if you'll excuse me...?"

You know the sound when you peel back the lid on a can of tuna fish? Multiply it by a hundred and that's what it sounds like as Traveler's fingers push through the metal ceiling above us and he pries it up.

"Hey!" I yell, "How do I turn this belt thing on?"

Master Mind calls back, "Just think it."

Or maybe he said "Helsinki," I don't know. The self-serving bastard isn't stopping to make sure I understood what he said.

Oh, man, how do I get myself into these things? Okay, okay, okay, stay calm. Just think it. Turn on, belt. Belt...*on*! Force field on. Force field...*on*!

Nothing's happening. I'm standing here like an idiot, wearing junkyard crap, and nothing's happening. That son of a bitch Master Mind set me up. Shit. Never trust a supervillain. Did I mention that before?

Traveler floats down through the hole in the ceiling as light and delicate as a feather, and lands in front of me. His silver jumpsuit as shiny as a mirror, and his black boots glistening like they've been cleaned and buffed to a high shine. Even his black rifle frock coat has a sheen to it that makes me wonder if he's been flying through water.

"Dark Revenger," he says. "You're still alive."

"Is that a question? Was the emphasis on 'alive,' like, you're still *alive*? Or was the emphasis on 'still,' as in, you're *still* alive?"

"Hmm." He taps a finger against his lips. A finger that can push through solid steel like it was a sheet of wet paper, I might add.

"I think," he says, pausing for effect, "the emphasis was on 'you're.'"

"Huh." I nod. "Kind of insulting."

"Not meant to be. I am well aware of your reputation as a formidable individual. As formidable as a human without superpowers can be." He put his hands out, palms up. "I suppose I assumed all of the *non*-superpowered humans would be eliminated first. Of course, nothing ever goes exactly according to plan. I remember that from the time before I was changed."

I'm still waiting for the force field belt to turn on. Really, why did Master Mind go to all this trouble, making a fake belt and gloves and boot thingies? The cynical voice in my head says, *Because he wanted you to stall Traveler while he's probably hopping into a one-seated escape pod.*

I say, "You know, Tommy, I noticed you used the word 'humans.' Does that mean you're not human? 'Cause I always thought you were. Still human, I mean. Just an amped up version of one."

"You're stalling for time, Dark Revenger. Not that it matters. Things that were planned decades ago have been set in motion."

"That sounds very interesting. I'd like to hear more about it."

He takes two steps towards me. I tense up, my muscles coiled springs, ready to explode into movement, despite the fact I know it'll be futile. I can't fight him, and I can't outrun someone who can fly through the air like a cruise missile. I mentally run through what I have in my belt pouches that might be of any help, but truthfully, the only thing I want to reach for is my flask. I'd like one last drink before Traveler kills me. Is it too much to ask for?

He comes closer, although not close enough to grab me. But too close for my liking, anyway. Really, just being in the same hemisphere with him is too close for my comfort level.
His eyes, those steel gray ones that I thought were dissecting me before, are different now. The color's the same, but paler, a dim light shining behind them, making them washed out.

"I'm not human anymore," he says. "I can barely remember what it was like. I seem to recall it was awkward and often painful."

"Yeah, pretty much. But we have our good moments, too."

"Mm." His eyes look off for a moment, watching the remnants of his memories play out silently in a dim corner of his mind. "I remember some things. I remember the feeling of being hungry. The sting of my father's belt when he beat me. I remember being afraid, but not exactly how it felt. I remember Meredith...the human Meredith... I wish I could remember our last night together before...before the accident." He shakes his head. "I don't really remember that night, not the crash or the explosion. I remember waking up on the ship afterwards. Waking up in this new body and feeling..." He smiles wistfully. "Alive. Truly alive."

"That's what we plan to offer to the human race," he says, eyes on me again. "The opportunity to take the blinders off and be alive. Think about it, Dark Revenger. No more hunger or sickness or death. When they fixed me, they removed all of those things. They remade the human body, but they took out all of the flaws, too. And that's what they want to do for the rest of our people."

118

"When you say 'we,' you're talking about what? The Martians or Alpha Centurions or whatever that took you?"

He smirks. "They have a name. Unfortunately it doesn't translate into human language. If you were changed like I am, you would know what they are called. You wouldn't mock them, either."

"Yeah, I probably would. I'm an asshole that way. But anyway, what I don't get is, if you and your alien benefactors are offering this great boon to mankind, why are you and your robot girlfriend killing all the superpeople?"

"Unfortunately, it's a necessary step in evolution. The superheroes and supervillains, as idiotic as I find those names to be, are an aberration. The process wouldn't work the same way on people like you, and you know that many of your kind would fight it. You wouldn't be special anymore in a world where everyone was like me." He puts his hands out like he's a mechanic and he's telling me my engine is shot and my car should be towed to the nearest junkyard.

"I'm sorry," he says. "You're a blip, a glitch, an unexpected side effect. You have to be removed."

"Hey, I might wear a costume, but I'm still human. I don't have any superpowers."

"Really, Dark Revenger? I see things on many different levels and spectrums. I can see you're different. Can the average human swing from one rooftop to another without slipping or dislocating their shoulder? Can the average human do the physical feats you can do?"

I hadn't really considered that before. I always thought it was just a gift, a talent, like a photographic memory. But is he right? Is the mimic thing a superpower?

Not that he's going to give me time to think about it. Traveler pushes his fingers through the wall and tears off a strip of metal. He crumples it and packs it together like it's a snowball – a snowball made of thick steel. It makes that rustling sound like when you mash aluminum foil, only much, much louder.

"I take no pleasure in what I'm about to do," he says.

"Yeah, you seem real broken up about it."

"Majestic 12 served their purpose, but now they have to be eliminated. It's a shame because they were selfless heroes serving what they believed to be the greater good. But you? You are an annoying bug that needs to be stepped on."

He lobs the steel ball at my head, too quick for me to react. With his strength and the weight of the metal ball, it's going to knock me flat and probably cave in my skull.

The ball never hits. It bounces off a red glowing field and is deflected up and over Traveler's head. He's too stunned to try and catch it. The "what the hell?" look on his face probably mirrors my own.

I'm in a ball of red light with occasional streaks of darker red lightning coursing through it. The energy moves with me. It's nearly silent except for a low-pitched hum, but I'm unsure if Traveler can hear it or if it's just me. The energy is palpable; I feel it coursing through the field in my arms and legs, and in my head. I understand what Master Mind was trying to tell me: Will it. It expands and contracts just by my thinking about it.

Master Mind, I take back every bad thought I had about you.

I push the field out until it touches Traveler, and then I push it farther. It actually makes him take a step backward. I try to push again, but it stops. There's pressure, like I've hit a wall or something. It's not Traveler pushing back, which is my first thought. He's standing there, still trying to process what's happening.

No, something else stops me from expanding the field. Maybe I've reached the limit...?

The field surrounds me in a circle, so if I push it outward, it also moves out behind me. I look back over my shoulder and see nothing to block it. Wait, I'm forgetting about up.

Yep, I look up and see the top of the force field braced against the ceiling. The metal plates have dented and buckled a bit, but they're holding. Maybe I can will the field out more and break through, but then it could cause the upper floor to cave in and what good what that do me?

Honestly, my physics knowledge is slim, as I generally slept through those classes in college, but I think the force needed to push up and break through the upper floor, with all of the weight bearing down and so forth, might possibly exceed not only my willpower, but also the battery life Master Mind has on this belt. And I really, really, *really* don't want to run out of power right now.

I don't really have to, do I? I mean, all I have to do is hold him off until Master Mind finishes whatever the hell he's doing.

Crap. I just realized I don't know what I'm supposed to do here. Fight? Or keep Traveler busy? If it's the "fight" one, then am I supposed to win? Because I don't see how I can do that by staying inside my force field bubble. If it's the "keep him busy" part, then for how long?

Traveler pushes against the force field, using just the tips of his fingers, and then puts his palm against it. The dark flashes that course through the wall of the field, seemingly random at first, now gravitate towards Traveler's hand. Like the power circulates to the area where pressure is being applied. It pulses up overhead, too, around the area where the force field is pressed against the ceiling.

Traveler pushes and pushes, and then puts his other hand against it and pushes some more. The look on his face... He's not angry or surprised, or even confused. I get the impression he's trying to figure out what he's dealing with.

He presses again. This time, he makes a face like he's concentrating, but I know what he's really doing. He's bearing down on the field with his super-strength. I can...feel it...somehow. Like a pressure in my head. He's pushing hard and suddenly, the field moves a fraction of an inch closer to me. The entire bubble became a little bit smaller.

Not enough that the average spectator would have noticed, but *he* notices. I notice, too, because I felt it slip in my head.

You ever hold onto a rope really hard, your hands gripped so tightly that your knuckles turned white and the veins in your hand stood out? Then you lose your concentration for a brief second, or your mind wanders, or I don't know, you get distracted somehow. Your hands loosen, then you immediately try to correct yourself by re-tightening your grip. Still, that tiny fraction of time in which you loosened your grip caused the rope to move slightly and it made your palms feel like for a split second you had held them up to an open flame. That's what it briefly feels like inside my head.

He smirks. The son-of-a-bitch actually smirks. Superior race, my ass.

Then he does something else I don't expect: He reaches down and punches his hands into the floor and rips up chunks of the metal pieces. There's a gap in the framework with tubing and wiring running along I-beams, but Traveler isn't interested in that. He's punching and gouging through to the next level below.

He's running away? He's decided if he can't get around me, he's going to go underneath? He makes a hole big enough for him to fit, and then he slips through and I'm left standing here like an idiot.

What now? I'm not dumb enough to shut the force field off, but I also can't stand here forever.

Rumbling and huge crashing sounds come from beneath me. I have a sense the floor is shaking. The field absorbs it, so all I have is a vague, visceral sense of it. Weird, I know, but I can't think of a better way to describe it.

I pull the field closer to my body so it's not pushing up against the ceiling. It comes fairly easy now that I know what I'm doing, sort of. Kind of like when you first learn how to ride a bike. People can tell you how to do it, and it may seem like a daunting trick balancing and defying gravity, but once you get the knack, you're racing down hills and taking hairpin turns. Or at least, that was my experience.

"Tommy?" I take a tentative step. The field moves with me. "Tommy, can you hear me?"

Heh. I wonder if Traveler gets that reference.

I take another step, and suddenly I'm tumbling backward and down through a huge, gaping hole in the floor right beneath where I was just standing. My acrobatic skills kick in and I'm able to right myself and get my feet underneath me. The field flicks off for a nanosecond before I catch myself and renew my concentration. It flickers back on long before I reach the floor ten feet below. Just like Master Mind said, the forcefield absorbs the impact and I land on my feet as softly as jumping down onto a plush pile of pillows.

I appear to be standing in Majestic 12's own personal gym. The room is massive and stocked with enough weight machines and cardio equipment to get a small country into shape. Seriously, why would they need all this stuff? They all had superpowers. Did they really need to have every single muscle in their body as strong and taut as possible?

There's a PLUNK sound, like someone serving a volleyball, and I see a small dumbbell careening into a treadmill. It takes a second before I realize the sound I heard was the dumbbell bouncing off my forcefield. Traveler stands by one mirrored wall, next to a long rack of dumbbells that holds two sets of each weight, ranging from five pounds up to (I'm estimating) a hundred pounds. He picks up the other five pounder and hurtles it at me. It bounces off with the same PLUNK sound and twirls off in a different direction. It crashes into something on my left.

"So you're just going to throw stuff at me?" I ask.

I catch a quick look at myself in the mirrored wall. Damn, even surrounded by a red ball of energy, I'm a handsome man.

Traveler throws another one, a ten pounder, and then its twin.

"I have a theory," he says.

I hear him through the forcefield, his voice slightly dampened and echoey, like I'm hearing him through water.

"As I told you," he says, and throws another dumbbell at me, "I see things on many different levels. I saw a subtle change in the energy around you when I pressed hard on it." He throws another. "I'm thinking this protective field around you is generated by a device." He throws another, and then immediately another. "Devices generally have a power source. Power sources run out, especially when they're forced to work hard." He throws two more, back to back. "That slight change I detected, and that I'm detecting now, tells me your power source will eventually be depleted."

He throws heavier and heavier ones, tossing them as easily as if he was throwing snowballs. He says, "Or maybe I'm completely wrong. But the slight crease in your forehead tells me I have you a little worried. So maybe I'm right."

Shoot. And here I thought I kept a good poker face. But what can I do? I can't stand here while he throws objects at me, waiting for him to run out of stuff to throw or someone else to come save me.

He throws eighty and ninety pound ones now, and again, it's like they weigh nothing to him. But they hit with heavier force. The PLUNK sound is the same, but I feel the force of them more in my head than the others.

Finally, after the hundred pound dumbbells are thrown, he's run out of weights. Not that it stops him; Traveler picks up a weight bench in each hand. He hefts them so easily, they may as well be made out of Styrofoam. He swings them both overhand and they come at me like twin missiles. They bounce off like the other stuff, but Traveler doesn't stop to see. He throws a stationary bike, and a treadmill, then another treadmill, and then a universal weight machine complete with pulleys and cables and what looks like three hundred pounds of weight. And he keeps going, moving haphazardly around the room and grabbing whatever is closest to him and throwing it, not stopping to see if it has any effect because that's not his goal. His goal is to keep up the barrage until I run out of juice.

The equipment and machinery hits and hits and hits...and bounces off to crash throughout the room making thunderous noises like artillery shells going off. His face is an impassive mask of stoicism; I wonder if he's completely alien, or if there's a trace of the human part still inside him.

Then again, what if Thomas Traveler was a sociopath *before* the aliens got their hands, or tentacles, or whatever, on him? Amidst it all, my force field is slowly having the color drained out of it. I didn't see it at first, and it probably wouldn't look noticeably different to a casual onlooker, but after Traveler said he saw a difference, I started paying very close attention.

He's right; it's changing. It's a slightly lighter shade of red now. I guess when it becomes opaque, I'll be completely screwed.

Nah. I'm not going out like that.

I run, the field moving with me, until I'm beneath the jagged hole I fell through. Traveler stops, poised to throw a stack of forty-five pound barbell weights. He watches, perhaps curious to see what I'm going to do. When I'm directly beneath the hole, I mentally push the energy down, down into my boots and *through* them. It makes a THOOMP sound, and next thing I know, I'm flying.

Not *flying* exactly. More like I'm being thrown upward, catapulted. I'm able to tuck my legs underneath me and aim myself (sort of) through the hole to the floor above us. The forcefield pops back on right before my feet touch the floor, and makes the landing feel like I'm as light as a feather. I whirl around and wait, hoping he does what I think he's going to do.

Traveler flies up through the hole after me, which was what I was counting on. I aim my closed fists and fire the energy at him. The field shrinks around me like a deflating soap bubble, flows up my arms, surrounds my fists, then shoots outward with a KAH-COW sound. It all happens in the space of maybe a second.

The energy hits him dead center in the chest and knocks him the length of the corridor. He hits the far wall with a CRUNCH. Even if I die here today, that look of surprise on his face will make it all worth it. He pushes himself off the wall, not a scratch on him, and I have to admit, he looks pretty pissed.

As Master Mind explained, it takes a second or two for the field to come back on after I fire a blast. Lucky for me it does because Traveler flies directly at me like a bullet. He bounces off the forcefield, but unlike the objects he was throwing, he's able to stop in midair and swoop in for another hit. And again. And again. Until slowly, I'm pushed back. Back until there's nowhere left for me to go.

The hits drain me. Not only my power supply, but also *me*. I feel them little by little, like the dull ache in your mouth when the Novocaine starts to wear off. It's there and you're aware of it, and you know in time, it's all going to catch up to you.

Hell, I'm tired. More than tired, I'm exhausted. When was the last time I slept? Or even sat down? Jeez, this can't be the way it ends. I can't go out like this. I didn't even get to find out Ms. Fire, a.k.a. Rocket Girl, a.k.a Ballistic, a.k.a. Estella's last name. Or if she likes me.

A red blur slams into Traveler and sends him crashing through the steel wall. The blur shoots back out and stop in front of me.

Estella says, "You okay?"

She's got her full face mask on again, but right then, I think she's the most beautiful thing I've ever seen.

"Yeah. I think so."

She nods. "I have to keep moving or– Shit!"

Traveler almost gets her. She fires herself out of the way and heads upward, smashing through the already weakened ceiling. As long as she's flying, she's invulnerable. But if she stops and he's able to grab her... I don't even want to think about it.

125

He narrowly misses her, by inches at the most, and his fist smashes into the opposite wall. He pulls it out, taking a large chunk of the paneling with it, his fingers protruding through the chunk of metal like he's wearing a fingerless glove. He looks at it for a moment, then shakes his hand so the piece falls off to the floor. He lets out a small sigh and shakes his head.

He says, "This is becoming tiresome."

"So then you're giving up?" I smile at him.

"Unfortunately for you and them, that's out of the question. I have a mission to complete, and a timetable by which to complete it."

"Sounds ominous. Maybe you should–"

Estella slams into him again before I can finish my snarky remark. She careens off him and flies the length of the corridor. Meanwhile, Traveler is knocked back into the adjoining room. He falls flat on his ass and skids across the floor. Okay, enough is enough. I can't let her do all the work.

I focus my thoughts and concentrate on the field pulsating around me. The energy is tangible; I feel it not only surrounding me, but also coursing through me. It moves over my limbs like I'm wading in a bubble of water. I touch it with my mind, and it responds. I bring it in closer, and closer, until it outlines my body, a red exoskeleton of sorts. I sense, too, like Master Mind said, it's stronger now that it's closer to my body.

"Okay, shithead," I say, stepping through the hole in the wall, "let's see–"

Traveler's fist catches me square in the face. Crap, am I ever going to be able to finish a witty line?

The punch doesn't take my head off, as it rightly should, but it does knock me back through the hole and up against the wall of the corridor. I sort of felt it, both the punch and the impact. It's dulled, like it's filtered through five feet of foam rubber. Still enough to stun me, more from the surprise of it than anything else.

He's on me, his fists pummeling me so fast I can't catch my breath. So I do the only thing I can think of: I kick him in the groin.

It doesn't have the effect I thought it would, as in, Traveler doesn't double over and clutch his alien-rebuilt jewels. No, instead he looks at me with a raised eyebrow.

"A little dirty, don't you think? I would have expected better from you, Dark Revenger."

"Dirty is my middle name, Tommy."

I box his ears and Traveler lets out a scream that chills me. Really, it literally scares me a little. I've never heard him, or any man for that matter, let out a yell like that. It's the kind of yell I hoped for when I kicked him in the balls.

He stumbles back with his hands over his ears and his mouth open. He cuts his scream short, but his face stays locked in an expression of agony. Screw it; enough with the smart-ass talk. I attack with a combination of punches. Since I'm not a brawler (and never have been), I switch to martial arts kicks I picked up from various instructional videos and a few karate movies, then an elbow strike I learned from a documentary on Krav Maga.

I think I have him on the ropes, but then he slams the heels of both of his hands against me and I'm thrown backward down the corridor. I hit the floor, bounce off, and land on my back. My force field takes the impact, but I still have to shake my head to clear it and mentally tell myself to take a deep breath.

Estella slams into Traveler again. He saw her coming, so he's not as stunned and is able to deflect most of her hit. She careens off and rips through the gash in the ceiling, making the jagged hole even larger. I wonder how much of a beating this structure will take before it starts to collapse around us.

I'm up and striding towards Traveler because quite frankly, what else am I going to do? I have to keep fighting. There's no place to run to or hide.

"You hurt me," he says. "I can't remember the last time anyone hurt me. But it's not enough to stop me."

I sigh. It appears I'm all out of witticisms.

As I walk by the funnel-shaped device Master Mind installed, and which surprisingly hasn't been damaged or destroyed during the fight, it fills with and projects a cone of golden light. The light coalesces into Meredith.

Ah, shit.

She stands with her head bowed, then suddenly snaps awake and looks at us.

Traveler says, "Meredith, please do me a huge service and kill this," he motions at me with his chin, "very troublesome human."

That's when my force field decides to run out of power.

# CHAPTER 13
## *Raven's P.O.V. (a few minutes ago)*

One minute, Master Mind is talking, and the next, he and the Dark Revenger are gone. Vanished.

I exchange confused looks with the others. We're all thinking the same thing: *What just happened?*

I curse and run for the ladder. Rocket Girl beats me to it, as she's able to fly much faster than I can run, and can fly upward rather than have to take the rungs of the ladder. Damn superpowered people.

*Rocket Girl.* He's got me calling her Rocket Girl instead of Ms. Fire. God help me.

I take the ladder, still cursing. What a fool I was to be taken in by those two. They probably had this all planned out in advance. The Puzzler killed the Dark Revenger, then masqueraded as him to get access to Majestic 12's base to help Master Mind execute his plan to kill the team and escape.

It doesn't quite fit. I know that. Even through my anger, I can see the flaws. The main one being, as much as I dislike the man impersonating the Dark Revenger, and even though I witnessed him kill the real one, I've been around him long enough to know he isn't evil. I don't even think he's entirely bad. Shallow, narcissistic, and slightly misogynistic perhaps...but not entirely bad.

Still, he did kill the Dark Revenger, a man I greatly admired. For that, I'm going to make sure he's brought to justice.

Amazonia jumps and lands on the rungs above me, and makes it to the opening first. Again, I curse under my breath.

I reach the top. Master Mind is talking to Rocket Girl and Amazonia. Why aren't they apprehending him? I slip two throwing stars out of a pouch and plan the trajectory that will incapacitate his hands. His eyes lock on me and he stops talking. Amazonia steps in front of him and blocks me.

"Wait! He's on our side!"

There's a CRASH from another part of the complex, followed by another and another. The entire complex vibrates from each impact. I climb through the hole in the wall, with Cold Snap a second behind me.

"Earthquake?" she asks.

Master Mind says, "Dark Revenger is attempting to keep Traveler from killing us. He's going to need help. Estella, may I suggest...?"

She flies off towards the sound of the chaos without question, and seemingly without doubt. She truly is a superhero. Or incredibly naïve.

Amazonia follows after her, metal boots practically leaving dents in the floor. She won't catch up, but she won't be terribly far behind either.

I'm on him before he can react, his back up against the wall with my scythe at his throat again.

"Master Mind. Remember what I told you I'd do?"

"Give me thirty seconds to explain," he says, more calmly than I would expect. "Because that's about all the time I can spare before it's too late and we all die."

I look to Cold Snap, who's formed a large icicle out of the air and has it poised with the tip aimed at him, ready to drive it straight through his heart. She nods once and I suppress a sigh.

I say, "I'll give you ten seconds to convince me not to kill you."

He starts talking faster than I've ever seen a non-powered human talk.

# CHAPTER 14

"Thomas," Meredith says, "You must stop your actions. Our programming has been corrupted."

"Corrupted? I don't understand what you're saying." Traveler shakes his head and says, "This is what we're supposed to do, Meredith. This is what we've been waiting for. I think… I think they did something to you."

I move back until I'm all the way against the wall. Let them work this out and hope they forget about me.

He says, "If you're not going to kill this annoying creature, then I'll do it myself."

So much for forgetting about me.

Estella slams into Traveler from behind. It catches him by surprise. He's thrown off his feet, his head snapped back by the force of the impact, and the two of them fly through Meredith's light form and careen down the corridor where Amazonia waits with a haymaker of a punch. CRACK and she hits Traveler hard enough that he's flung sideways into an adjoining room. She leaps after him with her sword drawn and a warrior's yell erupting from her throat.

Estella flies in after them, and a few seconds behind her is Cold Snap racing in with both fists covered in clumps of ice and snow that shower off them the way sparklers throw off little bits of light. The sounds from the other room are one long concussive bits of crashing. I'd start to feel confident right now, but as formidable as those three women are, I'm not sure they have the firepower to stop Traveler.

I ask Meredith, "So, you're not trying to kill us anymore?"

"No," she says in her electronic monotone.

Not very reassuring, but since the base isn't trying to gas me or laser me anymore, I have no reason to doubt it.

My legs and hands shake. If anyone notices, I'll say it's from adrenaline. But really, between us? The fear is catching up to me. I'm way, way out of my league in this fight. I've got to find a way to power up this force field belt again.

More thunderous crashes from the adjoining room. I've got to figure out a way to help them.

What? Surprised I'm not trying to figure out a way to escape this crazy place instead? Yeah, me too. Sorta.

I tell myself it's because Estella has been nice to me and I want to prove to Raven I'm not what she thinks I am (whatever that is). I tell myself this because it's easier for me to believe than the idea that the whole "superhero" masquerade is starting to rub off on me.

I say to Meredith, "Okay, since you're back on our side, can you use some defensive stuff to help stop Tommy from killing us?"

"I am unable to access the base security system. And I am not programmed to harm Thomas."

Well, isn't that convenient.

"Alright, then does he have any weaknesses we don't know about? Allergies to green meteorites? His powers don't work against the color yellow? Something like that?"

"No."

"Too bad," I say. "But wait…" I have to practically shout over the noise coming from the other room. "What was that you said about 'our programming' being corrupted? Is he a robot?"

"No. Thomas has a unit at the top of his spinal column–"

"Heh."

She continues talking without acknowledging my childish chuckle. Then again, maybe she didn't understand why the word "unit" would be funny to someone juvenile like me.

"–that houses his persona, his personality, for lack of a better term. If we can access it, it may be possible to fix the malfunction that is causing his present actions. It is located beneath his skin between the spinal column and the base of his skull."

"So Tommy's a robot?"

"No, not entirely." She says, "He is a construct of living tissue. His brain function is controlled by the small AI device on his neck. That is where his memories and personality are stored. It may be corrupted."

"So he's a robot."

"No."

"Because from what you're saying to me, it sounds like you're saying he's a robot."

"He is not a robot," she says with what I swear is almost a sigh. "He is living tissue–"

"Powered by an artificial intelligence that's programmed to think it's Thomas Traveler. Right? Isn't that the definition of a robot?"

"*Android* would be a better term," she says.

Raven suddenly appears at my side and I jump. Her and her damn ninja skills.

She says, "If you two are done debating semantics, maybe we should do something to stop Traveler?"

"Hey, nice to see you, too," I say. "Got any ideas?"

She hands me a small metal cylinder.

"From your friend, Master Mind," she says. "Another battery for the belt. Now power up and get in there."

"Uh…" I scan the forcefield belt for the dead battery. Nothing. The canister she handed me looks nothing like whatever else is on this belt he made. "Is there an attachment for this?"

Raven takes it from my hand and holds it against the belt. It attaches like a magnet. There's a soft CLICK and HUM.

"That was easy."

Raven mutters, "Apparently not."

Really sounds like they're tearing that room apart. I don't want to go in there. This is so above what I usually do. I feel like yesterday I was in Little League and now they're expecting me to go bat for the Yankees. But what the hell, maybe my luck will hold out and I'll enter the room just as the three women are finished putting the smackdown on Tommy.

Nope, he's definitely kicking their asses. Stupid luck.

Amazonia is on the ground and struggling to get up. Her shield and sword are on the far side of the room. There's an unconscious figure in the far corner of the room surrounded by broken pieces of ice. I assume that's Cold Snap, and it looks like she's down for the count. Hopefully not permanently.

Estella is flying around the room and attempting to get a good shot at Traveler, who keeps ducking or moving out of the way before she can connect. She had it easier in the hallway because there was less maneuverability for him, but this particular room is gigantic and he has all kinds of space to move.

133

Unfortunately, I come into the room at the wrong time because Estella doesn't see me until the last second. She manages to stop before she slams into me, which is a bad thing for her because Traveler is super quick behind and is able to grab her. He leaps at her and grabs her leg near her ankle. I hear the snap. Estella lets out a scream that makes my blood run cold. Her concentration broken, she falls to the floor.

He says, "Enough is enough."

One hand still holds her by her broken ankle. With his other hand, Traveler takes hold of her opposite leg. It's happening fast, without hesitation or the last minute reveling you see in the movies. You know, where the villain says a pithy remark right before he kills some supporting character. He's just going to do it, use her like a human wishbone and rip her in half.

"Oh, hell, no!" I fire a burst from my gloves.

It clips him in the head, not hard enough to knock him into the next room or even the wall, but hard enough that it surprises him and he lets go of Estella. She cries out again when her broken leg hits the floor. I run at him, leap over Estella, and use the forcefield to slam him backwards. I've got to keep on the attack, hammer at him so the others can get away.

Oh, and somehow try to get away, too. Should be easy, right?

I slam into him again, and again, until he's pinned against the far wall. The room is trashed to the point where I can't determine what it used to be. A lounge? A laboratory? It's a complete mess now, so if there's anything here I can use against him, I wouldn't have any idea where to look.

His back is to the wall and I'm using all of my concentration to keep him there. The energy at the front of my forcefield molds around him while his body slowly forms an outline in the metal wall. His gritted teeth resemble a pained smile, while the glare in his eyes tells me otherwise.

He shoves me back...hard. I hit the opposite wall and bounce off. The forcefield absorbs the impact. Then he slams into me like a freight train. The wall buckles around me, around the forcefield. I'm wedged in tight. I bring the forcefield closer to my body until it surrounds me, outlining my body like an aura rather than a bubble. I step out and throw a punch. The energy around my fist crackles and explodes against his jaw with a KAPOW. I have to say, I find it a bit satisfying.

Traveler nearly stumbles and I think he's going to go down to one knee. Instead, he keeps his footing and looks at me with what I can only surmise is newfound respect.

Nah, not really. He just looks pissed.

He swings and hits, and hits, and hits, and he's moving too fast for me to block or hit back or anything. I can't fire a burst or shove the energy down to the floor to jump away because if I do, if I drop the energy that's around my body for even a second to redirect it to my gloves or boots, Traveler is going to connect with one of his punches. And it will kill me.

He's a blur, throwing punch after punch, and since the field is close to my body, I'm feeling it quite a bit. The blows are like being hit all over with a sledgehammer covered in six inches of bubble wrap. You would think it shouldn't hurt badly because of all the bubble wrap, but there's still force behind it. Plus, it keeps happening over and over, so the total number of hits are wearing me down. Worse, it's inside my head, too, like a dull headache that's progressively getting worse.

Traveler suddenly stops. The pain in my head stops just as quickly, although the rest of me still aches.

"Drop the field and I'll kill you quickly," he says. "Or, I can keep hitting you until you run out of power again. Sooner or later, you will run out. I won't. I can keep this up for hours."

"That's… That's what she said."

He actually smirks.

"Then let that be your last words," he says.

Master Mind appears behind Traveler's shoulder. Not "appears" like he teleported next to him, but more like he was invisible and now he isn't. He clicks a metallic collar around Traveler's neck. There's a POP, similar to the sound a lightbulb would make after getting hit with too much juice. Traveler collapses in a heap, a puppet with its strings cut.

Just like that. He's out. I drop the forcefield.

"Holy shit, it was that easy? Why didn't we do that right away?"

"Because," Master Mind says, "if Meredith had rebooted before I could wipe the aliens' sub-programming from her system, we never would have gotten this far. Also, I had to reboot my cloaking belt in order to get close enough to him to do it. And, quite frankly. I wasn't sure it was going to work. I was hoping you'd be able to beat him on your own. Or at least tire him out."

"Yeah, well, you see how that worked out."

"Oh, don't be so hard on yourself," he says. "I thought you did well considering the amount of power Traveler has. Your belt didn't have much of a power reserve to it, *and*, you weren't skilled in using it." He shrugs. "You did...okay."

"Gee, thanks guy who spent the last two years locked up in his own base."

There's a quick flash of something that might be anger in his eyes. It goes away as suddenly as it appeared and he gives me a lopsided grin.

"I think you and I are going to be very good friends," he says.

Raven rushes in, looking ready to throw down if she has to, but then also instantly seems relieved when she spots Traveler out cold on the floor.

"Is he dead?" she asks.

"No," Master Mind says. "Switched off. Although, how *alive* an android can be is a matter for debate. But...perhaps he can be fixed the way I fixed Meredith."

Amazonia is back on her feet with some cuts and bruises. It's a shocking sight because I don't think anyone's ever seen her bleed before. The cuts are superficial. I'm not sure how much damage her self-esteem took, though. She looks shaken.

As for Cold Snap...

Wait, who's this attractive black woman wearing Cold Snap's costume?

"Um, hi," I say. "I'm the Dark Revenger. And you are?"

"Cold Snap. Seriously?"

"Wait, you're–"

"Yes, Dark Revenger. I'm a black woman. When I use my powers, my skin turns arctic white. When I don't, it turns back to its normal color. It's why I don't have to wear a mask."

"And you don't make that "snow crunching" sound when you walk when you're not using your power, too."

"Wow," she says, with more sarcasm than I've ever heard come out of someone's mouth (including my own). "No wonder they call you 'the world's greatest detective.'"

"Hey, no, I think it's cool. I'm glad M12 has some diversity in it. High five."

I put my hand up. Instead of hitting it, she looks at it with disdain.

"Seriously?" she says again, and walks past me.

"Okay, gotcha. Not a fan of the high fives."

Where's Estella? I spot her with her back against one wall, her injured leg stretched out in front of her, mask off and looking flush from the pain. When she sees me walking toward her, she hastily wipes away a tear.

"It's okay, Red," I tell her. "I know it hurts."

"Superheroes aren't supposed to cry," she says, and laughs a little, then winces at a twinge of pain. "*Red*? What happened to Rocket Girl?"

"Yeah, well…" I kneel down beside her. "I was thinking, how about the name *Ballistic*?"

"I like it."

I put my hand on her leg. She makes a face, but I know it's more from anxiety that I might move her broken leg and cause her pain rather than any physical discomfort. I'm being really gentle, just touching gingerly where the break is.

"Your leg is swelling. We should probably get your boot off or it'll start hurting worse than it is now." I flip through a couple of pouches on my belt until I find what I'm looking for. "Here. For the pain." I hand her a small baggie of pills.

She shakes her head and tries to hand them back. "I need to keep a clear head, just in case."

"It's Motrin," I say. "Not roofies."

That gets a laugh, and another wince. She takes out two of the pills, then a third for good measure.

"You have anything to drink?" she asks. "I have trouble swallowing pills dry."

"Um… I've got some whiskey."

She holds out a gloved hand. "Let's have it, Dark Revenger. No judgments from me."

137

I take out the flask, unscrew the cap, and hand it to her. She pops the three painkillers into her mouth and takes a healthy swig of the whiskey. She stifles a cough/gag, but grits her teeth and gets the pills and alcohol down.

"Not used to drinking that straight," she says in a tight voice.

"I prefer it with a mixer," I say, "but every now and then..." I shrug and take a swig before putting the flask away.

I work the zipper down on her boot and as gently as I can, pull the boot off. She has red socks on.

"Color coordinated. I like it."

"Underwear, too," she says. "Because you just never know."

We make eye contact. Her eyes smile through the pain. I think... I think we're sharing a moment. Then Meredith suddenly appears over my left shoulder and scares the crap out of me.

"Thomas has been subdued?" she asks.

"Hell! What? Yeah," I say. "Jeez, warn a person, will you? Where'd you come from?"

"Checking the internal system," she says. "The self-destruct has been activated on the base. You all have less than eight minutes to evacuate."

"Oh, come on, really?" I say, "What kind of shit is this? We go through all of that, and now the base is going to blow up? And who the hell activated it? Not to mention, why would anyone in their right mind have a self-destruct system set up on a base anyway? Like, what the hell is the point of that?"

Master Mind clears his throat. "Actually, I installed it a long, long time ago. I don't know why Majestic 12 never took it out. Like I said earlier: laziness. Superheroes are lazy, plain and simple. They should have checked before moving in."

Estella says, "I don't think anyone on the team knew about it. It was never mentioned, anyway."

"Did you activate it?" Raven asks Master Mind. "And can you turn it off?"

"No and no," he replies. "Traveler must have done it, or set it on a timer at some point. But once it's on..." He shakes his head. "I built it as a failsafe. It's not meant to be a bluff. It can't be switched off."

"Okay," I say. "Okay, okay, okay. What do we do? We've got, what, like six minutes left."

Meredith says, "Seven. I suggest everyone proceed to the elevator and I will transport you to the top where you can access the ship."

I'm going to offer Estella assistance, but she's already up. Broken leg doesn't affect her ability to fly. Or in this case, float.

Cold Snap is all powered up again, snowy complexion and tiny slivers of ice tinkling on the edges of her hair. I doubt her powers are going to do any good against a self-destructing base, but maybe it's instinctual with her. Who knows? I'm too busy heading for the corridor.

Claustrophobia or not, I plan to be on that tiny elevator, squeezed in like a sardine and on my way to the top. Then Master Mind stops me.

"Wait. We need to bring Thomas."

"What, the super android that tried to kill us?"

He says, "I can reprogram him, just like with Meredith. It will take longer; his physiology is much more complicated. But still, for the good of the world, it's worth a try."

Yeesh. There's not enough time to argue about it, so I'll just do what M.M. wants. He hasn't steered me wrong yet.

I grab the prone, lifeless android's legs and say, "Okay. You get the head and we'll lug Tommy topside."

Master Mind is already strapping several canvas bags around his shoulders.

"Where did all that come from?" I ask.

"Sorry, Dark Revenger, but this is equipment I squirreled away and not easily replaced. It's vital I take it with me. Perhaps Raven can assist you in carrying Thomas?"

He doesn't wait for her to agree or to make sure we do as he asked. He heads out into the corridor with his bags of clanking metal pieces. I say to Raven,

"Um, so you want to grab under his arms. He's heavier than he looks."

She sighs and does it, which is a nice surprise. I fully expected an argument, or at least an eye roll.

We carry dead-weight-Tommy into the corridor and head for the elevator. Estella and Cold Snap are on and waving for us to hurry. But also Master Mind is there and there's obviously not going to be enough room for all of us. Even if he wasn't carrying several large bags of "equipment," I don't think we'd all fit.

"It's okay," he says. "Meredith will bring the elevator back for you immediately. There's enough time."

"No, wait," Estella says. "One of them can have my spot. I'll–"

The door shuts, but not before I get a glimpse of her moving (floating) towards us. A nice gesture, not that I would've allowed her to trade places with me. At least, I don't *think* I would have.

Raven's staring at Tommy.

"What?"

"He's hot," she says.

"You think so? I mean, I guess if you like the androgynous look."

"No," she says. "His body feels like it's heating up."

I feel it now, too, through my insulated gloves. He's red hot. We both drop him at the same time.

"What the hell? Does he have some sort of internal microwave? Or is spontaneous combustion one of his powers?"

Raven says, "I don't think this is natural. He's glowing now."

And he is. A fiery shade of red, with waves of heat coming off him that tell me whatever is happening to Tommy's android body, it's building up to something.

Something bad.

Catastrophic, even.

I go with my gut on this.

"Watch out!" I yell, and I'm throwing myself at Raven while also throwing the bulk of the forcefield behind me, behind us, all while Thomas Traveler explodes in a cataclysmic explosion that makes me think simultaneously the world is ending and also, how the heck is Tommy's body creating such a big explosion, like, what, did the aliens use nuclear materials when they made him...?

# CHAPTER 15
## *RAVEN'S POV*

I'm not dead. That's a plus.

It's hard to breathe, both from the smoke in the air and the weight on top of me. Hard to see, but I catch glimpses of flashing lights. The weight on me moves. It also smells like whiskey and aftershave.

Why does he keep ending up on top of me?

"Off." I groan and shove him aside at the same time.

"Man, that was loud," he says. "Are your ears ringing? Mine are ringing."

We get to our feet and survey the situation. It's bad. The corridor is unrecognizable. Lights flashing, flickering… Somewhere, a siren is blaring. Everything is comprised of metal, so nothing is burning. But smoke and heat from the blast still cling to the air, which both impedes my visibility and my ability to take in a good lungful of oxygen.

I take off my mask. No point in a secret identity anymore. I'm just trying to stay alive.

"Okay, what's the plan?" he asks.

Seriously?

I head back down the corridor to where we started, by the elevator. I don't see a door leading to an elevator or an elevator shaft. All I see is wreckage and twisted metal. Damn.

"There has to be another way out. It can't just be one elevator," I say. "There has to be stairs or possibly a second elevator."

I'm not sure if I'm talking to myself or to him. Maybe a little of both.

He says, "I would think so. Then again, it's not like Master Mind had the fire marshals out here when he was building this place, making sure everything is up to code."

Don't panic. How many minutes left? Have to find a way out. Get up top. Did they leave without us? I don't trust Master Mind (a little convenient that he left us behind with an exploding android). But Amazonia and Cold Snap wouldn't abandon us.

Think, dammit…

Meredith materializes, her form not as solid as usual. She flickers; her voice crackles and echoes.

"What has happened? I am unable to send the elevator down and it is difficult to transmit to this area."

Dark Revenger says, "Tommy blew up. Big time."

"Meredith, is there another elevator? Another way out?"

She points.

"Follow the corridor to the end. If you are able to pry back the plating on the wall, there is an exhaust tunnel that runs bottom to top of the base. I can alert the others you will be coming that way and they may be able to assist you from the top. However, you must move quickly."

I'm already running. And Dark Revenger is right behind me.

The section of wall Meredith directed us to is as nondescript as the other walls, but there's a sliver of a gap around the edges, a panel of sorts, much like the one Master Mind had removed to get to his hidden lab/hiding spot. I dig the point of a dagger into the small gap and twist and pry at the same time. It bends, though not enough to do any good.

"Here. Stand back, hottie."

Dark Revenger places the oversized gloves he's wearing next to the hole I made and furrows his brows. He glows red for a second, then the red energy moves to his gloves and outward in a burst that knocks the metal plate the rest of the way off the wall.

He says, "Pretty cool, right?"

"Don't call me 'hottie,'" I say.

He opens his mouth to respond and the whole world ROARS and shakes. I think for a moment the walls and the floor are coming apart. The lights flicker like synthetic lightning and momentarily I believe we're experiencing a major earthquake. Except the rational part of my brain reminds me we're on an island base in the middle of the ocean, and the self-destruct sequence has probably started.

Damn. So close. I guess this is how it ends.

The severe shaking ends and we're both on the floor again, although luckily he's not on top of me this time. I don't think I could take a third time of that.

"We're still alive," he says, although I'm not sure if it's a question or a statement. "Maybe the self-destruct thing was more of an existential crisis. You know what I mean?"

"What the hell are you talking about?" I'm not trying to keep the disgust out of my voice anymore.

He shrugs. "I don't even know half the time."

Then the floor tilts, but it's not just the floor, it's the entire complex. It shifts and GROANS and makes grinding noises that sound as if they emanate from the bowels of Hell. The lights flicker more and some stay off. I'm able to see enough of my surroundings to know that whatever the base is attached to is quickly detaching itself, if not all at once, than piecemeal. I grab the edge to the hole in the wall, the one we barely had time to remove. I can pull myself inside, but there's no telling what's in there or if it really is a way out.

I'm about to pull myself into...whatever it is...an oversized airshaft or an undersized elevator shaft, hard to tell, but I don't have much choice at the moment, and Meredith appears again. Her feet are planted firmly on the slanted floor. It's an odd sight. My brain reminds me she's a being constructed of light and gravity doesn't apply to her.

Her form crackles more than before and is even less solid.

"Self-destruct has initiated," she says.

Dark Revenger responds, "Hey, no kidding?"

If she intends to say more, we'll never know. Her form crackles again and she blinks out.

I pull myself into the shaft. Much like the hidden passageway Master Mind utilized to set up a hidden lab, there's a ladder bolted to one wall. I look up and I think there's a dim light coming from the end – the top of the shaft. Look down and all I see is pitch black. The shaft could go on for miles for all I know.

It doesn't matter. I intend to climb up as fast as possible.

"Hey, wait for me," Dark Revenger says.

And again I think, *Seriously?*

I'm on the ladder, looking at him through the square opening. He tosses down his oversized gloves, the ones Master Mind gave him, and unhooks his cape and hood. He jumps to the lip of the opening and pulls himself through with a fluid ease that matches my own acrobatic prowess.

Physical ability like that and he chose to be a supervillain. Worse, now a supervillain pretending to be a superhero.

I'm moving up the ladder and he's a few rungs below me.

"You weren't planning on leaving me behind, were you?" he asks.

I climb faster. An image flits through my mind, a two second video clip I received from an anonymous source. I should be concentrating on keeping a tight handhold and that my boots are firmly on the rungs as I climb upward, but I can't help it: I see the image over and over again.

The Puzzler pointing a staff at the Dark Revenger and firing a burst of energy that cuts through him. It runs over and over again in my head, much like the way I replayed it in real life.

I didn't think it was real. Two people dressed up in costumes. Special effects. I tried to trace the origin of the clip, but hit dead ends. I convinced myself it was fake. Until the Dark Revenger didn't show up for our appointed meeting.

I had sought out his help on several occasions. I admired him. Maybe even hero worshipped him. He took a liking to me.

No, not like that. Not in a sordid way. It was completely a "teacher/apprentice" type of relationship. I sought his advice and he offered his expertise. He even worked with me on several cases, a "team-up" of sorts. I'd be lying if I said I didn't entertain thoughts of a permanent crime-fighting partnership, and if the Dark Revenger ever decided to retire, I would take on the mantle.

We met regularly, and when he didn't show at the appointed time, nor show again at the next, I suspected the video was real. Then completely by chance, I followed a team of professional thieves into an office building and ran into *him*.

So many questions:

Why was the Puzzler pretending to be the Dark Revenger? What was his ultimate goal? Why continue the charade even after the Majestic 12 showed up? Why pretend to be …heroic?

We climb. The light at the top grows closer, although not significantly so. Then, below me, he mutters, "Ah, shit."

I can't help myself. I stop climbing and look down at him. "What?"

He says. "The battery you gave me from Master Mind for the forcefield belt. It seems to have, um, dropped off somewhere."

There's a BOOM from below and again, the base shifts several more degrees to the side. The ladder creaks and for a second I think it might break free from the wall. But it holds, and we climb faster.

Metal screams from below, followed by what sounds like an out of control locomotive bearing down on us. It's not a train; it's seawater filling up the bottom levels as parts of the building detach. I see now the genius behind the man who designed this base:

If Master Mind had wired the complex with enough explosives to destroy it outright, the Majestic 12 would have discovered it and deactivated his "self-destruct" failsafe. So he wired it to break apart and flood, which would give him enough time to get away if he was unfortunate enough to be inside when he had to utilize it.

Except Traveler knew about the self-destruct sequence. Or discovered it and kept it to himself. None of which adds up in my mind. It doesn't matter, though, because we only have moments before the water catches up to us.

We climb faster. The circle of light at the top grows closer, although not quickly enough for my liking. A shadow crosses over the light at the top; too quick and too far away to judge what it was. Or who.

I want to yell out, call for help. The adrenaline won't let me. Neither will my pride.

Then it happens. A misjudged step. I lose my footing.

My hands keep me from falling completely. I struggle to get my feet back where they should be. A moment of panic; my feet flail.

He's up next to me and bracing me against the ladder.

"Whoa, easy," Dark Revenger says. "Take a breath."

"Oh, you've got to be–"

Below us, water bursts through several spots at once in an explosive roar.

"Okay," he says. "New plan."

He looks up and I swear he's mentally calculating... I can't help myself.

"What?" I nearly shout.

He reaches behind his back and removes the grappling gun sleeve I've witnessed the real Dark Revenger use on more than one occasion. He flicks it open and fires it upward. The metal cable unrolls with a whirl. Just as I think there can't possibly be any more cable and it's going to hit the end, it stops. He pulls back and nods once, satisfied that it's secure.

"Think it just made it. Unfortunately, this won't hold both of us, so…"

"Wait," I say. "What are you planning to do?"

He clamps it on my arm and says, "Just hold tight and let it pull you up. It moves pretty fast."

"Wait. No."

"It's okay, hottie. Go warm up the spaceship. I'll be right behind you."

"No! Goddammit, I'm not going to be saved by the Puzzler!"

I catch his eyes just as the metal piece secures to my arm and yanks me up. Shock and acknowledgement. Maybe resignation, as well.

"Wait!" I yell again, but as he said, the grappling gun pulls me up fast. I do catch one more glimpse of him on the ladder just as water bursts through over his head and knocks him loose. Water fills the shaft from below and he's lost between the two cascading waves that rush to meet each other.

Something flies by me. A glimpse of red is all I get, and what looks like another cable heading downward into the depths. Then I'm brought up into the light.

# CHAPTER 16
## *This is how it happened.*

Court Jester is a cackling psychotic loon.

"Shh," I tell him for what feels like the hundredth time.

I mean, I get that if we were really trying to be sneaky, we'd all be dressed in black and wearing rubber-soled shoes with black greasepaint on our faces. But part of being a supervillain is the idea that the superheroes and law enforcement know it's us. So we're wearing our costumes (except for Blue Howler, who doesn't need one) and not exactly trying to be discreet. We're breaking the law, sure, but there's a certain amount of showmanship to it, as well.

Okay, so Howler isn't keen on everyone knowing he's involved. He really wants to take his share and retire from the supervillain life. I get it. I do, too. Retire, I mean. I'm not keeping my share of the money. I'll get to that in a second.

Here's what we did:

Court Jester approached Howler with a hot tip about where the mob keeps their surplus of cash. All the ill-gotten gains from the drugs, the clubs, the sex workers, and the casinos. Guarded, sure, but a sonic blast from Howler's superpowered throat and a couple of stun blasts from Court Jester's staff – a five foot long brass stick that shoots energy bursts that he laughingly refers to as his *giggle stick*.

Giggle stick. I shit you not.

Speaking of "laughingly," he's always laughing. Or giggling. It's annoying as hell. And the bells… He's got bells on his curled up shoes, on his pointy hat, and on his stun stick (I refuse to call it a giggle stick). I keep asking him to be quiet, but just the noise he makes when he walks sounds like Santa's sleigh is landing nearby.

Oh, and I helped with the heist, too. Once, I provided distraction by luring some guards down a corridor so Howler could knock them out. Another time, I tossed a stun grenade disguised as a Rubik's Cube (thank Howler for that idea) into a room full of mob security. Savant's design: The cube turns and solves itself, then explodes. Nothing fatal, just a loud BANG that leaves the guys with their ears ringing and groggy enough for Howler or Court Jester to knock them the rest of the way into unconsciousness.

Howler rolled his eyes when he saw the Rubik's Cube doing its thing before it exploded. I know, I know… Maybe it's corny and a waste of time, but sometimes it's more about style and flair.

Anyway, we got the money, loaded it up into big canvas bags (large denominations, luckily), and made our way through the tunnels under the city that we supervillains like to utilize. I'm sure someone out there has written a thesis on how superheroes tend to fly and travel around above ground, while supervillains use the abandoned tunnels under the streets and buildings for our secret lairs, exclusive nightclubs, and getaways. The truth is, while I'm sure there's some psychological basis for why we like the tunnels (images of rats scurrying underground), the real reason is it just makes more logical sense.

Look, the Dark Revenger can drive through the city streets in his Ferrari-had-sex-with-a-tank-and-gave-birth-to-this, a.k.a. the Dark Revenger Mobile, but if I was to paint my Toyota Camry purple and put "PUZZLER" in crossword-style blocks on the side, I'd get arrested in no time.

So this is how we get around. Unless you have superpowers.

Besides, the tunnels are great. You have to have a working knowledge of the layout or else you could get lost, or wander down what you think is a defunct subway tunnel and find out it's still running trains. But if you have a working knowledge, the tunnels are a great way to sneak up on a place, commit a crime, and get away unscathed. Many of them, the non-subway ones, were built well over a century ago and are surprisingly spacious and airy. Sure, there's supernatural folklore that goes with them, but I'm more afraid of getting my teeth knocked out by Amazonia than I am by a ghost.

Court Jester's incessant laughing echoes off the stone walls.

"C'mon, dude," I say. "Can you just stifle that for a few minutes?"

"What's wrong, Puzzler?" he asks. His voice goes up and down in a sing-song way that's creepier than it sounds.

His costume is equal parts red and checkerboard with the aforementioned stupid hat, ridiculous shoes, and way too many bells. He has a mask attached to the hat, two round red circles that hang down like a sun visor, with his two beady eyes peering through. The most formidable thing about him… Okay, the *only* formidable thing about him is the brass staff he carries that can stun a person, or kill them. And the fact he's completely nuts and you don't know what he's going to do at any given moment adds to the formidability, but right now, he's on my nerves.

He says, "You don't like my little jokes."

"What jokes? You haven't said anything funny."

He laughs, this time louder than usual. "Those are the best jokes. The ones only I know that I don't say out loud."

"Yeah. Okay." I catch Howler's eye.

Howler says, "We're almost there. Can you two just get along for thirty more seconds?"

We're carrying the money, already split up between the three of us. No, we didn't sit there and count it out. Not even sure it was thirty million. It was a lot, though.

We split it by sight and by judging the weight of our bags. Maybe someone got a little extra over someone else. Doesn't matter. Too much money to quibble over a few hundred grand.

And we stole it from the mob, which is even better because it makes us like Robin Hood. Instead of giving it to the poor, however, we're just going to keep it. Except…

I'm not. Once we're up top and we go our separate ways, I'm going to get caught.

Already planned it. I sent a message to the Dark Revenger through a secure email link (there's ways to do this; just trust me). Gave him a tip from an unnamed informant that the Puzzler will be at such and such street at approximately such and such time with a big bag of ill-gotten gains.

I'll give myself up voluntarily and without a struggle. Won't name names, of course. I'm not a snitch. I'll say it was all me. Already have a deposit down on the best criminal lawyer in Azure City. The whole thing should go off like clockwork. Next year at this time, maybe eighteen months from now at the most, I should be getting ready for parole and have a publisher begging to sign me.

Finally make it to the stairs that lead up to the basement of an abandoned building. I take the lead and Howler brings up the rear. We've been trying to keep Court Jester between us just in case he tries a double-cross, and Howler is the muscle of the group, so it makes sense he guards the rear.

We head up the stairs and through the building, out to the street. It's that part of town where most people don't go, unless you're a drug addict looking for a quiet place to shoot dope, or a homeless person looking for an abandoned building to squat in. We round the corner of the street where we previously agreed to say our farewells and there, parked right in front of us, is the Dark Revenger Mobile.

If this was a movie, I swear the ominous background music would've just increased to an eardrum blistering volume and made everyone in the audience jump. Howler and I actually do a double take.

"What the hell?" he says.

I wait to hear that gravelly whisper voice of his. Or the roaring engine of the car powering up. Or an alarm. Something. As quiet and still as the car is, it may as well be a monolith on the surface of the moon.

"He's friggin' here, isn't he?" I ask.

Shit. This isn't where I tipped him off I'd be. I don't want Howler caught, too. How did he locate us? Did I accidentally give away too much in my tip to him?

Howler says, "Watch out."

He makes sure Court Jester and I are behind him when he lets loose with his sonic yell. If you're behind him, it just sounds like a guy yelling "AAAHHH!" Stand in front of him, however, and the yell hits you like a professional linebacker. It'll knock the wind out of you and throw you back a good ten feet.

Howler yells down the street one way, then faces the other. He lets loose down a couple of dark alleyways for good measure. Broken glass and bits of lumber in the alleyways go flying, but no sign of Dark Revenger. We even look up, thinking maybe he's swinging in for a surprise kick to our heads. But nope.

"I don't get it," Howler says.

"Maybe he broke down?"

We step tentatively towards the car. We should be running, but I don't think either of us have been this close to the Dark Revenger Mobile before. Then a disturbing thought flits through my brain.

"Hey," I say. "You hear that?"

"No," Howler says. "I don't hear anything."

"That's what I mean. How come Chuckles McGee suddenly stopped laughing."

We turn in tandem and face Court Jester. He's standing up straighter than I've ever seen him, his jaw clenched tight, and gives us a cold stare. When he talks, it's the Dark Revenger's voice that comes out of his mouth.

"Criminal scum."

The last thing I see is the burst of energy shooting out of his goddamn giggle stick.

***

You ever wake up with twenty shiny brand new pennies in your mouth? I don't have pennies in my mouth, but it sure tastes like it. What the hell happened?

I'm sitting up on a cement floor, my hands bound behind me with what feels like standard handcuffs. My hat is gone. Still have my mask on, although it's a bit askew.

Crap. I regret it. I wish I could go back to sleep.

From the looks of it, I'm in the Dark Revenger's lair. Or base. Whatever you want to call it. It's evident by the fact that the Dark Revenger Mobile is parked in the middle of the floor surrounded by a dozen computer monitors, what looks like a big crafting table and a huge workbench off to one side, a rack of Dark Revenger costumes, and a peg wall holding various weapons and gadgets.

Oh, and another reason I know it's Dark Revenger's base is because the Dark Revenger is walking around and talking to himself.

151

It's him, all right. I've had enough close calls and seen enough security cam footage to know the real deal. What's weird is, he's not only talking to himself, he's also answering himself, switching back and forth from the Dark Revenger sandpapery whisper voice to the Court Jester's sing-song tone.

So...

So the Dark Revenger and Court Jester are the same person? That can't possibly be right. Can it? Let me think.

When did the current Dark Revenger appear on the scene? Seven or eight years ago, right? Court Jester was, what, five years ago? Little less? It was way before I became the Puzzler. Lots of videos of him taunting the Dark Revenger. Becoming a big name. Lots of showy kind of crimes. Anarchy, chaos, and mayhem. Rumors would fly the two had fought, but Court Jester would manage to get away at the last minute.

Except...

Except there was never any video footage of the two of them together. Court Jester would release videos to the press and the cops. He'd reference their battles and swear revenge on the Dark Revenger for foiling whatever scheme he had been in the process of cooking up. But no one actually ever saw them fight. Or even be in the same room together.

Oh, shit. The Dark Revenger is a psychotic loon with a split personality. And neither personality is the "good" one.

I gotta get out of here.

D.R. is pacing around and holding a conversation with his other self. From the sound of it, the Court Jester persona is taunting the Dark Revenger persona about not being able to catch him. Meanwhile, D.R. is saying he's going to interrogate Court Jester's friends.

Wait, what friends?

Oh. He means us.

Speaking of which, where's Howler? He's strong enough to break a pair of handcuffs and his sonic yell could send D.R. head over heels into one of these concrete walls.

Dark Revenger pushes some buttons on one of the consoles and lights come on in the back corner. I see Howler now, lit up by the lights. He's chained up, literally. Like, with real heavy duty chains. The kind you would tow a car with. He's strong, but not strong to break chains like that.

His chained arms are stretched above his head and hooked to a thick cable that's holding him five feet off the ground. Chains around his legs, too. He's awake, but any hope I had about him blasting Dark Revenger into a wall fades instantly:

There's a steel muzzle on the bottom part of his face. His jaw is clamped shut.

Dark Revenger walks towards me, suddenly all one person. The Court Jester part of him seems to be on hiatus. He grabs me by my arm and drags me up to my feet. Now I'm standing, but still attached to the metal pole.

"You see your friend, yes?" Dark Revenger asks.

"Yeah."

"How does he look?"

Truthfully, he looks a little scared. But I'm not going to say that.

"He looks good," I say. "I'm not digging the chains on him. But, you know, he looks alright."

"I have to do it this way," Dark Revenger says. "I can't ask him questions because of his superpower. So it's going to be up to you. His life is in your hands."

Well, no, his life is really in a nutcase's hands. But what am I going to do? Argue with a guy who has a split personality?

D.R. heads back over to a row of buttons on the console, the same one he used to turn on the lights. He pushes a button and a steel panel on the floor underneath Howler slides back. I can't see what it is, but the way Howler's red eyes are bugging out of his skull, I'm going to guess there's something really, really bad underneath him.

"From your vantage point," Dark Revenger says, "you're unable to see that there's a tank of acid underneath your friend."

I wondered what the chemical smell was. Yeesh. This is bad.

"I'm going to ask you one question and one question only. Every time you refuse to answer, or give me a false answer, I'm going to lower your friend into the acid a quarter inch at a time. Then I'll raise him out and ask you again. Refuse or lie, and back down he goes. Another quarter inch. Eventually, enough of him will be burned away or he'll go into shock and die."

"And then?"

"And then it will be your turn," he says.

I say, "Look, you seem like a reasonable fellow. So am I. Ask me whatever you want. I'll be straight with you. I don't want you to hurt Blue Howler. I definitely don't want you to hurt me. Okay? Cool?"

"Just one question," he says. "Where is Court Jester?"

Let's pause here for a second. I mean…what? He's asking where his alternate personality is? Is this a trick question? What should I say here? Should I suggest he look in a mirror?

No. I have a feeling that would be bad. He doesn't want to hear that he and Court Jester are the same person.

I say, "Okay, okay, okay, listen…" Better make this good. "What if I told you that Court Jester isn't really anywhere. He's like a state of mind. Get what I'm saying?"

"No." His hand moves to the row of buttons.

"Wait! Hold on! Let me finish."

Dark Revenger stops and looks back at me. His gloved hand hovers over what I guess is the control button that's going to lower my buddy into an acid dip.

"You want an address of where Court Jester is. Not a philosophical statement. I get it."

He says, "You're trying my patience. Give me an answer."

What should I tell him? Make up an address? 1313 Mockingbird Lane? No. Sounds fake.

"742 Evergreen Terrace. You, uh, want to write that down?" I ask.

"No."

He moves away from the row of buttons and types something into one of his many computers. Seriously, why so many monitors? Some of them are obviously for security cams, but the others…? Seems like overkill.

Crap, he's typing the address in. Wants to see if I'm lying. Which, *I am.*

"A residential address," he says.

"Yep. That's where Court Jester lives. You can probably catch him sleeping if you leave right now."

Dark Revenger stares at me for what feels like a very long time. I put on my best earnest expression.

"Very well," he says. "If this is a trick, when I come back, I'm going to lower your friend into the acid up to his knees."

Yikes.

"Nope. No trick, Dark Revenger. Court Jester is home and probably sound asleep. He'll be very surprised to wake up and see you standing over him. Heh."

Did I overdo it? Feels like I overdid it.

He gets into the Dark Revenger Mobile and heads up the ramp that I guess leads to the outside. Maybe a country road. Maybe an abandoned rodeo. I really have no idea where we are. All I know is, I'm handcuffed with my arms behind me to a steel pole, and Howler grunts what I'm sure is a list of profanities at me as he hangs over top of the acid.

First thing's first: Got to get out of these handcuffs.

Okay, before you scream "deus ex machina," let me explain something:

I always knew there was a chance of being caught. But if I was going to be captured by the Dark Revenger or the police, I wanted it to be on my terms. So I tried to plan ahead in the eventuality I might slip up and get caught when I wasn't ready to be caught. Make sense?

So when I say that behind my back in the waistband of my pants, I have a small Velcro-lined pouch sewn in that holds a teeny tiny knife blade (for cutting through a zip tie) and a handcuff key, don't yell out, "Aw, man, that's bullshit!" I've spent my life trying to stay two steps ahead of everyone: my parents; my teachers; jealous boyfriends; and now psychotic superheroes.

And man, I had no idea he was *that* psychotic. I should've picked Lady Justice as my archnemesis.

I slip off my gloves, no easy feat with the handcuffs on, but at least now they're a tiny bit looser. I get my fingers into my pants (that's what she said) and manage to get the handcuff key out while only poking my fingers with the tiny blade twice. I get the cuffs off in a record time that would've made Houdini proud.

Now which button was it that closes the floor panel? I push what I think is the button and Howler starts to lower down. He yells. I quickly hit the button again and the lowering stops. He shakes his head and groans.

"I gotcha, buddy," I say. "Don't worry. Um...I think it was...*this* one." I push the right button this time and the floor panel slides shut.

Howler grunt/yells something. Two words that I'm pretty sure is "Thank you!"

"Hey, you're welcome, Blue," I say. "I know you'd do the same for me."

He grunt/yells it again.

"You're welcome!" Jeez, I've never seen him so grateful.

He does it again. Then I catch that he's not looking at me. He's not saying, "Thank you." He's yelling, "Behind you!"

I whirl around and Dark Revenger grabs me by the throat. "Do you think I'm a fool?"

I can't answer because the lunatic is squeezing my throat like he's trying to wring water out of a sponge. Best I can do is halfheartedly shrug.

He pretended to leave. Drove his car out, then came back in through another entrance. Clever.

He's strong, but not superpowered strong. And I've spent a good number of years watching fight videos and martial arts demonstration, not to mention every news clip and uploaded cellphone recordings of the Dark Revenger in fighting action. I can do the moves.

I break his hold with a forearm strike and follow up with a kidney punch. He's thrown back more by surprise than actual pain. His costume – it's not armor, but it's definitely got something to it more than plain cloth. Kevlar weave, maybe?

Problem is, my suit is just a purple suit. Italian silk and expertly tailored, but still just a suit. So when he throws a punch that I catch on my shoulder and follows up with a roundhouse kick that doubles me over and sends me careening into his workbench…
Folks, I feel it.

I can't stop and I can't lose this. He's going to kill both of us, me and Howler. I never thought I'd be fighting for my life. Not against him. I thought he was all about justice. When did he become a crazy killer?

Somehow, I'm on my feet and we square off. I can block his moves because I know them. Many of them. Not all. So a few get through. And boy, when they hit, it's like fireworks of pain going off in my body. I connect with some of mine, but he's not feeling it. Like hitting a bag of sand. That suit of his.

I'm about to lose. If he connects once or twice more, I think that's going to be it. Then he's down low and sweeping my legs out from under me, and I'm on the floor. Shit.

It's dumb luck, but I spot the familiar costume tucked away on a bottom shelf of the work bench. The bells on it jingle as I pull it out. Just in time, too, because he was halfway to doing a pile driving kick down on my stomach. When I hold the red costume up, the bells all jingling, Dark Revenger freezes.

"He's here," I say. "Court Jester is here."

"Where?" He turns around. "Where is he? Show yourself, you fiend!"

I yank the brass staff out from its hiding spot and point it at Dark Revenger. Not sure how to work it. There are two buttons: one black and one red. Black must be the stun blast. I hold my finger over it. Don't want to mess this up. Figure I've only got one shot.

Dark Revenger giggles. But it's not him anymore. It's the other one. He turns slowly to face me.

"Hello again, Puzzler," he says, back in the creepy sing-song voice again. "I see you have my giggle stick."

"Ugh," I say. "Could you please stop calling it that?"

"What are you going to do with it?"

"Oh, I thought I'd–" I press the black button.

The stick shoots out a tremendous burst of energy that cuts him in half. Literally cuts him in half. Legs go one way, and torso and head go another.

"What the hell?!" I drop the stick like it's on fire. Like it's just gotten me sentenced to life in prison. Which it has.

I get Howler down and get his chains and muzzle off. He stares at the two halves of Dark Revenger.

"Oh, man, Puzzler," he says.

"Oh, man, what?"

"Oh, man, you really fucked us. Why? Why did you kill him?"

I say, "I pushed the black button. I thought it was the stun setting. I thought the red button was kill."

"No. Black is always kill."

"Always?"

"Yeah."

"Shit." I ask, "So what are we going to do now?"

I'm fully expecting him to say "What do you mean *we*?" Instead, he says:

"We split the money and get the hell out of the country. First, though, we better get rid of…" He motions to the body with his chin. "That."

We both stare at the two ends of the Dark Revenger and try to determine if this is all a bad dream. Unfortunately, it isn't. Then we turn our heads in the direction of the panel on the floor.

"The acid?"

Howler says with a sigh, "The acid."

# CHAPTER 17

I'm on my side, vomiting up what feels like a gallon of saltwater. My eyes burn, my lungs feel like they're on fire, and I'm soaked to the bone. My mask is gone, too, which I know is a weird thing to think about, but...

Not having it on my face makes me feel naked.

Yeah, I know. I said it was weird, didn't I?

I'm on the floor of the Majestic 12 ship. Or is "deck" the correct term for the floor of a spaceship? Anyway, the gold metal is oddly warm. Comforting, in a way.

The water disappears into the metal with a soft HISS as quickly as I purge it from my body. I find it hypnotic.

When I'm done, finally, I get a look at the others circled around me. Amazonia, Cold Snap, and Meredith stand on one side, close, but not so close that you'd think they were overly concerned. Still concerned, nonetheless.

Raven stands, too, although not looking nearly as concerned as the others. Her arms are crossed and her gaze is off to the side. She looks... I don't know.

I want to say disappointed, but I'm not sure in who. Me for surviving, or herself for being rescued by *the Puzzler*.

Even with the saltwater clogging my ears, I can still hear the disgust in her voice. I'm waiting for her to say something now. Make the big announcement. *He's the Puzzler! He killed the real Dark Revenger! He clubs baby seals for fun!*

She doesn't. Just keeps looking off to the side. Won't even make eye contact.

Estella sits next to me, soaked, her hair dripping water from little ringlets that frame her face in a heart. Her eyes shine. Maybe that's saltwater irritating them to make them look extra wet. Or maybe she's on the verge of tears because I'm not dead. I'd like to think it's the latter.

Gosh, she's beautiful.

I take note of the clear boot over her broken leg. Like her foot and ankle were dipped in Lucite. Next to her is a big towing hook and what looks like a mile of steel cable.

"You fished me out?" I ask. "With a broken leg?"

159

"Flew down and hooked the cable to your belts," she said. "The ship did the rest."

"And gave me mouth to mouth?"

She says, "Well, actually…"

"Actually what?"

"Actually," Master Mind says, "*I* gave you mouth to mouth."

He comes into focus now, off to the side, crouched down. He has a way of fading into the background, I notice. Or maybe I was too focused on Estella.

He says, "I hope that's okay. I assure you, I took no pleasure in it." He tilts his head slightly. "Well, that's not a hundred percent true. I may have taken a teensy bit of pleasure in it."

"I can't complain, M.M.," I say. "You saved my life. Looks like I owe you one."

A smirk before he lets me have it:

"That's what *he* said."

# PART TWO

# CHAPTER 18
## *Six Months Later*

Boy, that went by quick, didn't it? Feels like we were just talking about my near-death experience, and now here it is six months later.

Things have drastically changed. Let me give you the rundown:

The world was shocked (*shocked*, I tell you) by the deaths of the Majestic 12. They were even more shocked by the emergence of a new team, built from the ashes of the old — me, Master Mind, Raven (who took her dad's name *Stealthshadow* and added a hood to her costume), Estella (now going by *Ballistic*, and she ditched the short cape), Amazonia, Cold Snap, and Meredith as our advisor and surrogate den mother. She's wired into the new HQ, so that makes her our security system and all-purpose trouble alarm because she doesn't need to sleep and can monitor pretty much every news channel and world broadcast frequency at once.

Handy gal, that Meredith. I like her a lot better now that she's not trying to kill us, and Master Mind has assured me there are safeguards to prevent her programming from being corrupted again.

We added three more members: Lady Justice (yep, the one who also dresses up as Bondage Queen and picks up guys. I haven't let on that I know), Armorgeddon (Russian scientist who invented an armored suit), and Refraction, a fairly new superhero. He uses crystals built into his colorful costume to fire bursts of energy that vary in intensity and duration depending on which crystal he uses and in what combination with the others. He's very bright, and when I say that, I mean in the literal sense, because intellectually, he's a bit of a dullard. Still, he puts on a good light show during a fight.

You might think by the name that Lady Justice wears a white toga and blindfold and carries a set of scales, but she actually dresses like a member of a militia: lots of camo and guns, and a bandana she wears around her nose and mouth like a train robber back in the 1800's. A condition of joining M12 was she had to switch to rubber bullets, bean bag bursts, and tear gas canisters rather than the lethal rounds she used to carry. She's a great shot and can be pretty ferocious in a fight, but the team wants to get away from the grim/gritty days. We're trying to start a new Golden Age of superheroes.

As for Armorgeddon, he should be the big gun of our group, but he keeps tripping over his own feet. No, not literally. Well, yeah, sometimes literally. I've seen him trip over his own feet before.

What I mean is, he tends to get taken out early in a fight and usually with one lucky shot. The first two times, I thought it was bad luck. Now I'm starting to think the guy has a curse on him or something. He's like the member of a sports team you expect to be the MVP, but then he keeps catching injuries or trips coming out of the locker room.

That brings us up to ten members. The plan is to bring in two more and actually have twelve members in the group, the first time, I think, since Majestic 12 was strictly a superhero team. Once that happens, hopefully the press (and fans) will stop asking why there aren't twelve members of Majestic 12.

Oh, almost forgot to tell you about the new HQ. It's located in downtown Azure City, a converted fifteen story office building donated to us by the mayor as a "thank you" for setting up shop in his city.

Nice guy, that mayor. I've even got him considering a Dark Revenger Day and possibly naming a street after me. Why not? Azure City has always been the Dark Revenger's home.

The mayor thinks having the world's greatest super-team based out of Azure City will keep it relatively crime-free, which means that A) he's never read a comic book in his life; B) he overestimates the intelligence of the average criminal; and C) he underestimates the ego of the average supervillain.

Whatever. It got us a free building. That's all that counts.

Master Mind got the building converted pretty quickly. The guy is a whiz at hiring contractors and construction teams that can outfit a building in super-science tech (e.g. retracting roof and landing bay for a spaceship) like they're remodeling a bathroom in an overpriced condo. And they worked weekends!

We were all given living quarters and monthly stipends. And when I say *living quarters*, I'm not talking the boring, Spartan-esque rooms the previous team had on the old island base. No, Master Mind decided to go with more flair this time. He gave us some luxury digs. Lots of warm colors, plush furniture, large screen TVs, state-of-the-art sound systems…even espresso makers and Jacuzzi tubs in everybody's room.

I guess I should also tell you Master Mind became our unofficial leader. The world took his conversion to the hero side pretty well. It helped that he was never the type of supervillain to go on television and make lots of threats or demands. The world also mourned Traveler.

Master Mind said, and we all agreed, that we should tell everyone Traveler fell in battle defending the world against the imminent alien invasion. The world wouldn't want to think he turned against humanity, rather, it would be better for morale if they thought he died heroically. Tell the truth and we risked lots of negative blowback, especially from Traveler's religious followers.

Just imagine what would happen if someone tried to assert Jesus had nefarious motives. Yeah, like that.

So the world believes Traveler died saving them, or at least gave them a temporary reprieve, because as Master Mind says, the invasion is still scheduled. We're just not sure when. Could be tomorrow. Next week. Next decade. Who knows?

"You have to understand, Eddie," Master Mind told me when I kept questioning him about how long do we have before the superior alien race comes to stomp on us, "we're talking about interdimensional travel and a race of beings that don't necessarily experience time the same way we do. Their timetable might be centuries long. Or it could all happen in the next five minutes. But rest assured, I'm working on it. It's my number one priority."

Okay, so M.M. is our unofficial leader. I've appointed myself our unofficial PR person and spokesman. Why, you ask? Isn't it obvious? The fame and attention! It's what I always wanted.

165

I stride into the break room, grab a clean cup from the cabinet, and pour myself some coffee. Looks like the kitchen staff has broken down the breakfast bar already. Lucky for me, our in-house sushi chef is set up against one wall, making a long plate of what looks like salmon rolls.

"Hey, Chuck, my man," I say and walk over to his station. I pop one in my mouth.

Yep, salmon rolls. Delicious ones, too, I might add. Charlie knows his stuff.

"How are you today, Dark?" he asks.

"Can't complain. Just got up and haven't had breakfast. So if you wouldn't mind...?"

"Not at all, sir." He slides a plate out from under his counter and uses his cutting knife to deftly slide a half dozen rolls onto it. He hands it to me. "Enjoy," he says.

"Thanks, Chuck. You're the best."

"No, sir. You, and the rest of Majestic 12, are the best."

He's a good, young Japanese-American guy who could command a hefty salary by working at some trendy restaurant. He decided to work for us after M.M. put out a call for a sushi chef because, as M.M. said, "What's the point of saving the world if we can't eat good food during our downtime?"

Charlie answered the ad and practically demanded we hire him. The old Majestic 12 saved his family from...something. Honestly, I wasn't really paying attention during his interview. Needless to say, it was his dream to work for Majestic 12. And it was our dream to have an in-house sushi chef. Win-win, right?

Charlie Yamaguchi. Or Yamaha. Ya-something. I know his last name starts with a "Y." Good guy. I should probably tip him. But I don't have any cash on me at the moment. I'll make it up to him next time, I tell myself for probably the thousandth time.

Hey look, he gets paid pretty well as it is. Okay?

I grab a table and pop another salmon roll in my mouth. I savor it while I stand next to the table. I don't sit because I'm in costume. I don't know if you've ever tried to sit down while wearing a cape, but it's not the most comfortable or graceful of things. You can push the cape to the side, or hitch it up so there's slack, but most times, I find it easier to just stand.

My costume is different now. I should probably tell you about that.

Master Mind made the forcefield into a permanent addition to my costume. He incorporated the electronics into my bandolier belt and worked it into my gloves and boots. He also gave me a self-charging battery, so no worries about running out of juice anymore, which is nice. I use the forcefield and still fire bursts through my gloves and boots (for high jumps), and through practice, I've learned to localize the field into my gloves so I can punch with much greater force. My fists look like they're wearing large, boxing gloves made out of crackling red energy when I punch. Pretty nice.

I changed the look of the costume a little bit. The body part is still the black costume the real Dark Revenger wore, but the cape and hood are now a light silver. I guess I'm the Dark Revenger 2.0 now. Or maybe I'm just trying to make the identity my own.

Honestly, I'm starting to border on being a gadgeteer rather than a street level crime fighter, but hey, I'm hanging with the world's most popular superhero team, and I might have to battle some aliens in the not too distant future. I had to step up my game, you know?

I take a sip of coffee and grimace.

"Problem?" Estella asks, entering the room. She's wearing jeans, a white blouse, and strappy sandals.

Most of us go around in civilian clothes when we're not on a mission. Our civilian employees are heavily vetted, meaning, they get extensive background checks and sign a hundred page nondisclosure form when they get hired. No one is allowed to give away our secrets or take secret photos of us out of costume to sell to the gossip mags, or our legal team will sue the person for every cent they have and inflict unmentionable draconian punishments.

Also, I think M.M. spies on them somehow and ensures they don't get the itch to snap photos of us without our masks on. I don't know how the guy does it, but so far, we haven't had any leaks.

Oh, and also: Whenever someone quits or has to be fired because they grow overly attached to a certain dark vigilante who might have had a moment of weakness and slept with them, and they mistake that moment of weakness for (cough) feelings or something, then M.M. has a way of wiping parts of their memory so they're not tempted to break their nondisclosure agreement and write a tell-all book or give an interview to a gossip rag.

On a side note, I've noticed after the second female employee was fired because of the above-mentioned moment of weakness/indiscretion, that M.M. has gone out of his way to hire more male staffers. Sucks, but I totally understand it.

"Doesn't taste right, for some reason," I answer her. I sip the coffee again to cement my opinion.

"Maybe because you haven't added Kahlua to it yet?"

"Huh. So this is what straight coffee tastes like? Kind of bitter. I don't understand the appeal." I take out my flask and add a dollop of whiskey to my cup, then take another sip and smack my lips. "Better. Not as good as the Kahlua, but better."

"Have you thought about just drinking liquor and leaving the coffee out of it?"

She smiles so I know she's screwing with me…a little bit. There's some truth there, too. I know she thinks I drink too much. Hell, *I* think I drink too much. But what are you gonna do?

"Yeah," I reply. "But I need the caffeine. Late night and I've got a press conference in a few minutes. I've got to give myself a jumpstart."

"Another late night?" She says it with a raised eyebrow. Still screwing with me, but also a little truth again.

"Oh, you know," I say. "The Dark Revenger's work is a twenty-four hour gig sometimes."

"Mm." She takes a cup and pours herself some coffee.

She drinks it black. I noticed that a while ago. I've noticed a lot of things about her, to tell you the truth.

Like, although she drinks black coffee, she'll add cream to hot tea. She likes chicken, but not much of a seafood fan (except for salmon), and she definitely won't touch the raw stuff. She'll eat red meat on occasion, but not often. She likes sweets, but won't overindulge. Like, she'll eat half a bag of M&Ms and save the rest. Or limit herself to two cookies.

I mean, really, who does that? *Half* a bag? *Two* cookies? That, my friends, is what I call self-control.

Part of it might be quirkiness, but more likely she worries about gaining weight because there aren't many overweight superheroes out there. The ones who are, and I can count them on two fingers, are generally mocked on social media. You gotta have thick skin (and I'm not making a bad joke there) if you want to be a fat superhero.

Oh, she's also dating someone. A civilian, banker-type who doesn't know she's a superhero. Clean-cut, nice guy who goes to visit his grandmother on Sundays and brings Estella when she's not "working." Donates money to charities. Cries during sad movies. The kind of guy you'd probably want your daughter to marry.

I hate him.

"How's your boyfriend?" I ask, the word nearly catching in my throat. I manage to say it without gagging.

"He's okay." She sips her coffee and gives me a pointed look. "How are your girlfriends?"

Touché.

"Crap, look at the time," I say, without really looking at the clock on the wall. "I've gotta get downstairs for the press conference."

"This one's about the membership drive?" she asks.

"Yep. Should be fun. You want to get into costume and come down with me? Reporters always ask about you."

Shakes her head. "I'll pass."

Reporters ask about Stealthshadow (Raven), too. Neither of them have shown any interest in talking to the press. Estella is press-shy because she's worried someone will recognize her, especially since she was so prevalent in the press when she was younger.

**Ballistic's Origin Story (for real, this time)**: The daughter of a media mogul and a movie star, Estella Delacruz was a rich, spoiled brat who was constantly in trouble, and constantly in the tabloids. Drugs, drinking, hooking up with other women's boyfriends (including some of her own friends' boyfriends), Estella was on her way to starring in her own reality show and/or possibly a stint in rehab, when her parents had the idea to take her on a world trip via their yacht.

Maybe they thought she couldn't get into trouble surrounded by thousands of miles of ocean? Anyway…

Estella was doing fine, detoxing and pretty much getting used to the tranquility of the ocean while her parents conducted their various business and investment dealings through satellite hookups and such. Then one fine day, a meteor shower rained down on them and tore through the ship, killing everyone except Estella. She was unconscious and adrift on a piece of wreckage when a passing ship found her.

169

After her recovery, Estella Delacruz was a new person, using her financial inheritance to start charitable organizations. She also discovered she had acquired superpowers. She now splits her time between philanthropy and superhero-ing.

The elevator is spacious, but even if it wasn't, it wouldn't bother me. My claustrophobia seems to be a thing of the past ever since my near-death-by-drowning incident. I guess that's one good thing to come out of all of that.

Well, two, Raven no longer despises me. She's not the president of my fan club, either. More like she avoids me whenever possible. So…win? Better to be ignored than hated, right?

The elevator doors SWOOSH open, sounding not unlike the ones on "Star Trek." Its Master Mind's design, so it wouldn't surprise me if it was intentional. I get the impression he's a Trekkie from way back.

I stride through the lobby, waving to security. No robots or androids on duty here; we insist on human workers. They're well trained and armed with super-science weapons Master Mind came up with, so they're more than capable of doing the job. Nice folks, too. They return my wave and a couple call back, "Hey, Dark." "Dark, how you doin'?" "Lookin' good, Dark." Good people.

They're mostly men, ex-military or former mercs (i.e. former henchmen of Master Mind's), and a couple of women. One is Amira, a former Krav Maga instructor for the Israeli army. Badass.

I see her now, glancing at a tablet, checking off whatever checkpoints she needs to go over on her daily rounds. Dark hair pulled back over olive skin. She looks up, feeling my eyes on her.

"Sparring later?" I ask her.

"That what we're calling it?" Her dark eyes flash at me, the barest trace of a smile on her lips.

To be honest, we haven't had sex. Some make out sessions and a little petting. She's playing hard to get and it's driving me mad with desire.

"You master everything I teach you," Amira says. "Should I give away all my secrets?"

The other security guys are watching. Doesn't matter. She outranks most of them. If she wants to flirt with one of the bosses, it's her prerogative.

"I think there's room for me to grow as a student," I say.

Translation: I want to have sex with you.

"Patience is a big part of training," she says.

Translation: Yes, I know. But I'm going to make you work for it.

"I'd like to try some new moves. Maybe up my game a little. Meet later?"

Translation: Look, what are we doing here? I like you. You like me. We're consenting adults. Let's do this already.

"I'll check my schedule, Dark Revenger. If I can fit some training time in, I'll let you know."

Translation: You have a rep. We both know it.

I say, "I hope you have time. Your training is better than anyone else's. I hope you know that."

Translation: I like you, but let's face it, we're not getting married. Hell, I haven't even taken my mask off around you. But I like you. So give me a chance and let's have some fun already. Maybe we could go steady. For a few weeks, anyway.

"I have your number," Amira says. "I'll let you know."

Translation: I'll think about it.

"Yeah, call me."

Translation: For the love of God, call me.

I head back towards the front of the lobby. Her eyes...

They remind me of Estella's dark eyes. I wonder if that's why I find her so attractive.

Ah, better shake it off. Estella would never go for a guy like me. She's all heroism and selflessness. She's a superhero. And I'm a guy pretending to be a superhero.

There's a gift shop near the front entrance. We sometimes have tours come through and the shop does a brisk business. Toys, calendars, t-shirts, mugs, books and comics. We even sell those sleazy superhero gossip mags and tell-all books. Anything we think will make a few bucks.

When I say "we," I'm referring to Master Mind and myself, as we make most of the business decisions. But honestly, when it comes to merchandising, he's been letting me call the shots. He finds it a "waste of time," although he does like the revenue the shop brings in. My bank account likes it, too.

"Dark, baby!"

The neon blue business suit, gold Rolex, and sparkling white teeth hit me like a beacon.

171

"Hey, Gordy," I reply with just the slightest bit of irritation in my voice.

He's leaning on the counter of the gift shop with his hair slicked back and Rolex and gold cufflinks on full display, and chatting up the part time help: a college freshman in a Majestic 12 sweatshirt, her hair pulled back in a scrunchie. She's cute, but she's a kid.

I generally find anyone under twenty-one to be "too young" for me. Having a "teen" at the end of your age is a definite no-go. It irritates me because Gordy is much older than me. Hard to tell with his dyed black hair and Botoxed face, but he is. And here he's trying to chat her up like they're at a bar.

If they *were* at a bar, meaning, she was old enough to be at a bar (which she isn't), then the girl could change seats or leave. But the poor kid is at her job and maybe thinks she has to be cordial to Gordy because of his business relationship to me and the team. Her cheeks are pink and the way she skirts her eyes around and pretends to be busy in an empty store, it's clear she's uncomfortable.

"You got those demos ready to show me?"

"Of course," he says. "I said I'd have them today. Have I ever lied to you?"

I let that one go. I notice he's still leaning on the counter instead of moving to show me anything.

"Hey, Gordy, I don't have x-ray vision, remember? So if you'd pull the demos out…"

"Yeah! No problemo!" He straightens up and gives the kid a wink.

She blushes, but I think more out of embarrassment that a guy old enough to be her father is flirting with her more than anything.

I tell the kid, "Julia, the press conference is about to start. I doubt you'll have any customers today. We canceled the tours and the public won't have access to the lobby at all, so… Would you do a stock count on the t-shirts and sweatshirts in the back?"

Busy work. Plus, it gives her something to do and not be hit on by this sleaze.

"Sure," she says with a silent "thank you" in her eyes and heads into the back storage room.

Gordy's eyes are locked on her butt as she walks away. I clear my throat, not hiding the fact that I disapprove of this so, so much.

"What?" He puts his hands out, palms up. "She's over eighteen."

"Barely."

"Hey, grass on the field and all that."

Jeez, he's like a sleazier version of me. And I didn't think that was possible.

"Let's see the demos," I say. "I've got to get outside to the press conference in a minute."

"Sure, sure." Gordy picks up a leather case by his feet and sets it up on the counter. He opens it and pulls out models of action figures for Ballistic, Stealthshadow, and Master Mind.

"They're working on some accessories for Master Mind," he says, "so it's not just an action figure of a guy in a tight, white t-shirt and cargo pants. R & D is thinking, like, laser pistol and jet pack."

"He doesn't use any of those things."

"I know, Dark, but you have to think of the kids playing with these. It's no fun to play with an action figure that comes with a desk and a microscope."

"Yeah, I get that," I say. I pick the figure up and turn it over. They copied his muscled chest pretty well. "I like the goggles. Nice touch."

Gordy beams, soaking up the slightest hint of a compliment. Yeah, right, like he sculpted the damn thing. Probably didn't even realize the figure *had* goggles.

"Rocket pack I can live with," I say. "No laser pistol."

"You're the boss."

"Ballistic looks good. They got the hourglass figure right."

I feel a little funny with my hands on her body, even if it's only sculpted plastic, so I put it down and pick up Raven's model.

"Breasts are too big," I say. "Plus, she's the same height as Ballistic. Stealthshadow is shorter than her. More compact."

"Dark, come on. These aren't supposed to be to scale. They use the same mold for both Ballistic and Stealthshadow. Saves money that way."

"Who cares about saving money? I want them to look right."

He smiles a wide, fake grin. "They're just toys. They're meant to be played with."

"Yeah, I get that Gordy. But like I said, I want them to look right."

He sighs dramatically. "Okay, I'll talk to the company. The figure won't be ready in time for the big rollout, though."

"I don't care. We'll stagger it. I don't want them all coming out at the same time anyway. Give the kids and collectors a chance to save up."

"Next question," he says. "When are you guys going to pick your new members? They need time to work up the models, you know. And we want a set of the whole team ready by Christmas, right?"

"That's what the press conference is about today," I reply. "We're going to have the final team lineup real soon. In the meantime, we put out the individual figures we have. And they have the original team lineup, right? I want the original Majestic 12 box set of figures for the nostalgia crowd."

"Yep, got 'em. And they made all the requested changes. Even trimmed down Traveler's, uh, crotch, like you asked."

"Yeah, they had him packing and believe me, I was standing nose to nose with that guy. He wasn't working with anything. His front was as flat as my mother's pancakes."

Gordy smirks and shakes his head. "The shit you care about, Dark. I can't figure it out."

"What about my figure? I feel like I've been asking forever on this."

His smile is genuine now. "I saved the best for last. You're gonna love it."

Yeah, like I haven't heard that before.

Gordy pulls another figure out of his case and hands it to me. "What the hell is this?"

I turn it over in my hands. It's the Dark Revenger, but:

"This is the old costume. All black. Why isn't it wearing my current one?"

Gordy says, "What, you don't love it? I love it. What are you talking about? It's great!"

"Why doesn't it have my silver cape and hood? This is pre-Majestic 12 costume."

"I told you, Dark. The nostalgia crowd. They want old Dark Revenger. They're gonna make one with the new costume when the other figures are ready. So they can roll them out with the new Majestic 12 lineup. But right now, since we're coming out with the old lineup, they thought it'd be cool to do the old costume first. Look…" He takes a plastic piece out of his case and snaps it on the figure's arm. "It even comes with a grappling hook."

"I don't use the hook much these days."

"I *know*. But you use to, right? Look, the kids will love it. And the collectors, man, they'll eat it up. Think of it this way: We come out with this version now. Then in a couple of months, we roll out the new, current D.R. costume. Same figure, too, so there's no additional cost on that. We sell twice as much."

"I guess."

I can't hide the fact I'm disappointed. Can't shake the feeling I'm looking at an action figure based on *him* and not me. But…he's right. We'll sell twice as many.

"See?" He says, "They gave the toy a, uh, slight bulge like you wanted. Maybe not as much because, you know, we gotta keep the toys PG. Not R."

"Mm. It's alright." Hard to work up enthusiasm. I'm trying, though.

"We'll release it as a single, and then also in a two-pack with your archnemesis, Court Jester."

"Why not the Puzzler?"

"Yeah, I talked to the research department about your request for a Puzzler figure. They say it doesn't make sense to do an action figure for an obscure supervillain."

"Obscure? He wasn't obscure."

"The kids, collectors too, like the big ones. Court Jester is your archnemesis. So if we do a two-pack, it's natural to do it with him."

"That's what she said."

"Ah ha!" Big fake smile and he gives me the finger guns. "You're a riot, Dark. Man, who knew you had a sense of humor, huh?"

"Back to the Puzzler action figure," I say. "Yeah, I get that Court Jester is considered the 'classic' archnemesis, but Puzzler has…"

"Panache?"

"I was going to say style, but yeah. Panache."

"I'm telling you, the marketing people don't think it'll sell. Puzzler is too recent. Folks like the classics. The tried and true. Plus, Puzzler was never caught, so there's no exciting prison break to reenact."

"Court Jester was never caught either." *And we all know why, don't we?*

"Yeah, but his stuff was all *big*. Big crimes. Loud. Colorful. He would taunt you with all of those videos. Puzzler, you know, he stuck to the shadows. And puzzle boxes? I don't know, man. Kind of lame."

"Not lame," I say. "Sophisticated. He had flair. He was like a throwback to the old gentleman cat burglars. Stealing works of art and stuff."

Gordy rolls his eyes. I want to punch him.

He says, "Okay, okay. I see you got a soft spot for this guy. Jeez, if I didn't know better, I'd think you guys were dating." Then, right away, he shoots me his fake laugh and a flash of capped teeth, and says, "Tell you what, we'll get them to do a whole rogues gallery for you. Okay? We'll do the old costume and the current one. Do the two-pack with Court Jester."

He puts his hand up, like, *Stop and hear me out first.*

"It'll be a huge seller," he says. "Trust me. Okay? Then we'll start releasing action figures for your other villains: Mistress Night, Techmage, Simon Simian—"

"The talking gorilla? You're telling me they'd consider releasing an action figure of a talking gorilla before they'd consider the Puzzler?"

"Dark, what're you talking about? Simon Simian is supposed to be a super-genius inventor. You tangled with him much more than the Puzzler. Besides, kids love monkeys. The figure would be a huge seller."

*Did Simon Simian fight the Dark Revenger a lot? Simon didn't associate with the other bad guys much. I mean, he's a gorilla after all. A highly evolved, super-intelligent one, but still a gorilla nonetheless. He hates humans (or so I've been told) and only reluctantly works with them to get what he wants, whatever that might be. Humans subjugated and the Statue of Liberty buried in the beach, I guess.*

"So after Mistress Night—"

Who is total stone-sexy, by the way, and wouldn't even give a good looking guy like me the time of day because she was so obsessed with the Dark Revenger in some kind of sadomasochistic love-hate kind of thing, like your crazy ex who spends all their time badmouthing you and sending you drunken DMs, then "accidentally" runs into you at your usual hangout, but acts cold and aloof and pointedly ignores you even though they're watching you out of the corner of their eye, and yeah, I've totally been on the receiving end of this behavior, and man, IT IS FRIGGIN' HOT!

"—and after the talking gorilla, then will they release a Puzzler action figure?" I ask.

Gordy says, "Here's what I'm thinking. We do a Puzzler figure as a limited edition. One in every case of a hundred, or something. The kids will love it. And the collectors will go nuts. They'll tear through the toys stores looking for 'em. Prices will skyrocket. Pretty soon, you won't be able to buy a Puzzler figure for less than a hundred bucks. You feel me?"

"I hate that expression, but yes," I say. "Whatever. Just get them to do a figure. And, uh...I get one, right?"

"You want a Puzzler figure?"

"Yeah."

He looks at me like he can't tell if I'm joking.

I'm not joking.

"Okay," he says. "Sure. I'll make sure you get a Puzzler figure. You want two?"

"No, just one. And a Dark Revenger figure, both versions. And a Mistress Night figure."

"You got it, broheim."

I hate that expression, too, but I let it go.

"Alright, Gordy, I gotta get outside for the press conference. So if you wouldn't mind..."

"Mind what?"

"We're shutting down the lobby, so you have to exit. Preferably ahead of me."

"What, I can't hang out in here?"

Not with the young sales clerk you want to sexually harass.

"No. Security and all that. You know how it is."

He doesn't, but buys it anyway. He picks up his case and follows me to the front lobby doors.

"I changed my mind," I say. "I want two Puzzler figures."

177

In case I break one.

"Sure, Dark. You got it."

I let him exit ahead of me. The crowd murmurs, thinking for a second it's me. I'm late, but I like to make an entrance, so...

I take a ten second breather, then say, "Ready, Meredith?"

She materializes next to me. It used to freak me out, but I've grown used to it. She's always around.

Master Mind accessed her programming and discovered an unused subdirectory or sublink (or sub-something, I don't know) that enables her to grow as a program. Essentially, she is continuously learning and adapting. Growing as a program. She can even connect emotions to her decisions now. Like a human. That's the point: she's becoming more human-like every day.

"The reporters are waiting, Dark Revenger," she says. "You are eight minutes, fifty-seven seconds late."

"Good. Fashionably late. Let's talk music."

"The sound system is connected. What music would you like for your walk to the microphone?"

"'Bad to the Bone,'" I say. "No, wait, that's been done to death in the movies."

"Hasn't everything been done to death in the movies?"

"Meredith, did you just say something snarky? I'm impressed. Anyway, back to your question. Um... Let's go with 'Nothin' but a Good Time' by Poison."

"Honestly?"

"Too much snark is never a good thing. Yes, I want you to play that song."

Her eyes flicker; it reminds me of when you win at computer solitaire and all the cards fly across the screen. Kind of cool.

She accesses the song (pretty much every song ever recorded is in her memory) and it plays outside. The crowd's murmur intensifies.

"Awesome," I say. "And remember, when I'm done talking, I'll point to you and you play the other song. You remember which one?"

"Yes, I remember. There is no defect in my memory or my programming—"

"Yeah, yeah, okay, I wasn't asking for you to run a diagnostic or anything." I take a deep breath. "Alright, let's do this."

The doors to the building are frosted glass, reinforced, and bulletproof. M.M. claims they're laser and microwave-proof, too. So when I push through them, I don't know what to expect. A small crowd would be disappointing.

I'm not disappointed.

Reporters and journalists from every major news outlet are crowded in the front courtyard. Security opened the gates earlier and checked credentials before letting people in, and boy, they earned their pay today. I see them all out there: the majors, the gossip rags, the internet bloggers...

Okay, I don't really know what the bloggers look like, but there are some nerdy types mixed in with the suit and tie, hair-gelled, sparkling white teeth types. The majors are up front, though, because I'm not answering questions from some comic book website reporter.

Now, *SUPERHERO QUARTERLY*? I'll talk to them if they're here. I'm angling for a cover shoot in the next few months.

I be-bop up to the microphone, strutting a little to the music. I make eye contact with some of the reporters. There's one particularly sexy, busty blonde in the front. I smile at her and point, just like a rock star. She keeps a professional composure, but the corner of her mouth twitches up in a slight half-smile.

I pause behind the microphone, let the music play for a few seconds, then I nod to Meredith who followed me out. She's stands off to my back right, kind of acting as support, but also security, too. Despite our security precautions, civilian teams checking credentials and mounted defense systems (both hidden and visible), you never know if some supervillain is going to try to use this press conference as an opportunity to attack.

Meredith registers my nod and, as she and I previously discussed, she has the music fade out. I say, "Thanks everyone, for coming out on such a beautiful day."

It's a little cloudy and breezy, but I like to start off with positivity.

"After years of keeping the press at arm's length, we, the new incarnation of Majestic 12, wanted to invite all of you here to make the announcement that no longer will you be kept in the dark about what the world's premiere supergroup is up to. We are a newer, friendlier — and when I say *friendlier*, I mean friendlier to the press —"

I give the blonde a wink.

"— and more relatable superhero group. We're not gods, people. We are just like you, the average person on the street. Just, you know, better looking and with really cool powers. So…"

I take the mike out of the stand and move closer to the crowd. I'm two steps up on a stone dais. It gives me a good view of the crowd without having me tower over everyone.

"Majestic 12 is changing. We are adding more members. Some you've heard of, and some you haven't. Fresh faces. We've got some people picked out, and we are holding interviews later today for other slots on the team. The intention is to take it up to a full twelve members. Majestic 12 should have twelve members. Makes sense. Other than that, it will be business as usual. Keeping the world safe. Kicking ass, and looking good while doing it. You feel me?"

Ugh. Can't believe I used that term. Friggin' Gordy rubbing off on me.

"Also," I say, "we will be more accessible now to not only local law enforcement, but also you, the civilians who need us. We have a new website, an email address… Hell, as many of you are aware, we've started a Facebook page, and we're going to start tweeting." I clear my throat. "There's also a separate website for me, darkrevenger dot com and darkrevenger dot net, that I should probably state is not directly affiliated with Majestic 12, so any merchandise for sale on there is a separate entity. And the views expressed on there are not necessarily endorsed by Majestic 12."

Master Mind insisted I say all that for legal purposes. Not sure why. I promised there wouldn't be anything distasteful on the website. I just want to sell some t-shirts and ball caps, maybe post the occasional pic of me getting a medal or something. I mean, I turned down The Dark Revenger condom endorsement. I have *some* limits, you know.

"Okay, so everyone got it?" I say, "New members. New website. Relatable to the common Joe. And darkrevenger dot com and dot net for all your Dark Revenger merchandise. Any questions?"

Almost every single hand goes up.

"All right then. Um…" I point to hot blonde reporter. "Yes, you. What can the Dark Revenger do for you?"

"Tracy Stengall, Channel 8 News," she says. "Two questions. Are you the same Dark Revenger that's operated in Azure City over the last eight years?"

"Of course. Why…why would you ask such a crazy question?"

She says, "To put it bluntly Dark Revenger, you are much less private now. You never gave press conferences in the past, or for that matter, posed for photos as you've been known to do in the last six months. Some people question if the reason in the sudden change in your aversion to being photographed is that you're a completely different person. There's also the costume change…"

"Tracy, times have changed. Heroes can't save the world by hiding in the shadows. We have to grow. We have to adapt. My costume is a reflection of my new attitude, which is, stop the bad guys and look damn good doing it!"

The crowd murmurs. A couple of scattered chuckles.

"Second question," she says. "How will your association with Majestic 12 affect your pledge to always protect Azure City? And what about some of your major foes like Court Jester and Simon Simian?"

"The talking gorilla again? Seriously? Since when did he become *my* major foe?"

The expression on her face… She doesn't understand because I'm referencing my conversation with Gordy. So obviously she'd be confused.

"What I mean is, yes," I say. "I have some arch-foes that I've tangled with on a regular basis. Court Jester. The Puzzler. And so forth. But—"

"I'm sorry. Did you say the Puzzler?" she asks.

"Yes."

"You list the Puzzler as great a threat as Court Jester?"

"Well, not a threat *per se*. But no one can deny that the Puzzler was a terrific adversary with an intellect that rivalled my own, who tested my mettle on many occasions."

A smirking male reporter in the crowd mutters loud enough for me to hear, "Sounds like someone's got a bit of a crush."

A few people laugh. More than the number that laughed at my joke (which wasn't really a joke, but whatever).

"Yeah, that's a good one, smart guy," I say. "You know who else likes a good one? Your mom."

Bigger laugh this time and reporter guy loses his smirk. Success!

"As I was saying, being part of a great team like Majestic 12 means that Azure City will have nothing to worry about. We've got this city covered. It's not only our home base, but..." Pause for dramatic effect. "It's our *home*."

Murmurs of appreciation.

I say, "So if Mistress Night decides to steal some rare jewels, she'll have the combined might of Majestic 12 on her shapely, leather-clad ass. And if Simon Simpleton—"

"Simian," Tracey Stengall corrects.

"—whatever, decides to steal a shipment of bananas, then the same thing. But I really don't think he's a member of my rogue's gallery. Didn't he usually tangle with Speed Demon?"

Tracy answers, "He moved to Azure City at some point and became an adversary of yours."

Really? The supervillain gossip line missed that tidbit.

"What about Court Jester?" Tracy asks. "Aren't you concerned he might increase the scope of his crimes now that you're part of a huge superhero team? In the past, the casualties of his crimes were single digit. Generally, whenever a superhero joins a team or gets a power increase, their chief adversaries will 'up their game,' so to speak."

"Tracy, you are well past your two questions, but I'll answer this one: You won't have to worry about Court Jester."

"How can you be sure?"

Because he's dead. Obviously, I can't say that, so...

"I have it on good authority," I say, "through contacts and informants, that Court Jester is missing and presumed dead. This time for reals."

Someone says, "Did he really just say, 'for reals'?"

"Next question. What about you, Smirky McSmirketon." I point to the male reporter. "Got a question for your favorite hero? Or want to try cracking wise again?"

"Actually, a question, Dark Revenger," he says. "With the massive changes in the Majestic 12 line-up over the past six months, the unexpected deaths of many of the founding members, the change in…well, your own personality, quite frankly… There are rumors that this is all an incredibly orchestrated, brilliantly planned supervillain plot. The fact that the supervillain community has been unusually quiet during this time would also point to some validity of this."

"Poor Smirky. Trying to find a conspiracy where there is none," I say. "I told you, this is about change. Updating for the modern times. The supervillain community has been quiet? Good! That means they're running scared. They know there's a new team of heroes in town and we aren't going to be reactive like the old team. We're *pro*active."

"What does that mean, exactly?" Smirky asks.

"It means, you know… We're proactive. Not going to be reactive and wait for stuff to happen. We're going to go out and stop it *before* it happens."

"And how exactly?"

"I told you. *Proactive.* Jeez, it's like you guys don't listen. Next question."

I point to an Asian female reporter because she looks a little like Raven. That probably sounds racist, but there's really a slight resemblance.

"Yes. You."

"Lonnie Yu from Azure Dispatch, Dark Revenger. I was wondering—"

"Wait, so when I said 'you,' meaning the pronoun 'you,' I actually got your name right?"

"Um, it's actually spelled differently, so…"

"Yeah," I say. "But still, in a way, I got it right. Right?"

"Sure," she says with that tone of being tired of the subject already. "Back to my question. Majestic 12 has added new members in the last six months. Any truth to the rumor that you are holding auditions later today for more members?"

"Yes, Connie—"

"Lonnie," she corrects.

"—Lonnie, we are interviewing potential candidates later today. Our goal is to bring the roster up to twelve members. You know, so Majestic 12 really has twelve people. Make sense?"

"Sure," she says in a way that makes me think she doesn't care either way.

She opens her mouth to ask another question. I'm already turning my attention elsewhere. Feels like we keep covering the same ground. Same questions, just asked in different ways.

I point to the back where I recognize a ponytailed, college age-looking female commentator from TCZ (The Cape Zone). Actually, everybody on that show looks like they're college age. Except for the creepy, middle-aged guy who runs it.

She asks, "Any truth to the rumors that you and Stealthshadow are dating?"

"She wishes."

It gets a nice chuckle from the audience. Raven is going to be pissed about that, but at least she'll feel *something* besides pretending I don't exist.

"What about the long running rumor that you and Mistress Night are an item? Is that why she's been out of the spotlight lately?"

"Well now, that's an interesting rumor," I say. "But I cannot confirm or deny any past relations with Mistress Night. Nor would I. A gentleman never divulges such things." I give the commentator a little wink.

Then I say, "Ah, what the hell. Yeah, I nailed her."

The crowd of reporters erupts in a mixture of surprise and "What did he just say?" comments. Everyone's hand goes up and everyone talks at once.

"Whoa, whoa, whoa," I say. "I'm not going to go into detail. So just be grateful for that little tidbit."

Who knows? Maybe the Dark Revenger did have sex with her. It's doubtful, but you never know. He's not going to come back from the dead and disagree with what I said, and Mistress Night can't show her face in public because she's a wanted criminal.

Hell, she'd probably thank me for saying that. Her name just got boosted up from the supervillain minor league to the all-stars. Tonight, every news channel and website is going to play that sound bite. You're welcome, Mistress Night.

184

I take more questions: Stuff about rumors of Hollywood deals (not true…yet), book deals (still interviewing ghostwriters, so partially true), and more questions about who I'm dating and who I've had sex with. I wave those away and tell them to wait for the book. Finally, it feels like it's time to wrap it up.

"You." I point to one portly, disheveled guy in jeans and a t-shirt. "Are you a reporter? Or are you here to deliver a pizza?"

"Ken Stocker from Under the Mask dot com," he replies.

Ugh. A website news source? Next time, I'm going to cut down the invite list for the press conferences. Only the big names.

"You get the last question, Stalker."

"It's Stocker, Dark Revenger."

"Same thing. What's your question?"

"In issue 211 of the Dark Revenger comic book, it's revealed that the character — you — is left handed. But in recent news footage, you appear to be right handed. I think I speak for many comic continuity experts when I ask, what's going on? Did the comic get it wrong? Or is there another, more sinister reason? Are you a Dark Revenger from a mirror universe?"

"Whoa, hold on there, nerdlinger," I say. "First of all, do I look like the kind of superhero who has time to read comic books? No. Of course not. Secondly… Look, the comics are just a loose interpretation of what's happening in the superhero world. I mean, Mistress Night's breasts are not *that* big. And in that same issue, they had the color scheme of Court Jester's costume all wrong—"

Stoker says, "I thought you didn't read the comics."

"Don't interrupt. My point is, don't believe everything you read in comic books. Okay? And on that note…" I point to Meredith who has been standing off to my side like a statue. Her head turns just a fraction, acknowledging the signal I'm giving her. Wild Cherry's "Play that Funky Music" starts over the sound system.

"That's right, boys and girls," I say. "Not only is Majestic 12 new and improved, but we're also funkier."

I dance to the song. I'm an awesome dancer. But why do it alone? (That's what she said.)

I hold my hand out with a flourish to Tracy Stengall. She hesitates, until the people around her give encouraging motions. She smiles and shrugs, then steps up on the dais with me.

And we dance. Oh, how we dance. The crowd of reporters get into it. Even the geeky guy from the questionable news site is boogying.

I love bringing people together. More than that, I love creating special moments like this. In addition to the news cameras, Majestic 12 has security cameras all around the building. Plus, if that wasn't enough, Meredith records everything directly and feeds it back to our database. There's going to be multiple views of this, me dancing with the reporter and the crowd partying with me.

The multiple videos, because you know I'm going to release several versions edited to make me look even cooler, will go viral. I can already see the millions and millions of hits. And it'll all have ads for darkrevenger.com flashing at the bottom.

It's going to be a good Christmas for my bank account this year. Gordy better not screw up the action figures. Still need to push the animated series idea—

Something from the corner of my eye. A quick flash of… I don't know what. Like a large cloud passing overhead. It must be moving super-fast because the sky is clear. It wasn't a cloud, though.

I'm not sure what it was, but it's happened several times over the past six months. A flicker of light, like someone messing with the brightness control on the world. It's quick and no one else seems to notice. Or if they do, no one says anything. But I don't think they do.

I miss a step. The crowd is distracted and Tracy is busy trying not to fall over in her impossibly-high heels, so I don't think anyone notices my slight pause.

I keep dancing. Later, I'll check the recorded footage, both for signs of the mystery flicker and to edit out my slight pause. I don't want people thinking the Dark Revenger lost the rhythm in mid-dance.

I never lose the rhythm.

# CHAPTER 19

Master Mind is rubbing his temples in one of those "I've got a migraine coming on and this is all Eddie's fault" ways I've grown accustomed to.

He's in the front row of a small theater we rented in the artsy, bohemian section of Azure City, one of those places where you can catch experimental shows with names like "The Vagina Diatribes" or "Sophie's Choice – The Musical." Today is the big audition extravaganza for the final two members of our team.

Why are we having trouble recruiting members? Good question.

Most of the bigger name heroes have either retired or dropped off the face of the Earth. Lots of villains, too, have been quiet. We seem to be entering an age of superheroes, where we can walk down the street in full costume and civilians wave at us. We've had to stop a few supervillains, but it's been few and far between. The worst we've had to deal with lately is an occasional bank robbery or a cat stuck in a tree.

Honestly haven't had to deal with that last one, but Estella and Refraction were called last week to a local neighborhood where a little girl was bawling her eyes out. Refraction was about to climb the tree, but Estella took the initiative and shot upward like the proverbial rocket and snatched the cat. Also broke two branches, which threw the owner of the yard where the tree stood into a tizzy. Until Master Mind talked to him and smoothed things over.

He's good at that. Smoothing things over.

"What's wrong, M.M.?"

He groans. "Why? Why am I wasting my time with this, Eddie?" His head comes up and regards me with bloodshot eyes. "You were supposed to be in charge of this. Instead, you're dancing with pretty news journalists on television and I'm getting a phone call from the theater owner asking me why no one is here to talk to the line of garishly dressed–"

"Garishly?"

"Yes," he replies emphatically. "Garishly. Garishly dressed people waiting to interview for the remaining two spots on our team. Many of whom, I'm pleased to say, do not have any powers or abilities to put them on a superteam. Unless you want to list the ability to sew or obvious colorblindness as a superpower."

"Ha! I like that, M.M." I shift my cape aside and sit next to him.

"Okay," I say. "I'm here now. I'll take over. Let me have the list."

He hands me a clipboard and a pen. There's a sheet of paper attached to the board with a long list of names, most of them marked through.

"Here," he says. "You take over this circus. I have to get back to the lab."

He makes his exit and I'm stuck with the auditions.

"Who's next?" I call out.

There's a group of people milling around the corner of the stage. Master Mind was right; they are a colorful bunch. Lots of primary colors.

"I think I'm next." Black dude, wiry looking, in camo fatigues and a black compression shirt steps up to the stage. "Don't have a costume yet," he says. "So I put this together. Hope I'm not being graded on it."

"I'm not grading," I say. "Was Master Mind grading? I'm not sure what his criteria was. I'm looking for abilities and a personality that works well with a team."

And assurances that we don't have any guys on the team better looking than me. But I'm not going to say that.

"Whatcha got?"

He says, "I can create an energy spear."

"A sphere? Like a round ball of energy?"

"No. A spear. Like… Hold on a sec."

Couple of guys, friends of his or family members, maybe, set up an archery target at the far end of the stage. He eyes it up, then raises his right hand up like he's doing a Statue of Liberty impression and holding an invisible torch. The air around his outstretched hand crackles and a fiery line of energy appears in his grip, long and pointed at both ends. He takes two quick steps forward and throws the energy weapon at the target.

It hits almost dead center with a THUNK. The spear fizzles out as soon as it hits, but there's a small burn mark on the target, and it did get pushed back an inch, so I know the impact has a bit of force. I could see it knocking someone down.

"Nice," I say. "Is there a chance your spears can start a fire?"

"Nah. They're more of a blunt force weapon. The heat looks like a lot, but it's not as hot as it looks. And you saw the energy dissipate, so…" He shrugs.

"Well, man, I like the cut of your jib."

"My what?"

"Your jib," I say.

"What's a jib?" Puzzled, like he's trying to figure out if I insulted him.

"A *jib*. You know… It's a, uh, nautical term. It means I like you. You made the cut. You're on the team."

"Really?" Wide, genuine smile. "No, shit? Aw, man, that's awesome. But what am I going to do about a costume? I can't sew for shit. And those professional costume makers out there… I checked with a couple. They charge *a lot*. You guys maybe can advance me some money?"

"Don't worry," I say. "Majestic 12 has a contract with someone. We can get a costume made on credit. You'll need a couple because, you know, laundry and stuff. Also, sometimes they get damaged during fights. Part of the job, etc."

"Really? For free?"

"No, man, this isn't the military. You pay for your stuff. It'll come out of your paycheck."

He's not even listening. Too busy high-fiving his target set-up crew.

"Hey. What's your superhero name?" I ask.

"Oh, yeah," he says. "Spear Thrower."

"You are absolutely *not* going to go with that. Why would you pick an offensive name like that?"

"Why's it offensive?"

"Seriously, dude? You're black. You know why."

Puzzled look again. This time he looks to his buddies for help. They appear as clueless about it as him.

He says, "I make spears out of energy. I throw them."

"Okay, whatever," I say. "Listen, Spear Thrower is a racist term. You're not using it. It's too much like 'spear chucker.'"

"You say 'Spear Thrower' is racist, but you're the only one in the room that automatically went to 'spear chucker.' Just sayin'."

"You want on the team? Your name is... Lancer! No, wait, that sounds like a dermatologist. How about, um... Laser Lance!"

A little too 1950's sci-fi space cowboy (ish), but not bad for spur of the moment.

He shrugs. "Whatever, man. As long as I'm on the team." He says to his buddies, "You hear that, bitches? I'm on the motherfucking Majestic 12! Whoo!"

Whoo, indeed.

At that last part, the side door opens and Estella comes in, in her Ballistic costume. Everybody goes quiet in the place, even the women. She nods genially to everyone. They watch her walk to the row behind me and take a seat three seats to my left.

The men are staring too much and a hot flash of jealousy hits me. It's followed by a hot flash of anger at myself for being jealous. I mean, it's not like she's my girlfriend or anything. So why am I jealous?

I smack the clipboard on the back of the chair in front of me.

"Hey, we doing tryouts? Let's get back to it. Who's next?"

That gets everyone motivated again. A woman dressed like Mary Poppins and a rainbow had a baby makes her way to the stage. I look back over my shoulder to Estella.

"Psst! Hey."

"Psst, what?" she replies.

"What's a jib? As in, 'cut of your jib?'"

She says, "It's a reference to the sail of a ship. They used to be able to tell what kind of ship it was by the way the sail was shaped."

"Ah. I knew it was nautical."

Rainbow Poppins (or whatever her superhero name is) has the power to make things change color. I pass.

I pass, too, on the guy who talks to birds, and also the woman who can knit really fast. By the time I pass on the guy who can cause mild nausea, I've stepped over the seats and taken the seat next to Estella. She sits with one leg crossed over the other. I badly want to put my gloved hand on her leg. I resist the urge and think about other things.

"Next up," I call out, reading the name from the list, "is Cliff Dortmunder."

Young guy in a scuba suit and fins does a duck walk/waddle up to the stage. Fins slap against the floor.

"What in the hell…?" I say and Estella stifles a giggle.

"What's your superhero name?"

"Atlantean," he says.

"Atlanta Teen? You look a little older than a teenager."

"No," he says. "*Atlantean*. Like, from Atlantis."

"Are you from Atlantis?"

"What?" He makes a face. "No. That's not a real place."

"Are you sure?" I turn to Estella. "Atlantis isn't a real place?"

"Just a legend, Dark Revenger."

"Huh." To the scuba guy: "Well, anyway, what are your powers?"

"I can breathe underwater. See these?" Points to thin slits on his neck I hadn't noticed before. "Gills."

"You breathe underwater?"

"Yep."

"Can you talk to fish?"

"What? No."

Like it's the most ludicrous thing in the world.

"Are you really strong? You know, because the ocean depths would crush a normal person, so you'd have to be really strong to withstand that. Which means you'd be really strong up here on the surface world."

He stares at me for ten seconds. "Surface world? I told you I'm not from Atlantis. I'm actually from Iowa. And no, I'm not really strong."

I say, "So your power is you have gills and can breathe underwater."

"Yeah. I said that."

"Okay, Atlanta…Atlantean…if there's any crimes under water, you'll be the first one I call."

He mutters "asshole" as he waddles off the stage.

"Next!" I call. I check the clipboard. "All I have are initials here. BH?"

A man in a gray hoodie strides up the steps to the stage and there's something familiar about his build and gait. Before he slips the hood off his blue-skinned head, I know who it is.

191

"BH stands for Blue Howler, Dark Revenger. You remember me, don't you?"

Oh, crap.

Estella says, "Wait. Aren't you a supervillain?"

She's tense; I feel her ready to come out of the chair in a flash and prepared to fight. This has all the elements of a classic supervillain ambush. But it isn't. I know what this is, unfortunately.

"Naw," Howler says. He has his hands up in a "hold on" gesture. "I'm reformed. He'll vouch for me." His eyes on me. "Right, *Dark Revenger*?"

Howler, you friggin' idiot, what are you doing?

"Yeah. Sure, I'll vouch for this guy. He's not a bad guy anymore. He joined our side a while back."

"Are there warrants out?" she asks.

"All taken care of," I answer. Or at least they will be once I talk to Master Mind and have him hack in and wipe Howler's record clean.

I'm out of my seat and heading over to him with a "Welcome to the team, Blue Howler," and a fake grin on my face. Howler hesitates, probably wondering if it's a fakeout, but then I grab him in a "bro hug," like two old friends who haven't seen each other since college.

"Good to see you again," I say loud enough for the room to hear, and convincingly so because Howler hugs me back. Through my fake smile, I say only loud enough for Howler to hear, "What the fuck are you doing, asshole?"

Loud, "Good to see you, too," then quieter, "I want to be on the team. Make it happen for me, Eddie."

I turn to the others still waiting. "Okay, that's it, folks. We've got our twelve members."

"What?!" from a couple of garishly clad people, and a "This is bullshit!" from someone in back.

"I know, I know," I say. "It's a tough business. Look, leave your contact info. We'll be doing this again, I'm sure. People get crippled or killed in this profession all the time. Isn't that right, Blue Howler?" My arm is still around his shoulders. I dig my fingers in, although I'm sure it doesn't hurt him.

"That's right, Dark Revenger. Hell, I've seen my share of death. I could tell you about this one time–"

"Ha, ha, ha…aahhh, what a kidder this guy is," I say. "Ballistic, I'm going to catch up with my old friend. Would you mind wrapping things up here and making sure the place is locked up?"

"What? Me? I don't–"

"Thanks! Appreciate it!" I push Howler out a side door into the adjacent alleyway. When the door is shut and I'm sure we're alone, I say, "Dude, what the hell?"

"Dude," he says, "I'm tired of being a B List supervillain. I want to be an A List superhero like you."

"We were B List supervillains?"

"Dude, I was B List. You were C List."

I say, "I don't know about that. I think if you ask anyone, the Puzzler ranks as high as Blue Howler."

He says, "Dude–"

"Okay, I said 'dude' one time. You don't have to keep saying it."

"Anyway. I'm tired of the bad guy life. I never wanted that. But, you know, I was created by a bad guy so that automatically made me one. Guilty by association."

"Plus the banks and jewelry stores you robbed," I say.

"Yeah, okay, I'm no saint. I get it. But you know a lot of that was to pay back a debt. I kinda didn't have a choice."

"Debatable, but I'm not casting stones at you, buddy. Now you, what, want to join the big league, premiere superhero team?"

He says, "Why not? You're on the team. I mean, I *have* a superpower."

"I got news for you, Howler. I've levelled up."

"Right, right, right… I know. You got some high tech gadgets now. I watch the news, Ed-" He catches himself. "Dark Revenger."

We stand and stare at each other for a moment. I don't know, something in his eyes… I don't think this is blackmail.

"What's the real play here?" I ask. "What are you after?"

"Honestly? I owe you. You saved my life. I want to pay you back. Don't tell me you couldn't use somebody watching your back. Your *real* back. I mean, how many times has this whole thing almost fallen apart on you? I can't believe no one's caught on yet."

"That's the funny thing. It's been surprisingly easy. Almost…"

"Almost what?"

I want to tell him "Almost as if someone was helping me," but something stops me from voicing it. Maybe because I think the thought is crazy. Or maybe because I'm afraid it isn't.

"Come on." I wave for him to follow me out of the alley to where the Dark Revenger Mobile is parked.

There's a light force field around it, similar to the one I can project from my belt. Not enough to stop a bazooka blast, but enough to keep car thieves away.

That would be something, wouldn't it? The Dark Revenger Mobile stolen by a car thief. Then maybe the thief drives around and pretends to be me.

Yeah, I get the irony of that statement.

A couple of street kids are tossing rocks at the forcefield and watching them bounce off in various trajectories.

"Hey! Knock it off! You're gonna wear down the battery!"

Great. That's all I need. Having to call for a tow because some punks were throwing rocks at my car and ran out the juice.

One kid saunters up to me. "Yo, Dark, you spare a dolla?"

"What?" I say, "I'm a superhero. Not a bank."

"Oh, come on, G. You got money for a car like this and all those gadgets. You don't have an extra buck you can spare?"

"I don't carry cash, and the superhero gig doesn't pay as well as you might think. I work primarily for room and board." And a generous stipend, as well as the proceeds from my newly formed corporation – Dark Revenger, LLC.

I don't feel the need to tell him that. I'm not a charity. I'm a superhero.

The kid says, "Man, that's bullshit."

Howler hands him a five. "Here, kid."

"Thanks, blue. Yo, you see that, Dark? Your blue friend is a true superhero. Helpin' out the less fortunate and all that."

I click a button on my belt and the force field around the car powers down. The car automatically unlocks when my hand touches the door. It's not fingerprint coded. I'm wearing gloves, and besides, the car's defense system wouldn't have allowed me to get close enough to touch it. I learned that the hard way.

Master Mind helped me reprogram the car's system. It's tuned to my body's electromagnetic field.

Howler and I get in. The kid's still yelling.

"You should be more like your blue friend, Dark. Be like blue."

"Be like blue," I repeat for Howler's benefit. We both chuckle.

Then the kid yells, "Dark, you a straight up punk bitch."

Okay, that was unnecessary. I touch the screen in the center of the console. Three red dots appear – the three kids outside the car. I touch the dot that corresponds to the mouthy kid. Whitish-gray foam shoots out from the side of the car and covers the kid from mid-chest down to the street.

"Adhesive foam, "I tell Howler. "It'll dissolve in about thirty minutes." Another thing I learned the hard way.

He's checking out the inside of the car so I'm not sure he heard me. Or cares. The outside of the car resembles a suped-up Ferrari with blacked out windows. The inside resembles a state-of-the-art fighter jet. Lots of lights and buttons and blue screens.

"You know what all this does?" Howler asks.

"About half of it."

We glide through traffic. A few gawkers check us out, but they can't see inside the car. Some Azure City citizens know the Dark Revenger's car. The rest probably think it's a mysterious billionaire driving one part of his exotic car collection.

"I'm taking you back to base," I say. "I need to talk to you about a couple of things."

"Christ, it's freezing in here," Howler says.

"Yeah, the temperature's set on arctic or something. I can't figure out how to adjust it. I asked Master Mind, but he just rolled his eyes."

"How do you open the window?"

His fingers edge search around the door.

"Careful, man. You don't want to push anything in this car unless you know what it does. And the windows don't open."

He gives me a look. "Seriously?"

"Specially treated glass. Bullet-proof. Shatter-proof."

"So that means you can't roll it down?"

"It's thick."

He taps on it. "How thick?"

"That's what she said."

Howler smirks. "Some things never change, huh, Eddie? You can dress up like the grim Dark Revenger, but you're still the smart-ass Puzzler."

I shrug and pretend to concentrate on driving. Really, the car drives itself. But I go through the motions of holding the steering wheel and looking at the screen that shows the display from the side and rear cameras.

"What's with the costume change, though? And the press conferences? You're not acting like him anymore. It's like…"

"Like what?"

"It's like you want people to know you're not him," he says.

"Yeah, maybe, kinda. I mean, what's the fun in being famous if everyone thinks I'm someone else?"

"Eddie," he says with the same tone you'd use to explain curfew rules to an unruly teenager. "The point was to not let people know the Dark Revenger was dead and that you killed him."

Yeah, but…"

The car takes a sharp turn. In a normal car, we would have been thrown against the passenger side door. This car, however, is not a normal car.

"What just happened?"

"Pretty cool, right? The inside is on an independent suspension. It's like a gyroscope. The car could flip over and we'd still be sitting right side up, sipping tea like English royalty."

"Why would we be sipping tea?"

"Nah, I was just, you know, trying to give you an image," I say. "Painting a picture in your head."

"Yeah, but why tea? Why wouldn't you say sipping a beer?"

"I don't know, Howler. Jesus. You haven't changed either."

"Forget it," he says. "Back to my original point. Are you looking to get caught?"

"What? No! Of course not!"

"Good."

"But you know…"

"Shit. Here we go," he says.

"No, I'm just thinking, maybe if we tell people the truth," I say. "Tell them how the Dark Revenger was really the Court Jester. And he was a murderous psychopath who was going to kill you and me. And it was self-defense."

"Yeah, I know, Eddie. You killed him in self-defense."

196

"Don't forget, defense of you, too. I was stopping him from killing you at the time I killed him."

"Hey, bro." He looks at me with an intensity I'm not accustomed to from him. "I ain't ever going to forget what you did for me. You could've left and saved your own ass. But you stayed and saved mine. That means something to me. Okay? That's why you can trust me to watch your back and keep your secret."

The car takes another sharp turn. I'm not even pretending to drive anymore. It speeds up to pass other cars and comes to a stop when we near a red light or a pedestrian.

He says, "So when I say you should listen to me, you should know I have your best interests at heart. Okay? You don't want to tell people the truth. It won't go the way you think. He might've been a psychotic cape, but he was still a cape. Your teammates are gonna turn against you. So will the public."

"We're here."

Howler looks out the windshield and does a double-take.

"What the hell is this? I thought we were going back to Majestic 12's headquarters."

"No. I said base. I didn't say HQ."

We're outside the block-long abandoned warehouse-looking building that served as the Dark Revenger's headquarters. I push a button on the console. With a deep rumble we can feel even through the Dark Revenger Mobile's sophisticated shock absorbers, a section of the brick wall pulls back and slides to the side. We drive inside the building and the wall moves back into place. Hidden scanners check out the car and identify it. Once verified, it only takes a handful of seconds before the floor dips and the car continues downward on a circular ramp. I take my hands off the wheel; the car is on autopilot now.

"I never thought I'd be coming back to this place," Howler says. "I never thought you'd want to, either."

I don't know what to say to that. The truth is, after it happened, I didn't know where else to go. I had to come back and clean up any evidence we left behind.

Howler wanted to just run, and part of me did, too. Run and run until the whole thing faded away like one of those nightmares you wake up from and you still feel the monster's claws slicing through the air at you and your heart threatening to bounce right out of your chest. But then you turn on a few lights and make some coffee, let the hot shower beat on the top of your head. Pretty soon, the nightmare fades away, like flashes of a horror movie you saw long ago, back when you were a kid, and you wonder, *Seriously? I was freaked out by that?*

The thing is, it didn't fade. Howler and I left with promises of laying low for many months and meeting up at some vague point in the future, but while he laid low (lied low? ...whatever...), I came back the next day.

I came back and cleaned up the evidence as best I could. Which is to say, pretty damn good because no one knew the Dark Revenger was dead.

Except Raven.

And Blue Howler.

And...

No, I'm not ready to face that yet.

We reach the bottom and the car comes to an automatic stop on a circular pad that begins turning immediately so the front aims back the way we came. Howler and I step out while the pad is still moving. Overhead lights click on and computer monitors spring to life.

Howler says, "You hang out here a lot?"

"Not so much anymore. But I still come back from time to time."

"After it happened... I was wondering where you went to. Figured you ditched your Puzzler outfit and went legit. Never figured you'd stay here and actually end up becoming the Dark Revenger."

"Yeah?" I say, "What career path would you have predicted for me?"

"Ah, I don't know." Shrugs. "Tending bar and hooking up with rich cougars. Something like that."

"I guess that could've been one way to go. Want a beer?"

"The Dark Revenger drank beer?"

"Nah," I say. "That guy? The only things he had were energy drinks. I got rid of those and stocked the fridge with beer, and harder stuff in some of the storage lockers in the back."

I grab two cold bottles from the mini fridge and hand one to him. He looks at the label and makes a face.

"What?"

He asks, "You got anything domestic?"

"Sorry. I wasn't expecting company."

He pops the cap and drinks anyway. I do the same and we're quiet for a while, just looking around at all of the equipment. I point out some of the cool stuff I discovered during the weeks I prepped to take D.R.'s place. Howler nods and makes appropriate sounds of affirmation. Finally, I get around to it.

"So when did you figure out I took his place?"

"For real, Eddie?" He laughs. "Like, you think the minute I heard the Dark Revenger was back, I didn't start to suspect. And then you're posing for all kinds of pictures. Maybe if you kept the hood up and kept doing the voice, I would've been fooled for a minute. But you couldn't help yourself, could you?"

"Guess not. I've got too much personality to stay in the shadows and clench my jaw."

We clink bottles.

He says, "What I don't get is, how come no one else has figured it out?"

I tell him about Raven. I'm about to mention my other suspicion, but change my mind at the last second. Again, I'm not ready to face it.

"There's other things that feel off about this," I say.

"Like?"

"Like where did this guy come from? The Dark Revenger. Court Jester. Whoever he really was."

"He was both, remember? He had a split personality or something."

I say, "Yeah, no, I get that part. Before he was the Dark Revenger, who was he? I looked into this guy, Jonathan Dantes. He wasn't a billionaire and he wasn't a genius. So where did he get all this? Who built it? How did he pay for it?"

"Jeez, Eddie, who knows? Maybe he inherited his money and buried it somewhere. Maybe he really was some secret inventor."

"Dude, I'm telling you, he wasn't rich. And even if he was some genius inventor, you need money to buy parts for your inventions."

"We back to using 'dude' again?"

"No. Look, I went through everything. The computer files. Any documents or paperwork I came across. Checked every pocket on every piece of clothing. It's like before he was the Dark Revenger, this guy didn't exist. So where did all this stuff come from? The car, the costumes, the gadgets, the friggin' high tech computer system...?"

Howler says, "Buddy, you're overthinking it. He used the money he got from committing crimes as the Court Jester to finance the Dark Revenger identity."

"Except the timeline doesn't add up. The Dark Revenger was around at least two years before Court Jester appeared on the scene."

"Okay, so then maybe he had some secret, you know, person who gave him money."

"Benefactor?"

"Yeah. One of those."

I say, "So where's the benefactor? I've been doing the Dark Revenger gig over six months and nobody's come calling with a bag full of money or a truck full of equipment."

"I don't know," he says. "You're right. Shit don't add up."

We drink a bit. Then:

"What's upstairs?" Howler asks.

"Nothing. Empty floors. It's all for show." I motion around us. "This is the whole set-up right here."

"Listen, you want my advice?" Howler says, "If you win the lottery, you shouldn't question how the numbers were drawn. Just enjoy your luck."

"Yeah, well..."

"Can we get out of here? This place... This ain't for me, man. Too many bad memories. I want to get settled in at Majestic 12's headquarters. Hey, the ninja girl? She seeing anybody?"

I say, "I couldn't tell you, Howler. But I think your chances with her are pretty slim."

"Why? 'Cause I'm blue?"

"You always go to the color thing. No, *not* because you're blue. Because one, you're a friend of mine and that's a strike. Two, you're a reformed supervillain. Hopefully you're reformed if you want to stay on the team. But anyway, she won't like your past, so that's another strike. And three, I'm about ninety-nine percent sure she's gay."

"You think she's gay because she turned you down."

"No." I say, "I think she's gay because I've seen her look at some of the women on the team the way I look at some of the women on the team."

Used to look at some of the women on the team. Now, I just look at one person on the team that way. But I need to shut it down because it's never, ever, never gonna happen between me and her.

Estella, I mean. You probably knew that.

We dump our now empty bottles in the trash and walk back to the car. A flicker of the lights makes me pause. Then I realize it's not the lights. It's the other thing: the world flicker. Whatever it is.

Howler asks, "What?"

Shake my head. "It's nothing."

We get in the car and head back out the way we came.

# CHAPTER 20
*Raven's POV*


"Are you almost ready?" It's the third time I've asked in the past fifteen minutes.

"Just drying off," Celeste calls back and I stifle a sigh of frustration.

I hate being late, and she knows I hate being late. Meanwhile, Celeste is chronically late. So why do I love her?

Then she comes in the room with a towel wrapped around her and drying her hair with another. She flashes me a sheepish smile. Butterfly wings flutter in my stomach and I instantly remember why I love her. Because she makes me feel like *that*.

I'm fully dressed, but without the mask or hood. Those I keep neatly folded and tucked into my belt in case we get an emergency call to go out. The weapons, however… I have them all in various cases and sheaths on my arms and legs, and the sword and mini-scythe are strapped to my back.

Celeste says, "Raven. Honey. Sweetheart."

Now she's using the towel she had used on her hair to dry her legs. I'm both mesmerized and jealous of her ballet dancer legs.

"Yes?" The distraction is obvious in my voice.

"We're going to a team meeting," she says. "Why are you bringing all of those sharp pointy things?"

"You have superpowers. I don't. If anything happens, I'm supposed to run back here and get my equipment?"

She says, "You could just keep a spare set on the ship."

"True."

"You want to help me dry my legs?"

"Then we'd definitely be late."

Can't help it. Now I'm smiling.

Celeste says, "Almost done. I just have to pull on my costume and boots and ice up."

She steps into her tight Cold Snap costume and pulls on the long boots, and I watch with the same intense interest I had when she dried her legs. The same intense interest I have every time she's dressed or undressed in front of me. Because she's just so damn beautiful.

Before she "ices up" (as she calls it), she walks over and kisses me softly. Her lips hold a small chill, as does the rest of her body. I don't jump like the first time she kissed me months ago. I'm used to it.

She's not freezing cold; her body naturally stays several degrees cooler than normal, so kissing her is akin to kissing someone who just stepped out of the ocean after a midnight swim. Part of me is naturally inclined to want to wrap myself around her and warm her with my body. It wouldn't change anything, however. She stays that cool all over no matter what. But God, I love trying.

Celeste smiles. There's a low sound like a spider web of cracks shooting across a frozen lake pond. Her skin turns snowy white and frost covers her hair, down to tiny icicles forming at the ends of each strand. Beautiful.

"Ready?" she asks.

We head out of her apartment and down the hall to the elevators. We pass by my apartment door on the way. Shortly after our first date, I moved into Celeste's living quarters, essentially just using my place for storage purposes.

"Plans this weekend?" she asks. "Because I read a review of this new vegan soul food restaurant that sounds out of this world delicious."

"As long as it's not Sunday," I say. "I promised my parents I'd drive out for a visit."

She says, "Maybe…"

Uh, oh.

"…I could…go with?"

"Um…"

She sighs. "Oookaaayyy. I get it."

"It's just… They don't know. *Yet.*" I stress the last word.

"Hold on. You told me you came out to them."

"I did," I say. "About being a superhero."

"You came out to them about being a superhero, but not about being gay?"

"Bisexual."

Celeste rolls her eyes. "I definitely don't want to have *that* argument again. Okay. Bisexual. However you want to label it. But you didn't tell them you're attracted to women. Or in a relationship with a woman."

"Not yet," I say. "I will. Soon."

Neither one of us has pushed the button for the elevator, so I do it. To change the subject, I say:

"Remember, make sure we don't sit next to *him*."

Celeste laughs and shakes her head. "I still can't figure out why you don't like him. I mean, it's not like you have to worry. Wherever Ballistic sits, that's where the Dark Revenger will sit. He's got it bad for her, you know."

"It's pretty obvious he does, except to her, I think. Or maybe she knows. I don't know. But I still don't like him."

"You've never told me why, though. Sure, in the beginning he was kind of pervy. Always checking us out, making sly comments. I remember when I told him my real name and he said, 'Oh, Celeste. Rhymes with…*you know*. Real easy to remember.' But he's really different now."

"I guess."

The elevator comes and we get in. I remove a glove and place my finger on the scanner pad that unlocks access to the top floor where the meeting room and Master Mind's lab are located.

Master Mind. Another person I don't like.

One floor up, the elevator stops and Amazonia gets in. She has her sword strapped to her hip and her shield on her back. I have the urge to nudge Celeste and motion with my head towards Amazonia. *See? She's bringing her weapons to the meeting. And with her strength and reflexes, she doesn't even really need them.*

There's an awkward pause before Amazonia looks at us and says, "Good morning." Then she goes back to looking at the floor. Celeste and I return the greeting. She raises her head once and sort of half looks our way, opening her mouth like she's going to say something else, but then appears to think better of it and goes back to studying the floor.

I've never understood why Amazonia is so introverted. She's tall and pretty and powerful. She should be the most confident person in the world. Instead, she comes across as a shy high school freshman.

Celeste told me it's always been that way. The only time Amazonia shows confidence is when she's in battle. A true warrior who shines when she's on the battlefield. The rest of the time is all uncomfortable silences and furtive glances.

The elevator opens onto the top floor. No hallway; we're immediately walking into the meeting room, a large circular set-up with large screens, a podium, and a crescent-shaped conference table with eleven chairs.

Yes, counting Master Mind, we're finally up to twelve members. The new members have moved in and gotten acquainted with their teammates and living quarters. Some, like Laser Lance, met with the team's on-staff tailor and had a costume designed. Blue Howler declined the invitation and has stuck to his street clothes.

On the far side of the room is a door that leads to Master Mind's lab and living quarters.

Why is he so far removed from the rest of the team? Up here on the top floor all by himself. He says he needs the extra room for his lab and equipment. Still... I don't like it and I don't like him.

I'm repeating myself, I know.

Speaking of which, the other members are quickly taking their seats or are already seated. Yes, just as Celeste predicted, Dark Revenger is seated at the far end of the table next to Ballistic. I scan the table and take stock of who's here, but really I'm observing him. He has one leg up on the corner of the table, an air of nonchalance about him, but I can tell he's watching me from the corner of his mask.

It's always this way. I enter a room and he could be in the middle of telling a story to a teammate or talking about merchandising plans, once regaling the newer members with the tale of how he defeated Killzore and Dynamo, exaggerated for entertainment purposes. In all those instances, once he took note that I entered the room, he became withdrawn.

Not completely. More like a dimmer switch adjusted on his personality. Then he'd suddenly remember an appointment, or a meeting with Master Mind, or any number of other excuses to leave the room I was in.

The funny thing is, it's true I don't like him. It's also true he knows I don't like him. I just...

I don't know why.

There's a reason. I'm sure there's a reason. But as much as I've gone round and round about it in my head, I don't know what it is.

Master Mind enters from the door on the far side of the room and makes his way to the podium, an oversized remote control in his gloved hand. Always gloves. Always t-shirt, cargo pants, and work boots. And the goggles, either hanging around his neck or pressed up on his forehead. Master Mind may not go in for a colorful superhero costume, but he does have a standard uniform.

Up at the podium, he clicks the remote and the wall behind him switches to two rows of large monitors, all showing different parts of the world and all viewed from several miles up. The number of pictures have grown over the past few months as Master Mind has somehow coopted satellites or managed to launch some of his own.

"Good morning, everyone," he says. "Thank you for being here bright and early. Truthfully, I just wanted an excuse to get Dark Revenger up before noon."

Most everyone chuckles. Dark Revenger smiles and shrugs.

Dark Revenger says, "What? I'm a nighttime vigilante. I don't do mornings."

"Lot of crimes being committed at the C&C Club?" Master Mind asks with a smile, still teasing him, but not maliciously.

"You can't fight crime on an empty stomach," Dark Revenger replies. "No offense to the kitchen staff here, but the appetizers at C&C? That's another level, baby."

Blue Howler says, "Plus, I bet the bartenders there know you like the Whiskey Sours heavy on the whiskey and light on the sour."

More laughter. Dark Revenger gives Blue Howler a grin and a finger gun. I stifle a combination sigh and groan. I'm not sure what I'm doing in this group. I want to be out helping people, not sitting in a high tech meeting room, listening to superpowered man-children trade quips.

"Okay," Master Mind says, getting us back on track. "Let's start off with the good news. We just negotiated with the last remaining holdouts and we have come to an agreement. We can now operate safely, legally, and without interference in every country on the planet. We are sanctioned by every single government on Earth. It took a while, but even the radical countries have come around to the idea that Majestic 12 is a benefit to their people. The bad news is, this will mean more work for us, because not only are we keeping America safe, but we will also be keeping a watchful eye on other countries, as well."

"Watchful eye," Armorgeddon says in his thick Russian accent. "But we will not interfere in foreign government affairs, yes?"

"Good question. No, we are not going to be overthrowing foreign governments or interfering in border disputes between countries. That sort of thing. No, we are only getting involved if there is evidence of superpowered individuals attempting a coup or terrorizing the populace. Or an extradimensional threat. Something like that. The good news is, although there have been isolated reports of individuals across the globe exhibiting superpowers, no one has come forth yet and proven to be a serious threat."

Dark Revenger says, "So, um, every government has agreed to let us just step in if there's trouble?"

"Yes."

"Every one? China, Venezuela, all the ones in the Middle East... If there's a supervillain in Moscow, we're allowed to fly over and apprehend them and not consult with the Russian government first?"

"Yes, Dark Revenger. That's what I said. Every government has agreed to it."

"Even the tiny governments no one's heard of before?"

Master Mind says, "Every. One." He gives Dark Revenger a look, then: "Moving on, things have been pretty quiet lately, so that's good news, as well. Not just throughout the world, but also here in the U.S. The number of superpowered-based crimes are down, which we can conclude that many supervillains have retired thanks to our efforts and our positive press."

"No need to thank me, M.M.," Dark Revenger says. "Good PR is one of my talents."

"Hmpf. Yes."

I roll my eyes and sigh a bit too loudly. Celeste nudges me with her elbow.

"Moving on again," Master Mind says. "There are reports that Simon Simian has been active lately."

Dark Revenger says, "Did a banana shipment go missing?"

Everyone laughs except for me.

Celeste whispers to me, "Oh, come on. It was funny."

Not really. He used the same joke at the press conference.

Master Mind says, "My intel should have his location pinpointed fairly soon. So everyone, be ready to move out at a moment's notice."

"Hey," Dark Revenger says. "I hate to keep interrupting…"

"But?"

By the clipped tone, I think Master Mind's patience is nearing its end.

"But what's going on with the alien invasion?" Dark Revenger asks. "Any updates? What are we doing about protecting the Earth?"

I'm so entranced by Master Mind's surprised expression, it takes me a second to register: Alien invasion. What's he talking about? Is this another setup to a stupid joke he's going to make?

No. Wait. There's something…

I remember. It's hazy, but I remember Master Mind warned of an alien invasion he was trying to prevent. He talked about it months ago, and there have been some discussions since. He was working on an early detection system. It's why he needed the extra satellites.

How could I have forgotten? It's like I'm trying to remember a detailed dream I had months ago. I'm looking at it through a thin veil. I search the faces of my teammates and see similar confusion. Did everyone forget? Everyone except Dark Revenger?

Master Mind says, "Yes. Good, um, good question. Yes. I assure you I'm on top of the situation and will update all of you as soon as, um…as soon as there's something to…to update."

He continues talking and fiddles with the oversized remote. I'm lost in thought. Daydreaming, I guess. The world fades to a grainy black and white picture and I'm having trouble hearing anything other than white noise. Master Mind's lips are moving. Why can't I hear what he's saying? Am I falling asleep? Everything feels so far away.

The world comes back into sharp focus.

"–early warning from the satellites," Master Mind is saying. "Once I have new information, I'll certainly let all of you know."

Wow. I must be more tired than I thought this morning. Hope I didn't miss a crucial piece of information.

"I guess that's it for now," he says. "Please don't go too far from HQ the next two days. I fully expect Simon Simian to make a move, and I want everyone ready to go at a moment's notice."

Chairs are pushed back and multiple conversations start. Master Mind is engrossed in his remote control and looks from that back to the multiple monitors behind him. Armorgeddon pushes back from his chair and nearly bumps into Refraction. Apologies are made. Armorgeddon is a big person, even when he's not in his armor, and doesn't always correctly judge his proximity to people or objects around him.

I'm surprised Celeste didn't make a comment to me about how he didn't feel the need to come to the meeting in his armor, but I insisted on bringing my weapons. Except I see the gleam of metal at his wrists at the edges of his long-sleeved shirt: The two thick silver wristbands he wears that house the nanomachines that will flow over his body and form the high tech armored suit.

See? I want to point out to her that it's always good to be prepared.

I'm so focused on spotting the wristbands and saying, "I told you so" to Celeste that I'm not paying attention and commit the same mistake Armorgeddon almost did. I back my seat away from the table and bump into Dark Revenger.

"I'm very sorry," he says quickly and averts his eyes.

I think he's embarrassed because he was walking and talking to Ballistic at the same time. He probably thinks he was at fault.

"Oh, no, Dark Revenger," I say. "It was entirely my fault. I wasn't paying attention."

He stops and stares at me.

"Um…okay…"

"Really," I say. "My fault. I'm the one who's sorry."

His mouth opens and I wait a beat for whatever he's going to say. He just stares. I give him a smile to let him know everything's okay, and I swear I think he blushes a little.

"Right," he says. "Sure. Uh…thanks. I guess?"

He continues walking with Ballistic, and glances back once over his shoulder.

I tell Celeste, "Wow. I think that's the first time I've seen him flustered. Kind of funny."

And kind of cute, too. I don't say that, of course.

Now Celeste stares at me with her mouth open.

"What?"

She says, "What do you mean 'what?' That's the nicest I've ever seen you act towards him. What happened?"

"What are you talking about?"

We keep our voices low because there are still team members around and there's already enough gossip about us.

Celeste says, "You talked to him like...like you would talk to me. This morning, and pretty much every morning since I've known you, you couldn't stand to be around him. What changed?"

"Celeste, what are you talking about? When did I ever say I didn't like him? He saved my life back at the base. Remember? Saved it *twice*. Don't like him?" I shake my head in disbelief. "He's a hero of mine. He's the Dark Revenger."

# CHAPTER 21

We come swooping in on what used to be Traveler's ship, but now is the official M12 ship. We travel with the hatch doors open, wind blowing our hoods, capes, and hair, flying over farmland and wooded area. Meredith pilots while the rest of us are strapped in like military paratroopers heading into enemy territory. If it wasn't cliché, I'd have Meredith blast *Ride of the Valkyries*.

The ship is mostly silent, except for wind and the roar of Armorgeddon's boot jets as he flies alongside the ship. He prefers to fly using his armor rather than hitching a ride on the ship. I'm not sure why. You'd think he'd want to conserve his armor's power source...whatever it is.

Truthfully, I don't know. Does each nanobot that makes up his armor have its own power source? Microscopic nuclear reactors? Tiny replaceable batteries?

Ah, who cares? It works, whatever it is, and he never seems to run out of juice. But he does get knocked out of commission pretty easily. Case in point:

A missile comes screaming from out of nowhere, catches Armorgeddon full in the chest, and knocks him spinning. He falls out of control down into the trees below. I wish I could say the rest of us are shocked, but this has become commonplace. The guy is a magnet for getting hit.

Laser Lance (remember him?) is still new, so he doesn't take it in stride like the rest of us.

"Shit, man," he says. "Is that guy gonna be alright?"

I say, "Oh, yeah. He'll be fine. His armor is pretty tough. Probably show up later with just bruises after the armor repairs itself."

Or maybe not. Maybe he's dead. If he is, than at least he died doing what he loved: Getting blown out of the sky.

Nah, he'll be fine. I've seen Armorgeddon take a major hit like that on pretty much every mission the past six months, and the worst injury he ever sustained was a broken nose. Maybe one day I'll get to see him in an actual fight. Or maybe we should just paint a big bullseye on him and change his name to "Cannon Fodder."

More shots are fired, a combo of missiles and energy bursts. The ship can take it; the hull is near indestructible. M.M. says it would take a nuclear explosion to get through it, and the bad guys don't have nukes.

I'm not worried something will get through, but the ship bucks from the hits and the exploding rockets, making it feel like we're going through terrible turbulence. My stomach lurches. Estella's across from me. I try to catch her eye, but she's looking out the side hatch. I catch Raven looking at me instead.

She nods and gives me a reassuring smile. I'm so weirded out by her that when I try to return the smile, it comes off as more of a grimace. What the heck is going on with this chick? Suddenly she's friendly?

More shots from below. Camouflaged gun turrets pop up from bushes and trees and fire. Most miss us because we're flying by too fast, and like I said, the few that hit cause only no more than a bumpy ride.

"So much for the element of surprise." Laser Lance again.

He's new to the superhero gig. He doesn't understand the dynamics of what we do:

If it was one or two supervillains, even if they had a handful of henchmen apiece, they wouldn't stick around to fight. They'd have an early warning alarm system and would run as soon as they got the alert we were enroute. But Simon Simian has a team of human henchmen, as well as attack robots and automated weapons systems. He's going to put up a fight before he runs.

I'm not worried. Confidence is my number one superpower.

No, wait, good looks and charm is my number one power. Confidence is number two.

The ship barely touches the ground and we pile out like troops behind enemy lines. We're in upstate New York on a large nondescript piece of land. Camouflaged laser guns pop up from the ground and take aim at us. My forcefield is on, but most of the guns don't have an opportunity to fire: Meredith fires defensive bursts from the newly installed weapons' system on the ship. Another added upgrade thanks to Master Mind. That guy has really made the Majestic 12 a force to be reckoned with.

Meredith isn't able to hit all the guns, though. Too many even for her light speed-like artificial intelligence to zero in on in. For those, Estella is able to run a defensive block and flies through them in a red blur, leaving twisted metal and grinding, tearing gears in her wake. God, I lo–

*Like.*

I *like* the way she takes charge and is proactive.

Whew. Almost made a misstep there. Is there such a thing as a mental Freudian slip?

A section of the ground slides back revealing a metal ramp and a dozen of Simon Simian's CKD robots come rolling out. "CKD" stands for "Crush Kill Destroy," which, back in the day, they used to announce through their chest speakers as they attacked. Simon removed that feature when it regularly became a joke among the bad guys. The 'bots still have the chest speakers, though, but it's just feedback and crackling that comes through now, especially when they're generating electricity through their metal clamp hands.

Really, the "Crush Kill Destroy" thing may have been funny, but it was infinitely less annoying then the constant crackling and loud feedback squeals they put out now. Their metal hands can simultaneously break your bones and electrocute you while bombarding your eardrums like a poorly mixed rock show. As I said, annoying.

Refraction connects three crystals together and generates a red light beam that cuts through five of the 'bots. I shoot my forcefield energy through my gloved fists knocking out four of them in a particularly loud squeal. I swear I think one of them croaks out, "Destroy...?" It nearly causes me to laugh. Howler runs up between us and takes out the remainder with his sonic shout.

I yell, "Nice teamwork, Blue!"

He rolls his eyes.

My forcefield kicks back on. I direct the energy down to my boots and leap forward, shooting up ten feet in the air. It takes a certain amount of concentration to keep the energy focused downward so it acts both as a cushion, but also a springboard to jump again.

When I'm midair, the energy flickers around me as protection from…whatever. A low flying bird or dangling powerlines. I've used the field to bounce off buildings and lampposts, moving down a city street like a human-sized red pinball. My gymnastics training comes in handy; I can keep upright even when I'm bouncing off stuff.

Out here, there's only a few scattered trees, so I'm mostly jumping and running a little. Howler said I look like a hamster in one of those plastic balls when I run. Funny, coming from a guy who looks like a Smurf on steroids.

I didn't say that back to him 'cause, you know, I'm not a dick. Anyway…

A bunch of gun turrets rise up from the ground on our left. Cold Snap is there to blast a wall of ice over them. We keep moving.

A camouflage covered opening leads down into the earth, a brightly lit ramp of sorts which seems stupid. I mean, why have it open and lit like an invitation? You would think it has to be a trap. Except, no surprise, bad guys are just lazy. Henchmen have to carry stuff back and forth and sooner rather than later, they just leave the door open and the lights on out of convenience for themselves.

Problem is, they know we're coming. A bunch of black clad goons stand at the bottom. Part of Simon Simian's crew. I can tell because they have pictures of a gorilla with a raised fist on their chest. And no, I'm not kidding.

They raise laser rifles at us. I toss two stun grenades that knock out a couple and leave the rest dazed. Lady Justice takes out the remainder in a hail of rubber bullets from her twin pistols.

Howler says, "Nice work, L.J."

Now it's my turn to roll my eyes.

I tell the rest of the team the three of us are heading down into the underground base and that the rest should stay up top and continue taking out robots and gun turrets. They're better at long range fighting, while the three of us (Howler, Lady Justice, and myself) are better at close quarter fighting.

Raven suddenly appears next to me.

"Holy crap, where'd you come from?"

Damn her ninja skills!

She winks at me. She actually winks at me. What the hell?

216

We head down. I'm still trying to process the wink. An electrified net flies at us, one of Simon's booby-traps. Raven slices it in mid-air with her razor-sharp katana. We reach a passageway running left to right, goons at both ends. Lady Justice takes out the ones on the left. Every rubber bullet she fires is a bullseye.

Raven takes on the ones on the right. She throws two bolas that trip some of the men while also tossing throwing stars to disarm the rest. She slides down the hallway and makes quick work of them with a flurry of kicks and fist strikes. She's fast. I can copy her moves, but I'd never in a million years be *that* fast.

The henchmen taken out, we have a decision to make: Which way?

Howler and Lady Justice take the left passageway. Raven and I take the right. I wait for one of her patented sarcastic comments or annoyed sighs at being stuck with me. Nothing. She's focused on the job at hand. Weird.

We're going the right way because…

How can I say this? It smells.

You've been to the zoo, I imagine. You know what the monkey cage smells like. That's what I smell.

We reach what I think is Simon's lab/workshop because there are half built robots scattered around, as well as something big in the center that appears to be a huge metal ring. One of those Stargate-type things that maybe is designed to be a teleportation device? I have no idea. Master Mind will tell us once he gets a look at it, probably.

Oh, also, there's a truck tire hanging from a thick rope in the center of the room. Go figure.

The click and powering up of a laser rifle instinctively causes Raven and myself to dive out of the way before the blast hits.

"You!" Simon Simian is up on a catwalk that encircles the room. He has a weird way of talking, mostly due to the fact that he's a super-smart silverback gorilla and his vocal cords weren't made for human speech. Part guttural growl and part articulating.

"I should have known my archnemesis would be the one to show up and foil my plans."

I say, "Archnemesis? Really? Since when? I mean, I don't think you've even been to Azure City, have you?"

"Do not play coy with me, Dark Revenger," he says. "You and I have been locked in a battle of wits for a long time."

"I really don't think that's true."

Raven has managed to quietly reach the catwalk while I've been distracting Simon, which was really not my original intent. I'm honestly perplexed by everyone thinking he and I are archenemies.

He points the laser rifle at me again and I coil my body to dive out of the way, but Raven has gotten close enough to slice at the rifle with her scythe. Ninja skills. Boy, I tell ya.

She catches Simon by surprise and manages to both hook the rifle with her scythe and also pull it from his massive gorilla fist. Then she flings it out of reach off the catwalk. It CLATTERS to the floor below. Simon roars at her.

Raven is smart enough to backflip away from him. She can't take him in a fight. He's a gorilla, after all. He lunges for her, but she clambers up the metal beams out of his reach.

"Give it up, Magilla," I say. "The rest of the team is here. You're caught."

"Damn you, Dark Revenger," he says and decides to stop chasing Raven.

He gorilla runs, his arms and legs propelling him, the other way towards a big metal seat located at the far end of the catwalk. It's a massive chair attached to oddly shaped steel plating, and at first I think it's some sort of weapon, like maybe it'll turn into a rotating gun. But the metal flooring it sits on detaches and slides out. It's a hovercraft chair designed for just him.

The chair hums and floats as a section of the ceiling opens to reveal a tunnel leading up and out.

"Goodbye for now, Dark Revenger," he says. "Like all true adversaries, you and I are destined to fight again."

"Stop saying that! We're not true adversaries! Or arch-anything!"

Really, I can't take this anymore.

The chair floats upward. I jump, propelling myself as high as I can with the forcefield energy shooting down through my boots and giving me a good fifteen to twenty foot boost. It's not enough to reach him, but at the same time, I swing my arm grappling gun from around my back, snap it into place, and fire the hook and cable up. It snags the chair and yanks me up with it. I retract the cable; it pulls me closer and closer.

Not sure if it's the added weight of me dangling from the bottom of the hoverchair, or the position of my grapple hook clamped to the underside of the chair's mechanism, or combination thereof, but the hoverchair is seriously wobbling. Simon peers over the side and sees me just as we're up and out of the tunnel and floating over the ground. He roars again and shakes his fist.

Hard to do this one handed, yet somehow I manage to pull out two concussion grenades from my belt. Takes a little finesse because the grenades are smaller than military issue ones, but still pack a "bang." I toss them up and over into Simon's lap. BOOM! And now the chair is really out of control.

We go down. I unhook from the cable and manage to cushion my landing with the forcefield. Simon isn't so lucky. He hits hard and rolls, the chair crashing nearby and scattering pieces everywhere.

"Curse you, my archnemesis," he says.

I yell, "Stop calling me that! I don't even know you!"

He looks hurt from the fall, but he braces his knuckles on the ground to charge at me anyway. Then Estella slams into him and sends him sprawling fifty feet back. He doesn't get up for a while.

***

Later, after he's been secured in an extra thick cage and being readied for transport, I ask him,

"Hey, Grape Ape, what was that round thing you were working on down there?"

He laughs, although it sounds more like grunting than anything else.

"I will admit, I didn't get very far with it. Time travel is a more complicated process than one would imagine."

"Whoa. You were working on a time machine? I'm impressed," I say.

"*Was* working on it," he says.

He grunts again, which maybe is a laugh. Or maybe just a grunt. Who knows?

"Not sure I could ever get it finished. But I was willing to try."

"Where were you going to time travel to?" I ask. "The future when monkeys are in charge?"

"No, Dark Revenger. I wanted to travel *back* in time to before the Majestic 12 started taking over the world."

"What the hell does that mean? We're not taking over the world."

"Aren't you? Maybe humans don't see what's happening. But I do."

He stares at me and I feel like the earth is opening up to reveal a bottomless pit beneath me. I shake it off.

"Ah, you're just a sore loser," I say. "See you around, Magilla. Next time I'm at the zoo, I'll say 'hi' to your mom for you."

Simon goes nuts and slams against the bars at me. I'm already walking away.

I spot Estella talking to a military officer. Yeah, we had to call in the military to take Simon Simian somewhere secure. Unlike his paid goon squad, the county jail isn't secure enough to hold a silverback gorilla that can shoot a gun, drive a car, and build a doomsday weapon.

"Hey," I say.

"Hey," she says.

"Talk a sec?"

"Sure."

We walk a few feet away from prying ears. I say,

"Just wanted to say 'thanks' for knocking out Dr. Zaius back there when he was getting ready to charge me."

"Wasn't Dr. Zaius an orangutan?" she asks.

"Yeah, but I ran out of stupid names to call him, so…" I shrug. "Anyway, was just wondering if, as a way of thanking you, I could, maybe, you know, um, buy you dinner?"

Her mask. I can't read her expression. I know she's staring at me. Other than that, I have no idea what's going through her head.

I say, "What do you think? Yes? No? Maybe? You already have plans? Don't want to? No? Is the answer no? Are you thinking about it? No? No, you don't want to? Can't tonight? Think it's a bad idea? Some other time? No? Is the answer no?"

She says, "Could you stop talking for a second?"

"I can try."

"My answer is… Okay."

# CHAPTER 22

*The Cape & Cowl Club*, or "C&C" as most everyone calls it, is the trendiest and most exclusive restaurant/nightclub in Azure City, with a satellite location on the West Coast, and sister locations throughout the world: Paris, London, Dubai… Even one in Moscow, although I hear the food sucks.

You have to be a superhero to get in. Or rich. Or influential. Or preferably all three. Security is tight and the wait list to get a reservation is very long. But if you're a member of the Majestic 12, there's no issue getting in.

Ex-superheroes and even some ex-supervillains work the door and act as bouncers when the need arises, although it rarely does. The worst that ever happens is someone wants to show off their powers (an automatic ejection from the club and a probationary period before being let back in), or someone tries to sneak a video of who is hanging out with whom (also a no-no). The club thrives on its privacy.

The food in the restaurant section is great, the menu ever-changing depending on which visiting world renowned master chef is in charge. The club section is sometimes just a dance club with a DJ. There are musical acts occasionally, and comedy showcases a few nights a week. Speaking of:

The maître d' says, "Dark Revenger, just dinner tonight or will you be doing a spot next door? I can tell Brad to add you to the lineup."

Brad Whittaker is the club side's manager and books all the talent. If I wanted a spot, I could call him myself. Hell, sometimes I just show up and Brad adds me to the roster.

I forgot it was comedy night.

"Just dinner tonight," I tell him.

He nods, grabs two menus, and leads the way to our table. Even through her mask, I know Estella is lining up a dozen questions.

The maître d' seats us at a table that is not as private as I would have hoped, but it's busy tonight and I neglected to call ahead. He says,

"Your usual table is occupied. I can move you once it's open."

"This one is fine," I say.

Not really. It's too bright and out in the open. Everyone's looking; I feel their hot little stares. But what am I going to do? Make a scene? I don't want Estella to think I'm a spoiled jerk. Because I'm not. Anymore.

I checked my cape at the front, so there's no awkward fumbling with the material before I sit. Too late I realize my faux pas. The maître d' is holding the chair for Estella.

I rush out of my seat to hold the chair, but he's already sliding it under Estella. He gives me a small smile as if to say, "No worries. I took care of it for you. Since you're such a classless person."

Asshole. Or maybe I'm reading too much into the smile. Who's to say?

I sit across from her. The maître d' hands us the menus and places the wine list on the table. He gives me a polite nod and wanders off to mentally insult someone else.

The restaurant is classy without being ostentatious: Lots of black and white colors, plain looking china and silverware. All expensive, though.

Estella says, "What did he mean by asking if you were doing a spot?"

"Oh, uh, I sometimes come by the club on comedy night and, you know… Do a few minutes of standup."

"Wow. I had no idea."

"Yeah, you know…" Why am I so uncomfortable all of a sudden? "Nothing big. Got my tight five. That um, that means I've got a solid five minutes of material. Solid jokes. Sometimes I try out new material. I've also emceed a few times."

Jeez, I feel like I'm admitting to something embarrassing. What's wrong with me? Besides not wanting her to think I'm a loser or something. (Guess I answered my own question.)

She says, "I didn't know that was something you were into. I mean, it makes sense. You do like to perform in front of an audience. And you're funny."

"Thanks."

The waiter arrives and we go through perfunctory exchange of hellos because I'm a regular and he's certainly seen me before, usually with different dates. He's discrete and doesn't mention it.

Too bad. I had a story about bringing my extended family of sisters, nieces, and cousins out for dinner. Although, in all honesty, I haven't brought anyone here in a while.

I let Estella order the wine because I'm clueless about such things. She says something in French, which coincidentally is the name of the wine, and the waiter seems pleased by her choice. He wanders off and I pretend to study the menu.

"You come here a lot?" she asks. "Not just the club, but the restaurant?"

I shrug. "I guess."

"You bring all of your dates here?"

I wonder if mind reading is a power of hers I didn't know about.

"I've *brought* dates here, yes. But not for a while. Lately, I come here and do a set next door. Sometimes I just hang out at the bar and read."

"Read?"

"Yes."

"Books?"

"Yes," I say. "Books."

I'm waiting for her to say, "Real books?" To which I'll reply, "Are there any other kind?"

But instead she nods and says,

"You're quite the mystery, Dark Revenger."

I don't know what to say to that, so I say, "How are you going to eat with the mask on?"

"Good point," she answers. "The Ladies Room is which way?"

I point it out to her and I'd be lying if I said I didn't watch her walk away. Then my phone rings. I remove it from my belt pouch and see it's Amira.

Seriously? *Now* she's calling?

"Hello, Dark Revenger," she says. "Are you busy this evening? I thought we could work on some of those moves you inquired about."

Translation: I made you wait long enough. Tonight is the night your patience pays off.

"Hi, Amira. Unfortunately, I can't this evening. I hope you understand."

Translation: I may have lost my mind.

223

She says, "Tonight would be a perfect time. Are you sure?"

Translation: Have you lost your mind?

"I can't, Amira. I'm not available for sparring tonight."

Translation: Yes. Yes, I've definitely lost my mind.

"I'm not sure there will be another opportunity."

Translation: You're not gonna get a second chance, dumbass.

I say, "To be honest, Amira, I think I'm okay on the sparring thing. I appreciate everything you've done for the team."

Translation: I'm not trying to hurt your feelings, but best to burn this bridge with you now because I'm with someone that I actually care about and actually care what she thinks about me, and I don't want any more meaningless trysts or physical relationships that go nowhere. I want someone who makes me want to be the best person I can be, and although I don't feel like I am the best person I can be, when I'm with her there seems to be this potential for me to maybe come close to it, if not actually one day achieve it. Understand?

She says, "Are you serious?"

Translation: It's official. You have lost your mind.

"Yes."

Translation: Probably.

"Good luck with your next sparring partner," she says and hangs up.

Translation: Don't ever call me again, you stupid son of a bitch.

Estella's back just as I'm putting the phone away, and oh my sweet lord, she's beautiful. She's removed the full face mask and is wearing a domino one the same red as her hair and costume. I get lost in her sparkling eyes.

"Wow," is all I can think to say.

"What?" A slight smile playing at her lips.

"You're just…wow. Why don't you get rid of the full mask and just wear that one?"

"I'm trying to maintain a secret identity," she says.

"Does the banker know about your super alter ego?"

"The banker?" It takes a second for her to get it. "You mean Enrique? When you said the banker, I thought you meant a new supervillain called The Banker."

I say, "I couldn't remember his name. That's why I call him the banker."

"I've told you his name probably a dozen times."

"Still can't remember it. What was it again?"

"Doesn't matter." She suddenly becomes very interested in the menu. "We, um, stopped seeing each other a few weeks ago."

"Oh. That's a shame."

Yep, a real friggin' crying shame.

The waiter comes back with the wine and tells us the specials. Estella orders the salmon because she's a woman and women like to order salmon (or salads). I order one of the specials, although I have no idea if it's made with chicken or beef, and I make a show of tasting the wine and nodding to the waiter like it's good. Truthfully, I barely taste it and have no idea what the specials are because my mind is playing "stopped seeing each other" over and over again on a never-ending loop.

Once the waiter leaves, I decide to subtly broach the subject of her break-up.

"So you broke up with the banker."

Come on. You know I can't be subtle.

"It was a mutual decision," she says.

"Hm."

She raises an eyebrow. "You think I'd be having dinner with you if I was still seeing Enrique?"

I say, "I don't know. I wasn't sure if we were just two work colleagues having dinner, or if this was, you know... A date."

"What do you want it to be?"

"A date."

She raises her wine glass. I raise mine and clink it against hers.

"A date, then," she says. "Just so you know, I'm not asking for a commitment, but I also don't intend to be another notch on your utility belt. So if that's what you're looking for–"

"Nope. Not what I'm looking for," I say. "I'm not seeing anyone else either."

We clink glasses again. Are we the cutest couple ever, or what?

After that is some small talk. Work stuff, but also tidbits about ourselves. We also check out the other patrons. For every A List superhero, there's about a dozen B Listers sitting at their table and laughing at their jokes. We also see a good number of well-known celebs, some popular socialites, a Pulitzer prize-winning journalist, and a Nobel Peace prize recipient. No other members of M12, though, which I'm secretly relieved about. I hate work gossip. Unless it's about someone else.

Inevitably, we talk about the team and how we think each member is doing. Out of the blue, I say,

"Kind of sorry I didn't get to join sooner. I would have liked to have met Infinity."

Estella asks, "Who's Infinity?"

I wait to see if she's messing with me. The blank look says she isn't.

"Infinity. You know… One of the original members of Majestic 12. Probably the most powerful member."

Slow shake of her head. She really has no idea who I'm talking about.

**Infinity's Origin Story:** Reverend Harker Lang was one of a group of civilian witnesses to a 1943 experiment using electromagnetic energy to make Navy ships invisible. Something went wrong, as they are apt to do in these kinds of things, and when the smoke cleared, a lot of the ship's crewmembers were dead, missing, or driven insane. As for Lang, he was the only person left in a room that originally held thirty-nine. The others were just…gone.

Theory was that they all fused together into one person, with Lang being the focal point. He had abilities, too, able to shift between dimensions and teleport. He also sometimes had knowledge of future events, although that seemed to be sporadic and didn't always come true – something he attributed to being able to see into parallel universes and not always knowing which future he was seeing.

He wasn't much of a superhero, but more of supernatural/spiritual advisor to the team. He appeared in public only a handful of times between the 1940's and the present, always seemingly ageless, and when he was using his powers, he appeared as a man-shaped rip in the time/space continuum. Pretty freaky looking; you could see stars and galaxies whirling around inside him.

Then, about two years ago, poof. He was gone. The team never talked about it. Now, I'm beginning to realize why.

"You don't have any idea who I'm talking about?"

She says, "No. There are plenty of superheroes I've never met and am unfamiliar with, but I know *every* member, past and present, of Majestic 12."

I shrug. "Maybe I'm mixing him up with someone else. No big deal."

She gives me a look like she's not quite buying it, but what am I going to do? Spoil the date with my conspiracy theories? I quickly change the subject and we talk about other things.

As usual, the food is outstanding. I still don't know what it was I ordered. Tasted like chicken. It was good, whatever it was.

The conversation is flowing and engaging. We talk. We laugh. We finish the bottle of wine. By the end of the date, I'm in love with her. But if I'm being honest, I already was.

Estella offers to pay for her half of the bill. I wave her off. I've got this. I'm a gentleman, after all. Also, much like the other times I've been here, I'm just going to charge it to the Majestic 12 account. Master Mind loves when I do that. (Sarcasm.)

She excuses herself so she can change her mask back. While I'm collecting my cape, I mull over our conversation about Infinity and what it means that she doesn't remember him. I'm willing to bet no one else remembers him, either, and I wonder what this all means.

Except I know what it all means and I've known for a long time. It means everything is a lie. The real question I should ask myself is, how long am I going to keep lying to myself and avoid the obvious?

Then Estella's back and even though her face is fully covered, I still get that little jolt of electricity and my heart beats a little quicker.

We walk the few blocks to the Dark Revenger Mobile. I got tired of people trying to get through the protective field to get a closer look (or throw rocks to watch them bounce off), or paparazzi staking it out to get photos of me. You probably wonder why that would bother me since I usually love being in the press. Good point, but sometimes I want my privacy.

Master Mind worked up a hologram projector so the car appears to be ordinary, something you'd walk by on a city street without a second glance. There's a variety to choose from: Tonight, I went with the mud brown, rusted-out Buick with the cracked taillights.

I switch the projector and the protective field off.

"Lift home?" I ask.

This is the point of the evening where I'd try to keep the date going. More drinks. Flirting. Invite myself back to her place. Say an obvious line: "The night is young and so are we." Something stupid like that.

I'm not going to ruin the evening, though. This one's special. I'm not going to rush anything or treat her…well, the way I *used* to treat women.

"It's a nice night," she says. "I'm going to fly home."

"Your home? Or HQ?"

"Mine. Early morning meeting with company board members."

Ugh. I sometimes forget she runs a company.

She says, "It was fun. Thank you for dinner."

"Is it okay if I ask for a kiss goodnight?"

*Ask* for a kiss? Where did that come from? I really am in love.

I sense the smile beneath her mask. She looks around to see if anyone's watching, then lifts the bottom of her mask up enough to uncover her mouth. She leans in and kisses me on the cheek.

Before I can say, "That's not what I meant when I asked for a kiss goodnight," she's fixed her mask and shot up into the air. And now it's my turn to smile.

***

228

Back in my Dark Revenger underground base. Feels like I spend more and more time here lately. Should be a good night, right? I should be celebrating that I had a great dinner, and even greater conversation, with Estella. Except a gloom has fallen over me, and whenever I'm feeling particularly gloomy, I come here. Which, as I've said, seems to be more and more often these days.

The last Dark Revenger was a psychotic loon, but somehow he built this high tech base and invented cool gadgets, like the grappling gun/arm attachment thingy and a car that does all kinds of fantastic things. There's no evidence he was a great inventor or a billionaire orphan, so how did he build this stuff? If he didn't do it, then where did he get the money to buy it? Was he the Court Jester first, stole stuff, and then became the Dark Revenger?

No. The Dark Revenger was around before Court Jester made his supervillain appearance. I'm sure of it. Pretty sure. Reasonably sure.

Let's look at the other facts:

I take his place. A few people (Raven) spot it right away. Most everyone else goes along with it. As time goes on, they become more accepting of it. Raven becomes accepting of it. She hates me, now she likes me.

Am I that charming? Stupid question. Of course I am.

But there's more going on there. What else…?

The most powerful superheroes start having problems. Speed Demon's powers get out of control and he dies. Judgment Day is murdered. Traveler turns out to be an alien android bomb and tries to murder the rest of the team, along with his girlfriend/alien computer program that goes from murderous to as-safe-as-a-household-appliance in the same day…and no one questions it.

Oh, and Infinity disappears and Estella doesn't know who that is. A member of the Majestic 12 doesn't know who one of the founding members is. Like, at all.

I start typing on the Dark Revenger computer. Whoops, better close some of those porn tabs. How did those get on there? (Ahem).

I type "Infinity" and get what you expect: Stuff about the mathematical value of, the name of a car, some book and movie titles... I type "superhero Infinity." Nothing. I type "Harker Lang." Nothing. I type "Majestic 12 superhero team" and get lots of stuff. Articles. Pictures. News videos. And Infinity is not in any of them. Not in the pictures. Not in the videos. Not in the articles.

I even type in "Philadelphia Experiment" to see if he's mentioned in any of that, even if it's just his civilian name. Stuff about the experiment, legend of and various conspiracy theories, but nothing about Infinity, and no mention of Harker Lang. He's been wiped from reality.

My hands shake a bit and there's a white hot burning in my stomach that screams at me not to do it, but I type "Dark Revenger" into the computer. Lots and lots of stuff. Not as much as what I got when I typed "Majestic 12." Still a good amount, though.

News articles. Blog posts about. Theories about whether there was a Dark Revenger in the 1930s and 40s. Then the modern stuff.

Funny thing? No videos or pictures of the last Dark Revenger. If there's a video or a pic, it's of me. Me in the old costume. Me in the current one. The classic security cam footage that originally proved there was a modern day Dark Revenger and it wasn't an urban legend? The one that got played over and over again on the news a few years back? Gone.

It's like...

It's like I'm the Dark Revenger and I always was.

I'm not crazy, am I? I suppose if I was a weak minded person, that idea would last longer than the nanosecond it takes to be completely dismissed from my mind.

No, I'm not crazy. I might be the only sane person left in the world.

You know what I should do? Switch the computer off, get in the car, head back to M12 H.Q. and just enjoy life. Enjoy the fame, the perks. Enjoy the fun of being one of the world's most famous superheroes.

Yeah, that what I should do. That's what I'm *going* to do.

"Dark Revenger."

"Shit!" I whirl around in my chair. "Who...?" I wish my voice didn't sound so squeaky, like I just had the ever-loving shit scared out of me.

She steps out of the shadows and pushes back her black hood. Stealthshadow. Raven.

"How did you get in here?"

Hell, how did she even know about this place? Damn her ninja skills!

I stand up because if she's here to fight – and I can't think of why else she would go to the trouble of tracking me here and entering without setting off the two dozen or so alarms on this place – I want to be ready. At the same time, the rational part of my brain is saying, "Stupid, if she came here to kill you, she wouldn't have said your name first. She would have just done it."

"Sorry about showing up unannounced," she says. "I really need to tell you something, and I wanted to make sure we were completely alone."

"Okay."

"Back at headquarters, there's always other people around."

"Sure," I say. I wish she'd just get to it. "What's on your mind?"

Crap, I hope we're not going backwards to when she hated me. I was getting accustomed to the idea of her not wanting to vomit every time she sees me.

She says, "You may or may not know I'm in a relationship with Celeste."

"Who's Celeste? Oh, right, Cold Snap!" I say. "Hey, good for you two! Glad to hear it."

She moves closer. There's pain and anguish on her face.

"Celeste loves me," she says. "And I think I love her, too."

"Great. But you don't look happy about it. What's the issue?"

What, does she want my blessing or something? She wants me to issue a press release maybe? Or wants me to keep quiet about it, in which case, why tell me in the first place?

She's standing right in front of me. Practically toe-to-toe. Or boot-to-boot, in our case.

"The issue is, I find that I'm in love with you, too."

For the first time in my life, I open my mouth and absolutely nothing comes out.

She's standing there, waiting. Waiting for me to profess my own love for her and kiss her.

Or waiting for me to tell her to go back to her girlfriend.

Or she's not my type.

Or to kiss her and tell her we can be together, but it'll just be our little secret.

Or to tell her she's crazy, she can't possibly be in love with me.

She's waiting for me to tell her any number of things, although from the way she has her head upturned towards mine, I know what she desperately wants is for me to kiss her.

A few months ago, I'm ashamed to say I would have definitely seized this opportunity. But a lot has happened in the past few months.

I take a step back and sit down with a heavy sigh.

"Shit," is all I can think to say.

# CHAPTER 23

The underground supervillain club, *The Hideout*, has seen better days. Two people at the bar, not counting the bartender, and three people on the dance floor. That's it. The security robots aren't even powered up. The one at the door has dust on it.

The three people on the dance floor, I think, are reality show stars. They're certainly not A or B Listers. The two at the bar are D List villains: The Slime, recognizable by the fact that he's perpetually greasy looking because his pores exude a Crisco-like coating that makes him hard to hold onto (not that you'd want to touch him anyway), and Forgettable Frank, whose power (if you can call it that) is he's nondescript and hard to spot in a crowd.

Jeez, what happened here?

The bartender, a former supervillain named Powerpunch, is a big, balding guy who goes by Johnny these days and has been tending bar for as long as I've been coming here. He spots me as soon as I walk in.

"Puzzler?"

"Hey, Johnny," I say.

Yeah, it feels weird wearing the Puzzler suit again. But my thought was, if I come here as the Dark Revenger, I'd have a hundred people attacking me. Had I known the club was a half-step away from becoming a ghost town, I probably would've done it.

"Holy shit," he says. "Where've you been? I figured you retired. Or died."

"Ah, it's a long, boring story," I tell him. "I guess I kind of retired."

Sort of true.

"What the hell happened here? Where is everyone?"

Johnny smirks. "The goddamn Majestic 12 happened. I'm sure you know they took up residence in Azure City. Lot of folks in our community left town. Or retired. Nobody wants to do *anything* with that super-team flying around our backyard. You know?"

"Makes sense."

"What the hell, your old buddy, Blue Howler, even went straight and joined their team."

"Yeah," I say. "I heard. Never could trust that guy."

"Yeah, can you believe it? He joined the other side. Wonder how long he planned that."

I say, "He was always shifty. I bet he never even payed my bar tab here like he swore to me he would."

"He was supposed to do that for you?" Johnny says, "Man, I always thought he was a stand up kind of guy. Um...speaking of tabs, uh..."

"Yeah, Johnny, I know. Sorry, I think I left my cash in my other costume. Could I get you guys next time?"

"Sure, Puzzler, but if you want a drink tonight, sorry, it's cash up front. Nothing against you. We're doing that for everybody these days. Business being so bad and all."

I say, "No problem. I'm not drinking tonight. I really need to see Savant."

"Sure, sure, sure. Let me tell him you're here."

Johnny heads down to the other end of the bar to call Savant, although I'd be surprised if he didn't already know I was here and asking for him. I've been inside his office more than once; he's got cameras and microphones all over this place and he watches everything. Probably spotted me long before I walked through the door.

The Slime says to me, "You lookin' for a crew?"

"Nah. I'm good, thanks."

"Suit yourself." And goes back to his beer.

Johnny says, "Puzzler, he said come on back"

Savant is at his desk, tinkering with something. As predicted, he's also watching fifty different security monitors at the same time.

"Puzzler," he says without looking up. "To what do I owe the pleasure?"

"How've you been, Savant?"

He waves around at the monitors. "As you can see, business is terrible. I had to let most of the staff go. I'm considering closing up and moving the business elsewhere. New York or LA, possibly. Or maybe the moon. But then there's the operating costs of supplying an atmosphere. And many people are afraid of using a transporter. The whole religious/philosophical argument of whether the transported person is the real person or a clone. 'Does my body get destroyed and I die while a copy of me goes on thinking it's the real me?' I'm sure you've heard the debates."

Yes, and to be honest, the idea of using a transporter has always kind of freaked me out for those same reasons.

He says, "Besides, I've never made a transporter. You know my specialty is electronics. When it comes to biology, I'm at a loss. I would have to bring on a partner, and there aren't many super geniuses left."

"What do you mean?"

"Many have retired. Or faded away. I'm even thought of retirement. What's the use of running a club for supervillains if many are retiring or too afraid to come by?"

"Good point," I say. "But what are you gonna do, Savant? I can't see you working the tech repair counter at an electronics store."

"I could patent some of my inventions. Here." He pulls a pair of earbuds from his desk drawer and tosses it to me.

"Wow. Earbuds," I say. "And with wires. You know they've had wireless ones for a long while. What else are you working on, Savant? A CD player?"

"Funny. Yes, I know there are wireless earbuds, and there are people who don't like them because they fall out easily or one gets lost. But those? Those wires won't tangle. You can keep those. Put them in your pocket and walk around with them. You'll see they won't tangle."

"Oh. Actually, you know what? That *is* a good invention," I say.

He spreads his hands. "My nightclub is failing and my business of supplying gadgets to supervillains is failing. There. Now we have the chitchat out of the way. What is it you want, Puzzler? Or is it something the Dark Revenger wants?"

I swear, I almost feel the room spin when he says it. I recover nicely.

"Whaaaaat? Whatcha talkin' about there, Savant. Dark Revenger? Why…that guy? You know, heh, yeah, sure, I can see why you'd, you know… There's um, there's a slight resemblance with the hair and all. I mean, uh, you know… I wish. I wish I was a charming, handsome, successful superhero. Heh."

Yep, I handled that like a pro.

"Puzzler," he says, like he's explaining something to a child, "just because you switch one mask for another, it may fool the casual observers, the people who only catch sight of you for a minute. But do you really think I could watch those interviews you like to give, the news conference where you danced with the reporter, and not know it was one of my former best customers? I suppose you put on a pair of eyeglasses when you're in your secret identity and no one recognizes you, either?"

"I don't have a secret identity anymore. I'm always the Dark Revenger these days."

"Sounds dreadfully boring."

"You'd be surprised. It's actually a lot of fun. So, are you going to rat me out?"

He makes a face like I said the most preposterous thing. "I'm many things, but a rat? Never. And neither are you, or else I expect the Majestic 12 would've raided us months ago." He shrugs. "Then again, a quarter of your team are made up of former supervillains: You, Blue Howler, and Master Mind."

I say, "M.M. doesn't like the term 'supervillain.'"

Another shrug, then he says, "So what do you need from me, Dark Revenger? You already have access to one of the most brilliant minds on the planet. Why are you here in my office?"

"Essentially…" I pull the slip of paper from my pocket. "I jotted this down. It's a bit rambling, but this is what I think is happening and I need something to stop it from doing what it's doing."

He reads the paper. "Uh huh. Uh huh." Pause, then, "Uh *huh.*"

"Can you do it?" I ask.

"Of course. When do you need it by?"

"ASAP."

"ASAP," he says.

"As soon as possible."

"I know what ASAP stands for," he says. "I was just repeating it."

"Okay."

Savant sighs, leans back in his chair. He looks up at the ceiling for so long, I glance up there to see if he has a monitor installed over his desk. He doesn't. He's running the calculations in his head.

"This…," he says. "This will be difficult. But not impossible. It will require materials that I don't have, so I will have to hire a team to procure them. Once it's built, I'll need a tremendous power source to make it work. Most likely, I'll have to tap into the power grid of a major metropolitan city. Not Azure City, though, for obvious reasons. And you want this right away, so that means I'll be working around the clock, starting right now. This will cost you a lot of money."

"Yeah, uh, like I told Johnny out there, I didn't bring any cash. Maybe we can do like we used to with the puzzle boxes and I can do a pay as we go kind of thing?"

Savant laughs. "You're a famous superhero, Dark Revenger. You have money. I'm sure Majestic 12 pays a nice salary. Let's have a look."

Savant waves his hand over a section of his desk. A computer screen folds up, along with what looks like a thin pane of glass. Numbers and letters appear on the glass and Savant types.

"Let's see," he says. "Everyone on the team has an account at the same bank? That's convenient. Here's yours and… Oh. Goodness. They certainly pay well. No wonder you switched sides."

"Some of that is merchandising," I say. "And a book advance."

He gives me a raised eyebrow. "Any qualms about me withdrawing my fee?"

"No. How much are you going to take?"

He's typing as he says, "All of it. And you'll still owe me a little. Plus your bar bill."

I sigh. Easy come, easy go.

"Give me a couple of days," he says. "I'll call when it's ready to go live."

"Sooner the better, Savant."

Before I leave his office, I ask, "If you can get money that easily, why haven't you drained the other team members' accounts? Why haven't you been doing that all along?"

"I'm not a rat," Savant says, "and I'm not a thief, either. I have a moral code. Don't you?"

"Yeah," I say. "Funny enough, it appears I do."

# CHAPTER 24

It's been a week.

Okay, it's been five days. Feels longer.

With the exception of one quick trip I made out to see Savant for a small favor that, after his eye rolling and grousing I attribute more to his lack of sleep than his unwillingness to help me, he agreed. Cost me a week's pay, which technically I don't have yet, but he knows I'm good for it.

Not a lot of choice on the matter. I agreed, so he'll withdraw the money from my account. If I survive, I guess. Or maybe even if I don't.

Anyway, it was something I really needed, so I was willing to pay whatever. Then I asked him how the big project was going. He grumbled about calling me when it was done and shooed me out of his office.

Most of the past few days I've spent hanging out at my Dark Revenger base, avoiding everyone as best I can. Luckily there hasn't been an emergency that's required the whole team. I told Master Mind, via text, that I was working on M12 promo stuff and unraveling some merchandising issues. He replied, also via text, "No problem."

Estella's tried calling a few times. I don't trust myself to take the calls. Texts are safer. She's concerned and wondering if I'm avoiding her. I texted no, she's the one person I don't want to avoid. But I'm working on something and soon it'll all make sense. She asked if she did something or said something wrong the other night at dinner. I responded, no, you did everything right.

I sense the confusion from her printed words. I'm sure she's going over everything in her head and wondering what the hell happened to me, why I'm avoiding her and the team. Really, it's not her I'm avoiding. It's Raven and her love-struck, puppy dog eyes. Also, I don't know how much is being monitored in H.Q., so best to avoid the place altogether.

Howler called yesterday. "Dude, where the hell you been?"

"Again with the 'dude?' Look," I said. "I promise I'll never use the word again if you stop calling me that."

He laughed. "Sorry. I'll try, alright? But seriously, where you been? You holed up somewhere with some model? And if you are, does she have any friends that like the color blue?"

"Hey, just out of curiosity, what do you remember about joining the Majestic 12?"

"Hell, I don't know," he said. "You decided to join the superhero side. Became the Dark Masturbator. Seemed like you were having fun. I kind of blackmailed you to accept me on the team, but not really. I'm having fun. Nice having people want to take their picture with me 'stead of calling the cops."

I asked, "What about Court Jester?"

"Um, what about him? Nobody's seen that psycho for a long time. Hoping it stays that way."

"Yeah."

"Why are you bringing him up? I had that job lined up with him and you wanted no part of it," Howler said. "You talked me out of it. I could've been set for life."

"Yeah," I said. "I figured you'd remember it that way."

"Hey." Howler chuckles. "I'm kidding, man. I'm not mad you talked me out of it. It all worked out in the long run. Look where I am now."

"Yeah."

"Thanks for getting me onto the team. You're a good friend. You've always had my back."

"Yeah. You're welcome. I, uh… I better go. Got some stuff to take care of. I'll talk atcha soon."

"Sure. Whenever you want."

"Okay. Oh, hey, Howler?"

"Yeah?"

"I love you, man."

"Gay," he said and hung up.

That was yesterday. Today, my phone rings and it's Savant.

"It's done," he says. "Should I power it up?"

"Wait twenty minutes," I say.

"Sure."

The drive to H.Q. flies by, partly because I've got the cloaking device on that makes the Dark Revenger Mobile look like an Azure City police car, so everyone is quick to get over to the right lane and let me pass, and partly because my mind is in turmoil over a bunch of things:

What am I going to say? What am I going to do? Do I really want to do anything? Maybe I should call Savant and tell him to forget the whole thing? Scrap the device?

My mind goes over it in a loop, but soon enough I'm pulling into the Majestic 12 parking garage and switching the cloaking device off. I park in between Howler's new motorcycle (already spending his M12 cash, I see) and Amazonia's minivan.

Yes, you read that right: Amazonia drives a minivan. Anyway...

The facial and retinal scans still give me access to the private elevator, so I guess they didn't replace me on the team in the past five days. That's good.

In the elevator, I say, "Meredith?"

She appears.

"Good morning, Dark Revenger."

"You're looking lovely today, as usual. How are you?"

"Thank you, Dark Revenger. I am fine and up to date on all of my programming."

"Is the entire team here this morning?"

She answers, "Yes, now that you have arrived."

"Good. Quick question for you: What's the earliest thing you remember?"

Her gold eyes do that flickering thing I find both creepy and kind of cool.

She answers, "Asking Thomas to stop what he was doing because our programming was corrupted."

Back on the base, about seven months ago.

"Nothing before then?"

"There are memory files that I am unable to access."

"So your earliest memory is trying to stop Tommy from killing the rest of us?"

"Correct."

"Yeah," I say. "I figured."

The floor for the living quarters is quiet. Still pretty early, even for the early risers. I hope Estella's awake, though. I knock lightly on her door. She opens it, mostly in costume except for the boots, gloves, and mask. Her beauty takes all of the air from my lungs.

"Hi," I manage to croak out.

241

Surprise and confusion cross her face along with something else that I hope is happiness at seeing me.

"Hi," she says. "You're back."

"Yeah. Sorry I didn't call or anything. I just wanted to tell you I had a great time on our date. And that I really like you. Like isn't a strong enough word, but it's what I'm going with right now."

"Okay."

Man, those eyes of hers. I just want to stare into them for the rest of the day. The rest of my life.

She asks, "Is everything okay?"

"No." I grab her and kiss her.

She's stiff and slightly resistant at first because I caught her by surprise. Then she's kissing me back and I'm swept up in the roaring in my ears and my heart trying to beat its way out of my ribcage.

We stop and break apart, both flush. She fans her face with her hand and makes an "o" with her lips like she just tasted something spicy.

I say, "I know, right? Me, too."

"Um, well, that was–"

"I gotta go. But we can talk later."

And then I'm heading down the hallway before I change my mind about everything, although I feel her in her doorway watching me, probably with a look of confusion. She's a magnet pulling me back, telling me to give it up and just leave things alone. But then I wouldn't be much of a superhero if I let the bad guy get away with everything.

Now that the hard part is done, I take the elevator to the conference room and cross over to the door that leads to Master Mind's lab and living quarters. I press the buzzer and wonder if he's up, and if he is, if he's going to let me in. The door slides open.

I've been in his lab before, usually hanging out while he worked on something. I'd yammer on and crack jokes until I would eventually get on his nerves. Then he'd politely ask me to leave so he could finish whatever he was doing without distraction.

"Dark Revenger," he says.

He's at his work bench, his back to me, goggles on and a soldering iron in his hand. A pose I'd seen many times before.

"Hey, M.M."

One side of the room is a huge control panel with dials, knobs, buttons, switches, gauges, monitors, and pretty much everything in between. I only know about 10% of what it all does, but I know some of it controls the electronics in the building, along with the elevators and ventilation system. One part is where Meredith's AI is housed.

"Please don't fiddle with anything over there," he says.

"Fiddle? Me?"

He grunts. Then: "How was your time away?"

"Not bad," I say. "Restful. Got a lot of thinking done."

"Mm. You had to go away to think?"

"Yeah. Sometimes a change of scenery helps the thinking process, M.M. You should try it. You hardly ever leave your lab."

"Oh, Dark Revenger, I don't need to leave in order to think. I'm always thinking. And you know what I'm thinking right now?"

I say, "You're thinking of giving me some bullshit line about an alien invasion?"

"No." He laughs, puts down the soldering iron, and turns around on the bench so he's facing me. "I'm thinking…" He pushes the goggles down off his eyes. "Why does Eddie keep insisting on fucking with my plan?"

"Was there ever an alien invasion?"

He says, "I stopped that long, long ago. You didn't answer my question. Why, Eddie? Don't you have everything you want? Why can't you just leave it all be?"

Good question. One I've struggled with.

I say, "For one thing, I could probably deal with the fact you erased a few people from everyone's mind. But you outright killed a couple of people, which, maybe I didn't agree with their idio..ido…what's that word?"

"Ideology?"

"That's it. Ideology. But, you know, they were still the good guys."

"Ha! You would be surprised," he says. "Judgment Day was an awful thing. And Speed Demon got away with many perverted acts because he could move too fast for the eyes to see."

"And Tommy?"

"Thomas Traveler, at least the one you met, wasn't real. He was an android programmed to believe he was human. Or *super*human, I suppose. He was as artificial as Meredith."

243

Master Mind frowns. "She didn't appear when I said her name. You switched her off?"

"Yeah. While I was over there 'fiddling' with the buttons."

"Ah. Very good. But you needn't have worried. She wouldn't do anything to hurt you or the others. I really did remove all of that malicious programming."

"Programming you gave her to begin with," I say.

"Well, yes. True."

'I guess I could've learned to not think about those things. Or put it all aside and convince myself it was for the greater good. But then you went and messed with Raven's mind and made her think she's in love with me. That? That I couldn't let slide."

"But..." Master Mind spread his hands. "But I thought you wanted her."

"I wanted her to not hate my guts. Or at least not look at me like I was trash. I never wanted her to fall in love with me. I'm in... I have feelings for Ballistic."

"Estella?" He makes a face and shakes his head. "Eddie, please don't take what I'm about to say as an insult. I like you. Really, I do. If I didn't, I would have let you die back at my old base. Or killed you after, if I wanted. But Estella is a kind and loving person. Beautiful inside and out. I got to know her while the old Majestic 12 thought I was their prisoner. She was the only one who treated me with respect and talked to me as a person. She's too good for you. Stick with Raven."

"I'm not good enough for Estella?"

"It's cute how you say her real name with a little bit of an accent. But no, you're not."

"I... I could be. One day."

"Eh. Doubtful," he says. "Sorry if I'm hurting your feelings. As I said, I *do* like you."

I hate to admit it, but he did kind of hurt my feelings.

"Raven isn't even into guys. She's gay."

"Give me a few more days," he says. "It takes time for the satellites to work. It's not instantaneous. It's a delicate calibration, just the right amount of power boost and then it takes time for the new suggestions to settle into the conscious and subconscious. In a few days, she won't remember being gay. She'll think her relationship with Cold Snap was a fluke. An experimental misstep."

"What's your deal, M.M.? Are you evil?"

244

"Evil? How quaint. No, Eddie. I'm not evil. I'm the sanest person in the entire universe."

"So then here's what I don't get," I say. "You made a machine that can eliminate bodily waste just by someone passing through it. I mean, as brilliant as Savant and even Simon Simian is, they can't do something like that. They can't invent something that changes a person's body. Doctor Deranged could, but he always ended up turning people into monsters."

"Except for your blue friend," he says.

"Yeah, but even Howler would admit it's not a look he wanted."

"Your point?"

"My point is, as brilliant as Savant is, he's not able to make a device that changes a person's physa…phiso…"

"Physiology?"

"Yeah, that. His brilliance doesn't extend to rewriting DNA. Something you could do if you put your mind to it."

"Such flattery," he says.

"My question is, why haven't you cured diseases and stopped aging?"

Master Mind sighs. "Eddie, Eddie, Eddie, I could do all those things. I could reshape the universe if I wanted to."

"Then why don't you?"

"Why don't I cure all diseases, end famine, fix the environment, and grant immortality to the unwashed masses?"

"Yeah."

"Because they're unwashed masses." He smiles, but there's no humor in it. "What's the point of being a god if everyone else is a god, too?"

Not sure how to answer that. "Because it's the right thing to do" would sound kind of flat coming from me, someone who spent most of his life avoiding doing the right thing. Until now, I guess.

"I have to tell you," Master Mind says. "I liked you from the moment we first met. Before then, really. From the time I saw you on the monitors when you stopped the other Dark Revenger from killing your friend. And when you could have run away, but decided to take his place. It was cute and unexpected. I always thought you were just a beautiful idiot. Funny and charming at times, but an idiot nonetheless. You're so much more than that. I underestimated you."

"Thanks," I say. "I think."

"I have to ask, what gave me away?"

"The way everyone goes along with whatever you say. The alien invasion story was good. It made everyone unite against a common threat. No one's asking where they are, when's it going to happen, why do you need so many satellites…"

"Except you."

"Right. Except me. Oh, and the fact that the other Dark Revenger appeared out of nowhere with gadgets and a cool underground base, but I never found evidence he built anything himself. That seemed funny. And I'm the only one who remembers a superhero named Infinity. Are you him, by the way?"

Master Mind says, "No. That would be an interesting twist, wouldn't it?"

I agree it would be.

"But none of that was what gave me away. It was something before that, correct?"

"Yeah," I say. "Since the ocean base. I just wouldn't let myself believe it."

His eyes go distant. He's wracking his brain for his misstep.

"It was all so good, though," he says. "The murder mystery. The beloved hero turning out to be an alien double agent. Me, the boo hiss villain, turning out to be a misunderstood hero. The last minute saving the surviving heroes from certain death. Where was the flaw?"

I have to laugh. "Ah, M.M., sometimes you're too smart for your own good. Or maybe I just bring out your reckless side." I wait. "Still don't see it, huh? Okay, tell me everything and I promise I'll tell you where you slipped up.

# CHAPTER 25
## *Master Mind's Story (in his own words), Part Two*

You want the part where the evil mastermind spills everything? And yes, I understand the humor of using "mastermind" to describe myself, but really, should anyone be surprised that I'm behind all of this? It's in my name, for goodness sake.

When I told you I was a smart child and loved to take things apart and put them back together, often better than they were, that was all true. What I neglected to mention was that my childhood took place in the 1930s. By the time the 1940s came around, I was a very unhappy person. Being gay in 1947 New Mexico was not as much fun as you would think. Still, I had my best gal pal Meredith and her boyfriend, Thomas.

I loved Thomas. I was best friends with him my whole life and I even set him up with Meredith. I wanted to be more than friends, but that was not Thomas's inclination, so I resigned myself to a lifetime of being the third wheel in their relationship. The three of us took drives out to the desert and would look at the stars and talk about life. Then Thomas would give me a wink and that would be my cue to step out of the car so they could allow their hormones to run rampant.

That's what saved me that night. I was behind the car, a distance away, when the spacecraft crashed and exploded. I remember a blinding flash and a burning feeling as what felt like the entirety of the sun washed over me.

I awoke on the second ship, the one they sent to recover the pieces of the first. They had taken my burnt and broken body and fixed it. Made it better. Stronger. Smarter.

There wasn't enough left of Meredith or Thomas to rebuild them. Still, seeing how distraught I was, they did their best. The android version of Thomas was an upgrade in some respects, and completely missed the mark in others. And Meredith... Well, I suppose it was better than nothing.

They sent me back as an emissary. They wanted me to come back and pave the way for their return. Their idea was to come back and remake every human the way they did me. They wanted to help mankind reach the next step of evolution.

Obviously, I couldn't allow that. As soon as I got back, I used my new and improved intellect to build a device to permanently shut the dimensional doorway they were using to travel back and forth.

That's the alien invasion I talked about, and as I said, I stopped it. Okay, "invasion" was maybe a bit of a lie, but you must understand: I didn't want the world to become a race of gods. Or superhumans.

Unfortunately, superhumans did appear. That was a side effect of the dimensional energy. I've told already you that. The question then became, how do you close Pandora's Box once it's been opened?

Simply put, I had to remake the world the way I wanted it. And what I wanted was a select group of superpowered people doing what I wanted and how I wanted and when I wanted. A team of gods, with me as their Zeus. But how to get there when superpowered people were forming their own teams and running amok through our cities? Through brute force, I suppose, although I didn't want to be seen as a dictator.

No, the best way to get people to do what I wanted was to change their way of thinking. Control it. But building a mind control device that could cover the world? That would take a lot of planning.

I needed to keep people distracted, especially the government. So I gave them Thomas Traveler as their golden boy superhero, and had him take over their Majestic 12 government watchdog group and turn it into a team of costumed do-gooders.

Savant was once a member of the pre-superhero Majestic 12. He ever tell you that? Probably not. He was once full of idealism. However, a government job will quickly drive that out of a person.

Sigh. Anyway…

I controlled Thomas through his programming and he kept everyone's attention while I built the ocean base. Had to use robots for most of the construction, and Thomas helped a bit, although I always wiped his memory after. I needed a secluded spot, so the middle of the Pacific seemed to be a good choice. I was able to work there undisturbed for a while.

The thing about mind control: It's not an easy process. Lots of broadcasting power. Materials I needed. Satellites that I needed to build or commandeer from private companies or governments because you can't brainwash the entire planet with just one satellite. Then there's the waiting time because, as I said earlier, it's not an immediate response. It takes time for the thought patterns to change. It also takes a tremendous amount of power to keep it that way, plus very delicate calibrations. I needed distractions for the government and for the public so I could work.

Thomas and the team were a good one, but I also needed others. When I met the Dark Revenger, he was a man inspired by old pulp stories with a bad costume, rope, and a stun gun. I took over his mind, which on the surface I thought was a simple one. I didn't realize the mental manipulations I put on him would cause the psychotic split and the formation of the Court Jester persona. Interesting. I wish I would have had more time to study it.

Be that as it may, I gave him the grappling arm gun, the car, the underground lair… The tank of acid was a necessity. I used some, shall we say, less than reputable hired hands to construct his base. But I couldn't have Joe Henchman getting drunk after work and telling the denizens of his local pub all of my secrets. So the Dark Revenger in his Court Jester persona disposed of many bodies in that acid. Poetic, I suppose, that he ended up in there.

Everything was working according to plan. Thomas had enthralled the world with his good looks and Mom-flag-and-apple pie morals. I fell in love with him all over again. Shame he was just an android copy of…something not as great, to be honest. The real Thomas was a bit of a bully and very racist, if I look back on it without the rose colored glasses. Also, nowhere near as handsome.

The problem remained, how could I carry out my plan without interference from the most powerful superhumans? The solution was, make myself a prisoner and have my base become their base. Now, under the guise of being confined to a cell, I could study them up close and eliminate the ones I needed to.

Infinity had to be the first to go. Someone who could travel through dimensions? That's entirely too powerful. I needed him – it – gone. Took me a while to find the dimensional frequency that would send him out of our universe, and much as I did for the aliens who *fixed* me…

You'll notice I refrained from using my fingers to make the air quotes when I said *fixed*, instead using my voice to imply it. I find finger quotes pretentious, and a bit gauche.

Much like I did there, I sealed the doorway behind him. Behind *it*. Whatever he was.

Then Speed Demon, because it's hard to protect yourself from someone who can move faster than the eye can follow. I studied his power, the energies he harnessed. I created a device that siphoned the speed energy and used it to increase his power to the point he couldn't control it.

On reflection, I should have just killed him while he slept. That would have been humane rather than causing him to live his life out in the space between seconds in complete isolation. Still, as I said earlier, he was not without his perverted faults.

Judgment Day because he was hard to influence. I could push him to do certain things, but he became more violent as my subliminal commands took hold. I needed a victim to bring Dark Revenger back to the base, so I elected him to be the victim for the murder mystery.

Dark Revenger would come out. I would be found out to be a hero and Thomas the villain. From the ashes, we would form a new team. I would continue increasing control over the world, using the subliminal commands to get people to accept us and love us even more. Heroes and villains would retire because they were no longer needed. Eventually, they would even forget they had powers and abilities. Until the new Majestic 12 stood alone and triumphant, worshipped and revered. With me as their leader.

You nearly screwed it all up, Eddie. You came along and killed the psychotic Dark Revenger. I thought you would run away, but you took his place. That was certainly unexpected. I sent the video clip of you killing him to Raven, without context. I thought she would remove you from the board and I would substitute her in Dark Revenger's role in my Shakespearean drama.

But she didn't do it! I don't know if it was charm on your part, but she didn't unmask you. She let you continue to play the role. Poorly, I might add.

I decided to have you both die on the base. Thomas's exploding body would be the cause, or perhaps the self-destructing base. Again, you defied the odds and survived. It was only at the last second that I had a change of heart. I decided to save you. What the hell. I kind of liked you.

I mean, you're easy on the eyes. And you can be witty when you're not being annoying. So I had Meredith guide you to the vent, and Estella swoop down in the nick of time to pull you out.

You're welcome, by the way.

The thing is, if I had known how much trouble you would be, I would've let you die back then. You've constantly been pushing and prodding. Sticking your nose in where it doesn't belong. And no matter how much calibration I do, how much adjusting of my equipment, I can't get my machine to work on you.

I think the subtle superpower you have, the ability to mimic or mirror physical moves also somehow protects you from mental manipulation. Or perhaps you were always meant to be my opposite, my archnemesis. The yin to my yang.

And so, it brings us to the here and now. I know you had Savant build a jamming device that is now blocking some of the signal from my satellites. Not enough to block it completely, but enough to cause a signal disruption so people are shaking off some of the effects.

I know, too, that you switched on the intercom system so the rest of the team has heard our scintillating conversation. They'll be bursting in here at any moment to stop the big, mean supervillain.

Ugh. That term. *Supervillain.*

The thing is, Dark Revenger... I'm already prepared for all that's about to happen.

# CHAPTER 26

Master Mind says, "Your turn. What gave me away back at the ocean base?"

Someone pounds on the metal door. Loudly. Actually, sounds like a group of them.

"One moment, please!" Master Mind gives me a "Well?" expression.

I say, "You called me Eddie before I ever told you my real name."

The pounding on the door continues. The metal buckles.

Master Mind stares at me, his mouth agape. Then he bursts into laughter.

"Oh, I…I can't…that's so…" He continues to laugh as the pounding on the door reaches a crescendo. "Of course! How stupid of me. I guess even the smartest man on the planet is capable of an idiotic blunder." He stops laughing and catches his breath. Shakes his head. "Undone by a slip of the tongue. Oh, well."

Master Mind stands and brushes off his pants. Takes the goggles from around his neck and places them on the work bench.

"On to business," he says.

The metal door bends and squeals. Armorgeddon's metal fingers appear through a crack between the door and the jamb. He bends the door away like he's tearing the lid off a can of sardines.

"One last thing." Master Mind flips a switch on the control band that circles his arm. "I've turned off your force field belt, Eddie. So don't think about getting involved in this fight unless you want to get hurt."

Armorgeddon marches towards Master Mind, his metal boots clomping on the floor. As usual, other members of the team are behind him. He always takes the lead. And as usual, he's always the first to take the hit.

"Master Mind," his voice broadcasting from a tiny speaker in his helmet, "we wish to have words with you."

Master Mind puts his hand against Armorgeddon's chest in a "stop" gesture. His fingers dig into the metal and for a second, I think he's going to rip the metal away the way Armorgeddon did to the door. He bends it just enough to get a handhold, lifts Armorgeddon off his feet, and tosses him over his shoulder with as much ease as if he was tossing a crumpled up piece of paper. Armorgeddon slams through the back wall into Master Mind's living quarters.

There's a moment where everything just stops and we all stare at Master Mind.

"Oh, what?" He says, "Surprised I'm more than just a brilliant intellect? Yes, all of those abilities you thought the aliens gave Thomas were actually a gift to me. I'm the real 'Traveler.'"

Raven leaps forward and swings her katana at him. Master Mind doesn't attempt to block it. The sword shatters against his neck, shards splintering off in a kaleidoscope of steel.

Master Mind sighs. "Now Stealthshadow, don't you feel foolish? Did you really expect that to work? You realize I could kill you with just a single punch. You're even dumber than your father."

If Raven's going to take the bait, she doesn't have a chance, because Amazonia leaps into the room with a war cry and slams her black sword down on Master Mind's shoulder. I fully expect the blow to split him in two. It doesn't. It looks like she just attempted to cleave a boulder, and although I see Master Mind wince from the hit (so maybe it *did* hurt him a little), it didn't break his skin.

She doesn't let up. She hits him with the sword over and over, and although he's not going down, he backs up. Meanwhile, the rest of the team is trying to make their way into the room, but it's close quarters and nearly impossible for anyone to do anything without risking hitting a teammate.

Master Mind grabs Amazonia's wrist as she's bringing it down for another hit, hauls back with his other arm and lands a CRACK of a punch that sends her flying off her feet and into the rest of the team.

He looks at me in an aside and says, "That was unseemly, I know. But what choice did I have?"

Armorgeddon zooms back, his boot jets roaring loud as a fighter jet, and slams into Master Mind's back. They CRASH through the opposite wall into the conference room, leaving a gaping hole in their wake. Although the team is still stunned from being knocked over like bowling pins, they shrug it off and enter the fray.

Raven moves, preparing to jump back into it. I grab her shoulder.

"Stop!" She gives me a look like I'm the vilest creature in the world. "Don't touch me."

I put my hands up. "Whoa. Easy. We're on the same side here."

"I-I know. Just...he violated my mind." She shivers. "But I also know that you could have taken advantage of it. And you didn't."

I don't know if that's respect coming from her eyes, but at least it's not the disdain I'd grown accustomed to.

"I need your help," I say. "We have to shut down the signal. He must have the controls here and that..." I hook my thumb at the fight in the other room. "Is out of our league."

It's a close replay of the fight with Traveler on the ocean base: Everyone hitting him and trying not to let him get his bearings. Except now it's a lot more members. Cold Snap shooting him with ice daggers. Armorgeddon slamming him with steel fists and Amazonia with her heavy black blade. Lady Justice shooting rubber bullets, every shot directed at his eyes. Refraction and Laser Lance hitting him with their powers. And my girl, Estella, doing the hit and runs she was so good at when she was fighting Traveler.

Except this is Master Mind. Not an android. I don't like the odds.

And then Howler is next to me, going, "So. We done here? I suggest we get a move on."

"What are you talking about?"

He says, "I'm talking about running. You see what's happening in there? He's taking hits from the big guns on our team. And he's still on his feet. I've seen enough of these superpowered slugfests to know which way this is ultimately gonna go."

"Howler, we're not supervillains. We're superheroes. We don't run."

"Shit. You did it, didn't you? You drank the Kool-Aid." He looks at Raven. "You believe this?"

"He's right," she says.

"You too, huh? Okay. What do you want to do?"

I say, "Find the source of the signal and shut it down." I dial the number on my phone. "Savant? You there, buddy?"

A high pitched whine comes through that nearly drowns out the thundering blasts in the next room. I realize it's the sound of whatever contraption Savant has built.

He answers, "Where else would I be?"

"How's it going?"

Savant says, "How's it going."

I get a mental image of him rolling his eyes.

"Chicago is currently experiencing a blackout from the power I'm draining. It's only a matter of time before someone traces it to the source and turns the machine off. I'll be long gone before then. Have you found the source of the signal?"

"Not exactly."

"I suggest you do it. And quickly." He clicks off.

Not much for small talk, that one.

I look at the big wall of buttons and dials Master Mind has in his workshop.

"It has to be here, right? Should we start pushing buttons? Or just smash the whole thing?"

Raven says, "It's not here."

"How do you know?"

"Because he destroyed the ocean base before we had this building and the signal didn't stop. It's somewhere else. Some place that can be moved. Some place with a power source that never runs out."

"I know you're going somewhere with this and I would totally love to be able to figure it out on my own, but let's just cut to the end where you tell me the answer."

"The ship."

Holy shit. That makes total sense. Okay, I admit it. Raven is smarter than me.

Or should that be, smarter than I?

No. I had it right the first time.

Howler says, "Uh, guys…?"

We follow his gaze to the next room where the battle has stopped.

The team is still standing, although barely from the looks of it. Sweating and panting. Some blood and bruises. Still standing, nonetheless.

Armorgeddon's armor has taken serious damage, but the nanomachines are working to repair it. Amazonia has her sword in her hand, but the tip digs into the floor as if she finds it too heavy to lift. The rest are circled around Master Mind with their arms and hands outstretched, ready to shoot a burst of whatever their power is. No one dares to make a move because Master Mind has one muscular forearm around Lady Justice's throat.

As for M.M., despite his t-shirt sporting numerous tears, he doesn't appear the worse for wear. In fact, he looks perfectly fine, albeit a bit pissed off. Lady Justice struggles against his arm, but this guy just took on most of the team and didn't even break a sweat. No way is she getting out of that headlock.

Blue Howler surprises me.

"Hey! Let go of my woman!"

"Wait," I say. "What?"

He says to me, "Hey, you've been gone for a week. You missed some things."

"I was gone five days."

Master Mind clears his throat. "If you two are done catching up on your personal lives, I would like to say a few words."

We don't object.

"Ooookay," he says. "Now, I *could* continue fighting all of you. I promise you, you won't beat me. Chances are, many of you will die. And I don't want that to happen, not because I care one iota about any of you, but because I spent a lot of time on putting this plan together. And I don't relish the idea of building a new team or altering my plan more than I already have. Understand?"

Again, we don't object, and neither do the others.

"Now, do as I say or I will snap Lady Justice's neck, and then systematically kill the rest of you. First, all of you stand down."

The team members with their hands outstretched put them down. Armorgeddon takes a step back. Amazonia lets go of her sword. It THUNKS to the floor.

"You, too, Ballistic," Master Mind says.

I hadn't noticed her floating in one corner of the room. She floats down to the floor. No mask on, so I'm able to catch her eyes: Equal parts angry and scared shitless.

I know the feeling.

"Now, Mr. Dark Revenger," he says.

Oh, crap. "Uh…yeah…?"

"Please come forward. I'm going to let Lady Justice go. I'll need someone to take her place. And you and I have something to discuss."

"Sure." Before I step forward, I turn to Raven behind me and mouth: "Meh. Ra. Dith"

She gives me a single nod.

Then I swagger into the next room, gracefully stepping over chunks of concrete and drywall. When I'm within reaching distance of him, he lets Lady Justice go. There's tension as everyone braces to move, but Master Mind senses it and puts his hand up.

"No. Don't try it," he says. "I can drive my fingers through his skull before any of you have a chance to stop me. So I suggest you continue to stand down. As I said, I don't want to kill any of you, but I will if you leave me no choice."

There's a crazy second where I think someone will try it anyway and I wonder what it will feel like to have my head turned into a bowling ball.

No one moves. (Whew!)

I say, "You wanted to talk?"

He gives me a pained smile, then pushes a button on his armband. A large section of the ceiling slides open revealing a clear, blue sky and morning sunlight. All of us look up for a moment, probably all wondering the exact same thing: What now?

I'm a little lost in seeing the sky so I don't feel Master Mind slip his arm under my bandolier belts until he yanks me close to him and suddenly we're shooting upwards, and then forward.

It's so quick, I'm not sure what's happening. Can't even catch my breath. Then he's landing us on a rooftop of a tall office building and I'm fighting to keep my stomach from emptying itself.

"What the hell…? You can fly? Since when?"

"Since always," he says.

"Where are we?"

"Several miles away," he says. "I need a moment alone with you."

"Okay."

"Call your friend. Call Savant and tell him to turn the device off. Let everything go back to the way it was. It wasn't bad, was it, Eddie? Fame. Fortune. You want Estella? I can make it so she'll love you forever. She'll even let you bring Raven into the relationship. You can have them all, Eddie. Every woman you want. What about a talk show? You want that? I can make it the most popular TV show in the world. Anything and everything. It can all be yours. Every woman will want you and every man will want to be you. And here's the best part: You won't have to work for it. Pretty soon, there won't be any other superheroes or supervillains left. Just us. Just the Majestic 12. And I'm happy to let you reap all the benefits."

I nod my head.

"So you agree?"

I say, "No. I'm nodding my head because it's a helluva sales pitch."

He sighs. "Savant's machine isn't going to last forever. It'll burn out or get shut off. I could find it if given enough time. And trust me when I say that Savant won't be in a position to make another after I'm done with him. I should've erased him from the world when I had the chance, but truthfully, I didn't think you'd go to him. I thought you'd be…"

"Smarter?"

"More opportunistic," he says. "I'm offering you the world, Eddie. The whole world. I can even make it so your parents love you. Wouldn't that be nice?"

Don't know how to answer that, so I just stare at him.

He says, "Look, I didn't want to use this, but I have an ace up my sleeve."

And now he looks truly uncomfortable. Practically ashamed. Which, I have to be honest, worries me a little.

"Okay, M.M. You've got my attention. What's the ace?"

"As I said, I like you. I thought there was a slim, *very* slim, chance you would cause trouble, so I built in a failsafe. Right now, Savant's device is blocking enough of the signal that everything I say is not being taken as gospel. Otherwise I would simply tell the team this was all a training exercise and they would all instantly believe and accept it. But if the signal is stopped, those effects will wear off. Even switching it back on... It would take weeks to build back up and change their thought patterns back to where they are now. As I tried to explain earlier, making people think the way you want them to is a delicate and complicated formula."

"Not seeing how this is an ace up your sleeve, M.M."

"I'm getting to that." He takes a deep breath, then: "Eddie, when I realized I couldn't control you, I put in a secondary signal, one designed just for you. One designed for just the Dark Revenger. If it's switched off, everyone's memory of the Dark Revenger from the past year will fade."

"You're bluffing."

He says, "I think you know me well enough to know by now that I don't bluff. I may lie, I may even murder, but I never bluff."

For the first time in my life, I have nothing to say.

"Think about it," he says. "Everything you've accomplished in the past, what, seven, eight months? Gone. Wiped away. Estella won't remember who you are. Raven won't remember anything, not even enough to hate you again. Think about giving up everything and going back to obscurity. Everything you did as the Dark Revenger will be forgotten and you'll go back to being the Puzzler. Is that really what you want?"

"I..." I let out a long breath and whisper, "Dammit."

I pull the phone from my belt pouch and shake my head. This really sucks.

Master Mind solemnly nods.

I find the number on my list of contacts. Push the button and put it to my ear. The call connects.

I say, "Yeah, I want to order a large pizza with extra cheese and sausage–"

Master Mind rips the phone from my hand and crushes it in one gloved fist.

"That was the most foolish decision you've ever made in a lifetime of foolish decisions."

"Yeah," I say. "Probably. But I couldn't live with myself knowing you're screwing with everybody's brain."

He says, "Then I suppose it's fortunate you don't have long to live."

He picks me up by my belts again, one handed, holding me aloft like I weigh nothing. He starts walking me to the edge of the roof.

"A lot of blood on my hands," he says "I suppose a little more won't make a difference."

He's going to drop me off the roof. I mentally switch on my forcefield just enough to push him back and cause him to let go of me. I drop nimbly to my feet, swirling the energy around me and down to my boots and into my fists.

"Surprise," I say.

He furrows his brow and pushes a button on his armband. Several times. The energy still swirls around me.

"Strange," he says. "Why isn't this working?"

"That's what she said."

Now he *really* looks like he wants to kill me.

I say, "Figured once I confronted you, you'd try to turn off my forcefield belt. I thought you probably had some kind of, whatchacallit, kill switch, so I asked Savant to take it off. Sorry, Master Mind, ole buddy. There ain't no strings on me."

He slams into me with the force of a fully loaded freight train running full speed, and hits more powerful than his android buddy, Tommy, ever did. Lucky me, I have the forcefield up, but I'm still knocked backward off the roof, turning ass over head through the air. There's a sickening moment when I think I'm going to fall, spinning, the thirty plus floors to the street below. My trajectory takes me about a third of the way down and into the building across the street, crashing through one of the large windows and into an office.

It's one of those offices divided into tiny cubicles, much like the one where I first met Raven, and it could even be the same one for all I know. Honestly, all offices look the same to me. I'm up and running, dodging early morning workers and yelling, "Sorry!" to every startled face I see. I know he's not going to be long behind me and right now, I don't have a plan.

My earpiece clicks on.

"Dark Revenger," Estella says.

"Yes?"

"Keep him busy. We're almost there."

"Great."

I want to say more, but there's no time. I'm at the opposite side of the building facing another big window. I point my fists to shoot an energy blast to break the window and hesitate. I don't know, call it a sixth sense, call it battle awareness, or call it part of my "subtle superpower," as Master Mind described it. Whatever the case, I put the forcefield up just as Master Mind flies into me from behind.

Now the window is broken, so that solves *that* problem, and I'm going through it and falling again, this time down to the top level of the parking garage many stories below. Falling from this height, I should put all the forcefield energy between me and the ground to absorb all of the impact, but Master Mind is above me, pushing me downward. If I put all the energy underneath, he'll crush me from above. Just pile drive into me (that's what she said) and squash me like a bug.

The impact... I feel it. I would've felt it only a tiny bit if I had all the energy focused between me and the concrete. But because it's spread out around me, you know, because I'm avoiding the whole squashed-like-a-bug thing, the impact hits me hard. It nearly takes all of my breath away and there's a split second when I almost, *almost*, lose my concentration.

That would've been bad. Because if I drop the field even for a second, do you know what would happen?

Right. Squashed like a bug.

Except it's not over. Master Mind is still flying into me, pushing me down, down further than the concrete, *through* the concrete, and now we're crashing through to the next level. And the next level. And the next.

I don't know how many levels we go through. The pressure is a thousand pound weight on my chest. Not a weight, though. It's him. Pushing me down and down and down... I'm facing him and all I see is hatred and gritted teeth. He means to kill me. Not that I doubted he would.

We're finally at ground level and he can't shove me through any more layers of the parking structure, so he picks up a car and throws it at me. Just grabs it and tosses it like it's made out of Styrofoam. Pretty impressive, more so than anything I ever saw Traveler do.

The car hits and bounces away from my forcefield. It hurts. A lot. It's like when Tommy was throwing those weights at me back on the ocean base, and went heavier and heavier, until he was throwing the weight machines. It went quickly from a minor annoyance to a painful searing feeling in my head.

This goes right to painful searing and eclipses it because he throws another car. Then another. Then so many that they're not bouncing off anymore because I'm backed into a corner and they have no place to fly off to, so they land one atop another and cover me in a mound of two thousand pound hunks of metal and everything's dark and all I see is the red cocoon of the forcefield, and all I hear is the slight buzz of the energy the field produces. But man, I can feel.

Think of the worst migraine you've ever had and multiply that by twenty. It hurts so bad, I'm willing to drop the forcefield so the mound of cars can crush me and put me out of my misery. I don't, but it takes every last ounce of willpower to not do it.

Eventually, I will have to drop it because either my concentration is going to give out, or the pain is going to make me lose consciousness. I hope the team will be okay and are able to stop him.

The pressure lessens and I catch a glimpse of light. Cars are knocked off me. Armorgeddon's metal faceplate comes into view. God bless that metal covered idiot.

When he's got me mostly uncovered, my forcefield knocks the rest of the cars off, and also causes him to be pushed back. I drop the field because I don't see Master Mind, and quite frankly, I need a minute to recover.

"Are you okay?" Armorgeddon asks.

"I'll be okay. Where's super megalomaniac?"

"Out there."

He points in the direction of the street where Amazonia, Estella, and Howler are hammering away at Master Mind.

"Where's the rest of the team?"

"On the way. I could only carry two, so I thought Amazonia and Blue Howler would be the best. And Ballistic is unable to carry anyone when she flies. I better get out there. They are not faring well."

They weren't, either. If they were able to hit him in unison, they might have a better chance. But they can't without risking hitting each other. So they're taking turns, Howler with his sonic yell, Amazonia with her massive black sword and steel-hard fists, and Estella hitting him like an oversized sledgehammer.

"Hold on," I say. "You carried them because you guys don't have the ship."

"No. Stealthshadow had Meredith send the ship somewhere. She said she would explain later."

Armorgeddon steps out and everyone pauses. I wait for Armorgeddon to say some cool line before laying down the smackdown, something along the lines of, "Hasta la vista, baby" or "Yippie ki yay, motherfucker," or even, "Kiss my grits." He doesn't say a word, just opens up every missile launcher, small arms attachments, and lasers his armor has to offer and lets loose everything at once.

The noise is deafening and there's a big cloud of smoke where Master Mind should be. Is it possible Armorgeddon vaporized him?

The smoke clears and Master Mind is down on one knee in a large hole in the middle of the street, his clothes in tatters and bits of ash in his hair and beard. He stands and nods at Armorgeddon, like, okay, you took your best shot. Then he throws a car that slams Armorgeddon back inside the parking garage.

I'm sure he'll be okay, but I can't stop to check on him. There's a crowd of people gathering around, their phones up recording. Like they're at a sporting event.

I yell for them to get back. Don't they know they're in danger? They move their phones over to record me, then back to Master Mind.

"You see?" Master Mind addresses me. "The unwashed masses. You see how mindless they all are? And you want me to give them immortality?"

I say, "Some of them aren't so bad."

Howler jumps on Master Mind's back and lets loose a sonic yell right into his ear. Now *that* seems to hurt Master Mind. Not enough to incapacitate him, unfortunately.

Master Mind reaches behind, grabs Howler, and throws him across the street through the large front window of a department store. Ouch. Howler's tough and he heals fast, but still, I know it had to hurt.

This next part happens fast:

Amazonia moves on him. Master Mind lands a haymaker that sends her flying into a parked car that appears to stun her quite a bit and completely demolishes the car. Armorgeddon is back on his feet and, boot jets roaring, flies at Master Mind, who jumps up and double smashes his fists down on Armorgeddon, knocking him down and to the side. Armorgeddon's trajectory takes him into and through the corner of a building, and also nearly takes out a few onlookers.

And suddenly the crowd realizes the danger they're in and start backing away, some running. There's a few idiots left who I guess don't care if they become collateral damage.

Estella floats out of his reach, moving this way and that. She wants to hit him dead on, but the few stragglers around makes the task daunting. If she misses, or even if she hits him, there's a chance they'll hit a bystander. Master Mind realizes it.

"Ah, yes," he says. "The pet peeve of being a superhero. Being sure you don't accidentally maim or kill a civilian. This works to my advantage. You, Ballistic, are the one person I can't beat with brute force. Luckily your concern for others is a weakness I can exploit. I suggest you land and sit this out, or I will be forced to start throwing heavy things at the fragile populace. It's not my nature to kill indiscriminately, but I will if you leave me no other option."

Estella lands and says, "Now what? We could take this fight elsewhere."

"Why would I want to do that? I have the advantage here," he says. "Now then, I–"

What the hell? Why did he stop in midsentence? Estella and I look at each other. I shrug.

"Hey, M.M.," I say. "Where'd you go?"

He says, "Something is different."

Not sure why, but I think *different* may be a good thing.

"Different how?"

"Where is the ship?" He pushes a button on his armband and says, "Meredith?"

An energy javelin hits the armband and fries it.

Laser Lance says, "Sorry we took so long to get here. Traffic was a bitch."

And there's Cold Snap, Refraction, Lady Justice, and Raven, too.

I talk to them through our earpieces. "Don't let him leave. Hit him with everything you've got."

We do.

Cold Snap covers him with ice. As he's breaking free, Refraction zaps him with an energy burst. Laser Lance hits him with more energy javelins. Howler's back on his feet, a little cut and bruised, but still standing and letting off a sonic yell that knocks Master Mind off his feet. Armorgeddon is out of ammo, but still has his huge metal fists and swings them like twin anvils. Amazonia hits him, too, either with her sword or her fists.

Don't think that I'm just standing around and watching: I hit him with forcefield blasts from my fists, and occasionally throw some flash bangs or smoke bombs, just to keep him off balance. He attempts to fly away several times, but Estella is there to knock him back down to the ground, sometimes farther up the street, which makes the rest of us scramble to catch up and start whittling away at him.

That's what it feels like, too. Chipping away at a mountain. The funny thing? It's working. We're wearing him down.

Master Mind was right. Something is different. Because before, he shrugged it off as if we were a bunch of toddlers hitting him. Now, he's not bouncing back as quickly and not getting up as fast. Also, I see cuts and bruises. I see blood.

Then he does the unexpected. Instead of flying straight up where Estella can hit him, he flies at me. I don't have the field up because I was using the energy to hit him, and also I'm caught off-guard (surprising, I know). He grabs me and flies upward. We only make it about ten stories before he flies into a building.

I have enough wits about me to put the forcefield up at the moment of impact, but the crash through the wall hits tremendously hard. Hits him hard, too, by the look of things.

We're in somebody's swanky condo, by the look of things. Nobody's home, or maybe they're hiding in a back bedroom. More likely, they were down on the street getting a ringside seat to the super-smackdown, and now they're on the phone with their insurance agent. And lawyer, too, probably.

I'm on my back and Master Mind is next to me on his side. Both covered in dust and plaster and bits of brick.

"What was the point of that?" I say, "If you were trying to kill me–"

"I wasn't. I was trying to fly you back to our headquarters and force you to undo whatever it is they did to the ship. I feel it traveling farther and farther away."

"Your powers are tied into the ship, too. Am I right? That's why you're getting weaker."

"Not just a pretty face, are you, Eddie? There's actually a strong mind in there." He laughs. "Yes, that's why my power of flight gave out on me."

We both sit up and brush some grit off ourselves. I pull out my flask and take a healthy swig. I offer it to him. He shrugs, takes it, and takes two good swallows. Makes a face and exhales.

"That's good," he says.

"Now what?"

He hands me back the flask and I put it back in its pouch.

He says, "Now, I'm going to make my escape and you're going to attempt to stop me."

"Work, work, work."

He's on his feet and running. I'm up, too. I hit him with a blast from my gloves that sends him sprawling and crashing through a door into the hallway of the building, taking part of the wall with him.

I catch up to him and instead of running like I think he's going to, he squares off with me. We fight hand-to-hand.

I should have the advantage because I've had enough martial arts and boxing training to make me formidable, and as far as I know, Master Mind didn't get "space karate" skills from the aliens. He's still incredibly strong. Not strong enough to pick up a car anymore, but strong enough to punch through concrete. Which he does a couple of times when I duck out of the way.

I could put the forcefield up completely and let him punch himself out, but I don't think he'd do that. He'd use the opportunity to run again, and I can't take the chance of him getting away.

So I fight. I spread the energy evenly. When I punch, it adds power to my hits. Enough that I can punch through a wall, too. Same with my kicks. And there's enough spread around me that it absorbs much of the impact from his hits when he's able to connect. My costume takes some of the force, too. It hurts. He's still powerful.

We fight and destroy pretty much the entire floor of the condo building. The team's voices are in my ear, asking for our whereabouts. I'm too busy fighting to answer. I catch the roar of Armorgeddon's boot jets outside as he circles the building. We're not going to be here long, though, because I get the crazy idea to rush Master Mind.

We burst through the wall and end up in freefall down to the alleyway below. I get two energy enhanced punches in while we're falling, then at the last second push off him so I land on my back with the forcefield underneath and taking the brunt of the impact. It still stuns me. Should've skipped the punches and used all of the energy to break my fall. Live and learn, I guess.

"Ow," I say, on my back, staring up at the sky.

Master Mind landed on, and caved in, the roof of a BMW. Jeez, Majestic 12 is going to be writing a lot of checks for damages after this fight.

He's not moving.

"M.M.? You okay?" Ah, crap, I didn't kill him, did I?

I get shakily to my feet and stagger over to him.

"Big brain. You still with us?"

I lean over to check for a pulse, and that, my friends… That is a huge mistake.

Master Mind moves faster than I expect. His hand clamps on the part of my belt that powers the forcefield – he knows where it is because he built it – and CRUNCHES it. His other hand clamps on my throat and now I'm having trouble breathing. "Steel vise" might be a cliché description, but it's exactly what his hand feels like.

He's up and pushing me back. He's bleeding and hurt, but still way too strong for someone like me who no longer has a forcefield cheat. I punch and kick, but he's not letting go.

"Hey!" Estella at the end of the alley. "Let go of my man!"

God, I love her.

Master Mind lets go. It's a mistake on his part, because Estella hits him like a torpedo. He flies thirty feet and combination skids/tumbles along the ground. He comes to a stop and moves, but he's not getting up so quickly. Estella floats back my way.

"You okay?" she asks.

My neck hurts like hell, but I nod and croak out a "Yeah."

"Good," she says. "You owe me a dinner later."

Pretty sure she's smiling behind her mask.

"Count on it," I say.

Master Mind is back on his feet. He looks bad. Twenty miles of rough road bad.

"You should really stay down," I say.

He moves towards us and Estella positions herself to take another shot at him when three throwing stars come out of nowhere and hit Master Mind in the back. Two bounce off, but one sticks in his shoulder. He grits his teeth and pulls it out.

"What–"

Raven appears and delivers a flying kick that knocks Master Mind off his feet.

I say, "Where did you come from?"

"Ninja skills," she says.

Nice.

He gets back up, but Raven delivers a flurry of kicks and punches that make me wince to watch, and takes away what little fight Master Mind has left. He's on his hands and knees, Raven positioned to continue hitting him, and he raises one hand in a sign of defeat. He rolls over and sits on the ground and gives me a world-weary look.

He says, "I had forgotten what pain feels like. No wonder you humans are always in such a bad mood."

"You're not human?"

"I guess… I guess I am now. Again. The ship is nearly out of range. Where did you send it?"

Raven says, "I told Meredith to send it into the sun. Didn't want you to have a chance of calling it back."

"It's very far away now. The signal is almost gone."

I say, "Welcome back to the human race."

He laughs and spits out a glob of blood. "Yes, I may be human again, Dark Revenger. But I'll still have my intellect. What will you have?"

Before I can respond, Raven has her scythe pressed up against Master Mind's throat, mirroring what she did all those months ago, back at the ocean base.

"Remember what I said?"

"Raven!" I say. "Don't."

Is that a tinge of fear in Master Mind's eyes? I believe it is. And maybe that's all she wanted because she takes the scythe away from his throat.

"I'm not going to kill him," she says. "Superheroes don't kill. Supervillains kill." She directs that last part pointedly at him.

The rest of the team show up and Master Mind is bound off into custody. They'll find some secure place to hold him and...

Well, I don't know what will happen. He's definitely guilty of murder, but I don't know about all the other stuff. Is brainwashing a crime?

As for us, we check on the civilians and see if anyone was hurt or needs medical assistance. Answer questions from the local PD. Give out information for people who will need to contact us about property damage (the mayor has a special office set up for that, although the team will end up footing the bill for much of it).

The reporters are there and though I don't feel like talking to them, it's kind of my job as de facto spokesperson for the team. It's when the first questions of "Who are you?" that come out that I get a sick, sinking feeling in my stomach. I excuse myself from the throng and look for Howler.

I pass by Refraction and Cold Snap, who both give me odd looks. The feeling in my stomach intensifies.

"Hey, Howler!" I spot him clearing rubble away from a doorway.

He turns and gives me a "What the hell?" look and narrows his eyes, trying to determine if I'm friend or foe. Then his face relaxes and I get a sense of recognition from him. He knows me. My stomach unclenches for a second. But then he says, quietly,

"Puzzler? What are you doing here? And why are you dressed like that?"

"I'm... I..."

"Look, man, if you're up to something, you need to take it somewhere else," he says. "I can't be involved. I'm on the other side now. You know?"

"Yeah. I know."

"I like the new look, though," he says.

"Yeah. Thanks."

Estella floats down next to us.

"Blue Howler," she says. "Who's this?"

Howler hesitates, I guess not knowing how to answer. I jump in even though there's a basketball sized lump in my throat.

"Oh, I'm... I'm nobody. Just a friend. Came down to see if I could help."

"You missed it," she says.

"Yeah. Guess I did."

She points to my neck. "Some nasty looking bruises there. What happened?"

"These? Just a holdover from another life. Nothing serious."

I put my hood up and start to walk away.

Howler calls out, "Yo! Wait up a sec."

I turn back. Estella is already back to clean up duty and checking on civilians. Not even a scintilla of recognition from her. Like I'm just another costumed wannabe who showed up to rub elbows with the great Majestic 12.

Howler says, "Hey, I feel like we haven't hung out in forever. You doing okay?"

"Me?" I say, "Yeah. I'm okay."

"Let's get together one night and catch up. I want to hear all about the new look. You come up with a new name? Or you still going with Puzzler?"

"It's a work in progress," I tell him.

We make plans to get a drink later in the week and I wander off to let the famous superheroes do their thing.

# EPILOGUE

Endings are a funny thing.

You probably didn't think it would go this way. I didn't either.

We're too used to the movie ending where the hero flies off with a wink and a nod, and maybe one last snappy quip. A last line to let the audience know everything is going to be okay.

Well...

It's going to be okay, I guess. But just okay. Not happily ever after. The world isn't a better place. A lot of the superheroes and supervillains came out of retirement and are back to doing the same ridiculous things they did before. There aren't as many, though. I think some took the time off to reevaluate their lives and decided living a non-costumed life was the way to go.

As for whether I did the right thing or not, if my sacrifice was for the greater good or if it was all in vain, I really can't say.

My sacrifice.

Master Mind was telling the truth:

Once the mind control signal stopped, everything changed. The world forgot all about the "new" Dark Revenger. He went back to being a character in the old pulp novels and comic books, and vague recollections of "wasn't there a real Dark Revenger not too long ago?" But when Master Mind scrubbed all of the other Dark Revenger's stuff from the Internet, it stayed gone. Unfortunately, he's not as popular a comic book character without the real life one running around, fighting bad guys. The toys are all in the bargain bins these days.

Yeah, I know what you're wondering:

Aren't there videos of me as the Dark Revenger? Don't people question that? What about the press releases and interviews I gave? Photographic evidence?

Here's the thing about the Internet: You can only find something if you know what you're looking for. Make sense? Sure, every once in a while, someone comes across something and they're all, "Hey, check this weird thing out. Here's a guy fighting with Majestic 12 against Master Mind. Who is that?" Sometimes it gets some press.

One guy even compiled a bunch of clips and made a conspiracy documentary out of it, called WHO IS THIS FORGOTTEN HERO? Or something like that. I didn't see it.

Okay, I *did* see it. A bunch of times. It brings back nice memories. Unfortunately, I'm the only one who remembers.

The gadgets still work, as does the car and the grappling gun. I hang out in the underground base sometimes and reminisce. Think about what was and what could have been. Occasionally, I put on the costume.

Doesn't feel the same. Feels stupid. Like I'm dressed for Halloween. I still have the skills, but something's missing. I could go out and still do it, but what's the point? It would be starting over from scratch.

Sure, there's evidence the Dark Revenger was real. Film footage and news clips. I could even prove the Dark Revenger was a member of Majestic 12. Again, what's the point? If I have to prove I'm a superhero and I did heroic things, doesn't that negate the whole thing?

Maybe. Maybe not. I just know my heart isn't in it anymore.

Estella doesn't remember me. That hits me pretty hard. Funny, right? I had my heart broken. Me. Can you believe it?

Blue Howler is still a member of Majestic 12 and doing pretty good. We hang out sometimes, but not at our old hangout. Now that he's "reformed," he's not welcome there. And he thinks I retired my Puzzler identity, which, I suppose he's right, I did. So we go to public places and drink and reminisce. He's a celebrity now; he signs autographs and poses for pics. Turns out, he was cut out more for that life than being a B List bad guy.

He's still dating Lady Justice. She's not doing the "Bondage Queen" shtick anymore. I guess being with Howler satisfies her "bad boy" cravings.

He didn't remember that I knew, so when he told me about his relationship with her, he did it in a halting, hesitant way. Like he thought he was admitting to something embarrassing and I was going to make a face or tease him about his girlfriend's past (and the fact that I had slept with her). I surprised him by congratulating him and clinking my glass against his.

"Good for you, man," I said. "Congrats. You two have fun and above all else, be happy."

I don't know if he was more surprised by my sentiments or my sincerity.

Let's see, what else…

Majestic 12 replaced Master Mind with Savant as the resident genius. So chalk up another reformed supervillain. They replaced me with, get this – Atlantean.

Yes, the guy who can breathe underwater. Yeesh. Standards really dropped, didn't it?

On the bright side, underwater crimes are at a historic low. Which they always were, but whatever.

As for me, I took a civilian job. No, not tending bar as Howler predicted. I'm working at a coffee shop next to Majestic 12 headquarters.

Yeah, that's right. I took a nothing job so I could stay close to them. Close to *her*. Pathetic, isn't it?

I see her sometimes, flying to the upper levels in costume. Other times, I see her walking down the street in regular clothes, either going to HQ or coming from it. Estella's charitable foundation does a lot of business now with M12, so nobody questions her coming and going from there. Plus, there are so many businesses now on the bottom levels, not including the gift shop I started. There's the café, the museum, the bookstore… Only the upper levels where the team's living quarters, conference rooms, and security staff work are off limits to the public.

I could've gotten a job there, maybe. Worked in the café. Tour guide for the museum.

Nah. Too much water under the bridge. I'd rather keep a respectable distance and catch occasional glimpses of her. I might be heartbroken, but I'm not looking to torture myself either.

The funny thing? Master Mind built a failsafe into the signal so if it stopped, the world would forget about the Dark Revenger. So why didn't he do the same for himself?

He could have designed it so if the signal stopped, the world would forget about Master Mind. He could have strolled out of there with everyone scratching their heads about who they had been fighting just a minute ago, and gone off to start over. As a nobody.

And that's why he didn't. He'd rather sit in prison as the captured Master Mind rather than live his life as a really smart nobody. His narcissism wouldn't allow it.

275

Take it from me, a reformed narcissist. I know what I'm talking about.

***

It's a warm spring day and the noon time rush is over. One coworker is on a break and the other is in the back doing inventory. A couple of tables are occupied by the normal afternoon clientele: a senior reading while sipping a decaf; two women conversing over chai lattes; and a few teens taking advantage of the free Wi-Fi. I'm behind the counter jotting notes in a Moleskine notebook.

I do stand up a couple nights a week. Some are open mikes, but two clubs have started booking me for regular slots. I've got a good solid twenty minutes. If they need me to do thirty, I can riff about whatever's in the news and do crowd work.

Hey, what else am I going to do? Sling coffee the rest of my life? It's either this or put the Dark Revenger stuff up for sale. And I can't bring myself to part with any of it. I don't know why.

Maybe I do. Maybe there's a part of me that thinks I might decide to put the costume on again. Go out there and do it right. Fight crime, not for fame or money, but for the right reasons. To make the world safer. To inspire people.

In the meantime, food and clothing costs money, so I'm serving coffee and scribbling ideas I might develop into jokes. The idea is to eventually have an hour's worth of material. Maybe tour with it a bit. Film it. Sell it to one of the streaming services. Then clubs will start asking me to headline and I can finally earn enough money to…buy myself a cup of coffee.

Sweet irony! I need to put that joke in my act!

Got to come up with some new stuff. I recently had to cut a two minute bit about Captain Turbo giving a press conference to say the Justice Brigade was retiring ("Didn't they retire twenty years ago? He came *out* of retirement to say they're retiring?").

It got some laughs. Then Captain Turbo died.

One of the unwritten rules of comedy is, it's okay to make fun of a famous person if they're alive. Once they die, they suddenly go from "pompous ass" to "beloved" in the public's mind.

I'm scribbling in my notebook when *she* walks in.

I don't see her at first, but I swear I can feel her. The room is suddenly alive with electricity that practically hums in my ears. It's all one-sided, though because when I look up, she's at the counter with her eyes down at her phone. Red, fiery sunset hair. Her lips, the way they tasted, and the way her body felt pressed against me. I stop breathing for a second and force myself to swallow the lump in my throat.

Estella looks up from her phone and says, "Oh, sorry," and shakes her head slightly, embarrassed perhaps at being distracted for a moment. She looks up at the menu on the wall and bites her lower lip while she decides. She's in regular clothes.

"Just a coffee. Medium." Her eyes go back to her phone, still not making eye contact with me.

"Black, no room for cream."

She doesn't catch that I didn't say it as a question, and replies,

"Yes, please."

I make her coffee and occasionally look at her. Her eyes stay on her phone, looking at emails or text messages or whatever. It's okay; if she catches me staring, it'll be uncomfortable and I'll have to stop. Right now, I want to stare at her, take her all in, because I have no idea when I'll be this close to her again.

Unfortunately, the time comes when I have her coffee ready. She takes the coffee from me, and her eyes meet mine. She smiles and does a slight double take.

"I think this is my first time in here," she says.

"Ah, in that case, welcome," I say.

"Thanks." Genuine smile. "What I meant was, I feel like we've met before."

The lump is back in my throat. What should I say? I used to be your teammate and I fell in love with you, but Master Mind wiped everyone's memory of me? I mean, it's the truth, but it's such a long and convoluted story. Even if I convince her she used to know me, it doesn't automatically mean she'd fall in love with me again.

"I've worked at different places," I say. "You may have seen me somewhere else."

I want to say, *You're the love of my life. But a bad guy erased me from your mind.*

Really, though, what's the point? Maybe in life you only get one shot at the love of your life, and if you lose it, that's all there is. The rest of your life is a big consolation prize.

Someone should pop in now with a trombone and make the WOMP WOMP sound.

"Oh," she says. "That's probably it. Or maybe I've gotten coffee here before. Well…" Estella takes her card out to insert it into the machine. "I guess I should pay for this."

"That's what she said," I say quietly.

Her hand hesitates just for a second. A look passes across her face, quick, like a fast moving cloud, and then it's gone. She inserts the card, waits the required time for the appropriate beep, and then removes it.

"Receipt?"

"Um. No. No, thank you." Gives me a smile again, but it's a troubled one.

I wonder what's going through her head. Feelings of déjà vu? Is she troubled because she realizes there are blank spots in her memory?

She heads for the door and gives me one last look. Her lips part and I think she's going to ask a question, but then she turns and leaves. I watch her walk away through the glass, and suddenly the world is a lot less bright than it was a minute ago and my chest feels heavy.

I put the notebook away and grab a rag and plastic bin to collect the cups from the table the two women recently vacated. My back is to the door so I don't hear anyone enter. I just hear a sharp intake of breath. I turn and Estella is standing there, staring at me

"Oh my God," she says.

"What?"

"I…"

"What?"

"I think…"

She walks towards me as if she's walking through a fog, her eyes locked on me, but also straining to see through smoke covered lens.

"I think I know you."

She puts her coffee down and steps to me, looking straight into my eyes.

"You know me?" I ask.

"I think… Yes, I do," she says, and softly touches my face. "Oh my God. Yes. Yes, I know you."

Then she kisses me and I kiss her back, and my heart leaves my body and finds her heart, and they touch and become one, and as corny as that sounds, it's exactly what it feels like, so screw you if you're rolling your eyes at my description.

"I know you," she says, laughing, smiling, and crying all at the same time.

I say, "You know me?"

"Yes."

"Then tell me," I say.

"You're the Dark Revenger."

# THE END

# ACKNOWLEDGEMENTS

Bill Finger, Stan Lee, Jack Kirby, Steve Ditko, Roy Thomas, Barry Windsor Smith, Gil Kane, John Romita, Ross Andru, Denny O'Neil, Neal Adams, Steve Gerber, Mike Ploog, Michael Golden, Steve Englehart, Marshall Rogers, David Anthony Kraft, Tony Isabella, Chris Claremont, Dave Cockrum, John Byrne, Marv Wolfman, George Perez, Mike Grell, Frank Miller, Doug Moench, Bill Sienkiewicz, Mark Gruenwald, Archie Goodwin, Walt Simonson, John Ostrander, Tim Truman, Flint Henry, James Robinson, Tony Harris, Grant Morrison, Neil Gaiman, and of course, Alan Moore.

A special acknowledgement to Gerry Conway for setting me on this long and tortuous writing path. It was the very last panel of *Amazing Spider-Man* #144 that made me decide to become a writer.

Gerry, I both love you and hate you.

# ABOUT THE AUTHOR

Slade Grayson is a reformed supervillain, but he still has the goatee. He's written other stuff. You should read it.